By the same author

The Falling Awake Mysteries:

The Invisible Body

The Long Lost Sunset

The Never Ending Fall

THE LONG LOST SUNSET

Jenny Cutts

STOPPED CLOCK PRESS

First published in 2021 by Stopped Clock Press
Copyright © Jenny Cutts 2021

The moral right of the author has been asserted.

All characters and events in this publication, other than those clearly in the public domain, are fictitious and any resemblance to real persons, living or dead, is purely coincidental.

All rights reserved.

No part of this publication may be reproduced, stored in a retrieval system, or transmitted, in any form or by any means, without the prior permission in writing of the publisher, nor be otherwise circulated in any form of binding or cover other than that in which it is published and without a similar condition including this condition being imposed on the subsequent purchaser.

ISBN 978-1-914001-05-5
Stopped Clock Press Ltd.
Company Number 12829670

www.jennycutts.com

THE LONG LOST SUNSET

PROLOGUE

'So, you're saying that Quentin, right now, is sleeping there in that bed, and I just can't see him?'

I'm standing at the threshold.

Reed has remained in the parlour and is looking towards the hearthside chair. I see that it is flanked by a glass of sherry on a side table.

'Actually, I think he might be sleeping in that chair.'

I feel a bit freaked out by this as I've circled that corner a few times.

'Looks like a comfy spot,' I agree, 'but how do you know?'

'I don't *know* know, but I'd put money on it. See those clothes – that's what he's wearing.'

I look closer and notice that what might have been a throw is really a silk robe and pyjamas.

Reed goes on. 'We can't know for certain, but that's usually what it means. It *could* just be a pile of clothes someone left there, but… you have to look at the context.'

I close the bedroom door as I found it.

'Awake people are just invisible to us,' he explains. 'It's like… we are in the same place but a different dimension to them… or something – who knows?'

We mirror each other in a dramatic, palms-up gesture, rapidly developing our shorthand for discussing this phenomenon that only we know.

'But sleeping people look like little piles of clothes,' he concludes.

'But *we* don't wake up naked?' I point out, glancing down at my clothes.

'Well, we're not really awake,' he reminds me. '*Your* sleeping body is still safely tucked up at home and that's where you'll wake up. If you fell off the theatre roof you'd still wake up at home in bed.'

'And you've tried this?'

I move away from the disturbingly empty-but-not-empty armchair, walk through the kitchen and out onto the roof. I pass the rabbit hutch, which is all wood and chicken wire and hay escaping onto the floor. I can see lettuce leaves but no Mrs Miggles in there.

Reed follows me, his footsteps crunching on the gun-grey weather-pocked felt. I'm standing by the railing at the edge.

'Please don't!' he implores. 'I'd lose you for the night.'

'But have *you* tried it?'

'I've tried lots of things.'

I stand there with my hands on a low railing, looking at the back streets below and thinking. 'But time still goes… normally?'

I'm looking up at the sky, but the narrow terrace is on the wrong side of the building to see any of the sunrise and, in fact, we are standing in shadow.

'Yes, normally. Or, if it's dilated in some way, there's no way of knowing. I just think of it as real world, real time.'

I recite the facts. 'We can open any door. If we move things, they stay moved. If we fall, we wake. Sleeping people – piles of clothes. Waking people disappear. Real world, real time.'

He gives me a wholesome, Agent Cooper-style thumbs up.

'If we wanted to, we could sit on that sofa and watch the fire going out, but I'd rather go somewhere to see the sunrise?'

He inflects his statement to ask the question of me. I smile and walk back inside as assent.

As we pass the armchair on our way out, I have to ask: 'Are you sure that isn't just a random pile of clothes he's just left there?'

'Well, it's just an educated guess. From all these years.'

I silently mull it over – how long has this been going on for him? How many places must he have been? I steal another glance at the chair.

Then I tell him: 'You know. This is all freaking me out. Quite a lot.'

'Yeah, me too.'

'But this is your life?'

'I just realised something,' he half explains enigmatically.

'What?'

'Tell you later,' he says, and sounds like he means it. 'Let's go and get some fresh air.'

***

Soon enough, we are down by the beach, sitting on the bench and looking out across the waves. The sun has barely risen, dashing out pinks and peaches along the bay.

'Warm, isn't it?' Reed asks me.

Although the sea breeze is fluttering my hair, I feel no early-morning chill to the air.

'Yeah.'

He's right. I look at him expectantly.

'Yeah, that's another thing. It's always warm in the... dreaming. It's one way to recognise where you are. You know: if you're awake or not.'

I hadn't imagined ever getting it confused.

'Not like you feel over-heated, just that little bit warmer, like always warm *enough*. It's an Indian summer, right, but this is England – it's always chilly at night.'

I nod to him, getting it. 'And not just warm, but sort of physically contented,' I add.

I didn't want to use the word 'sensual', for some reason, but that's what I mean.

'Yeah, I know what you mean.'

We sit there nodding and noticing our sensations.

'Why *is* that?' I wonder out loud.

'Who knows?' he answers in a comedy voice, and we both do the palm-shrug thing, without even looking at one another.

The wide bay curves away, indented with coves and clifftops and stretches of sand. The sea looks smooth in the distance but is choppier by the land, where rippling waves lap the rocks. There is a large canopy of clear, blue-ing sky above us and the sun peeps over the glowing horizon. Meandering sea scents reach us from the wet, plashing shore.

'So, what was it that you realised? That freaked you out back there?' I venture.

'Oh… nothing. It doesn't matter.'

'Hey,' – I take hold of his shoulder to make him look at me – 'we're in the *same dream*.' I hear wonder in my voice even though that's not the tone I was going for. 'Or whatever it is! It's like we're the only two people in the entire world right now!' I fling an arm out in gesture. 'I think you can tell me.'

He just looks down at his fidgeting fingers. 'Okay. I *will* tell you.' Then he glances at me sideways. 'But it isn't very nice.'

I turn my body to face him and lean my arm over the back of the bench. He warms up to whatever he's about to say. 'You know the little piles of clothing?'

'That's where a sleeping person is,' I say, as if trying to pass a test.

'I always thought so – and it's true – but I just realised: it also means something else.'

I just keep watching and listening.

'It must be the same for dead bodies.' His bright eyes look up at me to check my reaction. He bows his head. 'Like that woman in the garden shed.'

'Oh!' I almost put my arm around him. 'I'm sure Quentin is fine though!' And I do feel sure.

'Yes. But now I'm thinking of all those times – those little piles of clothes. Most of them – *most* of them – would have been sleeping, but some of them might – *must* – have been dead.'

I notice his skin has goosebumps and I know it cannot be from any kind of chill.

'And I never knew,' he continues, 'and I was right there. And I never did anything.'

What can I say? The places he's been, the night's he's spent like this, it's probably true.

'But you couldn't have known…'

All I can hear, like absolutely the only sounds, are the relentless waves of the sea crashing towards us. I feel the need to brighten the mood again. 'Best not to think about it too much!'

I'm sure he has said the same thing to me sometime this past night.

'So, *are* we the only two people in the world right now? In the whole entire world?'

'Put it this way,' he says, straightening up again, 'I've never once found another, erm… "dreamer" – until you.' He smiles faintly then looks back to the horizon. 'And I've been searching for a long time.'

***

We walk on for a bit, past the old hotel with its wrought-iron balconies, the sunlight shining orange on the windows.

'What about *your* parents?' I ask again.

'I don't have any. I'm all alone in the world.'

He spins around to look at the empty town and stops ahead of me.

'Almost literally – apart from you.'

He's looking at me funny, searchingly, his face serious in front of mine. I think I shuffle backwards and feel something like driftwood rolling under my foot. And then I feel like I'm falling but I never hit the ground.

CHAPTER 1

I open my eyes and scan the blocky Dublin rooftops ahead of me, the muffled blue-grey dawn at my back. I'm standing on top of the dome of the Museum of Archaeology and I'm feeling very alone.

The silent city spreads before me, oblivious. Everywhere, a bland backdrop of a morning, pungent with black brewery scents, unspools across the sky.

The normal sounds of city life seem sponged away by the muffling winds unfurling around me, but I know they just aren't there. I'm used to this, but still. Breezes catch at my hair with tingling twists and cool my skin with gentle moisture; a soft, impish tickle at my neck, a grazing kiss at my cheek. The slow rumble of the river floods my ears with its distant, rolling churn.

I see the city stretching out before me, shaded with precipitous crevices; perfectly pointed brickwork folding in origami angles, hidden ravines that plunge to the streets below. I wish I had the binoculars – but I let Zoya take them with her.

I pivot slowly as I scour the view, careful not to smash through the oculus or slip off the dome. I wonder, for a moment, if the low, whispered rumble is the sound of the distant river or the pumping of my blood. It's surprising how quiet a city can be when all the people have disappeared.

I make my way to the corner, where the round part of the building meets the square. Grappling with the Palladian wedding-cake cornicing, I clamber down to the storey below.

Here, I inch along the curving ledge, clinging to each marble column as I pass. I reach a position above the main entrance and stop. I'm about fifteen metres above the ground still, but I feel a bit more relaxed, tucked in here. I sit in the space under a window and let my legs dangle over the edge.

I look across at the mirror-image National Library, the same colonnade, balcony, columns and dome. I want to describe it as looking like a long-lost twin – but these buildings have been staring at one another for a century. Long, maybe, but not lost.

I let my gaze rise above the rooftops to the blank patch of sky. I think about the library and the museum and the all-sorts-of-everything that must be trapped inside: the shelves of books containing all those immortal thoughts of dead men; the discarded objects used by ancestors; the bones.

All those lives, preserved and packaged and catalogued, lingering long after death. And me, sitting among them, and nobody even knows that I'm here.

I laugh out loud at my own patheticness, suddenly splitting the silence. The sound echoes through the square.

A speck of movement behind the library catches my eye. I think I see someone darting along the far edge of its dome, mostly obscured from my view. It can *only* be her, can't it? I move position and crane to spot the disappearing figure and then I'm falling – the hard, thick stone of the balustrade hurtling, suddenly, toward my head.

***

The next moment, Reed wakes with a jolt, in a narrow single bed. He has been churning the sheets over and over in his sleep. The thin, grey morning tells him that it is still really early, and the small room reminds him where he is – the tatty bed and breakfast on the other side of the river. He decides to get out of there and go for a walk.

Hastily dressed in his clothes from the day before, he strides along the pavement with no particular plan. Gulls tug at fast-food wrappers. He walks along, lost in his thoughts.

Even now, as the city starts to shake itself for a new day, he is trying to outpace a loneliness he thought that meeting Zoya would have killed. If it *was* her that he had seen in the dreaming, why was she running away? She had said she wanted to travel solo for a while so why was she still in Dublin? And if it wasn't Zoya, then who else could it possibly have been? His thoughts loop while he walks. The soles of his Converse slap sonorously on the paving stones.

Crossing the O'Connell bridge, the wide green ribbon of the river interrupts his puzzling, strobed with the fall of daylight and churning its water against old algae-greened stone. He realises he must be heading to Kildare Street – drawn back there for no reason that makes any sense.

He notices the gradual swell of the waking city: delivery vans reversing; the whirr of street sweepers at kerbs; the hiss and growl of engines marking the incursion of bus timetables into the dissipating night.

Rounding a corner at a junction on the south side, he is stopped by a wall of air.

A dark blur has appeared at his feet. Now it is forming into a chillingly recognisable shape. A man lies spreadeagled on the paving slabs. A man who seemed to materialise out of thin air. A man whose crumpled frame looks like it fell from the sky, narrowly missing Reed's head.

Reed looks up and sees a scaffold-clad building. He looks down and sees the man on the pavement still, straggly, sandy hair flung across the face.

Reed makes the mental adjustment from the word 'man' to 'body'. His feet haven't moved an inch.

He remembers his own sense of falling and the impossibility of bracing for the impact of stone smashing into skull. It feels as though the dark-clad figure could be his own shadow self – but it just lies there, bleeding and becoming more real with every passing second. More real and more surreal at the same time.

Reed makes an effort to flip realities in his mind – the one where he idles on rooftops isn't real and the one where a dead man lies by his feet, *is*. A small crowd is gathering in the street.

He stares at the man, feeling thankful that he cannot see the face. This is Reed's second dead body and, apparently, they don't get any easier to see. He finds himself in a ring of people – early risers who have rushed over to help. He hears cars being left in the middle of the road and shouting and emergency calls being made.

Reed has no idea how much time has passed but sirens can be heard. A sergeant arrives and starts taking control. The group are encouraged away from the accident and Reed's feet finally unstick from the spot. The body is obscured by a tent.

'We'll be wanting to find out what any of you saw soon enough, but we need to move you back now. Are you alright, madam? It's a terrible thing, yes. Please move back now. Give the man some respect.'

Reed allows himself to be moved on with the crowd, but, in the jostling, slips away. He walks around a corner, turns up a dark alley and leans his forehead against the wall. Maybe he had had a premonition of this happening – a dream about a fall.

Reed catches himself before his thoughts stray into supernatural territory. He doesn't believe in any of that. For him, physical reality is weird enough as it is.

He gently bangs his brow against the wall. He's aware that a man has plunged to a messy death on the pavement and that he's still somehow making it all about *him*. The man landed close though, almost close enough to kill *him* too. He leans over and vomits against the bricks.

Reed pauses at the path into the cemetery and checks the newspaper clipping in his pocket – right place, right time, right funeral.

The graveyard is dotted with monuments of long-forgotten deaths. The dropping, age-softened headstones seem to sway in motley procession toward a once-distant boundary wall. Winter-shed, earth-baked plant matter mulches in the creases of graves and paths and roots.

The mossy stone wall beside him recedes over the rise of a hill, interrupted by small tangles of gnarled yew trees and sturdy, fluttering oaks. He can still detect the faint smell of warmed asphalt tumbling across the holy ground from the suburban streets beyond its clutch.

He can see the group of mourners near the top of the hill standing in twos and threes, gathering for the interment. He walks slowly toward them for a closer look but has decided not to join in. The sky is shining a bright, daring blue and strong sunlight cuts dark shadows at their smartly shod feet. It's inappropriately sunny for a funeral but many are clad in thick, black coats. Some are wearing dark glasses to protect against the sun's glare and to hide tear-swollen eyes.

Reed hangs back, staying away from their gravel-rattling, twig-snapping footsteps as they accumulate quietly at the place where the dug earth reveals its soft, dry richness and where their dearly beloved will be laid to rest.

He scans the crowd. A group of friends in black suits and skinny ties are wearing shirts so white they seem to reflect the spring sunshine. A family of five are arranged in a tight huddle, the parents looking glum and the teenagers bored. A couple stand sedately, side by side, tightly holding one another's hand. One man stands alone, periodically shaking his head.

Reed stops at the corner where the path joins the main thoroughfare through the graveyard and wonders what to do with himself. Noticing a fallen vase on a nearby grave, he bends down to right it, standing the clouded pot upright and replacing the scattered flowers. He reads the shallow, weathered inscription, now barely veined into the lichen-patterned stone: '*Love is a light that never dims.*'

When Reed straightens up again and looks at the mourners, he sees something that makes his mouth fall open in puzzled disbelief.

Standing apart from the women linking arms to one side and an elderly couple on the other, is a lone figure – a tall man, a little overweight, a head of springy curls. The man wipes a tear from his eye and looks across the sweep of gravestones. His chest rises and falls as he steadies himself emotionally with a sigh. The heavy physique, the sure-footed stance, the wayward hair – he is the spit of Dan Mather. *But what's he doing here in Dublin?*

Mourning at a funeral is the obvious answer, Reed realises, *but what's Dan's connection with the man who fell to his death?*

A lazy *caw* catches his ear and Reed becomes aware of crows perching, almost invisible, in the tallest oaks by the crematorium; a family of quiet shadows, shuffling in the leafy branches.

Reed sees a stone bench in cool shade, under the porch of the crematorium, and decides to wait for Dan there.

***

As the interment finishes and the group processes slowly down the path toward him, Reed watches for Dan in the crowd. He spots him, now wearing mirrored sunglasses, offering a supportive elbow to an elderly woman as they walk over an uneven patch. As he gets nearer to the crematorium, Reed can clearly recognise his friend. He only saw him five or six months ago in Shilly-on-Sea.

In the shadows, Reeds stands, planning to talk to Dan as he goes past. Further up the path, Dan pauses to polish his sunglasses with a hankie, turning away from the sunshine to see without squinting. Reed seems to have been beaten to it – one man is walking up the slope against the tide of mourners, making a beeline for Dan. Reed sits down again.

***

Holding up the glasses to check that they are clean, Dan sees someone approaching in the mirrored lens. The colours and shapes resolve themselves into a convex version of a very familiar face. He turns to see Marcus, as effortlessly handsome as ever, and wearing one of his naturally charming, broadest-of-broad smiles.

'I don't think I ever saw you looking so smart, Dan. It's like you're in fancy dress.'

'Didn't recognise me, eh?'

'No,' Marcus says, 'I'd recognise you anywhere.'

'Weren't you at the funeral…?' Dan asks.

'I was hiding at the back.'

The last mourners to leave the graveside walk down the path beside them, a couple of women linking arms. The one in her late thirties with long sandy-coloured hair slows by the two men.

'Oh, Marcus, I didn't see you. Thanks for coming; you too, Dan. Will we see you at the wake?'

'Of course, Nuala.'

Dan puts a comforting hand on her shoulder. 'The Claddagh?'

She nods.

'See you there,' Dan replies, echoed by Marcus.

The women walk on down the path.

'Nuala asked me to do a reading at the funeral,' – Marcus runs a hand through his wavy hair and seems to avoid Dan's gaze for a moment – 'but I couldn't… and I just couldn't… stand to watch… *that*.'

His eyes flicker toward the recently dug grave near the top of the hill.

'No, watching them lower your friend into the ground… It's not… great. Did you see much of him?'

'Off and on. I met up with Fintan a few weeks ago – well, a couple of months, I suppose… What about you?'

'Not for years,' Dan replies and sighs.

'What about us?'

'Too long, Marcus, too long.'

They turn and tail the other mourners, who are walking out of the cemetery in dribs and drabs. Reed sees them deep in conversation and decides not to interrupt. He stays in the shadows and consults the scrap of paper again.

****

Dan and Marcus are sitting by the duck pond in St Stephen's Green. Their black suits stand out against the greenery. The varnish-flaked slats of the bench they are sitting on shine sparsely in the sunshine.

Lunch-breakers have long since returned to work, teenagers sit on the grass holding hands, and older couples walk past, carrying their jackets. Spring is colouring the park.

They have found a quiet spot by the water, in a bright clearing where the afternoon sunshine pushes through the dappled foliage and the sky is framed with leaves. The city traffic is muted by a wall of tangled trees, their sharp-cut leaves merging with the feathery prickles of spiky bushes. Two swans glide elegantly by.

'Remember at uni that time the three of us tried to spend the night in Fletcher Moss?' Marcus asks.

'And when the police caught us breaking in and we were giving our names–'

'The two of us told them our names–'

'Like the obedient citizens we are–'

'But Fintan came out with some elaborate false name–'

'*Very* elaborate,' Dan qualifies.

'What was it…? Lord… something.'

'That's right, Lord Humphry…'

'Smythe.'

'Smythe!' Dan agrees.

The two mourners laugh.

There is a watery splash as a pair of ducks take to the green, silt-laden pond.

'No, Humphington!' Dan continues, correcting himself.

'Yes, Humphington. Lord Humphington Smythe.'

'What tickles me is that Humphington isn't even a name.'

The ducks glide by, casting arrow patterns in their wake.

'Got to admire his creativity.'

'Sounds like something out of a portrait,' Dan remarks. 'Well, you would know.'

'I don't think I ever painted a lord…'

'No, and you *still* wouldn't have,' Dan points out.

They laugh so loudly that the teenagers by the bushes disentangle themselves and slope away, holding hands.

'Do you remember,' Marcus continues, 'the police thought we were wrecked because we couldn't stop laughing?'

'Definitely one of those can't-make-eye-contact moments.'

'Yeah. For hours. You and me, we couldn't look at one another or we'd set each other off.'

'And I was so worried they would kick us out of university!'

'That's right,' Marcus concurs, remembering.

'Jesus, I was such a swot.'

Further along the path, a rabble of pigeons engage in beak-to-beak combat over some morsel of rubbish on the floor. Dan and Marcus are quietly remembering the old days. The leaves overhead flicker in the gentle breeze.

'That was such a Fintan thing to say though,' Dan says, after a while.

'Wasn't it?'

'Always making up names and far-fetched stories...'

'Telling people he was wildly implausible things he was not... Didn't he go into a lecture theatre once and start teaching the class?' Marcus wonders.

'I'd forgotten about that!'

'He didn't know anything about Victorian literature... God knows what he was saying to them before the real lecturer kicked him out!'

'"Assuming identities" basically,' Dan elaborates, 'though I'm not sure "impersonating an academic" is a crime.'

The friends laugh again. Marcus's buoyant waves flop forward on his brow and, as he pushes them back, Dan notices that recent years have begun to speckle the black with grey.

The scrabble and peck of the pigeons picking over the dusty, foot-worn path is scattered by the gentle panting of an old dog, his tongue flopping happily from a wide, canine smile.

'Yeah, Karen thought he was a geography student for three months – and she was actually going out with him!'

'Oh yes, Karen,' Dan says. 'I saw her at the funeral. Does she still work with you in Edinburgh?'

'She does.'

'I'll catch up with her at the wake.'

A sombre silence stretches around them. A pair of pensioners linking arms seem to sense it and cease their chatter as they pass. Beyond the frame of foliage, a pink streak is gradually colouring the sky, like the soft creep of watercolour on cotton paper.

'Looks like it might be a glorious sunset,' Marcus says. 'Can't we just sit here and enjoy it?'

Dan looks at his watch. 'We don't want to be too late. They'll be expecting us,' he counters, sensibly.

'Look.' Marcus points at a small, nondescript cloud. 'That one looks like Barbara Cartland.'

Dan smiles. He wonders how many surreal cloud descriptions they have swapped over the years – and how many years have elapsed since the last.

They look at one another and share the same rush of memories. It bubbles over into laughter that nobody else would understand.

They laugh again, even louder than before, falling about on the wooden bench before composing themselves with deep breaths and eye wipes and scale-descending sighs. Dan dares to look at his friend beside him, noticing a slight wiggle to Marcus's thick dark eyebrows that predicts the next wave of laughter. It breaks when Marcus sees the forced seriousness that Dan is willing onto his own face. They laugh again and look away from one another. Dan leans forward and covers his eyes with his palms. Marcus looks away, folding his arms and clasping his square jaw with a large hand that covers his quivering mouth.

Gradually, their mood calms to match the water's placid surface in front of them and their poses relax. Dan looks around, watching some people strolling across the small bridge.

'Catriona's not with you?' Dan asks, watching the cloud drift out of sight.

'No, Trinny couldn't get away.'

'Really?'

Dan remembers Catriona and Fintan chatting away in the corners of various parties in an assortment of student digs. He watches Marcus pulling at the neck of his collar and tie.

'I detest wearing ties.'

'Yes,' Dan agrees, taking off his own tie, 'this has got to go.' He looks at Marcus. 'You not taking yours off?'

'Better not,' Marcus replies, 'I don't want to upset anyone.'

'Who would be upset?'

'Oh, you know. Fintan's sister…? I already said no to giving that reading. I just want to do the right thing and not upset anyone.'

'Well, there is a dress code…' Dan remembers, a sunny glint returning to his eye.

'Oh yes.'

Marcus reaches for the bag beside him. 'Who do you want to be? The chimney sweep or the clown?'

Dan closes his eyes. 'Surprise me.'

CHAPTER 3

The Claddagh pub is full of people wearing interesting hats. They contrast with the black clothes that mark them out as mourners. A fluttering sonata of conversation swirls around the room, punctuated by the pressurised hiss of fonts filling glasses.

Dan and Marcus are standing by a wall, wearing a conical hat with pompoms and a battered top hat. Marcus looks dashing in his chimney sweep beaver, whereas the clown hat looks comical perched on top of Dan's unruly curls.

They look around the room, observing princesses, cowboys, jesters and more; the hat wearers displaying a selection of moods and expressions and drinks. Dan spots his old friend Karen wearing a black witch's hat and making her way toward them.

'Dan! Good to see you. Nice hat,' she says, smiling, 'I always thought of you as a pointy head.'

'You too,' Dan replies.

'You always thought of us as a witch?' she queries, raising an eyebrow.

Dan smiles. 'I meant – good to see you.'

Karen curls her vodka-tonic-bearing arm around Dan's shoulder and stands on tiptoes as they embrace. Marcus makes space for Karen between them. The three of them look around the room.

'Not your typical wake, is it?' Dan says.

'Fintan wasn't your typical man,' Marcus responds.

They all sip their drinks.

'No, he wasn't. I'm glad people are going along with the hat thing,' Dan says.

'Me too,' Karen agrees.

'It's what he would have wanted,' Dan summarises, cradling his beer.

'Yes, it's *literally* what he wanted,' Karen says.

The group are joined by a tall man in his fifties with a long face and a pint of Guinness.

'Never seemed the type of fellow to have a funeral plan,' he says.

'No, he just told us all the time, you know,' Karen responds. 'Sorry – this is… Mickey, wasn't it?'

She introduces them.

'Mickey Moran,' he confirms, shaking the men's hands.

'When he died,' Karen explains, 'he would want everyone wearing costumes, he always said. Nuala got us to tone it down to just hats, you know.'

'He wanted it all. The light and the shade. Such a luvvie,' Marcus comments, raising his whisky momentarily in memory of his friend.

'I didn't know he was into amateur dramatics,' Mickey says.

Dan thinks Mickey probably knew Fintan through work, whatever line he had been in recently. Not construction work though, he thinks, with a slight shiver, imagining the scaffolding and the pavement.

'Come on,' Karen responds, a bit too loudly, 'his whole life was one performance after another.'

Dan notices that her eyes are welling up.

'Sorry, I need another drink,' she says, looking toward the brass-edged bar.

She moves away before Dan can offer to get her one and Mickey closes the gap, forming a triangle with the men.

'The oddest thing about this wake isn't the hats,' he says, quietly angry, 'it's what nobody is talking about.'

'What do you mean?' Dan asks.

'Well, falling from a building like that, in the night, when you didn't even work there, it's not your normal sort of death, is it?'

'What are you getting at?' Marcus asks, softly.

'Well, look at us all, standing around, wearing party hats...' Mickey says.

Dan notes that Mickey isn't actually wearing one.

'... trying to celebrate his life... when Fintan clearly... didn't.'

Dan and Marcus look at him, feeling chills and thinking, again, about the horrible manner of Fintan's death.

'Sorry, lads. It's just, this country. Makes me angry sometimes. All these men... and everyone has to pretend it was an accident.'

Mickey contemplates the dark liquid in his glass, then takes a gulp.

'A cover-up, you mean?' ventures Marcus, quietly.

'Murder?' Dan says, his voice almost a whisper.

Mickey swallows and looks at them, shaking his head gently. 'No, lads. Oh, you probably don't know. You're English, aren't you?'

Mickey fixes them a serious look and lowers his voice to a hush.

'Suicide's illegal here. Excuse me.' Mickey walks away, perhaps leaving the wake entirely.

Dan and Marcus exchange a glance and, when they see the expression in one another's eyes, look away again. This time it isn't about trying not to laugh.

The wake has reached that point of the evening when alcohol-lubricated throats are opening up, gradually raising the volume. There is a collective change of key from minor to major, though some sit and think and sigh. Elbows fall heavier on tables, drops of whisky spill and peals of laughter swell.

Karen is returning to their corner with a fresh vodka swirling around in her glass. She looks composed again.

'Hey, isn't that that hippy woman from university? With Nuala?' Karen is pointing to a woman in a flowing pastel dress with silky, silvery hair. 'What's she doing here?'

'She's his godmother,' Marcus says, 'or was.'

Nuala and the willowy woman are making their way over.

'Hello all. Thanks for coming,' Nuala says in a strained voice. 'Do you remember Glenda? She was in Manchester the same time as all of you.'

'Hello. Dan, isn't it?' Glenda turns to Karen. 'I'm sorry, I don't remember you.'

'This is Karen. I'm not sure you would have met…'

'You were the scientist, weren't you?'

Actually, it was computer science, Dan thinks, so she's half-right, but he doesn't correct her. He greets her with a friendly expression.

Glenda continues. 'Sorry, that's just how I remember Fintan's friends. You were the scientist and Marcus was the artist. I remember, you two seemed like chalk and cheese on the surface but were always thick as thieves. Had you seen Fintan recently?'

'No, I'm sad to say,' Dan replies, 'not for years.'

'Not for years,' Marcus echoes.

'Well, I remember you,' Karen says, spikily. 'Didn't you hang out in our house for a while, waiting to hear if you'd lost your job?'

'Karen, it's probably not the time…' begins Marcus, trying to deflect the antagonism he can recognise in her voice.

'Something to do with Fintan getting access to one of your patients' notes.'

'Clients,' corrects Glenda.

'Glenda probably doesn't want to rake through all that right now…' Nuala asserts.

'That's okay,' Glenda cuts in, 'I like straight talkers.' She smiles warmly.

'Marcus,' Nuala takes his arm, 'can I have a quick word? Let's leave these straight talkers to their straight talking.'

Marcus allows her to turn him aside from the group for a more private conversation, though they don't walk out of earshot.

'Well, the truth can be painful,' Glenda is saying and proceeds to dish out some words of wisdom from the world of therapy.

Dan can hear Nuala raising a tricky topic with Marcus, at his shoulder. '…it's just that I can't help thinking he was in some sort of money trouble… You lent him some money recently, didn't you…?'

Dan's attention snaps back to the conversation he is actually in. Karen is being confrontational again.

'The truth? You look like you live in a fairy tale… Where's *your* hat?'

'Karen!' Dan interjects.

Glenda is laughing gently and doesn't seem to have taken offence. 'Oh, I didn't bring a hat. I don't really like pretence.'

At this, Karen lets out a guffaw and Dan realises that his old friend is quite drunk.

'*Now* I remember,' Glenda continues, her tone still pleasant, 'weren't you the girlfriend?'

'No, I wasn't. And, *whoever* I was going out with at the time, I wouldn't have been "*the girlfriend*". I'm not anybody's "*the girlfriend*"!'

'You're right. I'm sorry, that wasn't a very feminist thing for me to say.'

Glenda has a look of concerned empathy on her face. Karen's conical hat has slipped to one side.

'This fucking hat!' She yanks it off her head.

'Come on,' Dan says to Karen, taking her shoulder gently, 'let's get some air.'

He directs an apologetic expression to Glenda, who bows her head graciously and steps aside, then walks Karen out of the group and through the throng and onto the street.

***

Outside in the rapidly cooling evening, Reed sees Dan and a woman exit the pub. They lean against the wall and Dan helps the woman to light a cigarette. The woman looks like she is crying and talking intently. Dan rubs her shoulder. Reed hangs back and blends in with the background, not wanting to interrupt. The shadow of an alleyway covers him as he watches them talk.

***

Later, the remaining mourners have settled into groups around tables. Hats have been removed or swapped. Ties have been loosened and a few shoes kicked off. Faces are shining, hairstyles unravelling, and tables are wet with spilled drink.

A booth by the window empties as one group leaves.

'Shall we?' Marcus asks.

'Karen,' Dan calls, attracting her attention, 'want a seat?'

She whirls around. 'No. I think it's time I send myself to bed. Marcus, want to share a taxi to the hotel?' She looks from Dan to Marcus and back again. 'No. No, you stay. You two have got a lot of catching up to do. Dan – it was lovely to see you again, man. I hope the next time is under happier circumstances. Marcus – I'll see you for breakfast. Have a...' – she searches for an appropriate word, then shrugs – '...evening. Have an evening.'

'Will you be okay?' Marcus asks, 'Let me...'

But Karen has left the pub before he can finish the sentence. A minute passes when the men contemplate chasing after their friend.

'Will she be okay?' Dan says.

'Yeah. It's everyone else that needs to look out.'

They settle into the booth facing one another. They look each other in the eye and soft smiles spread across their faces.

'Okay,' Dan says. 'Well. Let's... have an evening.'

He holds up his glass of Glenmalure whisky.

'To Fintan,' Marcus replies, matching the gesture, 'he *really* had some evenings.'

'He certainly did. To Fintan.'

'To Fintan.'

They clink glasses.

Pausing with the whisky at his lips, Marcus adds the local salutation.

'Slainte,' he says, looking Dan deep in the eye.

Dan returns his friend's gaze.

'Slainte.'

***

Outside, Reed watches them through the window. He sees two drinkers leaning together over bright glasses and a shadowy carousel of bodies moving in the pub beyond. An amber glow colours the stone slabs around the frame and illuminates the window box of swaying flowers with a strange, day-for-night tone.

Shirted lads who smell of strong spicy aftershave briefly interrupt his view. They ramble past, shouting to one another, in search of the main drag and a young crowd. They don't notice Reed standing in the shadows, exhaling a miasma of smoke into the air, the sharp, bright point where tobacco meets fire dropping lazily in his fingertips. The drunken shouting of the young men seems at odds with the cosy scene playing soundlessly before him across the lane.

The rocky stone presses uncomfortably at his back and the night air prickles the follicles at the nape of his neck. One hand is warm in his pocket, the other cold around the cigarette. He stubs the butt out and raises his collar against the chill. He watches, wondering why he still hasn't gone inside to talk to his friend.

Within the glow of the pub, the two men look wrapped in conversation; leaning toward one another, animated and calm and jovial and intense. He watches them talking and laughing and mirroring each other, sip for sip, the bright, shining whiskies wetting their lips.

CHAPTER 4

The next morning, Reed is sitting on a small sofa in the lobby of a hotel, reading a newspaper. Clipped footsteps cross the shiny floor.

Waterfalls of gauzy curtain soften the plate-glass windows and mask the grubby traffic outside. The rising and falling cadence of street sounds swells with the uneven push and spin of the revolving door.

Over the top of the broadsheet, he is keeping an eye on the lift and stairs. The odd businessman, couple and tourist walk past. A neat-looking woman is checking out at the reception desk.

He turns the page and is confronted with an obituary of the man who died at his feet. The paper is a few days old. He scans the article but doesn't notice any details that he hasn't read before: Fintan O'Doherty, 41, a single man, Dubliner, well-liked, participant in many groups and clubs, nondescript office job, survived by a sister. The story has been running in the papers ever since the fall. The death remains unexplained.

Reed looks again at the photograph of Fintan – pleased to substitute the image of the healthy, smiling man for the abstract impressionist mess that he has been imagining lay under the straggly, sandy hair. The image of the body smashed into the pavement has stayed with him but seeing this photograph of the living person helps.

Then he hears a familiar voice carrying from the other side of the lobby.

'Thank you, yes, to the airport please.'

Reed lays the paper down on the low coffee table in front of him. There he is: Dan.

Dan is taking the handle of a small, wayward suitcase and turning away from the reception desk.

Reed is about to call Dan over, but, at the last minute, notices the photograph of Fintan face-up before him. Dan wins the fight with his luggage and heads for the lounge. Reed quickly turns some pages to hide the story about Fintan, sits back and calls clearly: 'Dan!'

Dan immediately spots him and beams. Reed notices dark shadows under Dan's eyes – but the dishevelled T-shirt is standard so he can't assume a hangover just from that.

Dan is moving toward the sofa in heavy-booted strides. His mouth hangs halfway between a beaming smile and dumbfounded surprise. He dumps the suitcase and comes to a stop.

'Reed!'

'What are the chances?' Reed asks, grinning.

Dan sits down on the opposite sofa. 'I'm just here for a funeral – it was yesterday actually – and now I'm on my way back home...'

Reed folds the paper in half and nudges it out of the way.

'What about you?' Dan continues. 'I thought you and Zoya went off travelling the world together. Is she with you?'

'Dublin is a place in the world,' Reed points out. 'Er, no, Zoya's… not here.'

'So, are you staying in this hotel too?' Dan asks. 'What happened to your camper van? I never did get that spin.'

'The van's still going strong.'

'So, come on, really, how did you know I was here?' Dan asks, narrowing his eyes.

Reed thinks for a second. *How much should he tell?* Dan observes the pensive look on his friend's face and continues talking before Reed can think what to say.

'Don't start that again…' Dan cautions, shaking his head more definitely this time. 'You just "knew", I suppose?'

Dan is leaning toward him, smiling. He seems to have already processed the coincidental meeting and is picking up where they left off.

Reed is still wondering how to play it. Would Dan rather hear that he basically stalked him from a funeral to a wake to a taxi last night, lurking in the shadows and acting weird? Why *didn't* he just go up and talk to him yesterday? Reed's explanation doesn't fight its way through his embarrassment quickly enough and Dan already seems resigned to his friend's enigmatic ways.

'Come to think of it, you remind me of him, in some ways – my friend whose funeral it was – he just seemed to "know things" too…'

Reed is on the verge of explaining himself – partly at least. He has already decided not to say anything about the body of Dan's friend falling at his feet.

'Doesn't matter,' Dan continues. 'How are you?'

'Oh, I'm good. So, how was the funeral? How did you know him?'

'Old uni friend. It was' – Dan's wide eyes roll – 'yeah, a funeral. So, are you here for a while? Wish I'd known – we could have met up. I could have come over sooner. I'm flying home today.'

'How's your sister and Matthew?' Reed asks, picturing them in the kitchen at Shilly-on-Sea, although he knows that they have moved in with Dan now.

'Great!' Dan exclaims. 'Really great! Both of them. Matty's got a lot of friends, still rides that bike you gave him, and is loving the magician's assistant thing they've got going on.' Dan loves gushing about his nephew.

'With old Quentin?'

'The very man! I think they've sort of adopted him, like a grandfather, really.'

'Does he still have that big rabbit?'

'Mrs Miggles? Yep. And Sarah is really making the most of her life now, which is all I ever wanted for her.'

'That's great,' Reed says, holding his friend's gaze.

'It really is. And she's dating a new man now, a friend she knew at university.' Dan's animated gestures come to a rest. 'Listen, man, it's so good to run into you. When are you coming to Kembleton?'

Reed takes in a breath and his face twists awkwardly. He doesn't really know what his plans are. Dan checks his watch.

'Do you have to get off?' Reed asks.

'I'm okay for five minutes. So… what happened with you and Zoya? Did you break up?'

'Oh…' Reed begins, reconfiguring his expression a few times before the rest of the sentence follows.

Dan watches him move his head to one side, running a hand through his floppy-as-ever hair. He waits to hear the answer.

'She just wanted some time travelling on her own. I don't know. I'll tell you about it some other time.'

'When?' Dan asks seriously. 'And where? Isn't there some way I can get hold of you – apart from posting wanted signs all over the… world?'

The two men give the matter some thought. Both sets of eyes have come to rest on the newspaper between them – randomly folded at the personal ads page.

They look back to one another and lock eyes with contrasting expressions on their faces.

'You've got to be joking,' Reed says. 'Personal ads?'

'Well, did you ever see that Madonna film? A few years ago?'

'The one about mistaken identity?'

'*Desperately Seeking Susan*, yes. If it worked for *them*…?'

Dan has a lopsided smile on his face and is raising his eyebrows. Reed knows his friend too well not to realise that his suggestion is a serious one and shifts in his seat.

'Well, what newspaper will we use? I don't think many places stock *Apparition Monthly.*'

'Very funny. I don't think they run personal ads anyway.'

'Evidently – or you wouldn't be single, would you…?' Reed jokes, softening the barb with a cheeky grin.

'Ha ha,' Dan says, flatly, in acknowledgement. 'But seriously… what's *that* paper?'

Reed exhales through his nose and checks. 'It's *The Register.*'

'*The Register*? That will do – it's got UK and Ireland distribution – it will do until you go further afield.'

'I'm not really planning to… for a while,' Reed states.

Dan notices a car pulling up outside the hotel. 'That might be my taxi. I'll have to make a move. So, we'll read *The Register* and look for messages?'

'As long as we don't have to use pet names,' Reed jokes. His mouth is pursed but his eyes are shining.

'No, we can use our real names, Reed – *is* that your real name?'

'Might be…'

The taxi driver is now identifying himself at the reception desk. The receptionist makes eye contact with Dan.

'Mr Mather, your taxi to the airport is here.'

Dan waves a hand and smiles in acknowledgement then leans forward to scribble his number on a corner of the newspaper. He rips it off and hands it to Reed. 'In case you lost it.' Dan stands. 'So, do we have a deal?'

He holds out a hand toward Reed, who is perplexed at the formality but extends his own in return. Instead of a handshake, Dan hauls his leaner friend up out of the sofa and into a surprise bear hug. It has been a while since Reed felt anyone's embrace.

'Do you want a hand with your suitcase?'

'No, I'm fine.'

Dan smiles and turns to leave. Reed watches him bustling out of the lobby, the taxi driver evidently making the same offer as he goes.

'No, I'm fine on my own,' Dan is saying, wrestling the handle back. Then he stops by the door and looks back. 'Stay in touch.'

Reed nods in return.

Soon, he goes outside and watches the taxi joining the busy city traffic and driving away. He looks at the scrap of newspaper that Dan scribbled on and retrieves the business card he gave him when they first met. He checks Dan's phone number against the one on the 'sceptic investigator and journalist' card. It's the same.

Then he slips something else out of his wallet to read. He turns it over. It is a photograph of a young woman with a beautiful smile. It reassures him to know that he has memorised her number, even though he knows that she won't even be there right now, in that eccentric house by a distant sea.

CHAPTER 5

Dan is pacing through the Departures Lounge at Dublin Airport, clutching his passport and a boarding pass for Heathrow. The bag he's lugging around is starting to dig into his shoulder, so he sets it down and glances up at the boards for information about his gate.

'Hey, Dan!'

He turns abruptly, not immediately able to recognise the source of the shout. He sees a bar curving alongside the thoroughfare, boasting a spray of flowers in a vase, shining glasses and one smiling patron – Marcus.

'Fancy seeing you here,' Marcus says once he has Dan's attention.

Dan picks up his bag and sits himself down at the neighbouring stool.

'It's barely lunchtime,' he says, glancing pointedly at the amber liquid swirling around in the bottom of his friend's glass.

Marcus shrugs.

'You're the second person I've run into today – but this is less out of the blue. Karen not with you?'

'No, she's catching a different flight.'

Dan glances along the row of empty stools and toward the tide of overcaffeinated air passengers making their way through the concourse. There is a single barman at the other end of the bar. Marcus signals to him for a couple more whiskies, but Dan shakes his head and orders an orange juice for himself.

Above the high, arching roof, he sees blue skies and puffy clouds and aeroplanes thundering to Europe and beyond.

The drinks are set down before them. Dan looks at the small glass of cold orange juice, finding its fresh, zesty allure more enticing than Marcus's dusky swirl of whisky. Even the smell turns his stomach. He's not sure where its distilled aroma ends and that of the cleaning rota begins.

'Didn't we have enough of an evening last night?'

'You sound like my wife,' Marcus jokes, channelling some old-school comedian.

'No, it's just that you look how I feel.' Dan sips his juice and props his head on his palm.

'No, Dan, with hangovers, you just have to drink through the pain.'

Marcus conjures an inspirational hand gesture to go with this piece of advice and Dan laughs but shakes his head.

'You know they won't let you fly if you're intoxicated?'

'Dublin to Edinburgh? I don't think they let you on if you're *not*!'

Dan mock-rolls his eyes. The joke is a bit more obvious than they would usually go for, but they laugh together all the same.

'Who are you flying with? Rye-anair?'

The pun was inevitable. Marcus looks at Dan with a nostalgic smile playing on his lips. 'You always could make me laugh, Dan. I've missed it.' His dark eyes flit away at the end of the sentence.

'So, isn't there a first class lounge you should be in somewhere? Famous artist like you?'

'I think you are misunderstanding the art business somewhat.' Marcus sips his whisky, twice.

'But weren't you the youngest ever *Moment* Artist of the Year?'

Marcus snorts a small, derisory laugh. '*Moment Magazine* Artlist, nine-teen-seventy-six!' He practically sings the date, pride and sarcasm tumbling over one another in the tone of his voice.

'Everyone has heard of you,' Dan points out.

'Well,' Marcus sips again, 'they haven't heard of me recently...' He looks at the glass.

'But you haven't given it up...?' Dan probes gently.

'No. No, I'm still working. In fact, they're having a retrospective of me next year. You should come up!'

'To Edinburgh?'

'You've never come to see us, have you?'

'Well, you were always flitting down to London – and that's a lot closer to me.'

'Come to Edinburgh,' Marcus commands, patting Dan's arm ever so slightly too hard. 'You can stay in the guest house, anytime.'

'I should. I've never been.'

'Well, it's a lot like Dublin, but taller.'

Dan gives him a sideways look.

'No, I'm not really a heights person either,' Marcus replies, 'but they are good for one thing…'

Dan's mind is suddenly coloured by the bright memory of a certain rooftop.

'… The views,' Marcus says. 'Remember that place in Palermo?'

'Just the three of us. You, me and Fintan,' Dan concurs.

'Remember that rooftop?'

Dan remembers. He swallows. 'Yes.'

'Best sunset in the world,' Marcus says.

They sit quietly for a moment, not even sipping. The shadow of an aeroplane cuts through the light.

'So, Edinburgh's a lot like Dublin then?' Dan enquires, picking up his drink.

'Georgian and gorgeous? Yes. Edinburgh's a bit twistier, I think. More surprises. Easier to get lost there, anyway.'

'Not sure you're selling it to me…' Dan jokes. 'I like to know where I am.'

'Yes, you're more of an A-to-B chap, aren't you?' Marcus teases in response.

'Listen, you're talking to someone who let you take him on – *not a few* – pretty *meandering* walks in our time…'

'I loved our walks and talks, didn't you?'

'Yeah, I loved them too.'

Marcus takes a long swill of his whisky. 'Puts it all into perspective, doesn't it? The first of our group to go.'

Dan's forehead furrows as he adopts an odd sort of smile. 'You're making it sound like we'll all be dropping like flies. We're all under forty' – Marcus looks at him –

'-five. Fintan… that was a horrible' – Dan searches for the word – 'thing. But *we're* all young, got most of our lives ahead of us…'

'Well,' Marcus considers, 'not young enough to win the Girtin Prize anymore,' he says, aiming to change the subject.

'So, things aren't going so well?'

'Oh, just a creative block… Put it this way, it's a good job I married someone who's stinking rich!'

'Yeeeeah,' – Dan stretches the word out – 'you're going to have to try harder than that if you want me to feel sorry for you. Some of us have to work hard for a living!'

Dan immediately registers the misfire as a flash of pain crosses Marcus's face. The expression makes him look more like a Roman god than ever and his dark eyes are ablaze.

'Art is hard work! I thought you, of all people, understood…'

Dan puts a hand softly on Marcus's shoulder to placate him and try to intercept the angry hurt. 'I'm sorry. I know. I know it is. Ill-judged joke.'

Marcus looks straight ahead but places his palm over Dan's hand to accept his friend's apologetic gesture, as if to seal a pact. Then he runs both hands across his head and stretches, his elbows pointing to the pale-blue sky. Dan spins on his stool to lean against the bar. The rim of chrome digs into his back and the frosted glass presses hard beneath his elbow.

'So, is it bottle washer or chambermaid we're talking about?'

Marcus smiles.

'It's just…' Dan continues, 'if I *do* come and stay…'

'Do!'

'… I want to know whether to expect you, wearing a bean-stained apron, delivering my full English in the morning.'

Marcus laughs loudly. 'It's a bit of a classier place than that. It's *full Scottish,* anyway, up there.'

'Oh?'

'It's the same but you also get tattie scones,' Marcus explains.

'I'm in!'

They both take a mouthful of their drinks.

'Seriously, though,' – Marcus swivels toward him – 'come and stay with us, anytime you like. Stay as long as you like.'

'Would Catriona be okay with that?'

'Why wouldn't she be?'

'Well… it's her business, isn't it?'

'Why don't you come up now?' Marcus asks, eyebrows flashing. 'The flight's not for hours yet. Change your tickets and come with me now?'

Dan breaks his friend's intensive gaze and watches the departure boards. 'Well, *my* flight is and I should really be getting to the gate now.' He finishes the orange juice, crunching a remnant of ice cube at the end.

'I mean it!' Marcus's voice is getting louder with excitement. 'What's stopping you coming to Edinburgh with me right now?'

'Well, you're drunk, and I've got work to do,' Dan says honestly. 'You'll probably have forgotten who I am again tomorrow. Be a bit weird over breakfast if I actually did.'

Marcus slumps slightly. 'Well, make sure you visit me soon. How is work anyway? Still a journo? What about the ghost hunting?'

'Yes, both.' Dan stands and reaches for his shoulder bag. 'Seriously, Marcus, I've loved seeing you. But I really have to get home. I've a deadline to meet.'

Marcus pulls at the bag to get Dan's full attention. 'They're all *deadlines*, aren't they? In the ghost hunting biz?' His breath smells of whisky. '*Dead*-lines…?' Marcus repeats for emphasis.

Dan hitches his bag and Marcus gets up from his seat.

'Hold on, I'll walk you to the gate.'

They walk a few metres in the direction of the British Airways gates, then Dan pauses. A big 'Departures' sign hangs above their heads.

'Hey, you don't have to walk with me. Look,' – Dan points back at the bar – 'your whisky is getting warm.'

'Okay, but we should arrange something.'

Dan turns to face his friend. 'We will.'

Marcus obediently plants his feet. 'Let's not leave it too late.'

The friends nod.

'Okay so…'

'Okay… so… bye.'

'Bye.'

Dan sets off toward the gate.

After a while, he hears his name again.

'Dan!'

He turns. Marcus is standing where he left him, under the sign.

'Dan, I would never forget who you are…!'

'I'm home!'

Dan lifts his bags over the threshold and closes the front door. The house is quiet, but they don't seem to have gone out. He checks the living room – nobody there. He ducks into the dining room, now used as his office, and notices that Sarah has tidied some of his stuff into piles. He reaches to the computer tower and monitor and turns them on. He steps back into the hall.

'Sarah? Matty? Are you home?'

He treads up the stairs and sees Sarah's bedroom door ajar, a couple of shapes arranged on the bed, above the covers.

Dan pushes the door open a touch more and leans on the jamb. Sarah and Matty are having an afternoon snooze. Dan smiles to see them curled up together, mother and son breathing in unison, their faces a picture of calm.

Dan moves toward the bed, taking care not to step on the creaky floorboard. He leans over to give his nephew a soft kiss on the top of his head. Matty's eyes shoot open.

'Uncle Dan! You're home!'

Sarah stirs and props herself up on the bedding. 'Hi, Dan, we were just having a nap.' Her hair has come loose, and she has a pillow crease on her cheek.

'Sorry,' – Dan pulls a faintly guilty expression – 'I didn't mean to wake you.'

'That's okay.' Sarah brushes it off. 'I'm glad you're back.'

She seems rested and watches her son hop off the bed to give Dan a welcome-home hug. Then Matty moves from the cuddle to the landing in the space of a sentence.

'I've learnt a new trick to show you, I'll just go and get it.' Soon, he can be heard rummaging about in his bedroom.

'Why, what happened?' Dan asks.

Sarah is sitting up, tying back her hair. 'Nothing, don't worry.' She slips off the double bed and neatens the bedspread. 'I just said to Nathan that if you came back in time – and were amenable to a bit of Matty-minding – that I might go out with him tonight.' She looks up at her brother hopefully.

'Of course. Where are you going?'

'Oh, just for a drink. Is that okay? You don't have plans, do you?'

'Not that involve leaving the house, no.'

'Great, I'll just give him a call.'

Sarah shuffles into her slippers and walks past Dan out of the room. At the doorway she turns around again, her smile fading.

'How was the funeral?'

'Oh, you know… At least I got to catch up with some old friends. You go tell your prince that you *shall* go to the ball.'

Sarah looks at him for a beat, sensing that he doesn't want to dwell on the funeral right now. 'Thanks, Dan.

You're a wonderful human being.' She bustles down the stairs.

Dan calls after her: 'I already agreed!'

He can hear her laughing in the hallway. '… and then I'll make a start on dinner.'

'You know the way to my heart, sis!'

Matthew is now calling him into the bedroom. 'Uncle Dan! I'm ready. I can make this Action Man disappear!'

***

Sarah is standing in the kitchen, having cleared the table, three plates stacked in her hand.

'*I'll* wash up, Sarah,' Dan says, taking the crockery from her, 'you go and get yourself ready for your date. Matty, you can help me dry.'

'Okay,' the boy replies.

Sarah strokes her son's hair before walking away.

'Mummy, are you meeting Nathan again?'

'Yes, is that okay?'

'Yes,' Matthew says, in a matter-of-fact tone.

Sarah uncocks her head and leaves the room. Dan hands the boy a tea towel. Soapsuds start to fill the bowl.

'You like Tom?' he enquires.

'Yes, he's got a brilliant dog. And I like it when he makes Mum smile.'

Dan assesses the intel.

'Then I'll like him too.'

***

A short time later, Dan and Matty are sitting at the kitchen table, each wearing a plastic visor and staring at a hand of cards.

For a minute, silence settles over the scene. Bare elbows are sticking to the plastic tablecloth and their dining chairs creak on the tiles. Jellies are arrayed on the table in colourful heaps of sugary treasure. They can hear the comforting noises of Sarah getting ready and walking from room to room.

Dan has pushed the sleeves of his shirt above his elbows and the peak of his plastic visor casts his face in orange light. Matty pulls a serious face, contemplating his cards, so Dan matches the expression with a narrow-eyed cowboy scowl. On the table, the jellies are piled in groups – one by each player and one for the 'pot'.

Dan stares at the caricatured faces on the bright Happy Families cards he is flexing in his hand and pulls another dramatic expression for Matty's amusement. The corners of Matty's mouth flutter in a small suppressed smile as he aims to match his uncle's game face. He giggles, eyes twinkling, to watch Dan's next move.

Sarah looks in on them, having changed her outfit and spruced herself up. She brings a fresh smell into the room and is wearing her hair down.

'Not *too* many sweets, okay?'

Dan looks at her. 'Me or him?'

They laugh.

'And it's normal bedtime tonight, okay,' Sarah adds, addressing this more to Matty. She straightens up and looks at her brother. 'We lost track of time over at Quentin's last night.'

'Have you got Master Squeegee, the window cleaner's son?' Matty asks.

Dan passes him a card from his hand and tosses a jelly ring onto the pot.

'Don't worry, I've got computer stuff to do.'

'Writing a personal ad?'

She has a wry smile on her face but leaves the question hanging like she wants an actual answer.

Dan glances back up at her and rolls his eyes.

'Happy Family!' Matty proclaims, laying the four Squeegee family cards on the table, his smile a mirror image of the bright rainbow motif on his T-shirt.

Dan mock-squints one eye in response and Matty giggles quietly.

'No. Just some work,' Dan continues, addressing Sarah. He looks up. 'You've gone dating crazy!'

A car horn beeps outside the house and Sarah pulls her jacket on.

'No, I'm serious – you deserve love as much as anyone – why not give it a try?'

Dan shakes his head, sighing.

'I'm fine on my own, thanks. I'm too busy with–'

'Work,' Sarah says, finishing his sentence. 'We've all got work, Dan.'

Dan watches her smiling from the doorway. She doesn't seem to be backing down on the matter.

'Hadn't you better get going?' he says firmly, then smiles. 'Have a lovely time.'

CHAPTER 7

A few days later, Dan is snoozing awkwardly on the sofa. A scatter of papers blankets his torso, a packet of biscuits nestles beside him, and a small notebook lies open on his face. His cheek has acquired a pen stain. The house is peaceful; children are at school and the street itself seems to have fallen into a quiet, suburban nap.

He jerks awake at the sound of the telephone ringing and the notebook crashes to the floor. He sits up and attempts to re-gather the papers in some semblance of order before abandoning his shuffling and re-shuffling to get up and quell the insistent ringing of the phone. His stocking feet pad across the carpet with a muffled swish. The telephone seems to ring louder and louder.

He picks up the receiver. 'Hello?'

A half-eaten fruit digestive tumbles from somewhere inside Dan's sleeve. He sees the biscuit land silently on the pristine floor. He pats himself down for crumbs, his palm rasping dully over his jeans.

'Good morning. Would it be possible to speak to Mr Dan Mather?' The voice is male, subtly Scottish and smooth.

'Yep. I mean, yes, this is he – me.'

'My name is Douglas Anderson and I'm the executive assistant to Marcus Reece.'

Dan's mouth falls open. 'He hasn't...?'

'I'm calling with a–'

'Is he okay?' Dan asks, interrupting.

'Yes, of course. I'm calling with an unusual invitation…'

Dan closes his mouth, setting it into a firm line, and narrowing his eyes. 'Go on…'

'Mr Reece wishes to engage your services as a,' – the young-sounding man takes a second to read the term – 'paranormal investigator.'

The cadence that Mr Anderson's accent gives the last word makes it sound more flippant than usual. Dan squeezes his mouth into a half smirk and glances about the hall. *Do fine artists even have 'executive assistants'?*

'Does he, now?'

'Very much so.' The assistant sounds earnest, but Dan raises an eyebrow. 'It is in connection with the guest house Mr and Mrs Reece operate in Edinburgh… The Gillespie.'

'Is he there? Can I speak to him?' Dan asks, tiring of the joke.

He swaps the telephone receiver to his other ear and leans against the wall. A loop of the pigtail cord slips behind the console.

'I'm afraid Marcus isn't here right now but, rest assured, this is a genuine offer of a job I've been asked to extend, Mr Mather.'

'Okay,' – Dan smiles, shaking his head slightly – 'but it's a joke, right?'

'No, Mr Mather.' The executive assistant ploughs on. 'Mr Reece wishes to engage your services in the matter of a – forgive me, I'm not sure what terminology your profession uses, but as it was explained to me – a...'

'Yes?'

The line is quiet for a few seconds and Dan widens his eyes impatiently.

'A haunted bed,' comes the smooth voice, sounding unconfident for the first time in the conversation.

'A haunted bed?'

'Yes, that's correct, or at least a haunted bedroom. In the guest house.'

'Really?' Dan says cynically, barely intoning the question mark. He shifts his weight on the carpet and puts a hand on a hip.

'Really, Mr Mather. Or at least that seems to be the case.'

'And there's no one closer to hand who can unmask the baddy in the white sheet?'

'This isn't a joke, Mr Mather,' the assistant chastises. 'As far as I understand it, guests frequently and independently report strange experiences when staying in that one particular room.'

'Lucky them.'

The man doesn't respond to the joke. 'So, I've been tasked with ascertaining whether you have capacity to take on the job for Mr Reece and whether this is something you are able to investigate.'

'Yes, I am *able* to investigate anomalous phenomena, but I am quite busy with some assignments for the next few–' Dan stops himself. 'Tell me again. Why didn't Marcus just call me himself?'

'Marcus is busy in his studio, and I expect, Mr Mather, that, as this is in connection with *Mrs* Reece's business, it was considered appropriate for *me* to place the call.'

'Marcus doesn't believe in ghosts,' Dan states, straightening the inky ballpoint pens beside the leather-bound jotter.

'I was under the impression that scientific investigation doesn't rely on belief.'

Dan's eyebrows rise. The voice sounds just as professional as before. 'And you'd be right, er–?'

'Douglas. Mr Mather, there is a fee attached to the assignment and you would, of course, be staying in the guest house free of charge. In another guest room, of course.'

Dan laughs, absent-mindedly scratching his scalp and tangling thick fingers in his curls. 'He's pulling my leg, isn't he?'

'No, I assure you, not. A letter detailing the proposition will be in the post to you by the close of business today. Am I able to report that you will accept the job in principle?'

Dan shakes his head. 'Um… no. Tell him I'll think about it.'

'Thank you, Mr Mather. Expect the details to arrive within the next couple of days. I'll look forward to welcoming you to Edinburgh in the near future.' The words roll off the assistant's tongue as if it is a done deal.

'I said I'd *think* about it.'

'Very well, thank you for your time, Mr Mather.'

'Okay. Bye.'

Dan drops the telephone receiver back onto its cradle. The garden flowers in the small ceramic pot wobble. He stills the shaking and nudges the vase back into its proper place.

'And it will be a *no*,' he says to the empty hall.

Then he wanders back through to the living room, shaking crumbs from his shirt as he goes.

***

Over the next few days Dan works in his study, eyeballing the computer monitor amid a growing sea of clutter. Sarah and Matthew leave for school and return from school, calling cheery hellos and goodbyes as they come and go. They pack up swimming gear and arrive back home, wet and pink, and carrying chlorine-smelling bags. They carry a picnic blanket and a kite out to the car and shake sand off their shoes in the hall, salt caught in the tangles of their hair.

Dan jabs away at his keyboard.

Sarah and Matthew carefully pack up buns for Quentin and sweet, fresh carrots for Mrs Miggles, then return with a box of new magic tricks for Matthew to learn.

Dan digs around in the piles on the desk.

Sarah and Matthew laugh over games in the living room and create delicious, sugary smells in the oven-warmed kitchen.

Dan stares at the computer.

Papers and books form hilly landscapes around crusted coffee cups and used plates. Sunshine blazes through a crack in the thick, velvety curtains, sweeping the undulating mess in a slow-moving searchlight that evaporates by nightfall.

One evening, Sarah pops her head around the study door.

'Still at it?'

The clatter of rattling keys stops for a moment.

Matthew, in brushed cotton superman pyjamas, runs in and gives his uncle a hug. Dan strokes the boy's back.

'Goodnight, Uncle Dan.'

Dan looks away from the monitor, the padded leather chair creaking as he moves.

'Night, Matty. Sleep tight.'

The boy runs out of the room and Dan looks back at the screen.

After a while, Dan becomes aware of Sarah's presence, still lingering at the threshold. He turns in his chair.

'Don't forget to put *yourself* to bed, Dan,' she says, smiling softly.

'I just have a bit more research to do.' He punctuates the sentence with a small smile of his own.

She still doesn't leave.

'You're working too hard.'

'I just need to get this article out of the way before starting the interview series for *Science Now*. Look, don't worry. I'm going to have myself a break,' – he grasps for a nearby coffee mug, lifting it in gesture – 'see!' Dan gets up. 'Taking my mug to the kitchen, right now.'

'Okay, well, I'm glad you're busy. Just. Don't forget to have a life.'

Dan rolls his eyes and moves into the doorway. He kisses his sister on the cheek.

'Night, sis.'

Sarah watches him amble into the kitchen, then unfolds her arms and goes up to Matthew's room.

***

Returning with a steaming coffee, Dan settles himself in the chair and fires up the modem. He sips the drink while he waits.

The fan whirrs and modem chords score a strange soundscape while the humming monitor seems to wait patiently for Dan's next command.

Once online, he clicks his way to SHERPA-net and logs in. The chatroom shows that *right_hand_dan* has joined the discussion.

He scrolls through the recent topics: Legal considerations for paranormal investigators; What is sleep paralysis?; Stonehenge and cultural suggestion; Psychic control and personal wellbeing; When worlds collide – Ufology and Demonology; Researching the history of a private residence; Poltergeist-faking syndrome; Parapsychological research methods; Borley Rectory and the relocation of local myth; Automatic writing and the dissociated state;

Cryptozoology and undiscovered species; Living with ghosts – what not to do…

A new thread pings into existence at the top of the screen: *CaptainK-man* on *Pareidolia and Pseudoscience: the methodological difficulties of replicating subjective human experience.*

Dan rolls his eyes and begins muttering under his breath. 'That prick again. No, Keith, the subjective human experience is the interesting part. Of course, we want to replicate them under controlled conditions. It isn't interfering with the scientific method, it's…' He shakes his head, casting off the knee-jerk reaction. They have been through all this – publicly – at last year's VIGIL conference. He scrolls on, ignoring it.

He remembers that his SHERPA membership is due and rummages in the pile of papers for the society's form, setting it to one side as a reminder.

He moves from the discussion threads to the case list, noticing a couple of standard ghost sightings, a disappearing farmhouse and a persistent chill. One heading jumps out at him: 'Haunted Bed in Hotel'.

'Must be all the rage.'

He takes another sip of coffee and opens his e-mail service. He has a new message from his editor at *Science Now* and opens it.

As his eyes scan left to right, his smile drops. He allows his head to descend slowly onto the keyboard, where it comes to rest with a clatter of keys. He raises his face again and peers closer at the screen, checking the message and shaking his head.

He clenches his fists.

'Well, maybe,' he hisses, through clenched teeth, 'you should have considered "whether your readership engage with the human angle" before commissioning a journalist to set up interviews with a load of humans!'

He is keeping his voice low in order not to disturb Sarah and Matty.

'Fucking pricks!' he whisper-shouts at the screen.

He shoves at a pile of papers in a small angry gesture not designed to actually topple anything onto the floor. He gets up and mildly kicks at a chair leg, then stands, hands on hips, in the middle of the room.

He cocks his head and looks back at the pile, knowing it is there somewhere. He picks out the letter from Edinburgh and flicks it open, re-reading the offer.

'Well, I'm not as busy as I thought I was going to be…'

He glances around the room, thinking it through. Gradually seating himself back at the desk, he clicks back to the SHERPA forum and finds the 'haunted hotel' thread. He opens the discussion. *CaptainK-man* has got involved again. He seems to be complaining that the Edinburgh and Lothians Chapter had heard about a supposedly haunted bed in the city, but that they hadn't been contacted by the owners and couldn't find out where it was.

Dan smirks and slowly shakes his head.

'Well, Keith, it's not what magnetometer you *have*, it's *who* you *know*…'

He takes a pen and circles the contact number on the letter, placing it dead centre on his keyboard, ready for the morning.

Then he turns off the monitor, modem, computer stack and light switch, closes the door to the study and sends himself to bed.

CHAPTER 8

Dan is standing outside the Arrivals exit at Edinburgh airport with two cases and a holdall. He can't see much of Scotland from here, but a cloud-dotted blue sky above him indicates a fresh, spring day.

From where he's standing, there's no sense of Edinburgh's beauty – no glimpse of its parks, volcanic hills or the estuary islands stepping toward the sea. Instead, Dan is confronted by a sweep of faded tarmac that meets the chamfered kerb of a lay-by and a stretch of unremarkable wall.

Marcus wasn't there to greet Dan's plane, but he hasn't been waiting long. Tourists, families and business travellers spill out of the building and disperse toward buses, cars and taxis heading for the city. Dan watches the vehicles pulling into and out of the pick-up area. He doesn't know what car Marcus is driving these days.

He pulls the collar of his jacket up. Powder puffs of spring cloud dash across the expansive sky like surf over a bright-blue sea.

After a while, footfall dies down and the frequency of pick-ups ebbs away – a lull between itineraries. Cigarette smoke wafts into his face so Dan moves further away from the smoker. The automatic doors intermittently swish open and closed, annoyingly. He endures the scraping sound of jerky suitcase wheels. The smoke seems to find him again, so Dan gives the smoker an unnoticed stare. His wind-blown hair tangles over his face. He leans against the wall and checks his watch.

***

Twenty minutes later, Dan is sitting on his suitcase and checking through his box of equipment to see if it has all survived the flight. A car pulls up in the lay-by. Dan doesn't know the man who gets out and goes back to zipping up his case. The neat brogues pass him on the paving. Dan starts thinking about where he'd seen the payphones.

Calling the guest house should be his next move, but he is wondering about the next flight back to London. He notices that one of his boots is becoming unlaced but can't be bothered to tighten it up.

He stands up and stretches. *Maybe he's forgotten I was coming.* Was it a joke after all? Dan suspected the ghost job was just a ruse to get him to visit, but where was Marcus? *Has something happened to him? Should he worry?*

The sliding doors open once more, and the shiny-shoed man reappears. He looks around then checks the time. The automatic doors keep opening and closing behind him. He seems to be retrieving a bit of paper from his pocket. It flaps in the breeze, catching Dan's attention. The automatic doors close. The man unfurls his small sign. Dan can see that it bears his name. The doors swish open again. He doesn't *have* to reveal himself, could still go home on the next plane…

Dan takes a breath. 'That's me.'

The man looks at him.

'*I'm* Dan Mather.'

'Oh.'

Dan flashes an expectant look and gives a slight shrug to go with it.

'They showed me your picture, but I didn't recognise you.' The young man is walking over. The doors close. He is holding out his palm offering Dan a handshake. 'I'm Douglas Anderson. We spoke on the phone.'

'Pleased to meet you,' Dan replies, taking his hand.

He processes the suited man's neat appearance. His manner is mature, but his face is that of someone in his twenties, and nobody's eyes have any business being that blue. Dan also notices that some sort of product is keeping his dark-blond hair in its precise style. Dan pushes his own wind-tangled curls off his forehead and puts the holdall strap over his shoulder.

'It's the Vauxhall Astra,' Douglas says, indicating his car. 'Let me take your case.' He's reaching for the equipment bag.

'Thanks.' Dan tips the suitcase handle toward Douglas instead. 'Take the suitcase. This one is my equipment, so I'd rather take care of it myself.'

'Of course, do you have any proton packs in there?'

Dan looks at Douglas, who is smiling.

'You mean, is it like ghostbusters? No, it's nothing like that,' Dan explains, in a weary heard-it-all-before voice.

They approach the car and put Dan's luggage in the boot. Douglas straightens and notices the larger man just standing and looking down at him.

'I apologise,' Douglas says. He fixes Dan with those eyes and adopts a gentle smile. He opens his palms toward Dan, a little like a television presenter. Or a politician. 'I didn't mean to upset you with my little joke.'

Dan gives him a lopsided smile. 'Don't worry.'

Douglas opens a rear door for Dan, who just looks at him.

'Fuck *that*. I'm not the queen.' Dan moves toward the front passenger door and folds himself into the car.

Douglas neatly closes the other door, dips his head to one side and serves up another placatory open-palmed gesture. 'Okay, Mr Mather.'

Douglas gets into the driver's seat to find Dan looking at him. '*Dan*,' he says, correcting him.

Douglas watches while Dan spends a few minutes moving his seat back and adjusting the incline. He pulls the seatbelt over his large frame and fastens it, then picks at a blob of tomato sauce on his T-shirt.

'I have to say you're not what I expected,' Douglas is saying, pulling his own seatbelt neatly into place. 'I didn't realise you'd be *so*...'

Dan opens a packet of crisps, then notices the handsome face observing him.

'What?'

Douglas shrugs. The blue eyes are shining with an almost-smile. He turns the key in the ignition.

'Actually,' Dan says, changing the subject, 'I thought Marcus would be picking me up. Where is he?'

Douglas releases the handbrake. 'I'm afraid Mr Reece wasn't available to come to the airport, but you're expected, don't worry.'

Douglas looks over his shoulder and pulls the Astra away.

***

After a long stretch of flat field, straight road and low, green hills glimpsed in the middle distance, Dan begins to notice brown signs for cultural attractions. The road becomes lined with white bungalows and he gets the sense that they are entering the city. Taller houses line the road with unfamiliar architectural styles. Dan looks at the crenelated gables, stone-seamed corners and many-chimneyed stacks.

Douglas notices Dan taking in the scenery. 'Is it your first time to Edinburgh, Mr Mather?'

'It's "Dan". And you can stop with the "Mr Reece" too – we're actually old friends. We were at university in Manchester together. Mrs Reece too.'

'Catriona?'

'So, whose assistant are you anyway? You said you worked for Marcus when you called…?'

Douglas's eyes are back on the road. 'They share me.'

The car passes the zoo, rising behind a set of steep steps, and then Murrayfield stadium which Dan has heard of, from a very passing interest in sport.

'Trinny must be a… difficult person to work for?'

'Not at all,' Douglas shoots back. 'Catriona has a very big heart.'

'O-kay,' Dan replies, drawing the syllables out slowly.

Dan watches shops and tenements whizzing past.

'But, what kind of assisting does an artist need?' Dan turns to look at Douglas. 'He's got an agent, hasn't he?'

Douglas's face lights up. 'He certainly has, Mr Mather. You do realise Marcus is quite a big name in the contemporary art world?'

Douglas seems to take delight in Marcus's status. Dan tries to ignore the condescension.

'I do.'

'Many people seem to think that being an artist is about having deep emotions and expressing them with paint and so on.'

'Isn't it?'

'It's a business. Believe me,' Douglas flashes Dan a curt smile. 'There's lots of executive assisting to do.'

'I didn't think belief had anything to do with business,' says Dan, echoing their previous conversation on the phone.

'Business has *everything* to do with belief,' Douglas replies, very earnestly.

He is starting to sound like an American business guru. Dan hopes to nip the ensuing conversation in the bud.

'But you also work on the guest house side of things?'

'I'm not in the kitchen, if that's what you mean. But I do some work for Mrs Reece – Catriona – so that means getting involved with the guest house side of things. I'm more of a personal assistant – it involves all sorts of tasks you might not expect. It's a privilege to work for two very successful business owners like Marcus and Catriona.'

'Didn't Trinny inherit the property, though?' Douglas changes gear.

'Nevertheless.'

Dan notices the pristine grounds and impressive architecture of some posh, private school.

'So, is it the hospitality side or the art side that most appeals to you? Are you an artist yourself?'

'No. I'm a businessman. Or I will be sometime soon.'

'Are you from Edinburgh?'

'I am.'

And suddenly they are in downtown Edinburgh: 'gorgeous and Georgian' as Marcus described. Douglas gestures around them with his gaze.

'Braw, isn't it?'

Dan looks around at the architecture and the new-leafed trees. 'Yes, beautiful, like Dublin, but taller.'

Douglas gives Dan a funny look then resumes concentrating on the road. Dan looks out of the window and catches his own reflection, smiling back at him.

The Astra sweeps past the iconic castle and away from the heart of the city, eventually turning into a very well-to-do street. The car curves along the sweeping cul-de-sac and pulls up outside a grand door. Dan's nose is almost pressed against the car window. He steps out onto the cobbled setts and has to retreat a few steps to take it all in. A Georgian townhouse stretches proudly before him; three tall storeys above the street.

Douglas is taking Dan's luggage from the car boot and setting it on the pavement by the door.

'I knew they were loaded but… wow.'

Douglas places the equipment case next to the suitcase.

'Careful with that.'

After watching Douglas place it carefully on the ground, Dan goes back to counting the windows, uncertain where the property begins and ends. Some of it must be neighbouring properties, surely. He notices that Douglas is back inside the car when he hears the door closing. He is winding the window down.

'Just go through that door there. It's unlocked until curfew at nine. They're expecting you inside.'

'Aren't you coming in?'

'No, I'm taking this to the garage.'

'Can't you park here?'

'They do own some garages around the corner – but I meant I'm taking it to be MOT'd.'

'Oh. Thanks for the lift.'

'Not a problem.'

Douglas drives the car in a wide arc around Dan and back the way they came.

CHAPTER 9

As Dan walks toward the house, the reflection of the cotton-wool sky blinks from the windows, leaving ranks of dark, impenetrable spaces. No familiar faces appear at any of them. He attempts to pat down his hair.

He reaches the pavement and collects his luggage, setting it down on the stone slab by the double doors. They are standing open and he sees a second set of glazed porch doors and a pale face that turns out to be his own. He shakes a few crisp crumbs from his T-shirt and tentatively pushes his way inside.

As he ventures within, the portico casts a heavy veil of shadow that cuts across the bright sunshine. The inner doors swing closed behind him, shutting the spring day resolutely outside. The sounds of the city are swiftly torn away.

His eyes adjust to the gloom. A burgundy river of brass-tacked carpet emerges from the darkness, drawing his eye up from the black and white floor tiles, past the dark bannisters and toward a spray of expensive flowers on a unit at the top of the stairs.

To the left of the staircase, the hallway opens onto a guest lounge replete with soft furniture. There is nobody sitting in the chairs.

A wooden plaque presents the word 'Reception' in elegant lettering and an arrow that points around the corner.

He pokes his head around the wall to see a reception desk. Still, nobody is to be seen.

'Hello?'

Nobody answers.

Back in the hallway, he decides to move his luggage. Gradually, he notices that the pale floral arrangement on the upper landing now forms a dramatic backdrop to a slight figure. He can tell before looking directly at it, that it isn't Marcus. He looks up to see Catriona, all poised and pencil-skirted and slim.

'Dan, I thought I heard you arrive.'

'I *am* expected, then?'

'Of course. Come on up.'

Dan adjusts his shoulder strap, takes a breath and picks up his two cases. Catriona watches as he lugs them up the flight of stairs. By the midpoint of the climb, Dan's heart is beating faster. He notices Catriona's neat, grey court shoes as he nears the top step. She still seems to stand like a ballet dancer. His bootlace is working itself looser.

He dumps the bags on the landing.

'Is that your equipment?'

'This one is, yes,' replies Dan, trying to suppress his panting.

Catriona aims a sculpted smile at him. 'How intriguing! Dan, we're glad to have you.'

The momentary wrinkles appearing around her eyes seem to be the only giveaway that she has aged at all, and they vanish as soon as her smile does. She seems also to be shaking Dan's thick hand with her petite one, so softly that he almost didn't notice. Was she always so formal with him? Dan tries to remember. He doesn't think so.

'We're putting you in a room on this floor – so you might want to park your suitcase there.'

Dan sees a corridor of bedrooms marching off to the right and leaves his luggage on the carpet, as instructed.

'… but we'll go up to the room we want you to investigate, right away, if you don't mind, because I've got to go out soon.'

Dan gestures with his arm. 'Lead the way.'

He picks up the case of paranormal investigating equipment and follows.

First, they sweep around the first-floor landing, passing a single door near the front of the building. Then they commence another flight of steps carpeted in the same deep burgundy. Dan has plenty of time to study the colour of the carpet as he struggles with the case. He is aware of Catriona's light footsteps disappearing swiftly ahead of him. His boot is beginning to rub now, and the bag feels heavier and heavier with every step.

At the top, the stairs fade into darkness. Catriona flicks a light switch on.

Dan rests the equipment case on the landing. He barely has chance to register another corridor running the breadth of the storey before Catriona has disappeared through a door.

'This way.'

Dan picks up his kit again and darts after her, finding himself in a large bedroom with an elegant metal bedframe and an impressive view over the city. He plonks the case down again, no longer quite so carefully, and draws the back of his hand across his forehead to remove some of the sweat. Catriona has already taken up a pose between the furniture – first position? – and looks as if she has been waiting there for hours.

'This is it. The Strathkeel – the best room in the house.'

Dan scans the room and sees a broad window, patterned wallpaper, wooden furniture and a soft bedcover delicately embroidered with wisteria blossoms. The ceiling is comparatively low for a grand eighteenth-century townhouse and it creates a comforting feeling that Dan did not expect. The sunny day casts a slowly sweeping shimmer that alights on the curved lacquered walnut of the antique dresser and drawers. An elegant wardrobe stands in the soft shadows, implying the scent of mothballs that never comes.

Although the task in hand is to survey the site of ghostly encounters, the sunlight catching the rooftops keeps drawing his eye outside. He walks over to the window to take in more of the view. Catriona watches him, with hands clasped expectantly.

'Very nice,' Dan says, making a show of looking around the room again.

'Yes, it's unusual to have such a grand room on the top floor of a house like this – once upon a time this would have been all servants' quarters but at some point it's been converted to create this boudoir. And who could blame them? Look at the view.'

Dan is already looking at the view. He recognises, in the distance, the unmistakeable outline of Edinburgh Castle.

'All the furniture in here is antique; some has been in the property for a long time. The older, the better, as far as the American guests are concerned.' She seems pretty pleased with herself.

Dan smiles politely. He doesn't really need to know any of this.

'So,' – Catriona points a willowy arm toward the double bed – 'that's the bed in question. A lot of people are telling us a lot of strange things.'

Catriona glances in Dan's direction but then her gaze flickers away from his. *Is she lying?* Her attention lingers on the bed for a while and she seems to retreat into her thoughts.

'Can I meet any of them?'

'Yes, we have a couple staying here still – but they asked to be moved to a different room because of...' Catriona pauses, choosing her words.

'Things that go bump in the night?' Dan offers.

She smiles. 'Exactly. So, you can leave your things here – nobody is going to be coming in and out – the room is yours to do with what you wish.' She checks the delicate silver watch on her slender wrist. 'Come on, I'll show you the family quarters.'

This time, they leave the haunted bedroom and turn left along the corridor. Catriona points out a bathroom door and family kitchen to the rear of the building as she whisks him to a smaller set of stairs that spirals to the storey below.

They hurry down the small staircase, Catriona leading the way. Dan hears her saying something about how they refer to these as the 'back stairs' even though they are at the side of the house.

Where the back stairs reach the middle floor, he sees another bedroom, evidently theirs. Catriona closes the door as they pass. Next to this is their study. The short passage leads to a large living-dining room with two tall windows that look out over the street.

Dan works out that they are above the guest lounge and reception. A dining table stands in one half of the room, lounge furniture in the other, and many shelves and cupboards line the room. Tasteful prints and paintings decorate the walls. Dan guesses that the other door is the one they passed on the first-floor landing and would bring them out by the main stairs.

Catriona is picking up the telephone. 'Hello. Karen, Dan has arrived. I'm going to leave him here in the family parlour. Can you come and settle him in? Okay, thank you. I have to go out now. See you later.'

She puts the receiver back in place and smiles.

'Karen is going to look after you – show you to your room and finish the tour.' She cocks her head to one side and the silken curtain of her blond bob parts around her slim, taught neck. 'You knew Karen manages the place for us, didn't you?'

'Yes, I saw her in Dublin the other week.'

'Yes, it's funny how things work out.'

She picks up a handbag from one of the seats. *Funny?* Dan feels a sudden chill. He just looks at her.

'Oh!' he says, realising, 'yes, you mean… Karen working here.'

'With all of us here, it will be just like old times!' Catriona says, checking the contents of her bag.

Clearly it won't, Dan thinks, *because you didn't used to be so... standoffish... and Fintan used to be a lot more alive.* He wonders why Catriona didn't go to the funeral.

'Well, not all of us,' he says.

'No. Listen, I must get off. Karen will be up in a moment. Make yourself at home.'

She moves toward the door. Dan is trying to work out whether he feels more like a babysitter or the child that needs to be watched. Catriona pauses and looks at him.

'Glad to see you again Dan.'

Then she leaves through the door that Dan was guessing about. All alone now, he stands in the middle of the room, looking at the world outside.

CHAPTER 10

Alone in the parlour, Dan has a look around.

The elegant room is busy with decoration but calmed by sage-green walls. It presents a strangely archaic world of letter openers, barometers and carriage clocks. A small, strategically placed floral arrangement casts its watery green perfume across the space.

The luxurious textures of the sitting room look inviting, but Dan stands tentatively, and doesn't sit down. A turning vehicle creeps quietly over the cobbled setts in the street below. The noise is interrupted by the soft chimes of a silvery clock on the dresser, drawing Dan's attention back inside the room.

He spots a record player waiting silently in the corner and crumpled albums jostling behind glass cabinet doors. At once, he remembers LP-listening parties back in the day and smiles.

As he moves toward the record collection with thoughts of a good rummage, a shiny frame on the telephone table catches his eye. He picks it up – Marcus and Catriona's wedding photograph. There they are, a young attractive couple, light and dark respectively, wearing swanky 1970s clothes. Marcus wears a large-collared shirt, Catriona in daisy-laced silk. He peers at Marcus's youthful, eager face particularly. *Did he look happy back then?*

A noise at the door startles Dan. He shoves the photograph back on the table and wheels around.

In bounds Karen with a beaming smile. She rushes straight up to Dan and gives him a big warm hug.

'Great to see you again,' Dan says.

'I'm so glad you came!'

'So, this is where the magic happens?'

'And the ghosts and the ghoulies!' Karen jokes. 'Sorry, was that an insensitive thing to say?'

'Not at all,' – Dan shakes his head slightly – 'the whole point is that I come with an open mind – and a case full of science.'

He winks and Karen laughs. 'Wow, I never knew science was so easy to carry around.'

'For some of us geeks, it's *all* about the kit.'

Karen laughs again. She opens the door to the hallway. 'Okay, let's get you settled in.' She beckons him to follow with a jerk of her head.

As guessed, the parlour door leads them to the first-floor landing and a choice between taking the main stairs up to the storey above or walking left, around the stairwell and into the corridor of guest rooms. Karen leads him around the corner and opens up the first room. She has already moved his luggage inside.

It's a nice room with a neatly made bed that overlooks the quiet cul-de-sac. Karen hands him his keys – one for the bedroom and one for the front door, which she tells him is locked after 9 p.m.

'So, do you want the grand tour now or do you need to… freshen up?'

Dan makes a show of looking himself up and down. His trousers are rumpled from the flight and his T-shirt still bears the small sauce stain. 'What are you implying?' he says.

Karen giggles. In her alto voice, the giggle sounds comfortingly matey, rather than girlish. 'The grand tour it is!' she says, holding the door open for him.

'Oh, just a moment.' Dan bends down and finally tightens his boot lace. 'And I'm done.'

'There are other guests staying on this floor – but we aren't full, you know. And the main stairs are your fire exit. Turn left out of your room, straight down the stairs and out the front doors to freedom.'

Dan looks down the staircase to show he is taking the information in. It looks sunny outside – at least, the stone setts look bright, even though he can't see the sky.

'She showed you the family apartment, didn't she? The living room – or "parlour" as she insists on calling it – their bedroom, study, stairs up to the kitchen, bathroom, my room is up there…'

'By the haunted bedroom?'

'The very same.'

'The servants' quarters?'

Karen grins. 'I know me place.'

She leads him down the stairs and into the guest lounge where the reception desk backs onto the wall. She gestures to a door behind the desk. 'And sometimes you'll find us hiding in that cupboard under the stairs.'

Dan looks at her.

'The office,' she explains.

Beyond the guest lounge and reception area is the dining room, which runs along the back of the building. They walk through and Dan sees that it is punctuated by tall windows and dotted with breakfast tables.

'That's the door to the terrace and garden. It's another fire exit, but the garden is enclosed by the neighbouring buildings, so you'll be stuck out there, but at least you won't be in a burning building.'

'Is there going to be a fire?'

'That depends' – Karen is leading him through a side door off the dining room – 'on what Muriel gets up to in here.'

At this, the man and woman seated at the kitchen table look up and the man laughs. The woman bats a hand in Karen's direction.

'Cheeky miss!' she exclaims but looks amused rather than annoyed.

The hotel kitchen is larger, more organised, and better equipped than the family kitchen he glimpsed upstairs. It is also spotless. The couple seated at the table in the centre are a man and a woman – barely fifty, he would guess – and have evidently been looking through holiday magazines. They are drinking from mugs.

'Don't worry, Karen,' the man says. 'I don't let her anywhere near the ovens. That's my domain, not my wife's.'

There is a twinkle in his eye, and he puts his arm around her.

'He's a wee joker, so he is,' Muriel says, affecting an insulted expression. Undisguised adoration lights her eyes.

'So, Dan,' Karen says, 'this is the business kitchen – I only brought you in here to meet Muriel and Rab. So, this is Dan; he's come to do something with the haunted room.'

Rab snorts and sips from his mug.

'Rab! *You* don't know what there is in heaven and earth,' chastises his wife, 'and don't be rude. This is Dan's profession.'

'That's okay,' Dan says, laughing. 'I'm a journalist in my real life. I just do this kind of thing on the side.'

'Well, I've never seen anything "supernatural",' Rab replies honestly, mostly to his wife.

'No, neither have I,' Dan says.

Everyone looks at him, inwardly juggling their assumptions.

'Actually, I'd probably like to interview everyone who works here at some point – about it – because that's what we do: talk to the humans first, then start with the data readings.'

'Of course,' Muriel says, 'I have seen some things in my time...'

'Here?' Karen asks. 'He means about the Strathkeel room, Muriel.'

'Are you going away?' Dan asks, noticing the holiday brochures.

'Yes – Turkey. We're just reviewing the brochures and choosing our daytrips,' Muriel replies.

'They do let us out from time to time,' Rab adds, an amused smile playing at his eyes.

'Och, cheeky!' Muriel says, playfully swatting Rab on the shoulder. She turns back to Dan. 'Is it right that you were at university with everyone?'

'That's right.'

'Our daughter Carolyn is starting university this year – Aberdeen.'

Rab squeezes Muriel's hand.

'First in the family,' she continues. 'We're so proud, aren't we, Rab?'

'We are.'

'I just worry she'll be alright.'

'It's a wonderful experience,' Dan says, reassuringly.

'What would you know?!' Karen exclaims, playfully. 'You were always too busy studying to be having all the *experiences,* man.' She touches him on the arm.

'I had experiences!' Dan asserts defensively.

'It's the experiences I'm worried about!' Muriel says. 'To listen to Karen and Marcus talk about those days…'

'Well, it was the sixties, you know–' Karen says.

'The very *late* sixties,' interjects Dan, making a joke of sucking his stomach in.

'Anyway, I'm sure it's different now,' Karen says, addressing Rab and Muriel.

They take thoughtful sips from their mugs.

'So…' Dan begins, changing the subject, 'is Marcus around?'

'I think he's at the studio,' Muriel replies. 'What did Catriona say?'

'She didn't,' Karen replies. 'Don't count him for dinner, Rab. I reckon he might stay over again, and he can fend for himself.'

Rab nods and drains his mug of tea. 'Okay.'

Karen turns to Dan. 'I thought we'd have coffee on the terrace, seeing as it's such a nice day.' She looks at Rab and Muriel. 'Will you join us?'

Rab waggles his empty mug. 'Thanks, but we've had our tea break.'

Karen shrugs. 'That's okay.' Her invitation still stands.

'Got to get on,' Rab says.

'Thanks, though,' Muriel adds. 'You go out there, I'll make them – coffee is it? You two go and sit down.' She tidies the brochures to one side and gets up.

'Thanks, Mur,' Karen says, smiling.

Muriel shoos them away.

'Thanks,' Dan adds. 'Nice to meet you both.'

On his way out of the room, he hears Muriel saying to her husband: 'Are Catriona and Marcus ever under the same roof these days…?'

He follows Karen back out of the kitchen and through the dining room, where she is holding the door to the garden open.

A strip of paved terrace runs by the rear wall of the guest house, edged by a grassy slope that drops away to a wild, tufty meadow that fills the large, enclosed space. A few patio tables have been set out, their chairs tilted to rest on the table tops. Karen is manoeuvring one to sit in and invites Dan to take the opposite chair. He sits and settles himself. He looks up at the towering wall above them: a sheer cliff-face cutting a hallucinogenic angle over his head.

'So, this is all very impressive,' he says, his gaze drifting over the short, steep bank to the sea of fluttering blades.

Tiny grass flowers are shimmering above the meadow, adding a powdery spray to the green.

'Isn't it?' Karen replies. Then she lowers her voice. 'And it's all Trinny's, you know.' She sits back in her chair looking at him with warm eyes.

Dan whistles. 'I knew she came from a rich family, but I never expected all this. You live here, then?'

'Yes, on the top floor.'

She points above her head to the upper windows.

'Oh yes, the servants' quarters.'

'That's me!'

They laugh, studying each other as two old friends. She is looking more and more familiar to Dan now: the same expressions and direct manner he knew from before; the same way she crosses one ankle over the other knee. He is also growing acclimatised to her Geordie accent again. He thinks that maybe it has softened due to spending so long in Edinburgh.

The muffled music of the unseen city tinkles in the distance – seeming as untouchable as the cirrocumulus clouds dabbing softly at the sky. The space is overlooked but it feels as though they are alone.

'So, back in Manchester, would you have ever imagined you'd be working for Marcus and Catriona and living in a mansion?'

Karen laughs. 'It's not quite a mansion.'

'It is, compared to my house!'

The sound of the terrace door opening makes Dan look around expectantly. He sees Muriel with a tray and settles back into his seat. As she nears, he smells the strong coffee and then it is before him, shining blackly, glinting with the wobble of the table as she sets down the sugar and milk. They thank her and set about preparing their drinks, spoons tinkling against the china.

'Didn't you want to go into the police force?' Dan asks her. 'What happened?'

Karen smiles and looks at the far corner of the garden. 'A detective really…' she replies, 'like Shirley Beck.'

'Too much *Ghost Squad*? What got you into the hotel management trade?'

She shrugs. 'I just fell into it.'

'Sounds dangerous!'

They laugh.

'I suppose managing a guest house is what happens while you fail to plan other things…'

They laugh again.

'Do you like it, though?'

'I do. I like working with people, and I get to live in Edinburgh, very reasonably.'

'Not to be sniffed at.'

'I don't get out that often – but when I do, I *really* get out.' She grins.

'I bet you do,' Dan concurs.

The white sails of a seagull carving through the swells above cast a shadow that first flickers across Dan's face then dives across the grassy sprawl.

'So, what's it like working for Trinny?' he asks.

They both know that Catriona has gone out for the day but continue speaking with hushed voices.

'Oh, she's okay. I think she sometimes forgets we were friends once upon a time, has got a bit… "superior" over the past twenty years. But it's fine, you know. Marcus is here too. Sometimes.'

She doesn't say anymore. Dan sips his coffee, casually.

'So… when is he coming home?'

'I'm not sure. You know what he's like when he's making art. Soon, I suppose?'

'Well, I'm glad he got over his creative block.'

Karen looks up at the bright sky then back to Dan. 'Was I too drunk and annoying when you last saw me?'

'No. Funerals are really hard.'

She nods gently. 'Are *you* okay?' she asks.

'I don't know yet. Are you?'

'I'm okay. But I'm still crying about it at night. Best to keep busy.'

'Yes,' Dan agrees sombrely, 'I suppose that's what we're all doing. In our own ways.' He is imagining Marcus painting passionately in a studio somewhere.

'Dan,' Karen announces, leaning forward to command his full attention, 'I've never known you *not* busy! The only person that could ever get you to come to a party was Marcus.'

'That's because,' – Dan leans forward to meet her gaze, conspiratorially – '*he* doesn't like them.'

'Well, he could have fooled me.'

They settle back in their chairs. A minute passes. They are each remembering moments from the past.

'I was hoping he'd be here when I arrived.'

He watches Karen thinking.

'I'm not even sure he knows you're here.'

CHAPTER 11

After breakfast the next morning, Dan is waiting for his interviewees in the guest lounge.

He sits in the corner by the window and moves a tweed cushion out of his way. He leans forward and places his tape recorder and notepad on the coffee table.

For the time being, he is alone. The polished reception desk stands by the wall, unstaffed, but the narrow door to the office behind is edged with lamplight. Karen must be inside. Dan amuses himself with the thought that it could easily be just a cupboard under the stairs. Marcus still hasn't returned.

Dan is waiting for a Mr and Mrs Jenkins, but they haven't appeared yet.

There is a sense of timelessness to the room that has nothing to do with the traditional Scottish decor. The silent turn of the wall clock's sliding hands is somehow both soporific and shocking; the endless slip of time through someone's grasp.

The partition between lounge and breakfast room is partly open, and Dan can glimpse the bright blur of flapping curtains at a window there. On a shelf in the lounge, a model yacht evokes memories of a distant sea but only smells of resin when he picks it up.

***

Soon enough, Arthur and Cherry Jenkins are sitting on the sofa next to his chair. Dan is holding the notebook and pen, ready to get started. Arthur and Cherry are holding hands.

Dan leans forward and presses 'record' on the tape recorder in front of them.

'Thanks for agreeing to talk to me,' he begins. 'As Karen has explained, I think, I'm here to investigate the anomaly in the Strathkeel room at the top of the house.'

'Oh, how exciting, Art. Did they call you in just because of us?'

'No,' Dan replies, 'I think there have been other reports of similar experiences guests have had staying in that room.'

'And you've come up from London especially?' says Art.

'Not quite. I've come up from the south coast, below London, well, never mind.'

'So, you've made a special trip. How did…?'

'Oh, Marcus twisted my arm. Anyway, I'm going to record our conversation just for my record – if that's okay with you?'

Arthur and Cherry nod.

'Can you just say that out loud for the tape?'

'Sure.' Arthur leans forward and speaks slowly. 'We are very happy for you to record this interview.'

Cherry leans forward too.

'Yes. We are Cherry and Arthur Jenkins – Sergeant Arthur Jenkins – hardware store owners from Maryland, USA.' Cherry looks to Arthur who nods encouragingly. 'And we are staying,' she continues, addressing the microphone, 'in the Gillespie Hotel, Edinboro, Scotsland...'

'*Scotland*, dear,' Art interjects.

'That's right,' – she pats his hand, gratefully – 'and very charming it is too. Oh, and we hereby agree to have our voices recorded for the purposes of this interview to investigate the haunted bedroom.'

She sits back on the sofa. Arthur looks from his wife to Dan who is trying to suppress impatience.

'Will that do?' Arthur asks.

'London is on the south coast isn't it, Arthur?'

'We haven't visited yet,' Arthur explains to Dan. 'We're doing our trip the backwards way around.'

'Okay. So. Can you tell me what you experienced on the night you stayed in the Strathkeel bedroom?'

'Do you mean me?' Cherry asks.

'He means both of us, honey.'

'Well. They do say that we women are closer to the spiritual, you know, a bit more sensitive to other dimensions and so on, so I just thought...'

'But it was me who felt it first.'

'Okay. I'm interested in what each of you experienced. So, please, let's just have one at a time. It is best practice to interview you separately, as I suggested, the most scientific thing to do, but, well...' Dan gestures for Cherry to proceed.

'Oh no! We like to do everything together, don't we, Art?'

'That's right,' – Arthur smiles at his wife then looks back to Dan – 'we wasted too much time not being together – so now we do everything as a two.'

'Okay. So, Arthur, er… sir, you can go first. Please describe all and any unusual sensations you had during your stay in the room.' Dan readies his pencil for taking notes.

'Well. We don't sleep so good, now that we're over the hill, you know that, but we'd had a long day of travelling to get here – to this fine city…'

'It really is beautiful, isn't it?' Cherry's violet eyes are shining.

'It really is,' adds Arthur.

'I'm so glad we finally came.'

'Me too, honey. Europe was on our bucket list, you see, Mr–'

'Dan, please. So, you were saying…'

'That's right,' Arthur nods. 'So, we were very tired by the time we got here, and so I went out like a light.'

'Me too; the bedding is so soft. The bed's a little smaller than we're used to, but it is such a charming room!'

'Oh, honey, that bed was plenty big enough – you're such a petite little lady. She's no bigger than the day I first saw her.'

'Oh, honey,' Cherry says.

Dan taps his pencil.

'It's true! I wish I'd married you first.'

'Oh, honey,' Cherry says again, this time looking into Arthur's eyes.

They lean together for a kiss.

'You know,' – Cherry addresses Dan – 'a lot of places, they just assume people of our age want twin beds in their rooms,' – she looks back to her husband – 'but we don't, do we?'

'No, we like to sleep all cuddled up.'

'Sometimes we hold hands – all night. It's true.'

Dan notices that they are holding hands now. He checks the time counter on the tape recorder.

'Okay. So, Arthur, you were saying you fell straight to sleep…'

'And I did too,' Cherry adds.

'Okay. So, what did you experience?'

'Well,' Arthur begins, 'first of all, I began to feel like there were other people in the room–'

'Did you know he was a staff sergeant? So, you must believe what he says is true,' Cherry interjects.

'I don't think that's relevant, honey.'

'*Sure* it is. An army man wouldn't be given to flights of fancy now,' – she turns back to Dan – 'and he isn't.'

'Go on.'

'Yeah, and it didn't feel threatening; just kinda… nice. And when I looked over to the corner of the room, it seemed as though there was a lightness, and figures, emerging from the light, two of 'em. I think they were holding hands.'

'Could you see who the figures were?'

'No, at least, not that I can remember.'

'Did they talk to you?'

'No, I don't think so. And, well, that's it.'

'Thanks, Arthur. So, Cherry, do you mind telling me what you experienced that night too?'

'Well, of course. So, like Art said, we went to bed quite early, all cuddled up, that's how we like to sleep.'

'You said that part,' Dan says.

'And I think we must both have fallen asleep within ten minutes of going to bed, wouldn't you say, Art?'

'Or the second my head hit the pillow!'

'They do have such nice pillows here – friends all told us we should pack our own – but they are so nice. In fact, I'm going to…'

'And what did you experience during the night?'

'So, like Art said, there was a light, happy, feeling, and it was coming from one side of the room. I don't know how it woke me up, but I was happy that it did.'

'And did you see any figures?'

'Why yes! The same ones Arthur did. Honestly, it felt like they were friends – *our* friends. It felt like there were friends in the room. You know, I can't remember what they looked like now, but they were as solid as you or me. It wasn't scary; it was… comforting, somehow.'

Dan's pencil scribbles away. Cherry continues.

'And the reason I know we weren't dreaming – is because I said to him, what did I say?'

'She said, "Well, I know we booked onto the ghost tour, but I didn't know it started in our room"!'

Arthur and Cherry laugh together, her high trill complementing his melodic double bass.

'I did! In the middle of the night. That's what I said to him.'

'She has always been a funny lady.'

'But you see – in the morning we both remembered it – so it *couldn't* have been a dream.'

'That's right. That's how we knew. Cherry's a very level-headed little lady…'

'And he was a non-commissioned officer in the US army…'

'So, you can see it's not the kind of thing we'd make up.'

'Mr and Mrs Jenkins, you don't need to worry about that. As a member of the Society for Historical and Empirical Research into Paranormal Anomalies, I am committed to undertake, without judgement, empirical methodologies of investigation within an ethical framework of social responsibility… The point being that we come with an open mind. Nobody is suggesting you are making any of this up – it is just that there may be a different explanation for the experiences you have had.'

'And when we told the lady at breakfast – the Scotch lady – she said we weren't the *only* ones who'd felt it.' Cherry gives Dan a funny, wide-eyed look and slow nod.

'And *that's* when we got chills!' Arthur adds.

Dan knows that this is the line that will feature every time they tell the story to friends back home.

'So, did you feel scared when you were experiencing it?'

'I could never feel scared with Arthur by my side.' Cherry looks up at her husband lovingly and Arthur puts his arm around her shoulder.

'Truth is, we were still so tired, we just rolled over and went back to sleep!'

'We did! It will take more than a Scotch ghostie to scare us out of our bed.'

'But you still requested to move rooms?'

'Well, we do like our sleep,' Arthur replies.

Dan reviews the notes he has made. 'Thank you. I do have some follow-up questions.'

'Okay, shoot,' Arthur says.

'Have either of you experienced anything like this before?'

'Nope.'

'Never,' adds Cherry.

'Do you believe in ghosts?'

'Well, we believe in God,' Arthur says, 'if that's what you're asking?'

'We believe in souls,' Cherry clarifies.

'Do you believe in aliens?'

'Little green men?' Cherry hoots. 'No, I certainly don't.'

'People get carried away thinking about UFO's – because they don't know how the military operates. No,' – Arthur leans forward to speak into the microphone – 'no, I do not believe in alien invaders.'

'Have either of you ever experienced anything like this before?'

'No, I can't say I have,' Cherry replies.

'No, sir, I have not.'

'Do either of you suffer from hallucinations?'

'No, sir,' Arthur says, 'we do not.'

'Are you taking any medication?'

'At our age?' Cherry replies. 'Shake us and we rattle!'

'I told you she was funny. Is it important? We can show you if you come up to our room.'

'Have either of you experienced a head injury?'

'Well, I can think of a few friends who would like to bang our heads together if they heard us telling this story!' Arthur jokes.

'Oh, Art! They would *not*.'

'Thanks. I think that's everything. You have been very helpful, Mr and Mrs Jenkins.' Dan turns the tape recorder off and closes his notepad.

'Art and Cherry, please,' Arthur says, reaching over to shake Dan's hand.

'Well, that was fun,' comments Cherry, clapping her hands in a small pitter-pattering round of applause.

***

'Oh, sorry, man. I didn't know you'd started,' Karen says, popping her head round the kitchen door.

Dan switches off the tape recorder and Rab and Muriel look up from their conversation.

'Actually, we've just finished,' Dan says.

Rab gets up from the table and puts on the apron. 'Well, we don't live here. Got our own bed at home,' he says.

'And I've never once seen anything when I've been cleaning in there,' Muriel adds. 'I think it must be the actual bed.'

'I forgot to ask.' Dan flips his notepad open again. 'Did you believe what the guests have been telling you?'

'Well,' – Muriel has a think – 'they all seem very genuine. And the thing is, they say the same sort of things.'

'Ghostly presences appearing at the foot of the bed?' Karen asks. She has wrinkled her nose and her mouth is pursed in a not-quite-smile.

Muriel gets up from her chair and picks up a basket of wrinkled napkins. '*I've* never seen anything, but you just don't know, do you?' she says.

'Okay.' Karen addresses Dan. 'Are you ready for me?'

'Lead on to your underground lair. Thanks, Rab, Muriel,' Dan says, exiting the room with his tape recorder under his arm.

Karen leads him through the dining room, its linen tablecloths half stripped. He follows her behind the reception desk and into the office.

Ducking through the frame, Dan feels like he is stepping into a cupboard but finds himself in a small, windowless office. They are unmistakeably under the stairs.

A swivel chair, computer desk and small table have been crammed in, leaving a narrow path from the door to a second chair at the far side, beneath the angled ceiling. Dan almost bangs his head on the pendant light as he folds his bulky six-foot-three frame into it. Karen takes the office chair, tucking herself neatly into the space by the desk. She waits for him to get settled, her hands on the desktop like a seance.

'What makes you think it's a lair? Do you see us as some evil genius?' she asks.

'Oh, sorry, ill-judged joke.'

'No! I'd take it as a *compliment*.' She smiles. 'So, here we are.' She gestures around them with a sweeping arm movement that is comically at odds with the tiny space.

'Like I said, it will be a quick interview – because I don't believe in ghosts and haven't seen anything.'

'That's okay. You don't mind working in here? There's no window.'

The desk lamp has been turned on and is edging the chunky keyboard in recessed shadow.

'It's okay, I'm barely in here. Just, you know, when I'm working on the dusty, heavy ledgers in the light of a candle and they won't let us out until I'm done…'

Dan looks around a bit more. There's a computer by the wall and a stack of dust-free ring binders.

'But at least I've got me fingerless gloves…' she jokes, in a mock Dickensian accent.

'Okay, Bob Cratchett. Anyone would think you do this job against your will.'

Karen smiles at him. It could be twenty years ago. She looks at the small tape recorder on the desk between them. 'So, is this your fancy-pants ghost-hunting kit? I mean, I used to record the top ten off the radio with one like this, you know.'

'Ha ha,' Dan says flatly. 'No, you should see my high-sensitivity infrasound kit.'

'So, are ghosts very loud or very quiet?'

'Doesn't matter – I can amplify them with my bionic ear. Shall we?' he asks. He turns the tape recorder on. 'Interview with Karen Harcourt, 19 April 1991, the Gillespie, Edinburgh,' Dan begins.

'Age thirty-nine and five quarters, single white female, five foot eight, brunette, real ale fan, winning smile...' Karen interjects.

Dan flashes her a look, half-admonishing, half-amused. 'Have you ever experienced anything unusual in the bedroom in question?'

'No, never.'

She smiles. Dan looks at her, hoping she will elaborate.

'I've never seen or heard anything weird in that room, ever. I haven't spent the night there, but I do go into that room from time to time and have never experienced any "anomalies" in there. At all.'

'And your bedroom is near to the room in question?'

'Yes, my room is on the same floor and I've never experienced anything spooky in there, either – except perhaps a few ill-judged one-night stands.' She smiles.

Dan tries not to laugh. He composes himself for the next question. 'They let you have boys over?' he says, finally.

They burst out laughing.

'Only if I've done my homework,' she replies.

Dan sits back in the small creaky wooden chair, watching her. 'Didn't you ever want to settle down?' he asks, forgetting about the interview and the tape recorder. There are so many questions he wants to ask about her life since their university days, he realises.

'I think that question's off-topic.'

'Yeah, sorry.' Dan picks up his pencil. 'So, you've never experienced a presence in that room? Any "figures emerging from the light"?' he asks, quoting from the Jenkins interview.

'I have not. Look, it's an old building – not as old as the Jenkins think – the Americans don't tend to know the difference between medieval and Georgian…'

'You mean about five hundred years?'

'But it's an old place – bound to have its own creaks and noises and whatever. People's imaginations run riot, don't they?'

'They do,' Dan confirms, 'that's why we record hard data when we try to figure out what's *really* going on.'

Karen looks as though she is about to tell him something but a slow thudding sound all around them makes her stop. It continues: a weird, disembodied, muffled thud.

They look at each other with wide eyes, pupils dilating.

'Oooh!' Karen says, quietly, a spooked expression on her face.

'What's that?' Dan asks.

Karen laughs. 'That will just be the Jenkins on their way out – we're under the stairs, remember. We moved them closer to the ground – I don't know whose idea it was to put them on the top floor anyway. We don't have a lift.'

'Those stairs nearly killed me when I got here.' Dan shakes his head, remembering. 'And the Jenkins have got thirty years on me.' Dan remembers the recording and hits the off button.

'No, wait,' Karen turns the record button back on. 'Interview terminated at 11:13.' She turns the tape recorder off again and sits back in her seat.

'It's not a police interview!' Dan says, laughing.

'I've always fancied myself as Juliet Bravo – you know, I used to think that was the character's name!' She swivels her chair back toward the computer and switches it on.

'Did you say there were some other guests I could interview about this?'

'Yes – Mr and Mrs Ogilvie. They only live further along the coast, but they're regular guests when they come to the city.'

'Because...'

'Because they've got too much money and can't be bothered to go home? They're friends of Trinny's, anyway. Apparently had some experiences in that room too. Apparently.'

'And I can interview them this afternoon? Where do they live exactly?'

'North Berwick. It's really not that far. I'm busy the rest of the day but Douglas has agreed to drive you out there.'

'Couldn't I just borrow the car? Or hire one?'

'No need. Douglas will be good for oiling the wheels – with the Ogilvies.'

'Well, he does *seem* quite oily,' Dan jokes, standing up and minding his head.

Karen laughs in agreement and watches Dan squeeze himself around the furniture and open the office door.

'No, but he is good for some things,' Karen adds, more seriously, logging herself into the computer. 'When he's not getting in the way.'

Leaving the Ogilvies' smart porch, Dan steps into the blustery wind and crunches down the gravel driveway. When he turns back to wave, they have already closed the door. He sees the pale faces of Mr and Mrs Ogilvie fading away behind the glass.

He makes his way down the drive, edging past their shiny car. Salty gusts of air immediately cool his cheeks and billowing grasses whip at his shins. He turns onto the pavement to find the street more exposed and riven with wraithlike winds.

He hurries to the Astra parked by the kerb. Douglas is sitting behind the wheel, reading a book titled *Be Your Business: Faking It and Making It*. When Douglas notices Dan approaching the car, he closes the volume and slots it neatly into a briefcase that he places on the back seat.

Dan opens the car door and plonks himself on the passenger seat, the weaving wind buffeting his curls. Somehow, Douglas's hair remains firmly in place. Dan tugs the door closed, shutting out the seaside with a thud.

Douglas is watching him with a questioning look on his face.

'Well,' Dan says, 'they clearly hate each other!'

'What makes you say that?'

'Um… the way he talked over her… the bitterness in her voice…?'

'I think they've just been married a long time.'

Dan wonders what such a young man could possibly know about it. 'Yeah, but you have to wonder, don't you, why some couples even stay together,' Dan replies.

Douglas looks at the house and the Lexus parked in the drive. 'Aye, right. The big house...? The fancy car...?' Douglas suggests, as if it's obvious.

'But is it worth being miserable for?'

'So, did you find out any useful ghost intel?' Douglas asks.

Dan looks at him. 'Are you interested?'

'Yes,' Douglas answers earnestly.

'Well' – Dan wets his lips – 'they corroborated what other people have experienced in that room, yes.' He flips his wrinkled pad open, reviewing his notes. 'Each of them had a ghostly experience in that room – but on separate occasions. Found it menacing...' Dan closes his notebook.

'Couldn't you have just done the interview by telephone?' Douglas asks.

'Maybe, but in real life – actually talking to people face to face – you get to pick up on things, things that aren't there in the transcript.'

'So, are you trying to tell if they are lying?'

'No, not lying, necessarily – but it helps to make sense of things if you find out what people believe, how susceptible they may be to... wayward ideas, what medical conditions they have...'

Douglas is watching Dan intently. He seems genuinely interested now. 'And you can tell all that just by looking in their eyes?'

'Absolutely. I can tell *you're* hiding a big secret, for instance.'

Douglas's blue eyes widen. 'Aye? What?'

Dan looks deep into his eyes, intensifying the moment. 'I'm just kidding, mate. I'm not a mind reader.' He chuckles to himself. 'I have this other technique that I use...'

'What?' Douglas asks, intrigued.

Dan smiles broadly. 'I ask them questions and listen to what they say!'

This time Douglas laughs, louder than expected. Then he looks toward the end of the street where he can see a corner of the sea. He relaxes against the head rest. 'You had me going there.'

'And that's how journalism works!' Dan says, as if closing an education programme with the line. He puts his notebook in the bag between his knees.

'But you have to do research and all?'

'Oh yeah, there's a lot of fact-checking. But people are the best source. Talk to people, ask the right questions, listen to what they say.'

It's unusual for people to take such an interest. A lot of the time, when Dan mentions paranormal investigation, people reveal their narrow minds. They seem to assume that Dan is a crazy believer and never ask what's involved or how he goes about it or why.

'Sounds like I should be careful what I let on around you,' Douglas quips.

'Aha! So, you *do* have something to hide.'

The two men laugh for a moment.

'So, in all your years of "paranormal investigation", have you ever found a wee ghostie?'

'Nope.'

'Or anything weird – that can't be explained?'

'Well, it does happen. Well, one time.' Dan watches the clouds being blown across the sky. Gulls are busy swooping over the estuary and soaring out to sea.

'Really?' Douglas probes.

'Well. A few months ago, I made friends with a guy – seems perfectly normal, well, *kind of* normal – but he seems to know impossible things.'

Douglas has a bemused look on his face. 'Sounds like some sort of con man,' he concludes.

'No, it's not like that.' Dan wonders why he brought it up because he doesn't want to say any more, but Douglas is still watching him, ever the learner.

'But there have been a lot of cons exposed over the years…'

'So, it's not a recent thing?'

'Oh no,' – Dan shakes his head – 'there has been debunking as long as there have been ghost stories. Some of it's a hoot. Dwarves dressing as ghost children, costumes dangling on coat hangers, people hiding in cupboards, people getting changed in the dark…'

Douglas seems interested to hear more.

'You know,' Dan says, 'telling people I'm a paranormal investigator is kind of a barometer for me – at one end you get the people who just outright believe in ghosts and ghouls and, at the other, you get the people who *know* ghosts don't exist so they think there's no point investigating any of this – but then there's the middle sort of people...'

'And what do *they* believe?'

'Well, it's not about belief, but it's just the understanding that ghosts and the paranormal is all about real, living human beings – and the reason you look into it is to look at human psychology and cognitive processes and social history and ideology and... everything. That's my kind of people – but they seem to be few and far between.'

'You don't care, though,' Douglas observes, 'what people think of you?'

'No,' Dan agrees, 'not much.' He puts his seatbelt on. 'Shouldn't we get going?'

Douglas's response surprises him. 'Are you in a rush to get back?'

Dan raises his eyebrows, questioningly.

'There are a couple of braw beaches here.' Douglas waves his hand around. 'We could get a walk?'

Dan looks at the shimmering slice of wave-dappled water they can see at the end of the street. 'I don't know.'

'Or there's a park with an aviary, cafés, fish and chips...? I just thought, seeing as you've come all the way out here... It's a nice place to go for a walk.'

'How far is it?'

'See that blue watery thing at the corner of the road?'

'Good one. No, I meant, how long a walk would it be?'

'However long you want.'

Dan thinks for a second. 'No, you're alright. I want to get back and write my notes up. Do you mind?'

'Not at all.' Douglas belts up and turns the key in the ignition. 'I was hoping you wouldn't – because I don't want to mess up my shoes.'

Dan laughs – loudly but not harshly.

Douglas drops the handbrake and sets off. After a few turns, the road runs alongside the estuary, offering a glimpse of expansive water, before cutting inland between buildings and toward the city again.

***

Later, in the dark little office, Dan is typing up notes. His fingers clack heavily on the keyboard.

The small lamp barely illuminates the desk space and Dan's dragged expression is tinged ghoulish green by the light of the computer monitor.

He flips a page over and unclamps his lips to release a small, growling sigh.

There is a brief knock at the door, which immediately opens. Dan squints at all the light spilling in. He doesn't appreciate the interruption. The outline of a figure in the doorway soon resolves itself into the tailored form of Douglas.

'You still here?' Dan says.

'I thought you might need this.' Douglas is holding a folded sheet of paper.

'What is it?'

'It's the history of this place, just a summary. Not much, but something to go on.'

Douglas raises his eyebrows hopefully and hands Dan the sheet of paper which is neatly folded and smooth. Dan puts it, unopened, on the desk beside him. 'Thanks, that's not really how it works, but thanks. Did you do this?'

'Me? Oh no. I don't have anything to do with history. More of a "future plans" kind of guy. I think Catriona had it from when her family bought the house a couple of generations back.'

'Thanks.' Douglas looks around. He doesn't seem to be leaving.

'Are you staying for dinner tonight?' Dan asks.

'Oh no, I'm out with Catriona.'

Dan is mildly intrigued. 'Like a' – Dan adopts a funny expression – 'date?'

Douglas laughs awkwardly. 'Like a personal assistant.'

'Needs someone to carry her handbag, does she?'

Douglas shrugs.

'Sorry – I'm just hungry. Is Marcus back yet?'

'Should have taken me up on the fish supper. I'm not sure.'

'But has anyone heard from him?'

'Don't worry, he just holes up in his studio sometimes. I'm sure he's still alive.'

'Yeah,' Dan concedes, 'it's only been a day.'

***

After dinner, Dan is in the Strathkeel room. His case of equipment is unzipped on the bed. He is checking the magnetometer, but it doesn't seem to be working. The digital display keeps reading zeros – which can't be true because there are *always* some ambient magnetic fields to detect. The bedside lamp alone should be registering around fifty hertz.

He switches the magnetometer on and off feebly, then lays it down on the mattress with the other boxes of kit. He shakes his head and sighs.

He walks out of the room, leaving everything behind. He stomps down to the first floor, strides past the family apartment and unlocks his door. Inside, he shoves his suitcase out of the way and then flops onto the bed.

Soon, there is a knock. He springs up to answer it and finds Karen there.

'What?' he asks.

'Just thought you'd like to know. Marcus called – he says he'll be back tomorrow, or the day after.'

'Did he?' Dan responds sulkily. 'Did he forget I'm here?'

Karen looks uncomfortable but tries to think of something helpful. 'It wasn't me who spoke to him.'

Dan is walking past her into the hall. She watches as he turns the corner and starts trudging down the stairs.

'Where are you going?'

He doesn't stop. Some of the steps groan under his tread.

'Out!' he calls, without turning to face her.

'"Out" where?'

Dan opens the front doors dramatically. 'Just out.'

He walks out into the street, leaving the porch doors ajar. Karen stands watching from the top of the stairs. The sounds of the city evening fill the hallway. Dan doesn't reappear.

CHAPTER 13

The next day, at a corner in Haymarket, Dan is checking a scribbled address against the street signs.

The thing with Edinburgh addresses, he is realising, is that there are too many parts to them: confusing sets of numbers balancing algebraically either side of a slash or dash.

Having followed directions away from the main road, he finds himself in a channel of tall tenements. The kerbs are lined with endless parked cars and the pavements seamed with railings.

He makes his way toward his best bet for his destination and finds that the door is flanked by a column of intercom buzzers. Tiny windows bear clues to the occupants. He peers closer at the cryptic labels. He finds it – a tiny brass name plate that says '38-9, SHERPA-ELC'.

His finger hesitates over the buzzer.

'I'm going to regret this,' he says to himself.

Then he presses the button.

'Yes?'

The sound is muffled. Dan positions his ear closer to the intercom, resting a hand on the wall.

'Hello? Is that SHERPA?'

There is just a fuzzy silence in response.

Dan speaks again before the connection is cut off. 'The Society for Historical and Empirical Research into Paranormal Anomalies?' he says, reeling off the name.

'Do you mean the *Society for Historical and Empirical Research into Paranormal Anomalies – Edinburgh and Lothians Chapter?*'

Dan sighs and looks up the street. A couple are walking along, laughing. The woman's heels clip the paving stones as they pass.

'Okay. *The Society for Historical and Empirical Research into Paranormal Anomalies – Edinburgh and Lothians Chapter.*'

'And who is this?' the voice continues.

'It's Dan – as you well know. Keith…? I just spoke to you, not half an hour ago – and by the way, your directions weren't up to much.'

'Well, you're here, aren't you?' the voice points out.

Dan takes a breath, watching the couple disappear around the corner.

'Evidently,' Dan says, sharply, then adds, more wearily: 'Just let me in.'

The buzzer sounds suddenly by his ear, causing Dan to flinch. Then he pushes the heavy door open and goes into the stairwell. He's been told that they are on the second floor, so he grasps the metal bannister and starts climbing, his boots stomping on the worn, grey flags.

Edinburgh, he thinks, seems to be mostly comprised of slopes and steps.

Once a tenement of residences, the building now houses a few offices of one sort or another. He passes a cheap-looking law firm, an agency of something, an association for such and such... He stops at the correct landing. A small sign lets him know that he is at the right door.

The door is open. He sees a high-ceilinged room with metal shelving along the far wall.

He pushes the door further ajar.

Inside, Dan finds himself cordoned off from the room by a waist-high wooden barrier. The room looks like something from a different age, perhaps a black-and-white screwball comedy – but there is no wise-cracking fast talk happening here. Behind the barrier sits a man wearing a black T-shirt. He watches patiently as Dan looks around.

The place resembles a sort of amateur local library – not quite business, not quite residence – and is shot through with the distinctive scent of sugary tea. Dan scans the row of mismatched shelving, discovering volumes, folders and boxes among the tangled clutter. He can assume that it will all be organised in some secret, esoteric system understood by a very select few.

The man in the black T-shirt speaks. 'Dan Mather?'

Dan opts for a gesture rather than replying verbally. The man is opening a ledger of some sort and seems to be waiting for a spoken reply. There is nobody else in the room and Dan would put money on being the only visitor all day.

He watches the man rest his book on the barrier then open it carefully, the wrinkled skin of the leather ledger revealing folios of smooth paper sewn tightly to the spine. The man lays a pen along the crease.

Two men enter through a doorway in the far wall. The one in front walks crisply to the centre of the room and comes to a stop, planting his feet wide in a military pose. The man sauntering behind carries a mug of tea. Dan notices that they are all wearing black.

'Alright, Dan,' the tea-drinker begins in greeting, shuffling closer.

'Well, if it isn't *right_hand_dan*,' the other says, talking over him.

'You know my actual, in real life, name… I'm not calling you *CaptainK-man* to your face.' Dan looks to the tea-drinker. 'Hi, Jim.'

'Alright, Dan. How's it going?'

'Alright. How are you? I haven't seen you since VIGIL '90,' Dan replies.

'Well,' Keith cuts in, 'let's not get carried away – there's protocol to be followed.'

As he turns toward Jim, Dan notices that Keith has actually clasped his hands behind his back. 'What's the first rule of SHERPA-ELC?'

Jim looks blank. 'I don't know, Keith.' He shrugs and takes a sip of tea.

'The first rule is…' says the man by the door. Dan had almost forgotten he was there. '…everyone has to sign in.'

Dan looks at the register.

'Yes, Gregor,' Keith affirms, 'everyone has to sign in.'

'I have to sign in just to come into your office?'

'It's not an office; it's a headquarters,' comes Keith's reply.

Dan shifts his weight onto the other foot. He spies a shelf bowed under the weight of printed computer paper and wonders what intriguing dataset it contains. 'The headquarters of SHERPA is in Melton Mowbray,' he says.

'No,' Keith counters, 'the headquarters of the Society for Historical and Empirical Research into Paranormal Anomalies – *Edinburgh and Lothians Chapter*.' He pauses. 'You're standing in it!' Keith adds, riled. He points at everyone's feet in turn.

'But if *I'm* already standing in it,' Dan asks, 'then why do I have to sign something to get in?'

'Just here,' – Keith instructs, pointing at the register – 'name, address, date, time – twenty-four-hour clock please – reason for visit and membership number – the full nine-digit number – here. You did bring your membership card, didn't you?'

'But…' Jim begins, in the background.

'No, visitors need to present their actual membership card so we can verify they are who they say they are,' Keith insists.

'We know who it is – it's Dan,' Jim says, shuffling toward them.

'Remember, you had that interesting debate about human subjects at the conference last year? Remember?'

'I simply don't think it is congruent for empirical paranormal investigators to include subjective human experience in our methodologies,' Keith says, snapping back into the old argument, 'let alone seek to influence or replicate it. Anyway, I'm waiting. You realise you are already eleven minutes' – he looks at his watch – 'and thirty-seven seconds into your appointment time?'

'Because your directions were terrible. Anyway,' – Dan makes a show of looking around the room – '"appointment"? Does it get busy around here?'

Keith folds his arms. 'That's how we operate. So, if you don't mind,' – he holds his hand out expectantly – 'membership card please.'

Dan puts his hand in his pocket and jiggles it around. Then he thrusts his left hand into his left pocket. A look of concern spreads across his brow. He checks his back pockets, then his shirt and jacket, rummaging more frantically now.

'No membership card, no entry…' Keith states, with a slow shake of his head.

'Just kidding, I have it right here,' Dan replies, taking his wallet out of his trousers, flipping it open and fishing out the card.

He hands it to Gregor to copy the details into the ledger, keeping his eyes fixed on Keith and smiling a broad smile. Jim laughs softly in the background and sits on the arm of a tattered, seam-ripped chair.

'Please state the nature of your visit,' Gregor says.

'You *know* why I'm here. We just spoke on the telephone. The,' – Dan grabs Gregor's pen – 'mag-net-om-e-ter,' writing the word as he says it aloud.

Gregor seems happy that the register has been completed at last.

'Oh, yes,' Keith chips in. 'Now, why do you need to borrow it again?'

'You *know* why,' Dan says, in an overly patient voice, pacing around by the door. 'I'm in Edinburgh investigating a reported anomaly and my own just packed up and doesn't work. I don't know anyone up here and, please,' – he grabs the wooden barrier, leaning toward Keith for emphasis – 'could I kindly, pretty please, borrow yours?'

'I find that regular maintenance checks prevent this sort of…' begins Gregor.

'Oh, yes? The haunted bedroom job?' Keith asks.

Dan sighs. 'Yes, as explained.'

'And why do you think you are best suited to investigating that one – when it is so clearly on our patch?'

'I thought we were all one association…' Jim says.

'As I think I may have mentioned, I am old friends with the proprietor and my services were personally requested.'

'I see. I didn't think it could be your personal reputation.'

Dan titters a bit, shaking his head and relaxing. He perches on the barrier like a seat. 'Look Keith,' – his voice is now earnest – 'I apologise. I'm sorry we got into all that at VIGIL…' Dan holds out his hand. 'Don't you think we'd be better off working as a team?'

'Well, that depends on the regulations about inter-chapter collaboration and…' Gregor rattles off some rules and regulations, but nobody listens.

'No, I don't,' Keith says, answering Dan's question.

Dan lets his proffered handshake fall away.

'You can loan our magnetometer to complete the job – we wouldn't be upholders of the mission statement if we didn't lend it to you – but you're not getting any help.'

'*I'll* give you a hand with the data readings, Dan.'

'Thanks, Jim.'

Keith wheels around.

'Actually,' Jim continues, thinking it through and gently scratching his head, 'I won't be here.'

Dan raises his eyebrows.

'Taking Sally up to Mull for a while – little holiday,' Jim expands.

'Are you? How is Sally? That sounds really nice.'

'But we must go for a pint if you're still here when I get back.'

'We must,' Dan agrees.

Keith, who has been flipping through another ledger, cuts across their conversation. 'You can have it – but we can't issue it until Monday.'

Dan looks crestfallen. 'Is someone using it?'

'I can't divulge that information. It will be ready for you here on Monday to collect.'

'Great!' Dan gets up off the barrier. 'That really saves the day. Should get some useful data out of this one.'

Keith hands the second ledger to Gregor.

'Thanks, Keith,' Dan says, 'you're a real...' The sentence runs out of steam as Dan can't think of an honest *and* appropriate way to end it. Keith's small smile withers alongside the unfinished sentiment.

'But first, you have to fill in this.'

Dan looks down to see Gregor pointing to the other book, his finger tapping the sticker that says 'Equipment Loans' on the front.

CHAPTER 14

The next morning, Dan is in the breakfast room, polishing off a plate of full Scottish breakfast. He's sitting by a window but not looking outside.

A swell of sunshine warms the room, glinting from silvery knives and salt cellars. Dan sits alone, casting a short, stumpy shadow that pools by the feet of his chair.

Dan chases the last piece of fried potato around his plate, tracing a bright smear of bean juice and yolk. He peers at his forkful, eats the last morsel of tattie scone and pushes away the plate. He picks up his coffee cup and enjoys the warmth flowing into his palm. It eases the tension in his writing wrist.

The only other guests remaining in the dining room are a young couple gazing into one another's eyes. Dan resumes flicking through his notebook.

***

After breakfast, Dan takes another cup of coffee to the guest lounge, where he sits in the armchair by the window, perusing the morning papers. It's becoming a routine.

He is skim-reading an article in *The Scotsman* about an apparently infamous crooked lawyer, Malcolm Duncan-Fox, who was jailed for defrauding hundreds of people, but has been denied early release. The story makes Dan strangely sad – can people not trust *anyone* anymore?

He looks up at the sound of suitcases and laughter gently descending the stairs. The loved-up couple approach the reception desk and begin checking out. Perhaps he is over-caffeinated but their giggling and pawing at one another irritates him. With a noisy rustle and flick, he raises his newspaper like a shield.

After the couple have left, Karen leans on the reception desk, looking toward Dan. 'What are you up to today?'

'Actually,' – Dan folds the newspaper in his lap – 'I'm at a bit of a loose end.'

'Well,' – Karen comes out from behind the desk – 'Auld Reekie is your oyster! What do you fancy doing?' She picks up a few leaflets from the rack at the edge of the desk. 'We've got aaaalll the information.'

She fans out the leaflets then peers over them and flashes her eyes with melodramatic excitement. She looks at the leaflets, about to work through them with the casual assessment of a local in the know.

'The Scott Monument is worth a visit – two hundred and eighty-seven steps, great view…'

'Oh, I'm not really a fan of heights. Or stairs. Actually, I think I'm just going to wait around here.'

He sips the coffee, which has cooled a bit too much. Karen puts the leaflets back where she got them.

'Up to you. Do you need anything?'

Dan puts the newspaper back on the coffee table, where it falls with a flop. 'Actually…' Dan says. Karen pauses at the office door and looks back. 'Do you get *The Register*?'

***

Later, Dan is knocking at the parlour door. The quietness of the guest house this morning is beginning to get to him. He opens it gently and goes inside.

Catriona is sitting in an elegant chair by the telephone table, her slim fingers delicately rifling through some paperwork. She looks up and switches on a decorous smile, the soft sweep of her hair caressing the finely sculpted parabola of her cheek.

'Come in, Dan,' she says belatedly. 'You don't need to knock.'

Dan walks toward her.

Inside the parlour, a new floral arrangement casts a fragrant lull over the still space. Outside, another fine spring day is blasting through the city and Dan edges toward the windowpane, following its bright trail.

He sees the sunshine dancing over the rooftops and falling warmly on the amber-tinted setts. Somewhere in the distance a flag is tugging at its pole. At the end of the crescent, a dog is acting much the same, pulling at the lead, full of passion for the park. The lively blur catches Dan's attention then pet and owner are gone.

'I didn't know if...' Dan begins. His gaze drifts once again to the city outside. He takes a breath. 'Is Marcus home today?'

'Very possibly,' Catriona says, resting her papers on her lap.

'I just wanted to update him on what's happening with the investigation...'

'Oh, yes?'

She seems more polite than interested. Dan can hear the whir of cogs in the distant carriage clock by the far wall.

'Or maybe, you can pass it on...?' Dan's eyes drift from Catriona's face to the world outside, once more.

'Oh, Marcus doesn't care about that,' she says quickly, with the brusqueness that wealthy people seem to get away with. 'It was *I* who commissioned you.'

Dan's attention snaps back to her slim face. He forces his mouth into a loose smile. Catriona resumes leafing through her papers.

'Oh... Well...' Dan begins, shuffling his feet on the thick carpet. A car engine trundles along outside. 'I've arranged to borrow some equipment tomorrow,' he says flatly, ploughing on with his report, 'because mine decided to pack up...' A black taxi is pulling up outside the guest house. 'But some acquaintances have come to my' – Dan recognises the passenger – 'rescue...'

He sees Marcus getting out of the taxi, carrying a small bag. His dark hair waves in the breeze as he leans on the driver's door, finishing a conversation with a laugh and a light tap on the roof.

Leaving the parlour door open, Dan finds himself jogging down the stairs. He has just reached the tiles when Marcus pulls open the porch doors and walks inside. He looks past Dan to where Catriona is standing on the landing above. Marcus stops walking and drops his bag gently to the floor.

'You're back,' Catriona states.

'I am.'

She places her hands on her slender hips. 'Did you get it done?' she asks.

'What?'

'Whatever it was you had to do.'

Dan observes them watching one another, feeling like an intruder. 'Marcus!' Dan's cheery tone is at odds with the atmosphere that has been settling in the hallway like dust.

'Dan!' Marcus steps back in surprise. He smiles uncertainly. 'What are you…?'

'Your haunted bed situation. I…'

The men look at one another.

'Marcus.' Catriona's raised voice cuts between them from the top of the stairs. 'Come up. We have some things to discuss.'

Marcus looks to Dan. He seems to have lots of questions on the tip of his tongue. He swallows. 'Sorry, Dan.' Marcus gestures with out-turned palms. 'I'll see you later.'

Marcus is still looking at Dan as his feet reach the stairs. On the floor above, Catriona turns sharply on her heel and returns to the parlour.

'I'll be here!' Dan calls after him. He watches Marcus disappear.

He stands in the hall, thinking, looking at the zipped holdall sitting on the floor.

He is still there five minutes later and can't hear anything from upstairs. *How long will they be talking for? Should he just go out and enjoy the day?*

He watches a man leaving a building across the street and stride into an exhilarating breeze. He becomes aware of someone walking slowly down the stairs.

'Are you lost?'

Dan turns to see Cherry smiling at him, her violet eyes, bright.

'You're lost in thought, aren't you, Mr Mather?' Arthur answers for him, kindly.

'*Dan*,' Dan says, not quite shaking his dark mood.

Arthur smiles. 'Dan.'

The couple have been walking down the stairs arm in arm and, as they wheel around into the guest lounge, Cherry links arms with Dan as well.

As the three of them enter the room, Karen sticks her head out of the office. 'Your taxi should be here in five minutes, Mr and Mrs Jenkins.'

'Thanks, Karen,' Art replies.

Dan finds himself taking a seat with the couple. From his now-regular spot in the corner, Dan has views of both the hallway and the street. The edition of *The Register* he was reading earlier is still lying on the arm.

'Do you want to join us, Dan?' Cherry is touching his knee and casually waiting for an answer. Dan processes the question.

'Oh, no, I…'

'We're off to the palace,' Art adds.

'The palace of Holy-Rood,' Cherry says.

'You'd be very welcome to join us,' Art offers.

'Now,' – Cherry presses her hands together – 'did you find the ghost?'

'I'm still working on it.' Dan smiles. 'So, are you enjoying your stay?' Dan glances to the hallway, then back to the couple.

'Yes, thank you – very much,' Art answers.

'Oh, sure, Edinburgh is such a beautiful old place,' Cherry gushes.

Dan keeps his eyes fixed on hers.

'We're here for another five days,' she continues, in full itinerary mode, 'and then we're off to England.'

'London, Windsor, Stratford, Bath…' Art adds.

'The Cotsles.'

'Cots*wolds*, honey.'

They are looking at one another, happily anticipating the subsequent legs of their trip. They don't notice Dan keeping his eye on the empty hall.

'We're doing it back to front, I guess.' Cherry's hand alights on Dan's arm. 'It's our wedding anniversary trip.'

'It certainly is.' Art reaches a long arm around his wife's petite shoulders and gives her a squeeze.

'Oh? How long have you been married?' Dan asks, mustering the required interest. He can't help his eyes flickering back to the foot of the staircase.

'Ten years on the fifth!' Cherry says.

Dan is surprised by the low number. He looks at the couple. 'Ten?'

Arthur leans in and almost winks. 'It's the second marriage for both of us,' he explains, then, looking at his wife, 'we saved the best for last.' Then comes the wink.

'Oh, Arthur, Nancy wouldn't like you saying that,' Cherry chastises him, but is beaming.

'But it's true, honey.' Art turns to Dan. 'I don't know why we stuck our first marriages for so long.'

'Oh, don't worry,' Cherry interrupts, thinking she sees something in Dan's expression. 'We're all still friends.'

'And we all still play bridge, same as ever,' Art continues.

'Oh, well… congratulations,' Dan says.

'I still should have married you first.'

'But you didn't want to hurt Nancy, or Emmett, and, look, Dan doesn't want to hear all about this… Are you sure you won't join us?'

'No, honestly, thanks for the invitation but I'm fine.'

'Looks like your taxi is here,' Karen announces, standing by the desk and looking out of the window. She points to the car pulling up outside, then goes back into the office.

The Jenkins get up, Arthur first, holding out a hand to Cherry. Once standing, she pats her dress down and puts her handbag over her shoulder. Dan stays where he is.

'You have a good day, Dan,' Arthur says. 'I hope you didn't mind listening to our story.' Then Art leans in, resting a hand on the wing of Dan's chair. 'It's just that I learnt life's most important lesson,' he says, by way of explanation, 'and I want everyone to know.' Arthur straightens up.

'Life's most important lesson?' Dan asks.

'It's short! Don't waste time waiting around and not living it.' This time, Arthur's wink is aimed earnestly at Dan.

'Are you coming, Art?' Cherry has reached the front door.

'See what I mean?' Art flashes his eyebrows at Dan before turning to his wife. 'Coming, honey.'

The Jenkins leave.

Dan looks around the room. He is alone. He tidies the newspaper onto the coffee table. He still can't hear anything coming from upstairs. The taxi drives away.

Dan leans forward in his chair, steepling his fingers.

Just go up there and talk to him.

Just as he is on the edge of marching up to the parlour as he wants to, a noise interrupts his thoughts. Swift footsteps are travelling *down* the staircase. Dan gets up from the chair.

He sees Marcus dashing through the hallway, grabbing his bag on the way. He doesn't stop and doesn't look in Dan's direction as he goes.

Dan sinks back into the armchair, then kicks out at the coffee table. It flips over.

'Are you alright?' Karen asks, having heard the commotion.

Dan rights the table and picks up the newspapers that scattered on the floor. 'Yes.'

He singles out *The Register* and turns to the personals section at the back.

'Karen, can I use your phone?'

***

After dinner, Dan is in the haunted bedroom with his ear to the wall – not his actual ear but his ceramic contact microphone.

He hears the strange, amplified sounds of unidentified slides and scrapes, the vibration of voices, the buzz of electrical wiring and the otherworldly clanking of water travelling through pipes. His boots butt up against the skirting board, leaving a tiny smear of black on the paint.

He spent a short time moping about in his room, packing and unpacking his suitcase, before relocating to the Strathkeel room to do some experiment prep.

It feels covert yet cosy being alone there, working in the semi-darkness. The light of the bedside lamp slides over the wall before him, the fleshy posies that decorate the wallpaper contrasting darkly with the sheen. The scent of lavender drifts from the shadowy furniture and everything is still.

Dan stands, listening quietly in the dark.

The contact mic is attached to a high-sensitivity acoustic detector which, in turn, is attached by headphones to Dan's head. It always makes Dan feel like he's wielding a stethoscope, like he's on the verge of asking the house to cough.

He moves the microphone to another part of the wall, being thorough in his groundwork. He is listening inside the building itself for any indication of unusual vibrations, moving parts or pest infestations that the owners didn't know were there. Dan's breath is shallow and controlled. Just once, he'd like to discover a secret compartment or hidden passage, but he never does.

Listening to the wall, Dan's eyes idle to the inky swathe of sky, high above the orangey fug of the city lights. He picks out the stars hiding there in plain sight.

If he heard something interesting, the bionic ear could also be wired up to his standard audio recorder. For the moment, the recorder is on the bedside table, taping the ambient sounds of the room, the wires twisted into a strange symbol like a code. It could be useful for noise reduction purposes, but the infrasound readings will interest him more.

He moves the contact mic toward the corner and hears something.

'*...it has to look like an accident.*'

Dan's eyes widen but he doesn't hear any more. He listens and waits for several long minutes, but the voice doesn't appear again. He knows he is on his own up here on this storey so the sound must have been travelling through the walls. It could have been coming from anywhere in the building then, or possibly, even from next door.

He peers out into the street for good measure, but doesn't see anyone down there. He closes his eyes, waiting to hear more.

Eventually, Dan removes his headphones and tosses them on the bed. He sets down the high-sensitivity acoustic box, picks up an exercise book and begins writing.

'Strathkeel Room, the Gillespie Guesthouse, 21 April 1991, 21:05: using the bionic ear, overheard but didn't record a voice coming from the wall: "It has to look like an accident". Unable to locate the source.'

His writing is a bit shakier than usual. He closes the book and turns everything off.

'*What* has to look like an accident?'

CHAPTER 15

In the morning, Dan is tapping at the parlour door again.

This time Catriona is standing. She seems to be alone.

'Dan, I told you not to knock.'

'I don't want to bother you, but I've some equipment waiting for me, to collect today, so I was wondering if I could borrow your…'

'Sorry, I… what were you saying?'

Catriona is moving around the room, setting things down, fingering through a drawer. Dan gravitates to the corner by the first window. The changeable weather is painting and repainting the scene outside with different falls of light.

'Oh, I was just asking if I could borrow your car to collect something…' He sees a familiar vehicle turning into the road. His face brightens. 'But don't worry, here comes my lift!'

It isn't a car, it's a late bay Volkswagen camper van – Neptune Blue and white.

Catriona looks over to where Dan was standing and sees only the door swinging on its hinges.

Dan is rushing down the stairs and out into the street. By the time he steps out onto the pavement, the van has pulled up. It looks out of place, parked in the smart street, the engine exhaling a slow, hot breath.

Through the windscreen he can see Reed unbuckling his seatbelt and leaning forward. He is looking up at the building's impressive facade with an uncertain expression on his face. Dan strides to the driver's side, opens the door and pulls his friend out of the vehicle. Reed's Converse pat the ground.

Dan enfolds him in a tight embrace.

A tumble of turning clouds gust across the sunny sky, dappling the shining camper van with waves of sunshine.

'I got your message,' Reed says, awkwardly, from inside the bear hug.

'That was quick,' Dan replies, still squeezing, 'I only placed it...'

'I was already in the country. Actually...'

Dan releases his friend.

'... I was already on my way.'

Their eyes meet and they laugh gently. Reed paces a little, stretching his spine. He can feel his shirt unsticking itself from the small of his back. He looks around at the quiet, stately street.

Dan begins a slow, sweeping shake of his head, looking at him. There he is, as if transported in the blink of an eye from that shiny hotel lobby in Dublin to the Georgian crescent before him, hair flapping in the breeze, the same enigmatic yet familiar half smile.

'Now, what's the point of me placing a personal ad when you're telepathic?' Dan jokes.

'I'm not telepathic.' Reed rolls his shoulders. 'Nobody is.'

Dan's beaming smile is infectious.

'Any idea where I can park around here?' Reed asks.

Dan walks around the van to the passenger door. He seems to be climbing in. A small crumple forms on Reed's brow.

'What's…?'

'Well,' – Dan settles himself in the seat – 'first we're going to Haymarket.' He fastens the seatbelt. 'We've got a magnetometer to collect.'

***

Inside the headquarters of SHERPA-ELC, the array of books and folders and printouts and kit is intriguing Reed.

'You're on the wrong side.'

'I'm not on anybody's side,' Reed replies.

'No,' Gregor says, 'you're standing on the wrong side.' He is perched on the stool again.

Reed and Dan look at one another.

'He means the barrier,' Dan explains, tapping it.

Reed is already standing in the middle of the room, drawn to the artefact-packed shelves.

'Oh, I'm with him,' Reed says, gesturing loosely toward Dan, who has remained obediently on the square of lino by the door.

'We're just here to pick something up, aren't we?' Reed continues, without turning to face Gregor. 'What is it? Is it this?' Reed picks up a small wooden box.

'Don't touch that. It's a spirit voice recorder from the 1920s.' The commanding voice makes Reed look up.

'Hi, Keith,' Dan says. 'This is my associate.'

Reed raises an eyebrow. 'You're very formal all of a sudden,' he remarks to his friend.

'You'll have to sign in,' Gregor states.

'I'll do it.' Dan smiles breezily, taking the biro. 'I'll sign for both of us…'

Reed's attention turns to a collection of books: *Margins of Reality: The Role of Consciousness in the Physical World.*

'You're early,' Keith notes.

'Okay… Well, we're here now so…' Dan is writing his details in the ledger.

'Okay, well, I suppose you can pick it up now.' Keith purses his lips sullenly. 'Here's the loan register to sign.' He lines it up next to the first book on the wooden ledge.

'Oh, that's good,' Dan says, signing. He puts the lid back on the pen and straightens up. 'I thought we were all going to have to stand around staring at each other until the appropriate time.'

Dan is smiling warmly but Keith shoots him a look.

'I'll have to see *his* membership card,' Gregor states, looking at Reed, who has cocked his head to read book titles on a shelf.

'Oh, look… Reed just gave me a lift. I'm the one loaning the magnetometer. You've got *my* details.' Dan puts a friendly hand on Gregor's upper arm. Gregor looks awkward at the touch.

'But he could be anyone.'

'I *could* be,' Reed pipes up, evidently celebrating the possibility. 'Membership of what?'

'The Society for Historical and Empirical Research into Paranormal Anomalies,' Gregor replies.

Reed laughs wildly for a second then stops abruptly when he realises that it isn't a joke. 'Oh. You're being serious,' he says, his voice now quiet.

He goes back to reading book spines: *The Holographic Universe; Free-Flight: How to Have an Out-of-Body Experience in 30 Days...*

Keith takes the opportunity to pace around the room. 'So, this man is quite clearly *not* a member of the Society for Historical and Empirical Research into Paranormal Anomalies—Edinburgh and Lothians Chapter or otherwise.'

Reed swivels his torso to look back at Dan. 'Nobody likes a pendant,' Reed says, quietly, referencing an old in-joke.

'*Don't!*' Dan warns, with a small shake of his head.

'Yes, everything this side of the barrier is for members only: our library of paranormal publications, the register of mediumship, census of apparitions...'

This time Reed turns all the way around. 'Shit, Dan, I thought there was only one of you...'

He makes a face intended to be comic. Dan has snatched up the pen to fill in the loan register under the careful supervision of Gregor.

'So, you'll have to fill out the agreed date of return,' Keith says.

'And we'll need an address for *him,*' Gregor says.

'I'm not signing anything,' Reed says matter-of-factly. He stands there taking in more of the room. 'So, what do you do, the Society for the History of Recently Imperial Paranormal Animals... something something Edinburgh?' Reed asks, raising the pitch of his voice and screwing up his eyes as he struggles to guess at the convoluted title.

Dan and Keith are going over dates for the ledger, but Gregor is happy to oblige with the answer. He even gets up from his stool. 'We research ontological anomalies by formulating hypotheses on the foundation of observed phenomena rather than belief systems, ideological assumptions or mythological frameworks.'

Gregor's tone is that of someone reciting from a document – but perhaps that is just how he speaks.

Reed considers Gregor's answer. He understood most of the *words*...

'We use scientific methods to investigate reports of paranormal activity,' Dan says, paraphrasing.

Reed adopts a wry smile. 'You mean ghosts.'

'Well the phenomena of "ghosts" is really only one aspect of categorically defined paranormality which...'

'And have you ever found one?' Reed asks, interrupting.

'We need your address,' Gregor reiterates, remembering the task in hand.

'No, have you?' Keith counters Reed's question, putting his hands on his hips.

'No, nobody has.'

'Ah, but you can't *know* that,' Keith points out.

'We are scientists…' Gregor begins.

'And historians,' Dan adds, quietly.

'By definition,' Gregor continues, 'the scientific method cannot prove a theory into facthood. No, that's a common fallacy. The scientific method is about empirical observation, unbiased hypothesis, testing hypotheses and refining hypotheses based on results. By providing replicable methodology and repeatable results, the scientific method is able to provide a wealth of evidence supporting – what *you* might call a "theory" – but that's its power, that it only *supports* and never claims to *prove*. *Disproving* hypotheses, yes, *that's* the achievement of science – we know that countless inadequate theories *cannot* be true thanks to scientific experimentation – but to consider a hypothesis – or explanation, if you will – to be proven, because there is an enormous amount of experimental data that continually supports the explanation, again and again, *that* would exhibit just as much mental rigidity as not testing assumptions in the first place.'

Gregor pauses a moment to discern whether his words have been sinking in.

'Science is an open thing, you see,' he concludes. 'Belief and assumption aren't part of it.'

Dan notices that Reed's pupils are slightly dilated – as if he is trying to scan the word-fog weaving in front of his eyes before it dissipates, like pot smoke in a squat.

Dan translates once again: 'We keep an open mind.'

Reed blinks a couple of times, snapping out of his puzzlement. 'Why are you assuming I've got an address?' he asks.

'Why are you assuming there aren't any ghosts?' Keith counters, raising his eyebrows.

Dan, meanwhile, has spied the magnetometer ready and waiting for him in a box on a table and moved toward it. He checks the contents, then tucks it under his arm.

'So, thanks for this, you're lifesavers,' he says, heading toward the exit.

He notices Reed standing with a bemused expression on his face, some retort brewing in his mind. Dan leads him away by the shirt sleeve.

'Open minds, remember. Come on!'

CHAPTER 16

By late evening, Reed is standing in the middle of the Strathkeel. The twinned bedside lamps light the room with an amber glow. Dan is bustling around him, setting up small pieces of kit at strategic points, tidying wires, twiddling knobs and jotting things down in his experiment book. The bed stands, neatly made, between them.

'If I knew we'd be having a sleepover, I'd have brought those paisley pyjamas...'

Dan turns to look at him.

'Remember?'

Dan laughs. 'I do. That seems ages ago.'

'Well,' – Reed pauses to think – 'September?'

'I suppose a fair bit has changed since then.'

Dan continues with his set-up. His measuring equipment has turned the dresser, drawers and desk into an experimental laboratory. His pad and precision-tipped pens lie ready for action beside an expensive-looking digital watch.

'You said,' Reed replies, remembering their conversation in Dublin.

'Anyway, I wouldn't call it a sleepover... but I did bring snacks.'

Dan presents a rustling plastic bag. He unloads packets of hula hoops, kettle chips, peanuts and ginger snaps onto the dresser. Reed walks over the creaky floor and places a bottle of Glenmalure ceremoniously in pride of place.

Dan looks at him.

'Present from Dublin.' Reed smiles, adding a couple of glasses. '*Now* it's a party.'

'It's not a party. We've got work to do.'

Dan strides over to the electromagnetic field meter. Reed ambles after him.

'I know. Taking readings, checking the equipment at time points… listening for things that go bump in the night.'

'You may get your SHERPA membership yet. So, I'll need to repeat this vigil on my own, taping the door, powdering the floor etcetera but, between you and me, this is more of an empirical data situation.'

Reed looks around the cosy, old-fashioned room. 'What's this one?' Reed asks, peering at another device.

'Oh, that's just a light meter. We won't really be using that – just, you know, something to turn on if we experience a bright light coming from the corner there, like the Jenkins did. Same goes for the infrared thermometer but, you know, with heat.'

Reed looks confused.

'The point is – with all this kit – to record empirical data so that, if we *had* any ghostly experiences, we could work out whether it was happening in the room or in our minds.'

Reed nods and puts the light meter back.

Dan begins pointing at everything again in an over-exaggerated way. 'Magnetometer, infrasound recorder, EMF meter, triboscope, and there's the audio recorder if we need to turn it on – but I'm not running it all night just recording our conversation.'

'Okay. I think I've heard of EMF…?'

'Electromagnetic fields… that's the gizmo that people think of when they think of "ghost hunting" – because they think ghosts are entities made of energy that can be detected in volts.'

'Got it. Listen, I'm happy to keep you company but do you *really* need me all night?'

Dan stops and turns. 'I just need your body.'

'O-kay….?'

'You can sleep right there.' Dan points to the bed.

Reed looks pensive for a moment before replying. 'I'm not sure I can sleep with you watching me… and the machines recording me…' Reed wonders what exactly the machines might pick up.

'But you wouldn't be worried about the ghost?'

They laugh.

'You don't believe in ghosts *either*,' Reed points out.

'No, but I like to find out what's going on. Whenever people start telling ghost stories and so on, there's usually something much more interesting going on. With physics.'

Reed thinks about his secret dream life. 'Physics – "interesting" you say…?' he teases.

'Oh, look, a poltergeist,' Dan says, neutrally, with zero enthusiasm, then throws a small cushion at his friend.

It bumps softly into Reed's shoulder before falling to the floor.

***

Reed is lying on top of the bed, his feet neatly together, arms crossed over his chest, eyes closed. Dan leans over to peer at him from the side of the bed.

'Come on, that's not how you sleep.'

Reed opens an eye. 'What's wrong with it?'

'You look like a vampire.'

'Hey, I'm just pale-skinned and interesting… there's no need to be rude…'

'I mean, roll around a little bit, turn over, stretch out your limbs… like I was doing.'

'I thought you were just building up your part.'

'The point is to take readings as if someone was actually sleeping in the bed.'

Reed moves into a sort of recovery position. 'How about this?'

Dan's watch beeps so he moves between the EMF meter and triboscope, jotting down their readings. 'And that's the hour. You have to get off the bed now. It's the…'

'Control hour, I know.' Reed sits up and shuffles off the mattress. Two small armchairs flank the bed. Dan takes the one closest to the window.

Reed is standing by the dresser, pouring a couple of glasses of whisky and carefully adding drops of water from a small jug. '*Lose* control hour, you mean.'

Dan rolls his eyes but concedes a half smile at the intentionally lame joke. 'Very good.'

He reaches across to take the whisky that Reed is handing him and watches his friend spread his lanky frame across the other chair. They sip quietly while the whisky's peaty aroma swells to the corners of the room.

'They won't arrest us, will they?'

'Because it's not Scotch?' Dan says. 'They might.'

He grins over the glass. Reed can see the city lights and inky outlines through the window behind him. 'So, why are we in Edinburgh anyway? Seems a long way for you to travel for this, now I know there is a whole underground network of "paranormal investigators" on the doorstep. Are you the best of the best or something?'

Dan looks at him seriously. 'I *am* the best of the best, yes,' he replies before breaking into a guffaw. 'But that's not why I'm here. The owners are old friends of mine from university.'

'Edinburgh University?'

'No, Manchester. But Marcus and Catriona were always going to end up back here because she inherited this massive fucking house.'

Reed cocks his head slightly. 'Catriona… she doesn't really seem like your kind of person.'

'Well,' Dan takes a sip, 'she was a bit more easy-going back then. But it's Marcus I was friends with, really. Catriona was just part of the group. Except for when she wasn't.'

'How do you mean?'

'Oh,' – Dan shrugs – 'nothing, they were kind of off and on. Everything was a bit more… fluid… back then.'

'And the friend? In Dublin?'

'Yeah, Fintan.'

Dan looks at the floor. 'He was very much in our group.' He looks back up to meet Reed's gaze. 'Somewhere in the centre, seeking attention in all sorts of interesting new ways…'

Dan's watch timer bleeps.

'Time.'

The two men put their whiskies down and attend to the machines.

***

Later, Dan rolls over on the mattress, tangling the covers, as Reed jots down readings from the machines.

'Is it getting scientifically spookier?' Reed asks.

'Well…' Dan begins.

Just then, Reed looks sharply to the corner of the room, gasps and jumps onto the bed beside Dan. 'Aaaahh!' he says, in mock fright.

The bed is bouncing a little.

'What are you doing?' Dan asks, jiggling with the rocking of the mattress.

Reed rolls onto his stomach and smiles at Dan. 'I thought I saw a ghost,' he jokes mischievously.

Dan checks the time on his watch. 'Weren't we going to make coffee?'

'I'll do it – in a minute,' Reed replies.

Dan notices Reed's eyes shining in the light of the bed-side lamp. He's never seen them looking so green.

'Talking of off and on relationships…' Dan begins.

Reed rolls over and sits up on the bed, wrinkling the bedsheets into twisted, awkward folds.

'… What really happened with you two?'

'Well,' – Reed sits back against the headboard – 'we weren't in a "relationship".'

'Oh, right.' Dan sits up and shuffles back into the pillows too.

'We were just travelling together.'

'Okay.'

'So, it's not an on *or* off thing…'

Dan adopts an understanding tone of voice. 'More like… a together-apart thing…'

'She just wanted to do some travelling on her own, alright?' Reed swings his legs over the side of the bed. 'I'll make the coffee – end of the landing, last door on the right?'

Dan nods and watches his friend dash out of the room.

***

Dan's eyes blink open. A buzzer is quietly going off. He is lying alone on the pillows at the centre of the bed. He looks at his watch and stops the bleeping.

'Shit.'

Reed enters the room with two more mugs of coffee.

'We just missed one,' Dan tells him.

'I'll do it. Here, take this.'

He hands Dan a coffee, sets his own down on the bed-side table and picks up the pad.

'So… I'll just make something up,' Reed says, from beside the triboscope.

'No, we won't "make something up"! Just write down that we missed the reading.'

He watches Reed writing for a while, listening to the flourish of the architect pen across the paper.

'What are you writing?'

Reed starts reading aloud as he writes. 'We… missed… the very important… reading because Dan… was un-pro-fess-ional and… fell… a-sleep.'

'Really?' One of Dan's thick brows is pitched at an acute angle.

'Yep, that's what I wrote.'

Reed shows him the paper as confirmation.

'No, I didn't doubt it.' Dan lifts the mug to his lips, the coffee sending bright notes from steaming surface to nose. 'These coffees smell suspiciously like whisky.'

'Do they?' Reed affects mock innocence with round, wide eyes.

'The point is to keep us awake, not make us drop off.'

'Well, maybe part of us will fall asleep then, and the other part will fall awake.'

Dan leans forward, cradling the mug. 'I didn't fall asleep, anyway, I was just' – he gestures – 'remembering old times.'

Reed sits on the edge of the bed and looks at him. 'That's a point. You keep asking about my love life. Let's hear about *yours* for a change.'

Dan looks at him intently, his mouth set firmly in a frown. 'I don't have – *or need* – one.'

'Okay, but what about back then? Was there something between you and Catriona?'

Dan folds his arms, resting the coffee mug by his elbow. 'No. Why?'

Reed pulls a face and wriggles his shoulders. 'You just seem a bit… like there's an atmosphere or something.'

'No. Really. No.' Dan shakes his head slightly.

'So…'

Dan looks at him. 'So…' he echoes, 'what are you asking me?'

'Well, have you ever been in love?'

'Look, I don't,' – Dan sets his mug on the bedside table – 'I haven't,' – he raises his palms and shoulders. 'Once upon a time. Maybe.'

'So,' Reed nods gently, 'who was the lucky girl?'

Dan turns to face Reed, with his whole torso this time, and locks eyes with his friend. 'When have I *ever* said I liked the ladies?'

'Oh. You're… gay, then?'

'You could say that – if I actually had time for a relationship – which I don't.'

'Okay. It's just, you never mentioned it.'

'And when did *you* come out? As being straight?'

'Point taken.'

The two men sit shoulder to shoulder on the bed, drinking their Irish coffee, immobile except for their right arms raising and lowering the mugs. Reed parts his lips to say something.

'You're…'

'Oh, relax, it *is* possible to share a bed with a friend, you know, without anything… romantic taking place.'

'No, it's just… I was going to say' – Reed gestures at the bed – 'you're on my side.'

***

Hours later, heads and shoulders nestled together against the headboard, the two friends are accidentally sleeping, mouths agape.

CHAPTER 17

I fall awake in the haunted bedroom.

It is deathly quiet. There are few ambient sounds in a city with no people – and you feel the silence in your soul.

It seems that Dan and I let the whisky put us to sleep. So much for the all-night data readings. I look around. The mugs and glasses and crisp packets are messing up the room. Patterns in the grain on the antique furniture seem to form faces full of reproach. The bedside lamps are still on.

I could set about waking myself and then I could get Dan up so we can carry on the experiment. I think about it, but it seems too late and I already know that I won't.

I'm now lying under the bed throw – I must have pulled it up to cover us in the night – and there's Dan's T-shirt by my side, like he just vanished. This is weird, lying in bed with Dan and also *not*-Dan, but it's comfy. I stay put.

I look outside at the night sky. It's the darkness before the dawn. I know there is a whole building full of unexplored rooms below me, but I don't want to leave the warmth and safety of the bed.

The meters still surround us, picking up things that people can't see or hear. I wonder if the machines can tell that I'm here – in the dreaming.

I'm glad Dan told me what he told me – but could I ever come out to him about *this*?

The room and city and night feel restful; no ghosts to trouble the peace. But what if I'm wrong? I don't know what's out there. I resolve to keep more of an open mind and stop making assumptions.

After all, I should have learnt my lesson. All those years of looking for another dreamer, all that time of being alone. And then, *she* was there. Yes, I was still going through the motions – wandering around, looking for someone, following reports of 'paranormal' happenings and hoping for a culprit like me, who can do just *this* – but I knew I would never find one. Yet, suddenly, there she was, running around with me in a shared dream.

She asked whether anyone could do this. I had assumed it was only me and her.

Physics *does* give rise to interesting things. I knew that – even when I was teasing Dan earlier. Nobody can know how weird physical reality is, as well as me. And her.

I wonder where she is now. Looking for other dreamers? Did I see one that night in Dublin on top of the library, or was it just a trick of the light? A ghost.

Bang. My heart thumps. The bulb by Dan's side of the bed just burnt out with a sudden crackling pop. I wonder if I can detect a low burning buzz coming from the other lamp by my ear. In any case, it now feels too bright and, for some reason, I don't want to draw attention to my being here. I reach my arm out of the warm covers and turn it off before a second blowout can make me jump.

At first it feels more comforting in the darkness but soon the room is streaked with witch-hat shadows, sharp stalactites and skinny, pointing fingers that stretch from the window toward me; menacing shapes cut by a high, bright moon. The wallpaper pattern by the headboard seems to pulse at the corner of my eye then stops when I turn my head.

That's what ghosts are, isn't it? People seeing things and hearing sounds and making them into a person in their mind. Especially if they *want* to see someone – someone who has left them behind.

I still haven't told Dan about it – seeing that body; his friend.

I calm down and survey the new roomscape around me, now bathed in moody blues and greys. Out of the window, the sky above the rooftops takes on a different hue. The folds of the city skyline form a chain, like painted theatre flats; rooftop stepping stones for night spirits to dance across the city like Peter Pan, pushing off from the castle top for some faraway magical land.

There's a noise on the stairs. I barely hear it above the sound of my own breathing but when you are the last person left, you pay adrenaline-flushed attention to house noises in the night.

I stay motionless and keep my breathing shallow, trying not to make the tiniest sound. There it is – a distant creaking. Houses do this. But it's rhythmical. I could turn it into footsteps in my mind. Soft footsteps creeping up the stairs. I hear them coming for me.

A trick of the mind?

No. Something is crossing over into my dimension – my nightly dream in which the whole world belongs only to me. Some uninvited thing is breaking into it. Is this what happens if you mock them – ghosts? They come to get you? If my dream world is possible, why *not* lost spirits too?

No. Really. There are footsteps out there.

A chill sweeps over my skin. I look toward the door handle. Am I imagining it starting to turn?

Slowly, I pull the top cover up toward my chin, a childish defence against night monsters. I tug harder at the covers, trying to disappear into the magic force field of the bed, but there isn't much give in them and it feels like my straining fingers might go through the papery sheet.

The handle clicks and I jump in my skin. My heart thumps louder as I watch it turn.

The door opens.

'Zoya! You frightened me to death!' My voice sounds raspy, so I clear my throat and resolve to bring it down a few octaves.

'Hi, Reed.' She smiles her beautiful smile. 'Of course it's me. Who else would it be?' She laughs, pacing into the room, perfectly at ease. My shoulders are still tensed.

Never before has she seemed so unreal. Have I magicked her here with my longing?

She reaches for the lamp on the bedside table and clicks the switch, conjuring the room back to an amber glow. Everything feels brighter now.

She is walking across the room and twirling around, noticing the little machines. Without even looking at me, she casually explains. 'Just thought I would come and say hello, check I've got the right place, before coming back tomorrow, in real life. What are these for?' She flicks a switch on and off.

'Don't!' I say, too late.

I relax and drop the sheet. I rest my forearm on top of the bedcovers, the silken fabric cool against my skin.

Zoya stops pacing. A twist of hair comes to rest against her cheek. I notice she is wearing a new shirt that I've never seen.

'What's going on?' She looks at me.

'It's one of Dan's experiments – but I think you might have just fucked it up.'

I'm not sure she has or not, but then think of me and Dan, back in reality, snoring our heads off in the bed. I don't think the experiment matters anymore.

'Oh, yes. Dan. From Kembleton? I saw his personal ad.'

My mouth falls open and I recompose my expression into what I think is a relaxed smile.

'That's how you know I'm here? Couldn't live without me, huh?'

I hear my thin joke falling flat.

'Yes and no,' she replies, 'I meant...'

'So, what are you reading personal ads for?' I ask her, suddenly feeling cross.

Zoya looks at me in the bed and notes the crumpled pillows. 'Oh, you're in bed with someone,' she says.

'No, it's just...'

'No, no, it's fine. You're… you can do what you like.'

She is looking all around the room again. There is a neutral tone to her voice and a pleasant expression on her face. I'm secretly pleased to note that both seem forced.

'It's Dan,' I say.

She looks at me. 'Reed, it's fine. *We're* not… Dan?'

I feel beside me for his T-shirt – or this dimension's version of his T-shirt, anyway – and hold it up. She watches as I hold it out to full capacity. It has a picture of a cartoon wizard pointing a magic finger to the skies. And it's extra large.

'It's Dan,' I say, again. 'It is possible to share a bed with a friend, you know…'

She looks again at the ghost-meters. 'Well, that does make sense.' She looks back at me and the T-shirt in bed together. 'Sort of.'

'We're meant to be staying up, taking ghost readings all night – but I suppose we fell asleep.'

'But you don't believe in ghosts.'

'No, but we're keeping an open mind.' I think for a moment before continuing. 'Do *you* believe in ghosts?'

'I never used to but…'

'Have you seen something?' I ask.

'No,' – she pauses – 'I *am* one.'

I look at her blankly, wondering if she has lost her mind. Maybe I don't know her as well as I think I do.

'I *mean*,' she continues, 'what if *we're* the ghosts?'

I'm not following. 'Me and you…?' I query, slowly.

She folds her arms casually. 'Yes.'

'I know it's bonkers that we can do this, but I think I'd remember frequenting a lot more old houses and dressing up as a Victorian child and stuff...'

'No, not *just* you and me – but people like us... who can do *this*.'

'It's a nice theory but... well, where are they? You know you're the only other dreamer I ever found, and I've been looking all my life...?'

'Yeah.' She starts walking around the room again. 'You think it's just you and me who can do it, or just us who share this particular bit of the dreaming, or something, but *I* don't.' She pauses. 'I mean, it *can't* be that,' she says. 'We're all human beings. There's nothing physiologically or psychologically... or anything *special* that links the two of us.'

I clench my jaw. 'Isn't there?'

'Well, that's sort of why I'm here, anyway, to find out if there are any others.'

I let my arms fall over the covers. 'Not to see me, then?' I wish it hadn't come out sounding so much like a stroppy child.

'I'm seeing you now, aren't I?' Zoya replies. 'Look, when we were in Ireland...'

'When? When we were there together or after you left me on my own?'

I sense she is wilfully ignoring my touchiness. 'Well, did you hear about that man who fell off the building?'

'Hear about it? He landed at my feet!'

'No! Did he? What…? Well, I followed the story a bit, in the papers, and I did a bit of… looking around.' She rests her hands on the armchair but doesn't sit down.

'I'm fine by the way, thanks for asking. It was horrible, but I'm fine,' I say.

'So, I was reading all about him.'

'Dan was friends with that man, you know. They all were.'

'Is that why Dan's here too?' she asks.

'No, he's here professionally.' I gesture around the room at the machines. 'As a paranormal investigator. Actually, I think he's a maverick. There's a local group who aren't very happy he's here…'

She perches on the arm of the chair. 'Anyway. The Irish police discovered someone had lent that man a load of money – someone whose address is right here – and then I happened to see Dan's message telling *you* to come here and so I thought I'd have to get here too.'

Listening to her story, I lean forward. My fingers trace the embroidered wisteria flowers on the bedspread. 'So, you are trying to solve the case or something?' I didn't know she was into that sort of thing.

'No,' she shakes her head a couple of times, slowly, 'not the money thing. Are you? Is that why you're here? I just thought it would be good to talk to people who knew him. And *you're* here.'

'Why? What are you trying to find out?'

'If he was one of us!' she exclaims, standing up. 'Look,' she continues, 'I'll see you tomorrow. I'll tell them I'm a friend of Dan's.'

'One of *us*? Based on the fact he died in an… unexplained way?'

'I would have thought, you, of all people, would be able to understand that life is weird.'

It stings when she says that because I had literally come to that same conclusion for myself, just before she burst in. I don't think she can hold *that* against me. 'Yes. And Dan and his people have made that the basis of a lifelong investigation. Physical reality *is* weirder than we think.'

'So, what's the deal with you two then?' She nods toward the bed. 'Are you Bert and Ernie now?'

'Please,' I say dismissively. 'Morecambe and Wise, at least…'

I notice that she is fiddling with the window latch.

'Zoya, what are you doing?'

What Zoya is doing is opening the window. The night air drifts in. I see the yellowing sky and the castle looming over the rooftops.

It looks like she is climbing onto the windowsill.

'We're three storeys up!'

'I know.' She turns back to grin at me, her legs already out of the window. 'That's why I'm doing it. See you later!'

Then she falls, vanishing into the night outside.

What?!

I push away the covers and leap out of the bed. Rushing to the window, I plant my hands on the sill and, as dread washes over me, take a panicked look outside. I don't want to see another body smashed onto another pavement – especially not *hers*.

The street is empty. No Zoya.

In the few seconds it took for me to get up and look outside, Zoya has slipped away into another dimension. I taught her that falling trick, but never so dramatically. Wherever Zoya is now, she has just woken herself up.

CHAPTER 18

By morning, Reed and Dan have folded themselves into a sleepy cuddle. They are tangled in the bedsheets, snoring and dribbling on the cotton.

The rude jab of sunlight jutting into the room and across the pillows makes Reed crinkle his face. He opens his eyes and sees, in extreme close-up, Dan's pillow-creased cheek and the dark bristles pushing their way out of his chin. A lone hair is escaping from his nostril, wiggling in the draught of Dan's snore.

A loud creak of the floorboard yanks Reed's attention to the space between bed and door. Two people are standing there, watching them.

'Ah!' he exclaims, with a slight jump.

The sound momentarily disturbs Dan but not enough to open his eyes. 'Reed… stop pretending to see ghosts,' he mumbles crankily.

Reed blinks a couple of times and the details swim into view. First, his gaze settles on Zoya, standing arms folded, her expression knowing and amused. The glinting pools of her eyes seem to communicate many unsaid things.

'Zoya!' Reed smiles and begins to sit up.

By her side is a slim, broad-shouldered man, no less handsome for the peppering of grey through his annoyingly luxuriant waves. He is frowning slightly.

Zoya smiles. She seems to be the embodiment of a clean, fresh morning. It makes Reed all too aware of the furry-toothed, sweaty-faced festering state of him and Dan.

'Marcus?' Reed guesses. It doubles as a greeting.

'Marcus!' Dan exclaims, springing to life, instantly aware of the odd-couple scene they are presenting. 'Marcus. Hey. Er… this is Reed.'

Should they be getting out of the bed?

Reed is wondering the same thing, but the soft mattress is still sucking him into its comfortable embrace.

'Hello,' Reed says.

'Hello,' Marcus replies, walking across the room.

When he opens the window, the slide of the runners and smack of fresh air finally wakes Reed's brain. A bright, breezy daytime flows eagerly into the room.

Marcus picks his way back across the littered floor to stand by Zoya's side. Reed props himself on his elbows and takes in the scene with narrow-lidded eyes. He notes the mindless scatter of strewn snack packets and the glistening rings that trace the whisky bottle's journey across the dresser through the night. And there, in wayward glasses, the dregs of their drinks, burning orange in the sunlight.

'Zoya? What…?' Dan begins, immediately pleased for his friend that she has turned up.

'Zoya's arrived,' Marcus announces unnecessarily. 'She said you'd want to be woken…' He looks around the room at the mess of snacks and whisky glasses.

'Yeah,' Dan smiles, going along with it, 'sure.'

'See, I told you it would be fine,' Zoya says to Marcus. Reed notices that she lays a hand on his arm.

'So… you were investigating the haunting?' Marcus asks.

'Yep,' Dan replies, very aware of the state of the room. 'Er, Reed's my–' He is choosing between the term 'business partner' and some better way of putting it when Marcus cuts him off.

'Shall we all have breakfast?'

'Yes, please,' Reed responds politely.

'Thanks,' adds Dan, 'breakfast would be great. All of us?'

'Well, it's brunch for everyone else,' Zoya says, a small, cheeky grin on her face.

'This way, just along the corridor, Dan, I'll rustle something up in the family kitchen.'

Marcus leads the way with Zoya following. Reed and Dan emerge from the bed with crumpled clothes. They stretch and readjust themselves, loitering behind. They take their time, lingering in the bedroom, so that they can talk.

'What's Zoya doing here? Did you invite her?' Dan whispers as soon as the others have left the room.

'I'll explain later,' Reed whispers back.

Dan puts his hands on his hips, looking over the room and the messed-up bed.

'I knew we shouldn't have started drinking.'

'I think we did a good job,' Reed answers, somehow reaching a different conclusion even though they are surveying the exact same scene.

***

They join them in the family kitchen. Zoya is sitting at the wooden table with a smile on her face.

Reed forces himself not to look at her for too long. In the daylight, he notices for the first time how uncharacteristically understated this room is; cosy and convenient instead of grand. The table in the centre is simple and sturdy, the oven gloves seam-worn and stained.

Marcus is clattering pans and bustling from fridge to cooker. Reed notes how Marcus is one of those annoyingly attractive and effortlessly charming people and immediately hates him. The loud scrape of a dragged chair makes him flinch.

Dan takes a seat.

'Zoya. It's so good to see you,' Dan says.

Reed knows that they barely know one another.

'Well, I am part of your team.' Zoya is looking at Dan intently, as if to say: 'Just go along with it.' Dan covers his perplexed reaction with a pleasant smile.

Reed slips into one of the other chairs. Dan notices the way he is looking at Zoya: 'gazing' might be a better word.

'Well,' Dan continues, 'I'm really glad you're here.' He seems to mean it.

'Does everyone want everything?' Marcus asks, igniting a flame on the hob.

'Yes, please,' Zoya says politely.

'Sounds good,' Reed concedes.

'The way to my heart!' Dan beams.

The kettle boils and Zoya leaps up to make the coffee. Marcus flashes her a smile. 'Thanks.'

'Can't help it,' Zoya says, pouring the water. 'I used to work in a café.'

Marcus and Zoya bustle around one another and bacon begins to sizzle in the pan.

Reed relaxes his posture. The small kitchen feels separate from the rest of the house, like they could be anywhere at all. The impression is underlined by the empty view from the window. From the table, all he can see is the sky. It makes him think of a plain, colour-washed canvas.

'So, you're the artist?' Reed asks.

Marcus pauses for a second, resting the cooking tongs on his shoulder, and looks at Reed. 'I suppose I am.'

'He's being modest,' Dan chips in.

'My grandfather was an artist,' Zoya says.

Marcus looks at her. She is laying cups and saucers on the table.

'What kind of art do you make?' Reed asks, but no one seems to hear.

'And this is your place? It's beautiful,' Zoya says.

'Oh, well, it's my wife's. I'm just the hired help, actually the un-hired help – but I cook a mean fry-up.' Marcus starts turning the rashers in the pan.

***

By the time breakfast is served, Reed has slunk to a teenager's sullen pose. He nudges the food around on his plate with a fork.

'So, you know Dan from university?' Reed asks.

'That's right. And you…'

'Reed's a friend. From back home,' Dan explains, a bit too quickly. 'Well, he helped my family out with something last year and… well, he's here to help me with the investigation.'

'Well, you're all welcome to stay as long as you want,' Marcus says genially. He bites a mushroom and looks toward Zoya. Dan, by her side, is assembling hearty forkfuls – a bit of everything at once.

'Did you say your grandfather was an artist?' Marcus asks.

'Yes, Michiel Minke,' she replies.

Marcus's dark eyes light up with recognition.

'You've heard of him?'

'No! Michiel Minke? I've studied his work!'

'Really?' Dan asks.

'Yes. Michiel Minke… great portrait artist,' Marcus says, turning toward Dan. 'I will have shown you some of his work, Dan. Wonderful textures.'

Zoya smiles. 'That's him.'

Marcus cocks his head a little, pleased with their connection.

'But you can't have met him though,' Reed states.

Marcus looks at Dan again. 'You know, I was thinking of getting back into portraiture – to get my creative flow back.' Marcus seems pensive. 'I must look out my Minke prints.'

'*I've* seen some of his paintings...' Reed says. Nobody responds. He concludes the sentence quietly, to himself. '... because *I* like art.'

Dan clicks his fingers. 'You should paint Zoya!' Dan seems so taken with the idea that Marcus and Zoya exchange looks. Then she laughs. Reed thinks it sounds more giggly than usual.

'Did you ever paint Dan's portrait?' she asks.

'I can't remember.'

'Now why would anyone want a portrait of me? Nobody wants to see my ugly mug every day – bad enough *I* have to see it when I shave!'

'That's not really what portraits are about, Dan,' Reed says.

Dan raises an eyebrow at his friend.

'No, he's right,' Marcus says. 'It's not just a painting of a person, of the way they look, but of a relationship between the sitter and the artist.'

'But you don't have a relationship with Zoya,' Reed says.

'But I would.'

Reed drops his fork and almost glares.

'I think he means that the sitting for the painting is the relationship,' Zoya tells him.

'But you'd make a wonderful painting,' Dan says, looking at her.

'I don't think Zoya would really appreciate being objectified as an image,' Reed says.

'Well, *I* think Zoya can speak for herself,' Zoya replies.

There is an awkward silence, filled with cutting sausages, chewing mouthfuls and mopping bean juice with toast. Zoya looks at Marcus with a gentle expression on her face. Her tactful tone of voice matches it when she speaks.

'So, were you also close to Dan's friend from Dublin?'

Reed shifts in his chair. 'They don't want to talk–' he begins.

'Fintan?' Marcus answers. 'We were.'

'I'm so sorry,' Zoya says.

Marcus puts his hand on her wrist. 'Thanks. I don't mind if people want to talk about Fintan.'

'No,' Dan agrees, 'it doesn't make it better or worse that he's gone.'

'You know what makes it the most unbelievable?'

Dan swallows. 'The… manner of his death,' he suggests.

'Well,' Marcus continues, 'all the scrapes and… adventures he got into… all the crazy things… he always got out of trouble somehow.'

Dan looks into the middle distance. 'He did seem to live a charmed life.'

Reed and Zoya find themselves exchanging glances; he knows what she is thinking.

'Yeah,' Marcus continues, 'he always seemed to land on his feet.'

Reed's eyes widen at the *extremely* poor choice of phrase. Zoya kicks him under the table. He forces himself to stare into his beans instead of reacting. He doesn't feel like eating any more.

'So, you realise that Zoya and her family are badass?' Dan says.

Everybody looks at him.

'Last year, Zoya and her dad apprehended a murderer by shooting him with a tranquiliser dart.'

'Really?' Marcus asks. 'Did you… Did he die?'

'No, he's in prison now,' Zoya replies, quickly and quietly.

'"Tranquilise" means put to sleep,' Reed is saying, almost under his breath.

'So, are you doing it? The portrait?' Dan asks eagerly.

Marcus and Zoya look at one another.

'I'd like to,' Marcus says. 'Are you game?'

'Won't that take ages?' Reed asks. 'Zoya doesn't like to be tied to one spot for too long…'

'Not long, just a few days…'

Reed is looking nauseated. She ignores him.

'I'd love to. However long it takes.'

'I love it when a plan comes together,' Dan says, quoting *The A-Team*.

He is grinning and looking from one face to another, almost double-taking when he notices Reed's thunderous expression. He doesn't understand why Reed wouldn't be pleased that Zoya's going to stay for a while.

'And how long are *you* staying, Dan? You can, all of you, stay as long as you like, as our personal guests…'

'Well, we'll have finished the anomaly investigation soon… and I'll have to see about work…'

'But you'll see Edinburgh first?' Marcus exclaims. 'How about you, Zoya? Reed? Have you been to Edinburgh before? I must show you the sights. We'll all go. Tomorrow! Make a day of it?'

Karen sticks her head around the door jamb. 'Hello again, I just wanted to tell Zoya – we've got your room ready. It's just along the landing on this floor.'

Zoya stands and tucks her chair under the table.

'I didn't want to interrupt your breakfast,' Karen says.

'No, I've finished – thanks, Marcus. I'd like to unpack.'

'But aren't you staying with me?' Reed's voice cuts through the conversation, louder than he's spoken during the entire meal. The unanswered question hangs over them all like a thundercloud until Karen breaks the tension.

'So, if you'd like to follow me, Zoya, I have taken your case to your room.'

They leave the kitchen and walk away along the landing. Dan and Marcus try not to be too obvious with the looks they are trading. Reed is slumped, arms folded and staring hard at nothing on the opposite wall.

They don't want to look at him too directly but can see his face is growing pink. The women's receding voices can be heard discussing Edinburgh's landmark volcano, Arthur's Seat.

The hands of an old-fashioned wall clock patterned with red cherries click quietly through the seconds. The clock reminds Dan of the one that Sarah has back home.

'Looks like her room is across the landing from yours,' Dan says conversationally.

He manages *not* to say anything about Reed acting like a moody child.

Reed just raises his eyebrows and nods, not looking at him.

'So, you're an art lover?' Marcus asks Reed.

Reed pushes his chair back to rise. It screeches against the floor. 'If you'll excuse me,' Reed mumbles and walks out of the room.

Marcus watches for a while to check that he has really gone. 'So, they were together then?' he asks, already knowing the answer.

'They *were*.'

'He doesn't seem to be taking it well.'

'You picked up on that, huh?'

They trade their old, suddenly familiar, smiles.

'Actually,' Dan continues, 'I'm hoping they'll sort it out, whatever it is with them. I mean she's *here,* isn't she, so...' Dan shrugs hopefully.

'Well, Auld Reekie might work its magic...' Marcus says promisingly.

'I just want them to be happy.'

Marcus seems amused, a crinkle at the corner of his eye. 'See…'

Dan looks at him, puzzled.

'… You always were a romantic at heart, interested in other people's love lives… but never in your own.'

Dan frowns, bashfully.

'You know,' – Marcus clears his throat – 'when I saw *you two*, cuddled up together this morning…'

Dan slowly and deliberately shakes his head.

'So. How are you doing?' Dan asks.

'About Fintan? Okay. How about you?'

'"Okay" just about covers it.'

'I can't help wondering what Fintan got himself mixed up in,' Marcus says.

'What do you mean?'

'Well, I hadn't seen him for a while and then he got in touch, asking for money, and I found it for him, somehow, and then we fell out, sort of, and… to be honest,' – his words slow and stall – 'that's the last time I saw him.'

Dan remembers Marcus telling someone at the funeral that he hadn't seen Fintan in years – but the cold drench of bereavement soon douses the thought away.

'Oh, man,' Dan says.

'And I'd give a hundred times that money just to be able to see him again.'

CHAPTER 19

I fall awake in my guest room on the top floor. The city sounds have all been sucked away. I get out of bed and stand by the window, the coolness of the glazing inches from my face.

My window overlooks the back of the property: the margin of terrace, the unkempt grass, the neighbouring buildings that ring the space. Silvery moonlight tumbles from the sky, lingering on the sea of scattering grasses.

I look to the ground. It seems a long way down. I watch as a figure emerges: Zoya is dream-walking too.

She paces across the terrace, weaving between the tables and chairs. Then she rolls down the small steep slope that drops away from the paving and comes to rest in the springy, wild growth below: not by accident, but for fun.

I leave my room and make for the stairs.

By the time I walk through the terrace door into the soft night, I see that Zoya is wading around in the meadow. In the soundlessness of the dreaming, I can hear, strangely magnified, the push of her footsteps tearing through the foliage and ruffling the plain of shimmering grass.

Then she sits down, leans back on her elbows and looks at the sky. I hurry – casually – toward her.

'Seen any new constellations?' I ask.

Zoya turns toward me and smiles.

'Do you mind if I join you?' I ask.

'Of course I don't mind.'

I sit on the ground next to her. The night, like all nights in the dreaming, feels tranquil and the surrounding buildings seem to buffer us from the cold, empty loneliness of the deserted city beyond. Above us, stars are revealing themselves, piercing through the city's ambient street-lit haze. The moonlight is strong, bathing us in a magical silver-trimmed light. I can see her clearly. She's looking up at the sky.

'You wouldn't know we were in a city out here,' I say.

'I know. It's nice.'

'Just us and the stars.'

Zoya laughs. 'And all the windows.'

'Well, windows with nobody to look through them,' I say.

She turns to me. 'There *could* be.'

Her voice has a slightly defiant edge. I stand up and cup my hands to my mouth.

'Hello! Is anybody there?'

Not surprisingly, there is no answer to my call.

'There isn't,' I say conclusively.

Zoya laughs again. 'Is that your method?'

She holds her arms out for me to help her to her feet. I pull her up.

'You drive about in your van, wake up in the dreaming, and shout?' she says.

We begin strolling aimlessly through the waves of grass.

'Pretty much.'

'But that's not how you found me. I don't remember any shouting.'

'No…'

'You were climbing up my house, if I recall… and then you ran away.'

We laugh.

'*Alright*.' I feel embarrassed. 'I was just surprised, that's all.' I wonder if she can see the flush of my cheeks in the moonlight.

'I know.'

'Well,' I say, 'about that, I don't think I ever said. That night… I did actually feel drawn to your house.'

'Did you?'

'Yeah. I really did. Because *you* were there.'

'It wasn't the fact that it's the craziest house in Shilly? On top of a hill–'

'… Big whale sculpture on the roof… No. Only a little bit. I felt drawn to go there that night.'

She narrows one eye slightly. 'You didn't.'

'I did!'

'How do you know you're not retrofitting your theory onto it?'

'My theory?'

'Yes. You think we share our dreams, or whatever it is, because… you and I are… a special match.'

I stop walking but she keeps pacing through the garden. 'Don't you think this is special?'

'Yes, of course.' She pauses and turns to face me. 'Of course I think it's special. And I've loved doing *all this* with you.'

'But… you think there might be others.'

'There might be!'

'There aren't.'

'What happened to keeping an open mind?'

She turns to continue her stroll. I catch hold of her hand. 'Zoya.' She turns and I take her other hand as well. 'The thing is, though, that *you're* the only one I *want* to be here… with me.'

She is looking up at me, her dark eyes shining in the moonlight. Will she let me kiss her? We draw closer and kiss softly. I've missed her lips against mine.

And then we are pacing through the garden again and I have kept hold of her hand. After a minute, I ask the question. 'What did I do wrong?'

'Nothing. I just wanted some time on my own.'

'No, really, you can tell me.'

'I just told you.' Then, she flails her arms in exasperation, breaking our touch. 'And I told you in Dublin too!'

I stop walking and put my hands on my hips. 'So, you came all this way, rocked up in Edinburgh, found out where I am, just to stay in the room across the hall?'

'Why are you taking it personally? I did think it would be nice to see you and…'

'Nice?'

'And there's this… idea I want to explore.'

'Your ridiculous idea about Fintan?'

'It's *not* ridiculous.'

'It kind of *is* – because, for one thing, how will you ever know if he was a dreamer, like us? He's dead now so *he* can't tell us. We can't bump into him on a night like this.'

'He might have told someone about it – just because *you* never would!'

'Well, *have* you told anyone yet? What about your dad? What would that be like if you told him that you have this whole other dream life when you're asleep? Don't you think he'll start looking at you like you're crazy?'

She folds her arms. 'You're starting to sound like a controlling boyfriend.' She starts walking back to the house.

'No... I... I'm just trying to stop you getting hurt. Come back... where are you going?'

By now she has reached the terrace.

'Out! Into the city. You know, there's a whole, big, beautiful city out there?'

'Zoya! Don't leave.'

To my surprise she comes walking back toward me. I'm glad she's changed her mind.

'I'm just going exploring.' Her voice is calm. 'It's important to me, that's all,' she continues. 'And the possibility of finding others – that's important to me too. Not everything is about *you*, you know. I'm not doing any of it "*at*" you. I'm just doing it.'

She kisses me on the cheek, standing on tiptoes because I don't move. She starts to leave again.

'Wait... I was going to ask for your help with something.'

She turns but doesn't come back. 'Maybe tomorrow? What is it?'

'I think there is something going on.'

'What?'

'I don't know. I just don't think Dan should trust these people–'

'His friends,' she interjects.

'–as much as he does.'

'Why?'

'Come on, falling from a building like that? It's weird. *You* know – you were following the story too. It's weird. But nobody seems to be questioning it. And you said something about some money…?'

'So, what are you going to do?' she asks.

I must be looking around at the darkened windows or maybe she just knows my ways too well.

'You're going to snoop through every room?' she guesses.

'Well,' – my shoulders rise – 'it's something–'

'You know, to really get to know people, you have to actually spend time with them – not just rummage through their things.'

'I can't very well ask them, can I? And I don't know what I'm looking for yet.'

'Okay, well,' – she walks away – 'have fun.'

'Where are you going?'

She is on the terrace by the door now. 'Out!' She sounds determined but not angry.

'Can I come with you?'

'No, thanks.'

She goes back into the house. The door remains closed behind her. She has probably left by the front door by now. She isn't coming back.

I flop down onto the grassy slope and look up at the stars. Lying back, I feel the tickle of the cool grasses at my neck. Gradually, the ground warms and I think about the ever-turning earth.

I remember a night we spent outside together, revolutions ago, with records and whisky and constellations. The first time we… everything.

It's fine, I tell myself. It will all be fine. She did just kiss me again. For a little while. She hasn't really rejected *me*; she's just… going through something. It's fine.

Okay, she has this need to look for other dreamers. I can't blame her – so did I. I suppose I'm just a little bit further ahead with all this than she is. She just needs to find out for herself. She probably thinks I'm bothered about being right, but it's not that. I could just save her some disappointment and some time. But it's okay. She'll get there. And I can wait.

I focus on a patch of stars above me. It doesn't seem worth it to think up a funny new name for the constellation if she isn't here to laugh about it with me. Fuck. I wish she'd dance back into the garden right now. I imagine her above me. We would be together in the moonlight then lie back, laughing, the silken leaves against our skin.

But it's all fine. I can wait.

I stretch my neck to look above and behind me. The hotel looms over me, as if descending from above. I think about the unexplored rooms again. Maybe tomorrow.

CHAPTER 20

The next day, Reed is standing at the base of the castle, squinting. The jagged rocks reaching up to the ramparts emerge from the purpled shade of tall trees into patches of strong, golden sun.

Dan, Marcus and a dapper gent in houndstooth tweed are walking off into the gardens.

'Shouldn't we wait for the others?' Reed asks.

'They'll catch up,' Marcus says, walking backwards for a moment. 'They know where we're going – or Douglas does anyway.'

Marcus turns back and keeps walking along the path. Dan is matching him pace for pace.

The tweedy man, Marcus's agent, stands waiting for Reed. His outfit and demeanour make him seem like a character displaced from a story set in a different time. The group have been sightseeing all day and Cameron Young has been acting like a tour guide for most of it, punctuating his descriptions with an easy smile.

'It can be really hard to get parked in the city,' he explains.

They walk on in pairs, skirting the elaborately moulded fountain. In the opposite direction, a highland terrier trots beside its owner, making a clockwise pass. The little dog is panting happily and looking with excitement to the hastily scarpering birds.

Cameron keeps making conversation as Reed scans the park.

Princes Street Gardens, he discovers, lies in the dip of a valley that Cameron tells him is the site of a drained loch. The green slopes swooping before them flutter with bright branches and the park swells with all the chlorophyll-richness of bloom-scented spring.

Cameron is telling the history of his professional relationship with Marcus.

Reed sees groups and couples slowly perambulating, the odd person in business attire cutting through the park.

'Oh, yes, way back,' the agent is saying, wrapping up. 'So that's when I started representing him. All I can say is sometimes it pays to take a chance.'

The smile spreads across his crinkled, distinguished face and Reed is momentarily mesmerised by the older man's piercing blue eyes. In another mood, he might have been less irritated by him. Not everyone can pull off a cravat.

A pitter-patter of accelerating feet sounds behind them, culminating in hands on Reed's shoulders that make him jump. He discovers Zoya bouncing up behind him. Douglas is in tow, gratefully slowing to a trot.

'We made it!'

Zoya beams. Douglas is now attending to his jacket, taking it off to flick out some creases then carefully slipping into it again. The afternoon is warm, for Scotland, but Douglas opts to keep the jacket on.

Marcus and Dan turn around, noticing their arrival, but continue talking and walking ahead.

'Did you enjoy your ride in the Porsche?' Reed asks.

'I did!'

'Yes,' Cameron says, somewhat campily, 'and *I* got stuck with the boring Vauxhall. I mean!' Cameron looks at Douglas. 'And they trust *you* to drive that thing?'

'Well, I'm planning on having one of my own, one day,' Douglas answers brightly, 'got to get the practice in!'

'Right,' Reed says, barely masking his cynicism.

He wonders if the polished young man has the same attitude toward Zoya, who he's been pairing up with all day.

'The Ross Fountain back there is cast iron, you know, all the way from France, by way of the Great London Exhibition, eighteen-sixty… something. Transported it in pieces – over a hundred of them – and reassembled it here. Of course, some of the religious men of the city found the nude female figures morally disgraceful…'

'Or *said* they did…' Reed mumbles.

Zoya briefly rolls her eyes – directed at the Victorians rather than his comment, Reed thinks – but she seems more interested in what lies ahead.

They are walking in the valley of the park, along a broad path lined with benches and trees. Bright petals dot the planted borders and new leaves stretch toward the sun. This would have been where the water was deepest.

To their left, Reed notices that the gardens are separated from the heavy traffic of the main road by a neat line of railings and a steep bank cut with loamy flower beds and dark-leaved roses beginning to bud. Their path, below the sweep of daisied slopes, affords a sense of quiet escape that Reed feels at home with. Squirrels dart between the trees.

'What's that?' Zoya exclaims. She is pointing ahead. 'That stage thing.'

'The Ross Bandstand. Finest in the country. Bands have been entertaining people from that stage since the 1930s…'

'Can we get in?' Zoya asks, walking on ahead of the little group.

'I don't think there's anything happening there today,' Cameron says. 'The gates will be closed.'

Reed has a flash memory of another stage they once explored together, in their uniquely secret way. 'Remember the theatre in…' he begins, but she has rushed off.

Reed and Cameron stroll on behind. Dan and Marcus are now far ahead. Zoya stops on the path, having spied a way in.

'I'm sure we can get over the railings easy enough…' She grabs Douglas's sleeve. 'Come on!'

'My jacket!'

'Come on…'

As Zoya drags Douglas toward the railings, he can be heard faintly protesting. 'I'm not really dressed for climbing over railings.'

At this point, the path curves upwards, skirting the amphitheatre and mounting the hill. Dan and Marcus are already standing on the top path so Reed and Cameron press on up the steep slope. Cameron is trying to tell him facts about the First World War memorial.

'...actually funded by Scottish diaspora in the United States – there are stars and stripes included on the frieze.'

Reed is barely listening to the facts pouring from Cameron's mouth now, but he does notice the haunting expression on the sculpted face of the kilted soldier seated on the plinth.

Cameron continues to talk about the memorial's relief design but Reed's attention drifts elsewhere. In the background, back down the hill, he observes Zoya and Douglas climbing up onto the stage. Cameron is saying something about the gardener's cottage.

They reach Dan and Marcus, who have been waiting for them on the top path. Reed looks to the stage and sees Zoya dancing with, or rather around, Douglas.

'You look like the kind of chap who might be interested in a flower clock...' Cameron is saying.

Reed looks at him blankly. 'Do I? Because that's literally the opposite of the look I was going for.' Reed stands there in his vintage black-and-grey shirt, looking genuinely pissed off, his hands on his hips.

Dan looks him up and down and grins. 'Yeah. You do,' he jokes. 'Look at him, all sensitive and willowy... mate, you've got "flower clock" written all over you!'

'Fuck off.' Reed makes a face in Dan's direction. 'And what the fuck's a flower clock, anyway?'

Dan, Marcus and Cameron are all laughing. They walk on along the path. Reed turns to face the stage. Zoya is indulging in some expressive dance moves. Douglas is not.

'What about *them*? Don't *they* have to look at the flower clock?' He turns and catches them up.

'Now, this floral clock has been here for nearly a hundred years. It has a real mechanism, you know, keeps accurate time. Minute and second hand. Every year, the gardeners plant it up – thousands of individual plants – takes them weeks. You can watch them doing it. Brainchild of the Superintendent of Parks and the renowned clockmaker, James Richie, of course. And a fine idea too. There's even a cuckoo that marks the hour…'

It seems that Reed is trapped in the conversation. He ambles along, listening to Cameron telling him about the mechanism, resigned to his fate.

***

Behind them, Marcus touches Dan's arm to stay him. He stops walking and looks at his friend.

'Actually,' Marcus says quietly, 'there's something I wanted to show you.'

Dan's thick brows rise slightly in curious anticipation. Marcus is reaching into his inside pocket, trying to fish something out. Some kind of letter.

'Well, *ask* you really,' Marcus says, handing Dan the folded piece of paper.

Dan opens it. It seems to refer to a contract.

The two friends stand elbow to elbow, reviewing the document. Dan skim-reads, noting the publisher's name – and a figure that seems to be a book advance.

He looks up to meet Marcus's eye. 'What is it? You're writing a memoir? Bit young, aren't you? Not remotely approaching the grave.'

Marcus folds the letter up and slips it away again. 'Well, more like a sort of biographical monograph, I suppose. An art book mainly. It wasn't my idea.'

'You can't *write*, can you?' Dan jokes, a long-standing tease.

Marcus laughs. 'Very funny.'

They walk on again, gaining ground on Cameron and Reed, who are standing next to the flower clock in the corner by the stone steps. Reed isn't even pretending to enjoy the experience, looking wearily at Cameron now, who is not at all put off from continuing his lecture.

'Actually, that's what I wanted to ask you about,' Marcus continues.

'Me?'

'Well, we had a writer, and he'd practically written the thing but then it, sort of, fell apart.'

'What happened?'

Marcus swivels his eyes toward Dan. '*I* happened. I wasn't enjoying it. And I thought, I don't actually want the world knowing all this, reading my life.'

'Well, you don't have to go through with it, do you? It's your life.'

'There is the question of the advance… but it would actually be a boost for my career, so, I'm thinking, I want to finish it. It's just…'

'You need a writer.'

'Yes.'

Dan starts absent-mindedly scratching his jaw, unintentionally resembling a mechanic sizing up a job. 'Takes a long time to write a book, you know…'

'We have most of it – chapters and chapters of the thing – it's embarrassing, really, but the editor said it wasn't… personal enough.'

'So, what's the plan?'

'We just need some rewrites really… More of an interview element to it, they said.'

'So, are you getting the writer back in?'

'No, I was hoping *you* would do it.'

Dan can tell from Marcus's clear, steady gaze that he means it. 'Me? I write newspaper stuff. And reports about haunted beds on the side.'

'You write features, though. And you're good at interviewing people. And, there'll be a fee.' Marcus's deep brown eyes stay on him. 'It shouldn't take that long.'

Dan opens his mouth but doesn't say anything. He's thinking.

'It's okay if you can't do it. It's just, I was hoping you would because… I can't really talk to other…' Marcus's sentence dries up.

Dan walks slowly along the path, one foot in front of the other, staring at the ground and mentally reviewing his work schedule. When he looks up again, his eyes meet Marcus's hopeful, questioning ones.

'Okay. I'll do it. Sign me up.'

They stand, mirroring each other, for a moment, considering their new plan.

'Did he say yes?' Cameron calls, optimistically.

'Yes,' Marcus says.

'Yes to what?' Reed asks.

Marcus and Dan join them by the steps.

'It's a writing job,' Dan tells Reed.

Cameron evidently knew of the offer before he did. 'Excellent!' He gushes, clapping Dan on the back. 'We should still be able to get it out to coincide with the retrospective.' He begins leading them up the steps. 'You're a lifesaver, Dan. Glad to have you on board.'

Reed hangs back by the flower clock. He studies the low, small-leaved plants arranged in precise seams of colour. The group presses on without him.

'Shouldn't we wait for the others?' Reed says.

*****

They cross the road, a group of six again, walking past the neoclassical gallery at the edge of the east gardens. A busking bagpiper is striking up. Reed finds himself dawdling at the back.

He can make out the odd snatch of conversation between Dan and Cameron ahead of him, all book and publishing chat. Zoya, Douglas and Marcus are marching on ahead. He can see her curls bouncing as she walks.

'That was the gallery, wasn't it?' he calls to the others.

Only Cameron responds. 'Indeed, Royal Academy at the front, National Gallery at the back.'

'Aren't we going in?'

'No time, Reed. It's a bit late in the day.'

'You can come back another day?' Dan adds, trying to brighten his friend's mood.

'Exactly,' Cameron agrees, 'you can't do all of Edinburgh in one day.'

They reach the set of steps near the Scott Monument and pause, ranged across the ascent.

'Here we are – the Scott Monument,' Cameron announces, ever the tour guide. He looks specifically at Dan who is standing further down the stone steps. 'Glorious to see writers being celebrated, eh, Dan?'

'Yeah,' – Dan looks up at the neo-Gothic folly – 'it must have taken a lot of work to build this thing.'

'There's actually a statue of Scott at the bottom – you should have a squiz,' Douglas says. 'Would be cool to have a statue of yourself, don't you think? I'd probably want them to make me better-looking.'

'Oh, I think you're handsome enough,' Cameron says, with a mixture of admonishment and aesthetic appreciation.

'It looks like a rocket,' Reed says. 'Can you get up there?'

'Two hundred and eighty-seven steps up to the viewing platform at the top,' Cameron states.

'Let's go up!' Zoya says, skipping up to the top path. 'They should put a helter-skelter slide around it for coming back down!'

'Actually,' Marcus says, at Dan's elbow, 'I always think it's like a big, looming gravestone.'

'That's a bit dark, for such a sunny spring day…' Dan observes.

They both laugh. Douglas has walked up the steps, following Zoya. 'We can always come back another day,' he tells her. 'It's my day off on Saturday – I'll show you more of the city, if you'd like?'

'Maybe, thanks.'

Reed stares at the back of the young man's head.

'Well, you could say it sort of *was*,' – Cameron's loud voice is addressing the whole scattered group; everybody looks at him – 'like a gravestone.'

They don't yet know what he means.

'Well, Scott never got to see it, of course – it was only thought up after he died, and completed twelve years after that.'

'So, what's the point of *that,* then?' Douglas asks. 'A massive big thing to show off about – *after* you're dead?'

'Are we going up, then?' Zoya urges, impatient with all the standing around. 'I bet you can see the sea from up there.'

Dan leans against the stone balustrade. 'I might stay at ground level.'

Marcus leans up too. 'I'll join you.'

'Of course,' – Cameron is continuing his oration – 'Scott didn't know anything about it. It's the architect I feel sorry for.'

'Why?' Dan asks.

'George Meikle Kemp. He died five months before it was finished.'

Zoya looks around with wide eyes. 'He didn't fall from the top?'

'No, he drowned in the canal, poor chap.'

'Poor guy,' Douglas says. 'Does anyone even know about him?'

'Just goes to show, doesn't it?' Cameron continues. 'None of us know when death's coming for us. Any day could be our last.'

The group stand around mulling over the morbid observation until they hear a quiet voice.

'But his art lives on,' Reed says.

They all turn to look at him, hanging back at the foot of the steps. Slowly, he walks up to join them.

'We're looking at it.' He nods to indicate the monument. 'Like Scott's novels do, too.' He draws level with Marcus. 'That's the point, isn't it?' Reed continues. 'That artists live on forever through their art?'

Reed and Marcus regard one another. For the first time yet, they seem to be in agreement.

'I always thought it was for the moment,' Zoya says, at the top of the steps. 'For people to enjoy there and then. I mean, not all art lasts forever, does it?'

'Like the flower clock,' Cameron says.

Reed squeezes his eyes shut at the mention of it.

'So, come on then. We're here now. Let's go up,' Zoya says.

'Actually,' – Cameron checks his Rolex – 'it's closing soon. I think you might be out of time.'

CHAPTER 21

The group bustles in through the front door, five of them laughing and chattering; one, not so much.

'Good day's sightseeing?' Karen asks when they reach the guest lounge.

'Really good, thanks,' Zoya replies, flopping onto one of the sofas.

Dan and Marcus are bringing up the rear, mid-conversation. Marcus's gaze flits from Dan, straight to Karen.

'Is Trinny home?'

Dan mumbles the end of his sentence and changes course. He sinks into the corner armchair by the window.

'No, Trinny's away now, until tomorrow,' Karen continues.

'At her sister's in York,' Douglas adds.

Karen manages her exasperation at his 'helpfulness' but it's still readable in her weary gaze.

'Sorry, Dan, what were you saying?' Marcus asks, locating his friend in the corner.

'Oh. Nothing,' Dan says, smiling a thin smile.

'Cameron – are you staying for dinner?' Marcus asks.

'Very kind, thank you. Yes – if you'll have me as I am?' Cameron makes a show of looking himself up and down.

'Cameron! It's 1991. We don't "dress for dinner" around here,' Marcus tells him.

'Just as well,' Dan says, looking at his own scruffy jeans.

'I'll let Rab know. Do you want drinks?' Karen offers, looking around the room.

'Thanks, Karen.' Marcus puts a hand on her shoulder. 'Do stay, Cameron?'

'Well,' – Cameron looks at his fancy watch – 'I do make it cocktail hour.' He smiles broadly.

Reed, who can't shake his habit of lingering on the outskirts, leans against the reception desk, glowering as he watches Douglas. The handsome young man hitches his smart trousers and takes a seat on the sofa, right next to Zoya.

Karen is taking drinks orders. Cameron stands, examining the beautifully constructed model of the yacht with small canvas sails. Then he takes a seat on a chair in the middle of the lounge.

'What's this?' he says, rooting about in the cushions and drawing something out. 'I just sat on this… watch.'

Cameron is holding up a slim watch for everyone to see. Nobody claims or recognises it, so he pulls a perplexed expression and takes another look himself.

'A ladies' watch. Seems to have stopped, anyway.'

Karen goes over to him. 'Mrs Jenkins's, do you think?' she wonders.

'No, I think she wears a silvery thing,' Dan remembers.

'Oh well.' Karen places the stray watch on the reception desk and disappears to fix the drinks. The whole time she is gone, Marcus stands quietly in the middle of the chatter, looking pensive. Reed is trying to read his expression. He is still looking at him when Marcus suddenly jumps.

It is just the sound of the front door being closed – no need for alarm. Then Marcus recognises the person coming through the hallway. 'Glenda!' he exclaims. 'You made it!'

Glenda is placing a couple of bags on the tiles.

Marcus charges through the lounge toward her and bends to give the slight woman a hug.

The rest of the group gravitate toward the hallway, interested in the new arrival. All except Karen, who has set down the tray of drinks and doesn't seem to care.

And Reed, who hasn't moved from his leaning place at all.

He takes the opportunity to look at the found watch. He notices that it isn't ticking and that both hands seem to have stopped exactly at the number 3, which isn't a time.

He hears Dan's voice saying his name and lays it back on the desk. Dan manoeuvres him by the elbow.

'And this is my other associate – Reed.'

'Hi.'

Reed finds Zoya standing by his side. 'Glenda is Fintan's godmother,' she says softly, leaning close enough that her hair falls against him. 'She might know something.'

Then she gives him a meaningful look with her dark, dancing eyes.

***

After a casual, chatty dinner, during which Reed manages not to say more than ten words, the group disperses with things to do and other homes to go to. Muriel confirmed that the found watch wasn't hers either and nobody mentioned it again. Reed wants to take another look at it, but when he passes back through the guest lounge, he discovers that the stopped watch is no longer there. Somebody has taken it.

CHAPTER 22

I'm standing outside Glenda's guest room on the first floor, about to start my snooping.

I push the door open. I haven't got my head around Glenda yet: Canadian and Mexican by way of Ireland and France; some kind of therapist; godmother of Fintan O'Doherty; has a strange effect on Marcus; Dan seems to know her too.

I have a poke around her room.

On the desk are a stack of therapy books – including her own. *Modes of Disrobement: Shedding Costume for Connection* by Glenda Fuentes-Tremblay. This must be her signature methodology. The volume has a lot of sticky notes in it. It looks like a working copy.

Opening the book jacket, I read the author biography and find the same tranquil, oval face, framed by somewhat darker hair. I scan the chapter headings. One grabs my attention: 'Beyond Social Nudism: Shared Experiential Nakedness and the Therapeutic Relationship'. Well, it would.

I skim read a couple of pages. I don't think the nakedness is metaphorical. I close the book and put it back on the pile.

I have a quick look through the drawers and wardrobe but find nothing out of the ordinary and soon leave the room. The next occupied room is Dan's. I don't go in.

I wonder if Zoya and Karen are enjoying their night out.

I go into the Jenkins' room and notice the tangle of pyjamas in the bed indicating the couple cuddled up, fast asleep. Their room has all the markers of wealthy septuagenarians on holiday: guidebooks, a fancy camera, expensive luggage, lots of cash. I close the safe and go downstairs.

I open the narrow door behind the reception desk and duck into the office. Here, I see the rota pinned to the wall, scrawled with staff holidays. Leafing through the bookings, I see that the Jenkins will be the last guests for a while.

I look through some paperwork half-heartedly. I wouldn't have any idea if anything was amiss. I don't discover anything interesting or any secret hiding places, and extricate myself from the ledgers and papers and unpaid bills.

I drift through the lounge and the breakfast room and into Rab's kitchen, where I steal a piece of flapjack from a plate under a cloth. I eat it, standing at the kitchen window, looking at the empty plains of fluttering grass beyond. I wonder what Zoya and Karen are up to now.

I finish the flapjack.

At least she didn't go out with that Douglas. Although I am aware he's not the only man in the city of Edinburgh.

When I walk back up the tall staircase, it creaks in a comfortable sort of way. I pass the landing window, ignoring the city outside, and keep going, up to the top floor.

Inside the haunted bedroom, I find that it doesn't feel any more haunted than anywhere else. I feel around the walls and look in the cupboard. There aren't any exciting secret passages in here. I get on my knees and look under the bed. Nope, no ghosts hiding under there.

Dan's kit is still up here. I pick up his experiment book and scan the pages. An intriguing note arrests my gaze: *'It has to look like an accident'*. Reading these words makes my skin prickle for the first time all night. He has recorded the time and location and then the observation ends, remaining unexplained.

I scribble an abbreviated version in my own notebook: the word 'accident' and the date and time. I thicken the question mark to remind myself that it was also puzzling to Dan.

I leave and close the door. Further along the corridor is Karen's room. I go in.

Karen lives in a modest room, big enough for a plump double bed, small enough to seem overstuffed. A chink of light falls through a gap in the curtains. Possessions are strewn over the small armchair, dresser and drawers; clumpy boots are lined up by a wall. The wardrobe teeters with stacked boxes, and jacket sleeves peep out, trapped between the doors.

The busy clutter and Blu-Tacked posters on the walls give it a sort of rebellious teenager feel, although nothing, on closer inspection, is frivolous or immature. I suppose the clutter is just what you get when you cram your forty-something life into one room of your employer's house.

I find this sort of personal mess troubling because I feel the need to sieve through all the things, coupled with the pressure to put it all back *exactly* as I find it so that people don't get freaked out.

On the dresser, on top of a pile of *things*, are a few copies of the same photograph – some fancy dress party from their university days. I move into the light and peer at the people in the picture.

I notice Dan first. He hasn't changed that much since then. He is wearing an odd sort of hat that might be a kitchen colander and seems to be dressed in tin foil. And then, I get it: they are doing *The Wizard of Oz*. The handsome features and swirl of dark hair sticking out of the lion costume identify Marcus and there's a scarecrow and a Dorothy standing nearby.

The slim-faced, gingham clad woman could very well be Catriona, and the scarecrow himself, I recognise as Fintan. I've spent quite a lot of time staring at his newspaper-print face.

This is how Dan described him – the attention seeker and connector of people, at the centre of things. Here he is, instigating an arm link and leg kick, the only one of the four looking at the camera.

I put the photo down and see a colourful document wallet. It slides out with a papery sigh. Inside I find some plane tickets – another trip to Dublin. I wonder why Karen might be going back but find no other evidence to explain it. I note it in my book.

I wonder if Zoya and Karen are still out dancing somewhere. I leave the rest of the room untouched; too much to deal with.

I haven't looked at the family apartment yet, so I make my way past the small kitchen and down the back stairs. In Marcus and Catriona's bedroom, everything is tidy and elegant and boring. The fitted wardrobes are lined with colour-coordinated outfits and there's only a neatly wrapped parcel under the bed.

Next to their bedroom is the study. I go in and sit at the desk. Through the window I can see the castle, shaded in charcoal planes.

Just when I think I've lost momentum I motivate myself to have a look through the desk drawers. In one I find an unopened letter stuffed toward the back. It has a Dublin postmark but remains unopened. I peer at the stamp and do some calculations; it seems to have been posted before Fintan died. Looks like the address was slightly wrong but it got here in the end.

I think hard about opening it. If I rip it open, it will stay ripped.

I stare at the envelope for a long time, looking at the address scribbled in wild, sprawling handwriting, then I find myself tucking it back into place. I can come back to it at some point.

I also find a couple of box files, pull these out and place them on top of the desk. They reveal a series of manila folders, each marked with headings, some with notes. I take these to be chapter headings. I think I've found Marcus's unfinished book.

I look out at the brightening night and the city skyline. I won't have time to read everything tonight but decide to take a look. What is it about Marcus that Dan even likes?

I find the notes about his time at university and start to skim. I am surprised to read a fair bit about protest marches and activism, even though a lot of it was going on at the time. I suppose it's easy to see people like Marcus and Catriona as very 'establishment', but they were passionate, change-the-world students once upon a time.

I sit back in the leather chair and look at the sky. The dawn has crept up on me. I must have been reading for a while.

I leaf through the other folders, knowing I don't have much more reading in me, but interested to see what other topics there might be.

I find one that bears the title 'Head over Heels' on the cover and lift it out of the box. The folder is very thin. It's empty except for a business card that falls onto my lap. I pick it up and notice that it is weirdly plain in design – just a telephone number. I turn it over; nothing on the reverse.

Looking at the telephone number, I notice something even more odd. The digits are hand-printed – added individually to the card, digit by digit, using stamps. Why not have it printed? Or write the number on by hand? Or put your name and business on it, for that matter? It's all very odd.

My impulse is to phone the number but that wouldn't work. Even if telephones work in the dreaming, who could possibly answer? Right now, there's nobody else in the world but me. So, I copy down the number in my notebook then sit back in the chair.

A yellow wash is spreading through the sky.

Carefully, I put the boxes of folders away and replace them in the drawer. And then I find the lost watch.

I look at it closely, confirming that the hands are still stopped dead at '3'. It still hasn't been claimed then – unless it's Catriona's, maybe – but as battered and cheap-looking as it is, I can't imagine it's her kind of thing.

I place it on the blotting pad and lean forward so that it's level with my eyes. I stare at it, thinking. My back starts to ache. I stretch a little and sit upright, casting my gaze to the castle.

A speck is moving along the outline of a rooftop. It is too distant for me to make out but looks like a person. It jumps off the edge.

If that's Zoya, what is she playing at? And, if not Zoya, who else?

The last time I thought I saw someone darting across a skyline in the dreaming, it was closely followed by some-one very real and very dead.

CHAPTER 23

Reed wakes up in his guest room. It's still early. He goes over to the window to draw the curtains and look at the day. He wonders if Zoya came home.

A pale morning hangs over the garden, casting the grassy meadow half in shade.

He sees something in the far corner – in a patch of watery sunshine; two shapes nestled in the grass. He realises that the shapes are people; Zoya and Glenda lying naked in the cool dawn sun, moving slowly, like driftwood turning by a shore.

He makes himself look away and then turns around, his back to the window, resolved not to play the peeping Tom. He wants to look at Zoya naked, yes – but he wants to look at her up close.

He closes the curtains and gets back into bed.

***

After the naked therapy, Zoya and Glenda are sitting at a table on the terrace. Zoya has slipped on a dressing gown and Glenda is wearing something that Zoya would guess was South American. The disrobers have robed.

Two green teas sit on the table between them. The women both look happy and refreshed.

'I must say, you are particularly receptive to therapy, Zoya. If only all my clients were like you.'

'I enjoyed it, thanks.'

'You're very welcome.'

'And it's about opening up, then?'

'Yes. Some people have real difficulty communicating authentically but it can change when they take off their clothes.'

'Men-people?'

Glenda sips her green tea. Her face flickers through an expression that dissembles, but her twinkling eyes seem to say 'yes'.

'I know someone like that,' Zoya continues. 'I mean, he doesn't hide his emotions or opinions, but just likes to keep things to himself – even when it would be better for everyone if he shared…' She glances up to Reed's window.

Glenda observes and smiles. 'Can't live with them, can't live without them?' Glenda suggests, inverting the gender cliché.

They laugh.

'You have to remember the paradox of their social conditioning, though,' Glenda says.

'The…?'

'On the one hand, society teaches men that their opinion is the most important thing in the universe…'

'Which is why they won't shut up about their opinions…'

'... and that simply *having* a desire entitles them to have it fulfilled – which is why they express their desires constantly – something women could do better at...'

'And on the other hand...?' Zoya prompts.

'Well, society also teaches men not to talk about anything that makes them look vulnerable, such as problems or feelings.'

Zoya nods, then smiles. 'I desire something.'

'Oh?' Glenda asks.

'Mmm, tea and toast in a nice hot bath and the sound of *no* men talking about anything for a while.'

***

Later that day, Dan and Marcus are walking over the sand at Yellowcraig, a long ribbon of biscuity beach edged with spiky grasses. Beyond a margin of marshland, the bay is flanked by a tangle of low, twisted trees. A postcard-ready island lies offshore, a red-and-white-striped lighthouse capping the scene.

'The wind is getting up again,' Dan says.

Marcus looks at him, his dark waves dancing around his face.

'Do we need to worry about the Porsche – and the salt?' Dan asks.

A wiry dog passes them in a breathy dash, its paws throwing up fine sprays of sand. Marcus shakes his head. 'I thought you'd enjoy the drive.'

'Oh, yeah. It's not every day I get taken for a coastal drive in the sunshine in a convertible. How long have you had it?'

'Well, it's Trinny's.'

'Won't she mind us taking it?'

'Not at all. She would want us to.'

Dan looks around. 'We should probably finish the interview. I'm just worried it might be too windy for the recording…'

The stretch of beach is sparsely scattered with sea-softened pebbles that roll along in their wake. They walk on, dislodging seabird prints that dissolve in the soft, sugary sand.

'What if I move closer?' Marcus suggests.

'Yeah, that should be okay. I don't want to finish the interview yet because I think we're on a roll.'

He looks to the horizon. The sky is subtly changing in tone and hue.

'Is this okay?' Marcus asks, sitting down on the sand.

Dan sits right next to him, placing his boots in the same dip. He notices how far they have walked along the long beach and how the view of the lighthouse island has changed. He can feel his curls being tightly knotted by the salty wind whereas Marcus's mane flutters attractively around his pensive face, as if designed for dramatic weather.

Marcus seems ready to resume the interview so Dan huddles toward him, sheltering the tape recorder with his body. Then he presses 'record'.

'Where were we?' Marcus asks.

'Actually, I don't think we've touched on your marriage yet. When did you two meet?'

'You know this. You were there! But for the tape… it was at university. At Manchester. You two were some of the first people I actually met there.'

'Were we?'

'Well, you first, I think. I remember when you came crashing into the kitchen with your Feynman book and your *2001* poster and your trusty stewpan and your spider plant.'

Dan smiles. 'But, back to your marriage. You met Catriona Gordon in Manchester in 1968 when you were studying art and she was studying dance, married in 1973 and have been together now for eighteen years.'

'Off and on,' Marcus says, by way of confirmation.

They watch the lapping waves. White veils of rushing swells lace-edge the shore and drag the wet sand smooth.

'Tell me about that. How many times did you split up and get back together again?' Dan leans closer so the tape can pick up the answer beneath the swirling wind.

'I don't think you should put it like that. In the book. I mean, we were always there for each other, and it was never that… black and white.'

'I'm trying to be tactful.' Dan thinks for a moment, choosing his words. 'Would you say that you had an open relationship back then?'

'No, but I think it's important that we had relationships with other people – I mean, imagine the poor sods who marry the first person they see and stay together and *that's* their life experience. I mean, you learn so much from *all* the different people you meet and… get to know.'

An unseen sun is dyeing the sky a rosy tangerine and painting shadows over the island rock. Fife has become a dusky seam in the distance and crimson waves are beginning to peak far from shore.

'How would you like to phrase it, for the book, then?' Dan asks. 'I mean, *I* know where the bodies are buried. Are we mentioning names?'

Marcus looks at him out of the corner of his eye. 'Was I that bad?'

'The way I remember it,' Dan says, 'you were always in monogamous relationships – but they just seemed to… overlap.'

The wind is now whipping through the tall grass and whispering through the wood. Marcus runs his fingers through his hair. 'I just… I just had problems breaking up with people,' he says, then adds quietly: 'I don't like to hurt anyone.'

'I know. You were just a boy who can't say no. But are we getting into any of this? In the book? What about Karen? I mean, she's still in your life.'

'Karen?' Marcus shakes his head briefly. 'That was just for a week or two. I hardly remember. And I think Fintan made more of a lasting impression on her than I ever did, anyway.'

'Well, she was going out with him for a whole three months... and all along believing he was a geography student called Clive!'

They laugh at Fintan's preposterous ways.

'We shouldn't laugh, though,' Marcus says, reigning it in.

'It was twenty-odd years ago,' Dan reasons. 'I'm sure she's over it by now.'

'Still. She was so hurt at the time. And angry with all of us.'

'Yeah, but it didn't stop her being in our circle.'

'Like Trinny was. That's what I mean. It didn't matter whether we were together or not, she was always one of us. *That's* what I want the book to convey. That despite our forays into other relationships and learning from life and all the things that happened, we kept coming back to one another, in some form or other...'

Marcus gazes at the darkening sea.

'It's like the waves, ebbing and falling at the shore, moving apart and coming back together. You can put it something like that.'

Dan's thick brows are set at acute angles. He turns off the tape recorder. 'You'll be saying I'm your rock next!'

Luckily, Marcus laughs. He stands up and dusts the sand from his clothes, then holds out a hand toward Dan. He grasps it and allows Marcus to help him up.

Dan looks at his shorter, leaner friend. 'You're stronger than you look.'

'I'm really not. Look. The sun is going down and we're three miles away from the car now. And that will be three miles of walking in the dark if we leave it too long. Come on, Trinny will be back from York and we've got guests for dinner.'

'Okay, I'm not ready to walk into the sea and disappear just yet,' Dan replies. 'Let's go back.'

Dan begins marching through the mounds of giving sand, back in the direction they came from. He feels Marcus's hand on his arm, pulling him back.

'But look,' Marcus says, 'how beautiful the sunlight's becoming, on the way down.'

C H A P T E R 2 4

Catriona is sitting at the head of the table holding forth, a petite yet commanding presence in a white silk shirt.

The breakfast room has been transformed for dining. Tables have been pushed together in a long row and swathed with thick cloth. Vases of swollen blooms have been strategically placed between the gilt-circled bowls and spoons. The room feels different this evening; windows shuttered, partition closed. The smell trailing from Muriel's trolley promises warm, homemade bread.

'I think we're all here. Muriel, you can serve now, thank you. Where was I…?' Catriona speaks with a quiet authority that gradually hushes the chattering guests. She looks at a lank-haired man sitting to her right and sporting a sage jacket and colourful bow tie.

'Douglas, you know, and this is our manager…'

'Karen. I actually have a name, you know.' Karen swings her glass of vodka tonic toward her mouth.

'I was just getting to that. And this is Glenda.'

Glenda nods graciously.

'And this is my husband, Marcus, Cameron, his agent…'

'How's the biography going?' Cameron asks Dan, who is sitting across the table from him.

'Oh, well, I think.' Dan and Marcus exchange glances.

'And my husband's friends: Dan, Reed – is it? – and Zoya. I think you all know each other. And, this is Dr Alasdair Duncan-Fox. Alasdair's a curator at Archive Repository Scotland. He's doing a spot of historical research for me – on this place.'

Catriona looks around the room, as if the familiar architecture will suddenly reveal secrets previously unseen. The elegant wall lamps spread a satiny shine over the wallpaper.

Muriel is ladling steaming soup into the bowls. Several of the guests exchange polite greetings but Dan just looks at his meal. Reed is carefully watching Zoya and Douglas, who are sitting next to one another.

Cameron opens a starchy napkin with a flourish and lays it on his lap. He leans toward the curator.

'Duncan-Fox? Aren't you a member of my club? I know the name…?'

'Ah,' – Alasdair steeples his fingers – 'well, that might be my black sheep of a brother's name you are thinking of. Malcolm Duncan-Fox.'

Cameron clicks his fingers. 'The crooked lawyer!'

'Cameron!' Catriona chastises, 'I don't…'

Alasdair waves her complaint away. 'It's quite alright. His crimes are nothing to do with me… That's why I always go by "*Dr* Duncan-Fox" – that and the many late nights I spent scribbling away at my PhD.'

'Dan,' Catriona says, speaking over the length of the table, 'I thought it was about time we bring science and the humanities together. Whatever Alasdair finds out about the history of this place might be useful to your investigation too. Wouldn't you say? Might explain a few things.'

'So,' – Alasdair looks interested – 'how is your research going, Dan? Have you found anything yet? I must say, it is fascinating to me that you do this sort of thing.'

'Well, we have some interesting readings, yes, but I wouldn't jump to any conclusions about a ghost,' Dan replies before getting back to his watery soup.

'Oh?' Catriona asks, managing to infuse the breathy vowel with a certain authority.

Alasdair raises a bushy eyebrow. '*Interesting readings*, eh? Well, I suppose we're more alike than it may first appear.'

A few of the other diners tune into the conversation.

'You might say that we are in the same game,' Alasdair continues. 'The archives make for "interesting reading" too!' His comment garners a few polite laughs. 'I jest, but there is an element of truth to it.' Alasdair looks around the table. 'We are both looking at traces of the dead.'

Dan shifts in his chair. 'I wouldn't put it–' he begins.

'*You*, scientifically detecting the trace of ghosts, as it were; *me*, studying the words of people who are now dead. That's what archives are, for the most part, the marks of people no longer with us. You can read the thoughts and deeds of people who aren't here – people you have never met.'

Zoya shoots a brief, meaningful look at Reed. He catches it because he was already looking at her.

'You know,' Alasdair continues, 'there's nothing like touching an old manuscript to connect you with the past – actually touching the same parchment that *they* touched when they were writing on it. Touching it with cotton gloves, of course!' He chuckles at his own joke.

Karen's irreverent guffaw is louder. 'Like a magic trick!' she announces.

Zoya laughs quietly at the comment but others just look embarrassed.

'So, how do you know my wife?' Marcus asks.

'Through the Theatres Trust. I think it was Douglas who introduced us at the Benefactor's Dinner, wasn't it?'

'Of course it was,' Karen says, cynically. She seems a bit too drunk for the early stage of the evening.

'I try to be of service,' Douglas says. 'Zoya, are we still on for Saturday?'

'Yes, please,' she replies, raising her spoon to her mouth.

Dan is on the verge of whispering to Reed that 'jealous' isn't such a good look.

Then Catriona shrieks.

'Oh, my God!' Everybody looks at her. Someone's spoon splashes in their soup. 'I nearly forgot! I didn't tell you…'

'Is everything alright?' Dan asks.

'Yes. Yes, I am now. It's just that, after I got back, off the train from York,' – her slim hands decorate the monologue with delicate gestures, inviting everyone into the story – 'I went out to check on the flat at South Queensferry, as the tenants are now gone, and well, I took the Astra because you must have had the Porsche out somewhere, and–'

'What?' Alasdair enquires, his eyes wide.

'Well, as you can see, I'm quite alright, but I was just driving along, and the brakes failed. It was just a mild crash really, but it was terrifying at the time. The car's okay too – apart from the burst brake pipes and a small dent. Douglas came to rescue me in a taxi and took me to the flat and saw that I was alright.' She smiles warmly at her assistant.

'I'll bet he did,' Karen says, out of the corner of her mouth, but not that quietly.

'And the car's fine. I'm picking it up from the garage tomorrow,' Douglas explains.

Reed has been watching Marcus throughout the story. He looks visibly upset. His wife has noticed too.

'Don't look so shaken up, darling,' Catriona says. 'I'm still very much alive.'

***

This place is really something.

Dr Duncan-Fox's apartment is crammed: small pieces of eclectic furniture; books, ornaments and scruffy-looking artefacts everywhere; prints and paintings hung all over the walls.

My detective skills aren't that impressive – I just listened in on Alasdair booking his taxi home and committed the address to memory. I see his distinctive paisley scarf hanging on the overloaded coat stand and know I'm in the right place.

I move along the passageway. A jigsaw of artworks overpopulates the long wall. There is a deep shelf over the door stuffed with peeling leather cases, cardboard boxes and dusty canvas sacks. At floor level, more clutter tucked tightly against the skirting boards.

Why did I get the feeling that Dr Alasdair Duncan-Fox is up to something?

I walk into the living room. It is small and completely overtaken by a couple of plush, cushion-packed sofas.

I peek into the bedroom and find a dark little cave stuffed with a queen-sized bed. A leather-bound volume lies open, page down, at the edge of the eiderdown. I think he's been reading in bed.

I close the door and look around again. I could spend several nights looking through all the *stuff* in here.

I move into Dr Duncan-Fox's study. A couple of desks are stacked with books and files and papers, and the shelves look precarious: over-stocked with heavy loads. I turn on a small desk lamp for a closer inspection. Immediately, there are too many things to look at. I don't really know where to start.

I find a letter cresting the wave of paperwork near the centre of the desk and spot the Gillespie's address. It isn't in the sender's spot of the letter but halfway down the page. Below the address, I read a red flag of a sentence:

'If you could "research" a similar story to the coach house property, that would be good, and if it can be discovered before the Americans leave, even better.'

It seems an odd way of putting it. To cloak the word 'research' in quotation marks that way can only mean it is a lie. It seems like Dr Alasdair Duncan-Fox might be crooked in his own way.

Then there is a passage providing a lead on Catriona's family history – the Gordons of Strathkeel – plus some other addresses.

Disappointingly, there isn't much of a signature to the letter, just a squiggle like a lazy autograph. It looks like a letter 'C' – or possibly a 'G' – I think, but I can't draw any conclusions about that.

I can't take the letter, can I? I mean, I *could* but… if we move things, they stay moved.

I leave it where it is and copy some of it down in my notebook.

I look at all the towering piles of academia again and the photo albums and slides and other boxes of… stuff. I glance at all the maps, drawings and framed facsimiles hanging from the walls in the hallway, many so low you would have to crouch to see properly. I look at the stacks of novels piled on the tables and floor. I spy cardboard boxes groaning with old typewriters and unidentified junk.

I find it all overwhelming – because I want to look at it all but can't. I don't know how anyone can live like this. All this stuff: it would weigh on me. I realise I'm missing my van and the open road.

CHAPTER 25

Reed walks softly along the landing. The house is quiet except for a couple of now-familiar creaks. It's early and nobody stirs.

He pads along the hallway, passing closed doors, the carpet muffling his tread. He emerges from the dim corridor into a patch of brightness at the top of the stairs. Dust motes speckle the air. He looks out of the window and sees seagulls perched on the building across the road.

He walks on, accidentally nudging a print hung on the wall. The hard frame presses his shoulder as he corrects his course.

Rubbing his arm subconsciously, he passes the Strathkeel room, the bathroom and Karen's bedroom before finding soft light again at the family kitchen, its tall, never-shuttered window awash with peach and grey.

He walks down the back stairs, treading lightly to minimise the sound. At the ground floor, he grabs a banana from the bowl and weaves through the breakfast tables to the back of the house. As he folds back the door, the hinges release a small sigh on the still, morning air. A dew-sprinkled day is waiting for him outside.

He steps onto the terrace, unprops a chair and sets it into place. The leg scrapes gently against the paving. He takes a seat and opens his novel.

***

After breakfast, Dan is working in the dining room. The tablecloth is covered in papers and he is listening back to one of his tapes. Zoya enters and takes a seat at the other side of the room, near the kitchen. Dan switches off his tape player. She is putting on a pair of hiking boots.

'Oh, don't mind me, I'm just lacing up.'

Dan watches her pulling the laces tight and catching them on the right hooks, making the boots snug around her ankles. The terrace door gently swings open and Reed appears, holding a paperback. He leans against the door frame.

'Going for a walk?' he asks her.

'Oh! Where did you come from? How long have you been out there?' Dan asks.

'A while.'

'I never thought of you as an early bird. Why are you up so early?'

'No reason. Might have a nap later.'

Zoya continues tightening the laces but her focus switches to Reed by the door. She knows that Reed's sleep behaviour is unlikely to be random but that he won't tell her what he's up to in front of Dan. Reed avoids her gaze. He knows that she knows. She switches to the other boot and Reed looks at Dan.

'Working hard?'

Dan replies with a gesture indicating the spread of papers in front of him. He is holding a pen.

'Where are you going for your walk?' Dan asks Zoya.

'Arthur's Seat. You know, the big volcanoey thing.'

'On your own?' Dan says.

'Yes, on my own. And I want to get up there before it's too full of tourists.'

'Will you be alright?' Reed asks.

'Yes,' she replies, 'I'm brilliant company.'

'But will you be safe up there?' Dan asks, continuing the questioning. 'I mean, you don't know who's about.'

Zoya stands and tests the fit of her boots. 'Yes, I'll be fine. On my own. Don't worry.' She sighs. 'See you later.' She picks up her backpack and leaves.

Reed drifts further into the room and watches her walking to the front door and then, through the windows, he sees her pass by in the street. He returns to the breakfast room and takes an interest in Dan's work. Dan neatens his stack of papers in response, cutting off the inspection.

Marcus appears, walking breezily through the room. 'Morning, Reed. Good book?'

He passes Reed and makes straight for Dan's table, not waiting for the answer.

'Are you ready for our next "date"?' He means the biography interview.

'Ready when you are,' Dan says.

Reed wanders off with his novel.

'I thought we could go to my studio today?'

Dan puts the lid on his pen and smiles. 'Perfect.'

***

In Marcus's studio, the two friends are sitting on a sagging sofa by a low, battered table that bears mugs, plates and a muddle of photographic prints. The aroma is an odd mix of coffee, turpentine and paint but doesn't stop Dan enjoying his sandwich.

Marcus picks up a print from the array of photographs and holds it up for Dan to take a better look. 'So, this is the 1972 group show I did at the Hayward – *Communication* – see, I was telling you – there's that piece I sold to David Oaks… and…'

'… the rest is history,' Dan says, talking with his mouthful.

'History, indeed.' Marcus's lively gesticulation pauses and Dan catches a slightly sad tone to his voice.

Dan shakes his head and swallows. 'Don't. Don't get onto this again. It's just a phase.' He shakes his head again. '*I* get writer's block sometimes,' Dan says, in a tone of encouraging solidarity.

'No. I think I've given all my art to the world now.' Marcus looks at Dan. 'I've nothing left to say.'

'Don't do this to yourself.' Dan lays a hand on Marcus's arm.

Marcus sits quietly, looking up to the rafters. His eyes seem moist. 'Okay.'

He snaps back to the matter in hand, forcing some dynamism into his demeanour. 'So, where did we get up to?'

Dan looks through his notepad. 'You were just getting into the international shows…'

'Yes!' Marcus jumps up from the sofa. 'I've got some pieces from *Re-Figuration* over here. You finished?'

'Yep.'

Dan puts his empty plate down and follows Marcus to one edge of the room where he is pulling canvasses out of narrow storage slots. Folded easels, wooden frames and sheeted canvasses are leaning against a wall and the units are littered with piles of paper, sticky bottles and crusted jars.

Marcus sets a couple of paintings on the floor, propping them up for display.

It has been a while since Dan saw any of Marcus's paintings in the flesh. The colour choices cast a spell that takes Dan back in time. He kneels to take in their full power. Dan is impressed all over again at how accomplished they are. They really deserve to be seen.

'Oh,' Marcus is saying, already in a different part of the studio, 'there's another one, wait, I'll bring it.'

He flits by the rickety ladder and disappears around the corner. Dan takes another look around.

The studio stretches in awkward planes that define an oddly shaped space with an L-plan floor, rhomboid walls and a sloping roof. A mezzanine crouches below the high ceiling. Specks of paint have been splattered over the white walls.

The place feels both balanced and ramshackle – airy spaces and tight corners, the steady metre of organised storage covered with the colourful clutter of craft.

A wooden door closes them off from the small mews street outside and the skylight frames a clear patch of sky and a glimpse of towering wall. It feels like a happy, hidden little space; dynamic yet settled, busy and calm.

You couldn't design a studio this way from the outset, Dan realises. Everything has accumulated and found its place over years and years and years, forming like desire-lines that map Marcus's mind.

He's still waiting for him to reappear.

Dan shuffles around the corner where Marcus was last seen. He seems to have vanished. Then the sound of muffled movement draws his attention to a recessed store. Is Marcus waiting for him to follow him in? Gently, Dan pulls back the curtain.

He sees metal racks and more art materials and stretched canvasses and Marcus himself pushing a sports bag to the back of a shelf. Marcus turns. 'I'll bring it out,' he says, smiling.

'I thought I'd lost you then.'

Dan holds the curtain aside as Marcus carries another painting out from the cubbyhole and watches while he sets up some easels. It feels good, standing there in the middle of the sunlit studio, having Marcus show him various paintings he has made – but Dan can't stop wondering what is in the bag.

***

I'm standing inside a grand dome, unsure where to go and unused to the dreaming in daylight. I mostly do this at night.

The round room is imposing, lined with mysterious tomes, ringed by the gilt ribbon of a delicately wrought bannister and capped with a high domed roof. It would be intimidating in the waking world. If it wasn't all just for me alone, right now in the dreaming, I might feel like I shouldn't be here.

I shuffle around somewhere near the centre, taking it all in.

Tiers and tiers of russet volumes stretch from the ground floor to ladder-high shelves on the storey above. Lines of matching red labels run in rings across the thick and thin spines circumnavigating the edifice with the span of centuries.

The shadowed curves of shallow stone arches resemble firmly pressed frowns. I clear my throat and discover the sound's sliding, circular echo slipping softly around the walls.

The dome is barely set back from the main street, but the thick layers of eighteenth-century stone muffle the noise of the city, trapping a timeless, solemn silence in the still space.

I look up to the ceiling and find an oculus revealing blue sky. I smile to imagine a pair of webbed gull feet alighting there, or – thinking back to the museum in Dublin – the clumsy soles of a man like me.

I should be getting on with my search. My early rising worked as planned and I am making the most of an afternoon nap. I've got my own private dimension – but I don't know how long it will last.

The dome is incised by compass-point doors leading off, multiple-choice style, to the rest of the institution. I imagine a maze of parchment, paper and ink and set off, guessing at the route.

I find myself roaming through endless corridors and corners and doors. Some of the doors reveal small offices, others lead to shelves and shelves of *stuff*.

I know what Dr Duncan-Fox would call this *stuff*: archives.

I go into a storeroom, aware of my hesitant feet which are trailing slow, purposeful footsteps on the stone floor. I don't normally creep around like this – don't need to – but there's something about this place.

The floor space soon shrinks to a slim passageway that twists around stone corners and through short, stumpy doors. I am intruding on history. I retrace my steps and escape.

I try another storeroom and another. Shelves and shelves and boxes and boxes. I see rows of marshalled books with wobbly spines and cotton bags containing long parchment rolls; everywhere, doors and shutters protecting dark stores of papery treasure.

I begin to linger and look at things.

A numbering system seems to scamper across the shelves, running enigmatically through the bays and rooms.

I can't quite follow it; some kind of narrative I don't understand, sweeping in and out of view.

I touch my fingers to a volume, making contact with the past, then walk further in.

I pull at a book spine that gives way, revealing itself loose at one side. I panic and pat the fragment back into place and push it back into line with a leathery slide. Some of the books have brown clumps of sticky tape unfurling in curls, I notice; others are neat and perfect and newly conserved.

I pick up a box and see mysterious numbers scribbled on it in pencil, like a code. Inside, I find wobbly papers encased in neat, plastic wallets, scrawled handwriting dancing over the sheets in thick and thin strokes. Other boxes contain hard, curling parchment or shining photographic prints. I open another and find a document nestled protectively in a precision-cut foam bed and daren't disturb it. I put everything back as I found it on the shelves.

This is a distraction and I should get back to the task in hand. I don't know why I thought Dr Alasdair's office would be easier to find. I had no idea that there could possibly be so many rooms or so much *stuff*.

Stuff. Historical documents. The marks of people no longer with us, he called it. The trace of ghosts.

If I found Alasdair's apartment oppressively cluttered, this is a whole other dimension. I don't have enough years left in my life to read all *these* documents. Not even just to peer briefly inside every book or box or scroll.

It would take many lifetimes.

The observation is apt, I think, because it all *contains* many, many lifetimes too – the words and deeds and thoughts of so many dead people. When *I'm* gone, my life won't be traced in any archives I can think of. I shiver. It's cold in these small, stone rooms.

I try and comprehend all their deaths: these ancestors of Scotland. They didn't all slip peacefully away in old age. There was lots of disease in the past, wasn't there? Lots more accidents, lots more death in childbirth, lots more war.

I consider the war memorial in the gardens and how those lists of names are just the neat face of all those lives and stories and damage and death. If you could see all the documents about each of the people listed there – and read their thoughts and get to know their families – you couldn't comprehend it. It's probably the only way to contain the debilitating significance of it all – hiding all these traces of life behind closed doors and neatening the awful mountain of death into tidy rows of names.

I want to read something. I take a volume down from the shelves. As I open the pages of the book randomly, the paper releases its antique, inky smell. Scanning the contents, it seems to be a list of crimes or trials. The curling, sloping handwriting lists out various terms I don't recognise – some in Latin – but I also read the word 'murder' written out again and again.

I ease the volume back into its place on the shelf and remind myself that I only have the duration of a nap.

Finding my way into a series of interconnected offices, I cast about, looking for Dr Duncan-Fox's name on one of the brass plates. Eventually, I spot it and slip through the open door. His office is much like his home study and, again, I see his distinctive scarf hung on a peg.

There are tall, bright windows and a twist of graphite scents the air. It's so strange to see everything by the light of the day. I feel confused and panicky, as if, at any moment, someone might walk in.

Well, they might be – *will* be – walking in; it's a working day at the archives, after all. There *will* be people walking all around me in that other dimension – the waking world. It creates a strange, choppy sense of interference – but in my mood or in reality, I can't tell.

Much like in his home, there is a sediment of folders, books and papers veiling the furniture. I identify the main desk by the jacket slung over the back of the uncomfortable-looking chair. Alasdair might be sitting and working there right now – why wouldn't he be?

I edge over to the desk to take a look at the historical documents lying on it – although, by now, I realise I'm out of my depth. I don't know what it is I'm looking at.

I see some archival documents in translucent wallets and oatmeal folders, together with some working notes. There are slips of paper brass paperclipped to the folders, bearing mystical strings of letters and numbers, and some photocopies underneath.

I move to the curator's side of the desk and see that the pile has magically spread itself out. My skin prickles.

This is why I don't do so much of this sleep-sleuthing in the daytime. If waking people move things, they *also* stay moved. And *keep moving.*

It's not that I can ever see something in the process of being moved by someone. It's not like some disembodied floating, carried thing. It's just that things can move around when you aren't looking. It's disconcerting. It feels like I might catch it happening in the corner of my eye – but I never have and don't think I ever could. When waking people are moving things, I just notice them resolved in new positions, different to how they were a moment ago, but always after the fact. It makes my head swim.

I think that Alasdair *is* right there, right now, working away at his desk. The clues are all there – open door, scarf and jacket hung up, documents trading places on his desk. If I touch anything it would really freak him out. That's what Zoya said, isn't it? Maybe *we* are the ghosts.

Peering over where his shoulder might be, I realise that he is busy cobbling together a document from various photocopies – cutting and gluing bits of paper together on a page. Maybe the next step is a few more rounds of photocopying, I don't know, but he's clearly faking up some kind of document. I'm pretty sure this isn't what people mean when they say they are witnessing history being made – but it is the exact thing I came expecting to see.

I look out of the window. His office has a pretty amazing view. And then, without anything at all moving, I see that the chair is in a different place and the stuck-together page is missing from the desk.

It doesn't seem very ethical behaviour for an archivist. Who is this con job for, I wonder?

I look out of the window again and up to Calton Hill. I can see the facade of the unfinished neoclassical building and half expect to see Zoya on top of it. High places seem to be her thing.

But she isn't there and *couldn't* be because I know that she is on the other side of the barrier between us – the one between sleep and waking.

***

Back in Marcus's studio, time has moved on. The strip of skylight is showing a pinkish glow to the sky above. The glimpse of the neighbouring building looming above them, shows that the inhabitants have turned their lights on but the streetlamp on the corner remains dark.

The easels are bearing portraits now.

After listening to Marcus explain the paintings for a while, Dan feels like he is beginning to see them in a new light.

'See what I did with colour there,' Marcus says, pointing to a detail of a painting that Dan didn't know he was seeing. 'Zoya's granddad taught me that.' Marcus looks at Dan to check he is noticing the right bit. 'Or his works did, anyway. See, you cut your teeth as an artist with this stuff, long before you can invent something of your own.'

'Like, finding your voice?'

'Exactly.'

'So, when are you starting her portrait?'

'Sunday,' Marcus says, scrutinising his own work, re-living choices he made in the details, a long time ago.

'I was going to ask if you don't mind me sitting in when you do it?'

Marcus wheels round to look at Dan again. 'Not at all. Not if Zoya doesn't mind.'

'I think it might be a good framing device for the book, you see…'

'Pun intended?'

'Actually, no.' Dan smiles. 'It might work well for the structure of the book for me to have seen you at work and…'

'Yes, yes, of course, I don't mind.'

Marcus begins taking the paintings down and putting them safely back in their storage spaces. He folds the easels and stashes them against a wall and then turns off the standard lamp and moves it back to some corner, out of the way.

The room is not dark, but the shadows change without its light. Evening has been creeping up on them outside.

Dan watches Marcus putting things back where they are kept. There is some kind of organisation to the clutter but only Marcus could ever know it.

'You did my portrait once,' Dan says.

Marcus is filing some prints in a drawer with his back to him.

'Do you remember?' Dan asks.

'Oh. Yes.'

'Do you… still have it?'

'Er, sorry, I don't remember what happened to it. I'll just find that other box of prints I was going to show you.' He starts climbing the ladder up to the mezzanine.

'I'll just use the facilities,' Dan says, walking around the corner.

On the way to the toilet, he passes the curtained cubbyhole, and, as he listens to Marcus creaking about above, can't resist a quick look.

He ducks behind the curtain and reaches straight for the sports bag. His fingers close on the zip.

'I found it!' Marcus is saying, making his way down.

Dan jerks away from the bag and dashes from the store to the toilet, quietly closing the door.

When he emerges, the studio seems a shade darker and Marcus is standing facing the wall. The long rectangle of window running above the front door reveals dark edifices crowding out a strip of sunset sky, the fall of night riotous in the frame.

Dan walks over and stands next to Marcus, joining him in gazing at the light. Minutes pass.

'It's getting late,' Marcus says. 'We should go back.'

CHAPTER 26

The sun is disappearing behind the buildings when Marcus and Dan arrive back at the guest house, closing the night outside. It sounds oddly quiet for dinner time.

Walking into the guest lounge, they see that pretty much everyone is there, and Catriona is pacing around in the middle of the room. She notices everyone looking at the friends as they walk in, and swivels on her heel.

'What's going on?' Dan asks, addressed more to Marcus than anyone else.

'Been having fun?' Catriona asks them. Her voice is oddly icy.

'What's happening?' Marcus walks toward her, Dan tailing behind.

'I don't know.' Catriona crosses her arms.

Dan looks to Karen, then to Rab and Muriel, for a clue but only catches their awkward expressions. He notices that Reed and Zoya are also there, seated in one corner of the room. Even Glenda is involved, sitting poised in another. Marcus looks around for a few seconds.

'What are you all waiting for?'

'We're just discussing something,' Catriona answers, looking straight at Marcus.

Douglas is seated by her elbow, doing the same.

Marcus shrugs, puzzled. 'What?'

'You tell me?'

Dan walks a few paces to Marcus's side and uses his rational mediation voice. 'What's going on, Trinny?'

Karen, who has been sitting restlessly, fidgets her hands on her lap. 'We've found another watch,' she explains helpfully.

Marcus shrugs.

'That will be the same one, surely,' Dan says, looking around the room.

'It isn't,' Douglas states. 'The last one was a ladies' watch whereas this one is a gent's Tissot. But the mechanism has stopped.'

This time, Dan's shoulders twitch – his turn to shrug. *What is the big deal?* He looks at his friend in the corner. 'Do *you* know what this is about?'

Reed shakes his head. He has noticed that the hands of the watch both point exactly to the '2' – but hasn't said anything.

'And nobody has lost this one either,' Douglas continues, crossing one leg over the other.

Dan notices how shiny his shoes always are.

'The point is,' Catriona says, addressing her husband, 'what if it's a thief? We've the Gillespie's reputation to think about…' There is some pain to the expression flashing across her face. Dan wonders what is *really* bothering her.

Marcus answers with bemusement. 'It's nothing to worry about, just some lost property or something. Why are you making a big deal about it?'

Muriel and Rab rise from their seats – just enough to begin inching their way out of the room. 'We'll be off then, seeing as it's our night off,' Muriel says. Rab escorts her away with an arm around her waist.

'Night,' Karen says, 'see you tomorrow.' Her right knee is bouncing a little. She seems keen to make her own exit.

In the corner, Zoya starts speaking to Reed. 'Come on, let's go out for a bite.'

Reed nods and they stand and begin weaving around the furniture. They pause when they draw level with Dan.

'Dan, are you coming?' Zoya asks.

He shakes his head.

'But how would I know if there *was* something to worry about if you don't tell me anything?' Catriona is demanding of Marcus.

Everyone starts to leave.

'Come on Dan, let's…' Karen begins.

'Oh, you don't *all* need to make excuses,' Catriona says, brusquely. 'Come on, Marcus, let's go upstairs.'

Catriona walks purposefully through the guest lounge and toward the stairs. Marcus follows. Their discussion can be heard as they go, although people are trying not to listen in.

'But… there isn't a problem…' Marcus says, chasing her swift footsteps.

'Well, you don't think anything is a problem, do you?' she is saying. 'Or do you? I don't know. Because you don't talk. Or not to *me* anyway.'

She seems to look directly at Dan as she turns the corner and commences the stair climb. Whether she means anything by it or not, he takes it as a warning not to follow them up.

'But it's nothing. I didn't want to worry you...' Marcus's voice says, as they disappear up to the first floor.

'You didn't think the money would be a problem either...'

Dan hears Catriona say this but everyone else now seems too busy milling around. Karen, Douglas and Glenda come into the guest lounge, exchange glances and sit down.

***

Some time later, Dan is sitting in his regular seat by the window, reading the papers, when Glenda passes through the room.

'Are they still at it?' she asks.

Dan shrugs and barely looks up from the article he is reading. Everything has been really quiet upstairs.

Plates and napkins are dotted sporadically around the lounge, the remnants of suppers quietly eaten by those still about. Karen is collecting them.

'Want to go out later, Dan?' she asks. 'Once the Jenkins have gone out to dinner, I'll be at a loose end.'

'Er, don't you have managerial stuff to do?'

'We're winding down for a break so they're the only guests here – apart from you lot.'

'Er... no, it's okay. I don't feel like it.'

Karen looks across to Douglas who is also sitting there. 'Are you waiting for anything in particular?' she asks him.

Before he can answer, there are noises from above: the sound of the parlour door being opened; Marcus and Catriona talking; and something else – luggage being set down at the top of the stairs. The situation reveals itself. Catriona is lugging her own suitcase down the stairs, letting it rest every other step with a thud. It could well weigh more than she does, Dan notes when she comes into view.

'You don't need to go!' Marcus is saying from the landing.

'Oh, look,' – Catriona's voice sounds really calm – 'I was always going to go and stay at the Queensferry flat soon, to get it sorted. I just feel like going there now.'

Douglas rushes from his seat and halfway up the steps to take Catriona's bag off her and carry it down the rest of the stairs.

'Thanks, Douglas.' Then, to Marcus: 'I'll be taking the Astra, as I want the boot space. They replaced the cable.'

'I'll drive you and get a taxi back,' Douglas offers eagerly.

'Thanks. Oh, look, we've got an audience.'

Karen, Dan and Glenda have congregated by the stairs.

'There's no drama,' Catriona tells them. 'I'm just going to the flat, now that it's empty, to plan some renovations.' She doesn't seem angry or upset.

'For how long?' Karen asks.

'Oh, I don't know, as long as it takes,' Catriona replies.

The small crowd observe the scene playing out, not really knowing what to say. Karen holds the doors open for Douglas to carry the suitcase outside. Catriona follows and waits next to it on the stone step as Douglas jogs away to fetch the car. Karen and Glenda watch her, one cynical, one concerned.

But Dan is looking in the opposite direction – toward Marcus, who is standing forlornly at the top of the stairs. Then Marcus walks away.

Dan is just about to follow him when he feels Karen's hand on his shoulder. 'I think he might want some space, you know?'

Dan affects an expression of agreement. 'I'm just going up to my room.'

Taking the staircase slowly and steadily, Dan reaches the first-floor landing, and turns, not left to the parlour, but right to his room.

***

Later, Dan is lying on his single bed. He has been mindlessly watching the plaster ceiling turn sepia overhead. Soft, sloping shadows have settled where the light from the streetlamp fails to reach. There is nothing to see, but Dan stares at it, all the same.

He strokes his forehead and nestles ink-smudged fingers in his tangle of hair.

He has been oblivious to the footsteps of the evening – carpet-muffled inside the guest house, clattering on the pavement as someone passes outside. But then there is music; muted by stone walls but becoming recognisable as it seeps around the crack of his door.

He becomes aware of a familiar cycle of twangy chords and a curving line of melody that carves wobbly questions that he can't make out – but *knows*.

He recognises 'Box of Rain' from the *American Beauty* album by the Grateful Dead – a record they have listened to together countless times. He hasn't heard it for a while, but it's still in there; etched on the grooves of his memory.

At the swell of harmonising voices, Dan rises from his bed and follows the sounds where they lead. He makes his way around the corner.

As he pushes open the parlour door, the music is suddenly loud. He walks into the spinning cycle of tangled guitars, vocal harmonies and percussive clashes.

He immediately smells the punch of whisky. A single lamp is casting a cosy glow across the sofa. One of the cushions has tumbled onto the shadowy floor. He sees Marcus reclining, one foot on the table, by the bottle.

Dan scans the room. The far reaches vanish into velvety darkness but there is nobody else here. His attention swings back to the amber-lit plushness of Marcus's party-for-one. The varnished coffee table shines like a dark pool between them.

Marcus notices Dan in the doorway and his eyes thaw with a warm smile.

'Are you okay?' Dan asks, nudging the door closed behind him.

Marcus immediately greets him, his voice loud and enthusiastic over the sound of the record. 'Dan! Dan, come in! Have a drink!'

Marcus immediately rolls toward the side table to retrieve another whisky glass, yanks the stopper from the bottle and pours an unreasonably large measure with a splash.

The lyrics spin their cryptic narrative about distant dreams.

Marcus bangs the newly filled glass down next to his own, too hard.

'Careful, don't hurt yourself.' Dan feels he has to shout over the music and goes to turn the volume down.

'Come in, come in. My home is your home.' Marcus is indicating that Dan take a seat beside him on the sofa, where the large whisky has been placed.

'Do you know,' Marcus continues, 'I've lived in more homes with you than I have with Trinny.' Then, as a delayed reaction, he points to the record player.

'It was just a bit loud,' Dan says, gently.

'Do you remember this record?' Marcus asks.

'Of course I do.'

Dan, still standing, picks up the record sleeve and looks it over like an old friend.

'Remember the Wembley concert? None of the others came; it was just you and me in the end, remember?'

'Well, we are the best ones,' Dan says cheekily, trying to cheer his friend up.

'I've got all the Dead albums around here somewhere – maybe at the studio – we should have a listen to them… sometime.'

Dan watches Marcus take a large gulp of his whisky. 'Yes, we should.'

Next, Marcus is pouring even more whisky into each of the glasses. Dan's – which hasn't been touched yet – now stands perilously full. He gently takes the bottle from Marcus, as if simply tidying, but places it far away on a cabinet across the room. Marcus flops back on the sofa, nearly spilling his drink.

'Whoa, watch it!' Dan cautions, somewhat pointlessly.

Marcus sticks out his arm toward Dan, insisting he take the drink.

'Er, thanks.' He takes it, carefully. 'That's a very full glass.'

Dan sits, not on the sofa within range of Marcus's flailing gestures, but on an armchair to the side.

'Glass half… one and a half times full!' Marcus says. 'You always were the optimist!'

Marcus closes his eyes and hums along to the record. Dan silently puts his glass down on the table and wonders how to pry Marcus away from his. Then he notices the intensity of the feeling Marcus is giving his hum-along and watches him, only speaking when Marcus reopens his eyes.

'Are you okay?' Dan asks, gently and seriously.

'Okay? The best record, the best whisky, my best friend…'

'What happened with Trinny? She hasn't left, has she?'

'You all saw her with that suitcase…'

'No, I mean…'

'She'll be fine. She's fine without me. And I'm glad.'

Marcus pulls a strange sort of smile, but his eyes look watery. They lean back and listen while the record washes over them for several songs, sharing the music wordlessly.

Dan remembers that concert in '72: hairy; weed and sweat-smelling; Marcus laughing; the chill streets of London; talking long into the night.

The swelling organ and harmonies make Dan aware that the side is coming to an end and he is about to get up, ready to turn it over, when he notices that Marcus seems to be dropping off. He leans over and rescues the whisky glass before it drops, and places it by the bottle – a long way out of reach.

'Come on, I think it's your bedtime,' Dan says.

He attempts to coax Marcus off the sofa by taking hold of his arm, but Marcus doesn't seem like he will be easily moved. The record has reached the end of its spin, so Dan switches the turntable off.

'I'm fine here. I'll just sleep here,' Marcus is saying. 'I want to stay here with you.'

Dan thinks for a moment, then takes one of the crystal glasses to fill with water. By the time he gets back, Marcus is lying on the sofa. Dan squats by his head.

'Marcus, are you asleep? Drink this water, will you?'

Marcus opens one of his eyes. 'If you stay here…'

'Okay. Here.'

Dan guides his friend, who dutifully drinks his glass of water, spilling only a few drops toward the end. Marcus's eyes open like slits above his impish grin.

'This whisky tastes like…' He is trying to make a joke. Marcus's voice changes as he watches Dan get up and make a move to leave the room. 'Where are you going?'

'I'm just getting you a blanket.'

Marcus's arm darts up to grab at Dan's shirt. 'Dan, Dan…' He is whispering now. 'Dan, Dan, Dan…'

'What is it?'

Dan allows himself to be stayed and leans closer to Marcus to hear what he seems urgently about to tell him, although he suspects Marcus is now just repeating his name as a game and can't remember what it was that he wanted to say.

'I *do* remember that day,' Marcus says.

'That day?'

Marcus keeps his eyes closed, perhaps lost in a memory. 'The day I painted your portrait.'

Dan swallows. He remembers to breathe. He can remember it too.

'I remember everything about that day in Palermo,' Marcus says, his hand still gripping Dan's shirt and his dark eyes opening.

Dan watches, his own pupils dilating.

'The rooftop, the painting… you…' Marcus whispers, his eyes closing again.

Dan watches as the pause stretches longer and his friend's grip loosens and falls away. Marcus seems to be asleep.

Dan rises from his haunches and makes his way to their bedroom, where he scoops up pillows and a duvet in an awkward armful higher than his head. As he walks back into the parlour, an eye is watching him through the thin slit of the slightly open door.

Zoya has paused in the darkness. She watches a pile of bedding with Dan's legs make its way to the sofa. She decides not to go in, but to wait and ask him about it all once he's finished taking care of his friend.

She finds herself quietly watching as Dan makes a bed for Marcus on the sofa, covering him with the duvet and carefully manoeuvring a pillow under his head. She wonders how many times this exact thing has happened before. Whatever is going on with Marcus and Catriona, at least he has his old friend around. Dan has always struck her as big-hearted and Reed has told her how caring he is with his sister and nephew. Tonight, it's Marcus's turn to be looked after.

Then she sees Dan lean closer to Marcus and softly kiss him on the cheek. The kiss lasts a few long seconds before Dan sits back on the floor. Zoya pulls the door to, ever so gently, and makes her way up to bed.

CHAPTER 27

The next day, Dan is sitting at a breakfast table, working on his notes, as usual. His face is set in an expression of concentration, his mouth clamped shut.

The table he has chosen today is standing just where the shadow cuts across the room and the morning light tapers away. His breakfast plate has been cleared but he is still working on his second cup of coffee. There are puffy bags under his eyes due to the fact that he had stayed up, finishing the glass of whisky, watching Marcus sleep and listening to the record again and again.

The smell of sausages is fading, and the room is otherwise empty. Dan hunches over his work.

Reed walks in and makes for the coffee pot. 'Morning,' he says.

'Morning,' Dan replies, scribbling a note on the transcription next to something that Marcus said.

'Want a coffee?'

Dan looks at his cup then swiftly drains the remaining amount before holding it at arm's length toward Reed, ready for a refill.

Reed pours.

'Thanks, that makes three.'

'Big night?' Reed asks, leaning against a chair back and sipping at his own cup.

Dan doesn't seem in the mood to chat.

Reed meanders toward the window, lifts the voile and looks outside. 'Have you seen Marcus?'

'Not to speak to,' Dan replies, without looking up.

'No. Have you *seen* him? He's with Zoya outside. Looks like the portrait painting has begun.'

'Oh. Right.'

Dan continues writing, his pen scratching at the paper. Reed watches Marcus and Zoya on the sunny terrace. She is perched on a stool, swinging her leg, while Marcus darts about before a small canvas. Paints are laid out on one of the patio tables.

'He's painting like his life depends on it!' Reed observes.

'Sketching, then.'

Reed lets the net curtain fall and turns away from the window. 'Can I join you?'

'I'm working… Oh, okay.'

Dan moves some of his papers, tidying things up just a bit. Reed sits in the opposite chair. Dan becomes aware of Reed staring at him.

'I wanted to ask your opinion on something,' he says.

'No,' Dan begins wearily, 'I don't think Marcus is going to seduce Zoya over the easel…'

'No, not that,' Reed says, then a worried look shoots across his face. 'Does he do that?'

Dan slurps his coffee, shaking his head. Reed resumes his intense scrutiny.

'Jesus, what happened to you?' he says.

'Just a spot of whisky and Grateful Dead. What is it?' Dan asks.

'I know he's your friend but…' Reed looks out of the window again at the gauzy silhouettes of Marcus and Zoya, who are laughing in the sunshine.

'Yes?' Dan prompts.

'How well do you know him? I mean, after all these years?'

Dan sits back in his chair and considers the question. He decides to adopt his tried-and-tested tactic of letting the other person say too much.

'I just think,' – Reed looks around to check they are still alone – 'something really dodgy is going on and–'

'Because someone's lost a couple of watches?' Dan asks, sceptically.

'No. Not that but… something.' Reed looks down at the table for a while. 'Do' – he begins the next sentence slowly – 'you think… that he might be trying to swindle her out of this property or… something worse?'

Reed's green eyes flash toward Dan's during the sentence but end up staring down at the tabletop again.

'Worse?' Dan asks, after a pause.

'This whole ghost thing… That curator is going to come out with a load of bollocks that tells a ghost story. Don't ask me how I know but–'

'But you do. But what has that got to do with anything?'

'I don't know,' Reed says, 'but there'll be a fake bit of historical research and…'

Dan is remembering the holdall he saw hidden away at the back of a shelf. He wants to ask Reed if he has seen Marcus with it, or if he knows what's inside.

Reed is still speaking. 'Well, that car accident…?'

Dan leans forward on the table to speak quietly. 'What else do you know?'

Reed ponders the question. He actually does know some more – the ladies' watch stuck at the '3' in the study, the business card with no name – but nothing that makes any sense. He can't quite figure out a way to explain that he has rooted about in Marcus's locked desk or begin to touch on *how*.

'I just think,' Reed says, 'you should think about leaving.'

Dan's gaze falls to the table and he gathers his notes into a pile. He sighs. 'Look, I've actually got a paying job to do.' He gestures with the papers.

'Well, that's another thing,' Reed says. 'Isn't this whole memoir and retrospective all a bit… desperate?' Reed rests a forearm on the table and leans closer to Dan. 'And don't you think Catriona and Douglas are a bit too… close?'

'You're just jealous. He's a handsome fella.'

'I'm not. Is he? I suppose you would know,' Reed says, swapping his anxiety for an attempt to engage Dan in a provocative joke.

'I would,' Dan says coolly, puncturing it.

'Reed, look, thanks for your concern but, if you don't mind,' – he indicates his papers again – 'I have to get on.'

'Okay.' Reed stands up and leans on the chair frame.

'But just consider it... *Something*'s going on. There must be some reason for the fake ghost story.'

Dan cocks his head. 'Which you know about because...'

Reed just looks at him, not answering. He lets go of the chair and walks away. Then he pauses and comes back to Dan's table.

'Something else?'

'Just one thing. What were the "interesting readings" anyway?' Reed's focus flickers from Dan to Zoya outside and back to Dan at the shaded table again.

'You want to know?' Dan sets his pile of notes neatly to one side and puts down his pen. 'I'll tell you,' he says, simply. 'Remember the magnetometer?'

'Yes. It measures magnetic fields.'

'Remember, I told you it is an especially sensitive one? Can detect very low frequencies?'

'Ye-es?'

'Well, we got some.'

Reed is still wearing a puzzled expression.

'Oh, well, magnetic fields of a frequency between, say one and thirty hertz, especially if the pattern varies randomly, can produce hallucinogenic effects on people's brains. We also got some infrasound – which can be connected, come from the same source – you know, very low frequencies of sound. You can't hear them. Has the same effect.'

Reed's brows remain low, making him look suspicious. He's not sure if Dan is pulling his leg. 'And the low frequencies and whatnot are coming from a ghost?'

Dan snickers briefly.

'No, no, no, the environment effects people's brain function, causes hallucinations. Well, in some people. Makes them think they've seen and heard things that aren't actually there in the room. And when the thing they hallucinate is a person, well, they – we, society – tend to call that a ghost.'

'So, where's it coming from, all this magnetism?'

Dan smiles. 'Easy. The iron bedframe. The scientific method won't allow me to conclude that with certainty – but, between you and me, it is.' He sips his coffee, triumphantly.

'That's why,' Dan continues, 'they've only had "ghost" sightings in that one room – it's localised, the low frequencies are created by vibrations in the springs and frame when people move about on the bed and they can't sustain over distance, so the only people who get the hallucinations are the ones sleeping in the bed.'

He raises his cup again, then draws it away from his lips, not having finished the explanation.

'And not everyone, and not all the time.'

He looks expectantly for Reed's reaction.

'That *is* interesting,' he says, thoughtfully, with an undertone of surprise.

'Told you,' Dan says in a sing-song voice.

'So, how come *we* didn't have the hallucinations from lying there awake?' Reed asks.

'Maybe the whisky, maybe the talking... And not everyone's brain is susceptible in the same way. I was going to write up a proper report first, but I'll just tell them now, I think. Give them chance to get a new, modern bed-frame ordered. I don't envy whoever it is has to lug it up all those stairs…'

Reed puts a hand on Dan's table and leans over it. 'How about we wait?' he says quietly. '*Don't* tell them – until the fake history comes in – and see what happens?'

Dan sighs but his features relax. 'Okay, Columbo.'

Reed looks wryly amused at the reference and straight-ens up.

'Reed,' Dan begins, having decided to mention the bag.

Just then Marcus appears at the terrace door.

'Doesn't matter.'

Marcus's face barely looks tired, but his waves are wilder than ever.

'Are we still interviewing today?' he asks Dan.

'Yes. Sure. Why wouldn't we?'

'Great. No, that's great. I'm just finishing up with Zoya's sketches.' Marcus gestures with a paintbrush. 'She's going out with Douglas for the day soon – he's showing her the sights.'

'Yep. Whenever you want me.'

'Okay, won't be long.' Marcus goes back out to the garden.

When Dan looks back to Reed, he sees a whole new mood written on his pale face.

'And you're not jealous, you say…?'

***

It's becoming Dan's routine to follow breakfast with a visit to the guest lounge. Today he has eschewed the morning papers and is scribbling on his pad, sipping from another coffee.

'Hey, Dan. Working hard?' Karen asks.

'I've been turfed out by Muriel.' He nods toward the breakfast room.

'Aren't you interviewing Marcus today?'

'Yes, but I needed a fifth cup of coffee first!' Dan jokes, but not about the number of coffees.

'Hard going, is it?' Karen smiles. 'I mean, this is basically what happened all through university – with the two of you following each other around.'

Dan rolls his eyes from his pad to look at her, his face wearing a lopsided smile. 'He was painting – in the garden – and now he's gone to get changed.'

'I bet you wish you'd recorded all those conversations back then?'

Dan laughs gently. 'Yeah.' He lets his pad fall on his lap. 'Actually, it would be good to listen back to them, if we had. Is it today you are going away?'

'Yep. Everyone's leaving except you lot.'

She begins moving things around on the reception desk. Muriel walks in.

'Sorry about that, Dan. I just want to get it all sorted so we can leave on time.' There is a glint in her eye – the long-anticipated holiday.

'You're off too? Oh, yes, Turkey!'

'That's right!' Muriel replies, then turns to Karen. 'So, it's just the two guest rooms to do and that's everything.'

'Thanks, Muriel. This sounds like the Jenkins now.'

Dan hears them coming down the stairs. Karen nips out from behind the desk and into the hallway.

'I said I would fetch your bags for you.'

It's too late – Arthur has deposited them on the tiles at the foot of the stairs. 'No,' he says, 'I wouldn't hear of it.'

Cherry taps him lightly on the arm. 'That's my Art…'

The three of them walk into the lounge and Karen slips back behind the reception desk.

'I've ordered your taxi to the train station – it should be here in five to ten minutes.'

Arthur goes over to settle the bill while Cherry takes a seat next to Dan. As she does so, there is the sound of more footsteps coming down the stairs.

'Well,' she says, 'we're off to London! We've got five days there and then, let's see, where's next on the itinerary…'

Glenda and Zoya round the corner into the lounge. Zoya has been carrying Glenda's luggage and sets it down neatly by the reception desk.

'Then Bath, I think, and we've a trip to Stonehenge…'

'Stonehenge? My favourite place on earth,' Glenda says.

'I thought *you* might be a Stonehenge fan,' Dan mumbles.

'Such a magical place,' Glenda says with a faraway look in her eye. 'Did you know it is a harmony of male and female? Yes, the ley line channels the power of Mother Earth – but it is aligned for the summer solstice, which is the male solstice…'

Behind the desk, Karen also seems to be looking into the middle distance, pondering something quite different. 'How come we never hear about any of the other types of henges?' she says.

'Like chocolate henge?' Zoya asks.

Reed has also ambled down the stairs unnoticed, and overhears them. 'Or cheese henge?' he adds.

Zoya laughs.

'Hey, Dan,' Karen calls across the room, trying to bring him in on the joke, 'what's *your* favourite henge?'

'I'm not really your Stonehenge type of guy.'

'Aren't you going out with Douglas today?' Reed asks Zoya.

'I am.' She perches on the arm of the sofa.

'I forgot my book,' Reed says, and wanders off to get it.

'And that's why Stonehenge is such a powerful place for healing and fertility,' Glenda adds.

'Actually,' Dan says, with some authority, 'Stonehenge was a harmony of work and play for the Neolithic peoples who made it. They dragged some of those stones – the bluestones – 150 miles to that site. Probably rolling them over logs. 150 miles! From Wales, in fact, those ones. And expertly tool-worked too. This is thousands of years *before* your druids came along with their spirituality and god-worshipping. So don't go crediting the Druids with Stonehenge. Please! I've read that it was a place for partying, actually – people from all over the British Isles travelling hundreds of miles to get together there, feasting and socialising and having a good time. And it wasn't about your Druidic otherworlds – it was about celebrating life in the here and now.'

'And you're *not* a Stonehenge type of guy, you say?' Reed says, passing through the lounge having retrieved his book.

Dan almost looks embarrassed.

'Sounds like you *might* be *somewhat* of a Stonehenge type of guy…' Reed adds, with a friendly, teasing smile.

There is the sound of a car pulling up outside.

'Is that the cab?' Arthur says.

Karen looks toward the street and recognises the car. 'It's just Douglas.'

Zoya hops to her feet. 'He's here to pick me up,' she says, remembering her plans. 'Glenda, I hope you have a nice trip to Stockholm, and you too, Mr and Mrs Jenkins. I hope you enjoy the rest of your holiday… and you too, Karen…'

Douglas beeps the car horn.

'Oh, *everyone,* have fun!'

Zoya concludes her well-wishing and goes out to the car. Most of the group watch her go then turn back to one another as the front door closes, except for Reed, who watches unhappily as she gets into the car and as Douglas drives off.

'So,' – Cherry looks at Dan – 'have you ever been to Stonehenge?'

'Me? No… It's not really my… I wouldn't mind seeing it but… I've never really had the time to…'

'Oh, you should go!' Cherry taps him sharply on the arm. 'Go wherever your heart takes you!' She seems particularly full of the joys of spring today.

'My wife, the free spirit,' adds Arthur, 'and I wouldn't have it any other way.'

Karen spies a car driving up the close. 'This is your taxi, Mr and Mrs Jenkins. Yours,' – she looks at Glenda – 'is on its way too.'

The Jenkins give a round of hugs and handshakes as the taxi driver comes in and collects their bags. Dan can hear Cherry instantly making friends with him as they get in and on their way.

'I totally agree,' Glenda says to Dan, still considering what he has said about Stonehenge. 'Who doesn't love a party?'

Karen pauses what she is doing for a minute and nods her head. It looks as though with these words she has found a whole new respect for the woman. She spies another vehicle making its way toward the house. 'Oh, that's your taxi too.'

Dan stands and moves toward her luggage by the desk. 'Let me…'

'Oh no, I can manage.'

She gives Dan a soft, slight, considered hug. 'Dan, it was so nice to see you again, so it was. Remember, there's more to life than work!' She picks up her own bags and leaves.

'And *that's*' – Karen sits on the reception desk – 'the end of my shift. The next taxi that comes is for me!'

'So, where are *you* off to?'

'France.'

Then she hops off the desk again and springs lightly up the stairs.

She must have passed Marcus on his way down because he pops his head around the corner. 'Oh, there you are!' he says, spotting Dan. 'Shall we begin?'

'I was waiting for *you*,' Dan says.

'Oh! I was waiting for *you*.'

***

Zoya is standing between a coat stand draped with feather boas and a gorilla suit, in the middle of a vintage clothing and costume-hire shop in the centre of town.

Douglas reappears wearing a red gilet. 'How about this one?'

'Yeah, good,' Zoya says, nodding. 'I think the ski one was better, though.'

She smiles, holding up the other choice: a blue, chevron-seamed eighties gilet, coloured yellow and orange at the shoulders.

'Really?' he says. 'But this one's a better colour, though. Not exactly orange but... I suppose it's a bit... big.'

'Mmm, orange puffer vests have probably been like gold dust since 1985.'

Douglas wrinkles his nose.

'Well, they both work… if you've got the double denim. So, up to you.'

Douglas is turning this way and that, looking at his reflection in an old mirror that is thronged with vintage ties. Zoya shifts her weight and glances up at the sky-high tower of second-hand clothes rails.

'But does it say *I'm in fancy dress*?' Douglas worries.

'What do you mean?' she asks.

'Just, I always think' – Douglas turns around, checking out his rear view – 'with fancy dress, you want people to *ken* that you're in fancy dress. And not that you just like the clothes. You know, like I might just look like I'm out of fashion.'

Zoya is just looking at him speak.

'Like,' he continues, 'I want people to know that I'm intentionally dressed like Marty McFly, rather than, you know, this is how I dress…'

'You mean,' Zoya begins, trying to tease out some meaning from his rambling, 'you are going to the fancy dress party in costume as someone who is wearing fancy dress?'

They both laugh but Douglas soon stops, puzzled. 'Are you… laughing at me?'

'Not at all. I just never knew it could be so complicated!'

'Oh, okay. Sorry I'm taking so long.'

Zoya dismisses it with a small shake of her head.

'Thanks for chumming me,' Douglas continues. 'This probably wasn't what you expected from our day of tourist fun.'

'It's fine. We have done a fair bit of sightseeing!' she says tactfully. 'Anyway, I like going to real, local places.' She looks at the riot of random garments hung as high as the rafters. 'Happy to help.'

'So, which one – say really – which one's best?'

'Well,' – Zoya purses her lips – 'do you want to look *right* or look *good*?'

Douglas considers the question, rolling his tongue around in his mouth. 'Tough choice... Oh, I'll get the ski one.'

He marches off purposefully to a changing cubicle behind a colourful curtain. Zoya resumes her wandering around the racks and rails, spending some time by the knick-knacks and novelty items by the shop window. A man walks in, so she makes space for him to pass. She picks up a glittery platform shoe.

'Hey, Callum!' the man is saying, sounding like he has recognised a friend.

She moves on to some Aladdin slippers. She sees Douglas standing talking to someone at the rear of the shop.

'I thought it was you!' the man says. 'How's things, man? I've not seen you since...'

Zoya sees Douglas and the man talking by the suits. The man picks up the sleeve of a tweed jacket to inspect it, chatting away, but Douglas doesn't look that comfortable, maybe aware that he is keeping someone waiting.

The other man leaves and Zoya joins Douglas by the sales desk. He puts his outfit on the counter, ready to pay. The sales assistant rings it up on the till, folding the garment into a carrier bag.

'Just bumped into an old pal,' Douglas tells Zoya.

'Is he going to the party too?'

Douglas hands over his money and collects the receipt. 'Oh, no, it's a different group of friends.'

They make their way out of the shop.

'Are you sure you don't want to come to the party?'

'Oh, no, thanks, but I'm going to the Cameo with Reed.'

Douglas holds the door for her. 'Did I hear him say something about your dad?'

'Erm, not really.'

A noisy truck drives passed.

'Just in passing, maybe,' Douglas continues. 'My dad's dead.'

Zoya is sitting in the middle of the studio, Marcus working away at the canvas beside her. The illumination from the skylight is perfect for painting and fills the white-walled space with a soft, bright light.

Dan is there too, sitting on the shabby sofa, observing Marcus at work.

'So, what's the craziest thing he did?' Zoya asks.

'Ooh, tough question.' Marcus looks around. 'What do you think, Dan?'

'Maybe… He crashed a performance of *The Importance of Being Earnest* once.'

'You think?' Marcus narrows his eyes, considering it. 'No. That sort of thing was just fun and games for Fintan.'

'Yeah. Like he said at the time… they should have given him that part to begin with…'

'Come on, he did some properly "out there" things. With consequences.'

'Really?' Zoya asks, trying to remain in position on the chair.

'Like… the therapist appointment?' Marcus suggests this story tentatively with a slight wince crumpling his face.

'Oh yes,' Dan replies, 'that was quite serious in the end.'

Marcus faces Zoya and begins to explain. 'Yes, so, the reason we know Glenda is that she was Fintan's godmother and was also working at the university when we were there,' he says.

'As a therapist for student services,' Dan adds.

Marcus puts his paintbrush in the jar of white spirit, listening as Dan recounts the story.

'And one day, he went to see her, to meet for lunch or whatever, and he found his way into the counselling rooms...' Dan continues.

Zoya shifts in her chair, about to get up, but Marcus gestures softly for her to stay put. He sets about mixing a new colour.

'... and started conducting a counselling session with an actual student...' Marcus says, looking up from his palette.

'...who had made an appointment,' Dan says.

'I don't know how far it got...'

'... or why they didn't question why they got this guy instead of the woman they were expecting...'

'Or why the counsellor looked young enough to be a student!'

'No!' Dan says in agreement, laughing. 'But it was taken *really* seriously by the university.'

'I think because she had left the client's notes out.'

Dan looks at Zoya, summarising the story with a big-eyed expression. 'Yeah, there was quite a big drama about it,' he concludes.

'Bigger than the play crashing thing,' Marcus points out.

'And *that* one was actually on stage!' Dan jokes.

'So, what happened?'

Marcus's expression becomes more sombre. 'Well, she was going to lose her job.'

The paint mixing seems to have stopped. Marcus stands, legs planted wide, arms folded, still casually clutching a brush.

'Oh yes. Do you remember that day?' Dan says, leaning on his thighs and looking up at Marcus.

'Yeah. She basically camped out at our house all day, waiting to hear what they would decide. We were all just sitting around, or maybe *you* weren't but we arts and humanities types were.'

'No. I was there too,' Dan says. 'I think I missed a couple of lectures…'

'*Must* have been serious!' Marcus is teasing and Dan acknowledges the in-joke with a wry half smile.

'Shall we have a break? Are you tired, Zoya?' Marcus puts his brush back in a pot and offers her an arm to get down from the high chair. 'Let's stop for a while,' he says.

Dan wriggles his way up off the sagging sofa. 'I'll make us coffee.' He goes over to the kitchen corner and sets to work.

On her feet again, Zoya commences a few stretches and rolls of her neck. She catches sight of Dan's notebook lying neglected on the sofa cushion.

'Sorry, Dan – *you* were meant to be asking the questions!'

'No, it's all fine. We were focussing on uni days today, anyway,' he says, reaching for some mugs in the low cupboard. 'Actually, I've got lots of notes.'

Marcus, meanwhile, has turned the easel more to the wall, away from Zoya's prying eyes. 'Is it okay if you don't look at the portrait yet?' he asks. 'It's in its early days and I'd just rather prefer–'

'Yes, no problem.' Zoya smiles broadly. '*Dan's* seen it though,' she adds cheekily.

'Oh, that's okay. What was Reed up to today?' Marcus replies.

'Oh, Reed? I'm not sure.' Zoya's curious wandering has taken her to some racks near the kitchen.

'But you're not avoiding each other?' Dan asks.

'No. I went to the cinema with him last night, actually.'

'Oh?'

Dan's 'oh' comes with all the gossipy questioning tone possible.

'Yep,' she answers matter-of-factly. 'He wanted to take me to see *North by Northwest*. I think it's one of his favourites,' she elaborates, just as nonchalantly, peeking at a pile of drawings on a shelf.

'And?' Marcus asks.

'And… it's a lot of bother over a mistaken identity.'

Dan's laughter crashes around the walls of the studio. 'He didn't mean it like that,' he says, composing himself.

'What's up there?' Zoya asks, her hands on the bannister of the ladder.

'Up where?' Marcus asks, crossing the room to look up through the skylight at the neighbouring building.

'No, this ladder thing.'

Dan is stirring some milk into the coffees and placing the mugs on a small tray.

'Oh. The ladder thing goes up to my mezzanine thing where I keep my printed–'

'… things,' Dan says, finishing the sentence and carrying the tray between them to the coffee table.

Marcus smiles then looks back to Zoya. 'And other bits and bobs. Oh, that reminds me!' He dashes over to another corner of the studio and scrabbles around. He comes back holding a photograph which he shows to Dan.

'Do you remember this? Karen gave me a print of it. After the funeral. I think it came from Fintan's collection. She got prints for us all.'

Dan peers at the black-and-white photograph and Zoya leans in to see what they are looking at.

'Look how young we were,' Dan remarks, studying it.

'Was it a stage play?' Zoya asks.

'No, just a party,' Marcus says.

'Oh yeah, you're matching, aren't you? From *The Wizard of Oz*.'

'Definitely Fintan's idea,' Dan says.

Marcus points everyone out to Zoya. 'There's me… Dan's the Tin Man… that's Fintan dressed as the Scarecrow… Trinny.'

'How did you decide who would be who?'

'I don't know,' Marcus says, simply, 'I suppose we just fell into our roles… though, of course, Dan wanted to be Dorothy.'

The three of them laugh but Dan removes himself from the huddle to go and sit down again, shaking his head as he goes.

'It's funny,' – Marcus holds Zoya's gaze – 'because it couldn't be *further* from the truth!'

It sounded like he was going to say: 'It's funny because it's true.'

'You should put it in your book. Can I go up?' She gestures to the ladder with her head then commences the climb carefully. 'Was it a good party?' she asks, watching her feet find the slats.

'Yes,' Marcus says, sitting beside Dan on the sofa. 'Just be careful, it's a bit rickety.'

'Was it a good party?' Dan says, echoing the question, pensively. 'Erm…'

Dan and Marcus look at one another.

'If you can't remember, then it probably was!' Zoya jokes.

A smile spreads across Marcus's face as he remembers his friend fondly.

Then she almost loses her footing on the ladder.

'Careful!' Marcus calls. 'Are you okay?'

Zoya nods and continues her climb. The men watch her move.

'Do you remember…' Dan begins, unearthing another story from his memory.

'Palermo.'

They both say it at the same time. Zoya has clambered onto the upper floor and is watching them, her chin resting on a bent knee.

'What happened?'

'Fintan disappeared,' Marcus says, then, explaining: 'We somehow took a holiday.'

'The three of us. Stayed in a lovely apartment.'

'With amazing views from the rooftop, do you remember?'

'Must have been a good view if the vertigo didn't get to us,' Dan says.

'Oh, *Vertigo*?' Zoya says. 'I think Reed wants to take me to see that one too.'

'Ah, yes, great film,' Marcus replies.

'*That* film, Zoya,' Dan calls up to her, 'it's just a lot of bother about a looky-likey!'

Zoya laughs.

'So, did he go missing?'

'Yes,' Dan says, 'we were up on the roof. *You* were painting…'

'Well, that's why we were there.'

'And *I* was drinking…'

'We were *both* drinking.'

'And listening to the Grateful Dead over and over again.'

'And Fintan came up to the roof to say he was nipping to the market or somewhere.'

'And he was gone all day and didn't come home.'

Marcus breaks off from the back and forth with Dan to look up at Zoya.

'I don't think we were worried until the next morning,' he says.

'And then, at breakfast, he came home to the apartment.'

'And he *still* wouldn't say where he'd been!' Marcus is illustrating the story for her with big, artistic gestures.

Dan remembers another detail and grabs at Marcus's arm. 'But he had completely different clothes on – and a load of dinar!'

'And a black eye!' Marcus adds.

Zoya dangles her legs over the edge and leans back on her arms, watching the friends lose themselves in the telling of the story below.

'And we didn't even ask, did we?' Marcus says.

'And *he – ne-ver* told us!'

'That's right' – Marcus nods repeatedly – 'we just sat around cooking eggs and not saying anything.'

Dan touches Marcus's chest with the back of his hand. 'Just exactly like we'd done the morning before.'

'As if *no-thing* had happened,' Marcus concludes, drawing a slow, wide line with his hands to illustrate the word 'nothing'.

A loud crash makes Zoya clutch the handrail. Her heart thumps as she steadies herself against a fall. She is safe, it turns out, but she sees, almost in slow motion, Dan diving over Marcus as if shielding him from falling glass.

The sound ebbs away and the dust settles. She sees that shards of skylight *have* scattered over them from the roof. A substantial piece of masonry has also fallen heavily, denting the wooden floorboard by the sofa. She slides down the ladder to join the men, who are dusting themselves down and establishing that they are okay. They seem to have avoided any glass cuts.

The three of them look up to the smashed skylight, feeling cool from the shock, and from the chill air tumbling in.

CHAPTER 29

They unlock the front door and pile inside. The guest house is dark.

'You have to take your keys with you, remember. Now we are closed, the door will be locked,' Marcus says in the hall, flicking the light switch on.

The lounge is empty, filled with an unexpected sense of foreboding.

'Everything already feels different,' Dan says.

More lights are turned on and the place slowly comes back to life.

'It's so quiet now everyone's left,' Zoya observes, hugging herself.

'Are you sure you're okay, Dan? The glass didn't get you?' Marcus asks.

'No, I'm fine… What's that?'

'What?' Marcus asks, his voice full of dread.

'It's a note,' Zoya says, picking it up from the reception desk, 'from Reed.'

Zoya switches the desk lamp on to read it.

'I thought it might have been…' Marcus mutters quietly.

'Oh, shit!' Dan says. 'We didn't call him!'

'That's what *he* says,' Zoya adds.

Then she reads the note aloud: '*You said you'd be back by 6. I waited. You didn't call. Have gone out now. Got a key.*'

'It was the window smashing – distracted us,' Dan says.

'Sorry, but we needed to board it up or the rain would get in,' Marcus says.

'No, of course,' Dan agrees.

'Do you think he'll be alright?' Zoya asks.

'Yeah,' Dan replies. 'He'll just be watching some Hitchcock film or something.'

'I meant alright being on his own.'

***

Later, in the parlour, Zoya is standing by the window, looking outside. 'Yes, it's just Marcus leaving,' she confirms. She turns away from the window and looks over at Dan. 'Did he say where he was going?' she asks.

'No, I didn't catch him, anyway.'

'Maybe *he'll* leave a note. Did he say what time he's coming back?'

'Marcus?' Dan says.

'No, *Reed.*'

'It just said he'd gone out, didn't it?'

Zoya lets the thick drape close with a heavy swish and resumes her seat on the long sofa next to Dan.

'So, you're becoming quite the film buff,' he says. 'What did you make of *The Innocents*?'

Zoya yawns and pulls the blanket over her legs which she has curled up beneath her.

'That bad, eh?' Dan says.

'No, I'm just,' – she yawns again, pointing at herself as she does – 'yawning.'

'Put yourself to bed,' Dan suggests. 'I think I'm going to stay up and watch the second one.'

'Me too.'

Dan freezes like he's heard something. 'What was that?'

'I think it was on the telly.'

Dan relaxes again. 'So, what happened with you two after the cinema?'

'Nothing,' Zoya replies. 'We went to bed.'

Dan arches an eyebrow.

'Separately.'

Dan doesn't press her. He looks around the room.

'It's spooky now nobody's home, isn't it?'

'I think that might be the horror film talking,' Zoya says, extending the blanket for Dan to slip his legs under, as if the lambswool could protect them.

The back of her neck prickles. Anything could creep out from the shadowy corners far behind them.

'What's next, *The Haunting*?' Zoya asks, focussing on the entertainment.

'I'm just going to check the front door is locked,' Dan says, standing and going over to the door.

Zoya pulls her knees and blanket up under her chin. 'Turn on all the lights!' she calls.

'Don't worry. I'm a big boy… And I'm going to.' Dan heads out onto the landing and down the stairs.

'Hurry back!' Zoya calls after him.

Dan walks swiftly down to the front door and ensures that it is, indeed, locked. Then he darts straight back up the stairs. They both feel better when he is back in the parlour and the landing door is closed. The television is running adverts in the background.

'He *has* got a key, hasn't he?' she says.

'Marcus?'

'No, Reed.'

'I wonder,' Dan begins, 'if he's gone to visit his van?'

'Maybe,' Zoya says, 'I think he *was* missing it. Do you think he's coming back?'

'Reed?'

'No, Marcus.'

'I don't know. He might have gone to stay with Trinny. Or, maybe back to the studio. Do you think I should ring around?'

'No. He's a big boy too.'

'Yes, but…' Dan's words trail off. Zoya has been watching him closely. Dan just points his eyes at the TV.

'You love him, don't you?' Zoya asks.

Dan turns and looks at her, silently holding her kind gaze.

The film's opening music blares from the television.

'It's starting,' Dan says, watching the screen intently.

CHAPTER 30

I found my way into the studio. It's not so far from the garages, once you know the shortcuts. Sleep could have come quicker but, at last, here I am.

I'm in the middle of a funny-shaped room. There are odd shapes and corners and a looming, pale drape, motionless in the grey light. It looks like a ghost costume made out of a sheet. On closer inspection, the peaked cloth drapes a skeletal frame. It can only be a painting on an easel – a particular portrait, I expect.

I switch a lamp on. I don't want to start tripping over stuff.

I approach the easel and take hold of the sheet. I can smell the paint. I decide to lift it and have a look. Even though the portrait has been barely begun, it is unmistakeably Zoya. Turns out Marcus is as talented as they say.

I start looking around the studio with a systematic sweep.

I see the accoutrements of the artist: encrusted palettes, chalky scraps, water-bubbled paper, tubes of paint congealed with crusts, jars of brushes – stiff-bristled and soft, and the stab of palette knives glinting in the dark.

The studio is pretty much as I'd imagined it and I'm not going to root about in all his stuff. I quite like being in here, though. I can see why Marcus would be happy spending days cosied up here, shutting the world out.

The familiar night-dreaming makes me feel comfortable too. Not like at the curator's office. That really freaked
me out. Once again, alone and safe, untroubled by the
awake. Just me and 'Zoya'. I slip back toward the painting,
remembering what Marcus said about portraits depicting
the relationship of artist and sitter. There's nothing unsettling about it. No sense of seduction. It isn't finished yet,
though. Early days. I fold the drape back over the canvas.

Right. I'm going to touch as little as possible but I'm
here to check whether anything seems odd or unusual.
Fuck knows what that would be, but I don't trust Marcus
and I had to come and see.

One thing I notice is that a skylight has been boarded up
and there is a bucket of swept glass by a dustpan and brush.
I also see a dent in the floorboards but nothing horrible like
the stain of blood.

I start climbing the intriguing ladder, which leads to a
small mezzanine furnished with a mattress. I crawl onto
the mattress – it would be a cool place to sleep after a hard
day's painting, or anytime. Is it the scene of passionate
affairs, I wonder. Whatever, it is a good vantage spot for
contemplating the room below.

Clearly, there's a lot of stuff here: drawers and racks and
shelves and boxes. It's like the inversion of the archives,
I think – that place, neat and organised; this one, cluttered
and messy – and I'd still need more than one sleep to look
through it all. I lie on my back for a moment. I bet Marcus
knows where every little thing is; things he's made and put
his heart into, stories and experiences he's expressed.

The night rolls on silently beyond the strip of window. The studio feels peaceful and hidden away. I can see why Marcus might prefer it here – especially because his actual house is a hotel. We all need our private spaces – to share or not share as we choose.

Calm spreads through me. I might have been acting like a dick. I consider that all my suspicions might well be down to jealousy. My ideas about Marcus trying to swindle his wife out of her property were fucking stupid. He's not the type to concoct some fake historical ghost story or whatever *that's* all about. I was being childish and stupid. I can see it written all over Dan's face.

Isn't there that thing – Occam's razor? Simple explanations are the best. The reason Marcus wanted to paint Zoya's portrait is that he's an artist. Simple as that. And Dan is writing the book because he's a writer. There's nothing more to any of it than that.

It actually makes me feel better, realising how idiotic I've been. I can feel layers and layers of paranoia falling away from me. I feel… sort of… clean.

I get up off the mattress and swing my legs over the edge. I take my time climbing down the wobbly ladder. I *bet* Zoya has been up and down here.

My feet touch the ground and I go around the corner and find a small kitchen area, a toilet door and a curtained storeroom with shelves. My attention falls on a sports bag behind the curtain – maybe because sport has bad connotations for me. Always has, but now especially – after what happened last year in Shilly-on-Sea.

I decide to look inside, intrigued as to what sport Marcus could be into. He's all slim and dynamic and everything, but organised sports *really* don't seem like they would be his thing. But. I am keeping an open mind.

Inside the bag is a shitload of money. It takes me by surprise. I plunge my hand between the bundles of notes, wanting to know how deep the money goes. I find a folded piece of paper containing an intriguing set of instructions. I have to copy them down for myself.

I pull out my notebook but realise I must have dropped my pen. I duck back into the main room and search around. You would think an artist's studio would be full of pencils, but I have to settle for a stubby piece of charcoal instead. I quickly scribble the instructions as I remember them but then go back into the recess to check my copy against the note.

In my haste I look on the wrong shelf and realise my error when the bag's not there. But then, the bag isn't *anywhere* on *any* of the shelves. A shiver races up my spine. Somebody has taken it. The bag, the money and the instructions are now gone. Somebody has *just* taken it – probably passing right through me like a ghost.

First things first, I have to get out of this dream dimension. I leave by the front door and wedge my notebook behind the drainpipe. I clamber partway up the wall, then fall to wake myself up.

***

Reed wakes up in his camper van, parked a few streets away. He jumps out onto the cobbles and starts running along the street to the studio, racing to see if the bag mover is anywhere about. He comes to a stop, realising that he hasn't been quick enough, as the mystery person is no longer around. His heart thuds and he looks up and down the street, panting. Not a soul about.

Then he retrieves the notebook and re-reads the note. 'The dustbin on Mitchison Square.' He's pretty sure he got that bit right.

CHAPTER 31

There is, indeed, a dustbin by the statue in Mitchison Square. Reed has been watching it for hours.

He's trying not to *look* like he's staring and hopes to fit in with the tourists who are bustling around the busy square. He would be a tourist himself, but he has barely left the hotel, except for that one day of sightseeing. He decides that the couple of nights at the cinema and the couple of dreams spent poking around don't count.

He sits on a bench, trying to look casual. He rests an arm along the back of the seat, reminding himself to relax. The dark sunglasses help him to keep his watch without being too obvious about it, he thinks.

He stretches his neck by looking up at the moss-channelled stone building towering above him, the high ledges populated by restless pigeons and menacing gulls.

Above the high buildings that surround the small square like dark cliffs rolls a strip of tumbling, changeable weather. Thin beams of sunlight make occasional forays to the paving slabs below.

So, how long to wait?

The day is at its busiest now, bubbling with coach parties and school trips and subcultures hanging out in the square. People sweep past his bench like foaming tides, the hubbub of their chatter, buoyed like flotsam on the swell, echoed by the rumble of suitcase wheels on cobbles as they go.

A group of Spanish teenagers in quilted jackets and backpacks have congregated nearby. He hopes that they won't obscure his view but thinks they probably won't be there for long. The turnover of people seems to be quite fast in the centre of Edinburgh when you're not far from the Royal Mile.

Couples and friends and families seem to come and go, but Reed is only interested in anyone who goes near that one bin.

Some way to spend a morning.

His gaze wanders once more to the architecture above street level. This city really is something else. A flock of pigeons scares and scatters before floating back down to the ground. A busker is starting up. Nothing else appears to have changed.

Reed begins to wonder if the woman sitting beside him is wondering about *him*. She seems to have been there a while. So has he. He shifts position, leaning forward, resting on his knees. The woman rises and greets a friend with a hug.

The thought did occur to him that anyone who recognises him waiting here would probably change their plans, but he's convinced that the drop-off would have happened long ago – right after the bag disappeared – and he is watching for someone else.

It is reasonable to assume, he thinks, that the person removing the bag of money from the studio would be none other than Marcus himself, but Reed is still trying to keep an open mind.

He checks his watch. The instructions were specific about leaving the bag in the rubbish bin before two o'clock.

Neither Dan nor Zoya know where he is today. They would find his suspicions ridiculous, now they are both Marcus's friend. Deep down, he doesn't really believe it either. Reed thinks back to being in the studio last night and the affinity he felt, lying on the artist's bed. It didn't *have* to be Marcus who took the bag.

But something is happening here – before 2 p.m.

He considers lighting a cigarette to make it look like he has a reason to be sitting there. Then he remembers that everyone is too busy thinking about themselves to notice or have any thoughts about him at all. Everyone's a loner in that way.

But not in all the other ways. He thinks about how different he and Zoya are, the way she immediately befriends people and gets involved in things and how he never could. He remembers her sitting next to him in the cinema, re-members how he wanted to hold her hand but kept that desire to himself.

Alone in the crowds, he realises something very simple: Zoya isn't actually thinking all the things about him that he imagines, because she is just busy *being* herself. Like everyone is.

He remembers to concentrate on the bin. A hefty man dumps a burger box inside it and walks away down the street. His thoughts turn to Dan.

He remembers their conversations over a crumb-littered table in the beach café. He remembers the chase through the muddy field and the sleepover and the beers and the couch.

He realises that, recently, Dan hasn't been quite the same. After the night in the haunted bed, Dan has seemed withdrawn. He thinks about Dan at the dinner table. He doesn't even eat with the same gusto as before. And Dan loves his food.

Reed kicks himself for not noticing that perhaps Dan isn't alright.

And he almost misses it – a City of Edinburgh refuse collector, parking his hand-pushed cart by the rubbish bin – even though the man is wearing a grubby, luminous tabard and should really stand out. There he is, beyond the stream of tourists, quietly emptying the bin.

Is this it or has Reed missed something? Was it meant to have been picked up before this?

The bin is emptied and replaced with a new bag and the binman pushes the cart off along the route. Reed gets up, his knees cricking, and commences a slow, meandering tail. The side street slopes downhill and the cart and binman pick up pace. The man cuts behind some ancient-looking stone steps. Reed follows.

When he sees the abandoned cart in the short alleyway, he skips to a jog. Around the corner on the next street, he almost misses the man because he has removed the council tabard and blends in. But he spots the sports bag he is carrying and follows him down the road.

The man disappears into a car – a small pink one, dotted with girly stickers – and slings the bag onto the passenger seat. Reed keeps walking and pulls out his notebook. As he nears the bottom of the hill, he hears the engine coming to life and looks back at the registration number before subtly scribbling it down.

CHAPTER 32

....

They are sitting at the kitchen table, Dan, Zoya and Reed, much as they did the morning she arrived, except that Marcus is not there. Fading orange light drops soporifically through the fogging window.

Reed looks from Dan to Zoya. They are waiting to hear whatever it is he wanted to talk to them about. He glances over his shoulder at the doorway before leaning toward them, hands pressed seriously on the table.

'Are you sure he isn't here?' he asks very quietly.

'Yes, why? Where is he?' Dan says, resting his chin on his hand.

Reed pauses for a beat before imparting his next thought. He looks directly at Dan and takes a breath. 'I think we should leave.'

'Why?' Zoya asks.

'We need to get out of here... Something bad is going to happen.'

Zoya makes a small, breathy snort and Dan's hand falls to the tabletop with a knock. 'This again. What makes you think that?' he asks, with unmasked exasperation.

Reed looks around and listens to the silent corridor yet again. 'Someone is paying someone off. For something.'

'That's vague,' says Zoya, shifting her weight in the chair.

'Who is? And who are they paying? What facts do you actually have?'

'Look, it's Marcus, okay? He's up to something. I saw a… collection being made.'

'A collection? And you saw Marcus there?' Dan is entirely unconvinced.

'No…. But…' Reed is thinking hard. There must be a way of telling it that can show Dan he knows what he saw without freaking him out about the whole dreaming thing. Or perhaps now is the time to tell him everything – except that would divert them from the matter in hand.

'What did you actually see?' Zoya asks, cutting into Reed's thoughts.

'Yeah, how do you know all this?' Dan adds, sounding sceptical.

When Reed's attention flickers to Zoya he sees that she has a slightly challenging look on her face. He can practically read her thoughts: *Why don't you just tell him about everything?* She has always been an advocate of not keeping the dream-walking a secret, not with people they trust, but Reed hasn't seen any evidence of her putting her opinion into practice yet.

'Do *you* know what he's on about?' Dan asks her.

'No. I think maybe Reed is just being paranoid.'

Reed's eyes flash imploringly before a look of betrayal settles on his face. *Why wouldn't she, of all people, believe him?*

'Come on. Have you just found something and made up a story about it?' she says.

'Made up a story!?'

'I mean… jumped to conclusions, maybe.'

Reed shakes his head firmly and sets his mouth in a resolute line. 'I think we should leave. We can all go in my van…'

'Would be a bit of a tight squeeze…' Dan says.

'I'm sitting for the portrait…'

'And I'm working on the book…'

'*You* could leave though, Reed,' Zoya says.

He shoots her a particularly hurt look.

'No.' Dan shakes his head. 'Stay.'

'What if' – Reed's voice takes on a new tone: he is trying a different approach – 'you're in danger here?'

'That's crazy. Why would *we* be in danger?' Zoya replies.

'Well, *we're* the only ones here,' Reed points out.

'Or *are* we…?' Zoya says, looking seriously from one to the other.

They turn toward her.

'Just kidding,' she says.

Dan relaxes and begins to explain. 'I'm not ready to leave yet. I'm–'

'Who's leaving?' Marcus asks.

He has appeared at the kitchen door. He looks at the three guests sitting at the table but mostly focuses on Dan. He doesn't seem to notice the little involuntary jump Reed gave when he heard him speak.

'You'll be back for the party tonight, won't you?' he continues.

'Party?' Zoya asks, brightening at the word.

'At the gallery. You're all invited. *You're* coming, aren't you, Dan?'

'If you want me to?'

'Of course I do! All of you. Dan, I found my Deadhead collection. I've got the records downstairs in the parlour. I thought… after the gallery, we could listen to them?'

'Yep. Count me in.'

They share smiles.

'Great,' Marcus says. He casually grasps the door frame before leaving the room entirely.

'I'll see you all later then.'

Reed, Zoya and Dan look at one another, processing the invitation.

'Not really your thing, is it, a party?' Dan says to Reed.

'Oh no, he can do a party,' Zoya says, remembering. 'Shall we go?'

Reed shrugs. 'Might be interesting to see who's there…'

***

Later, Dan finds himself standing at the edge of the fancy party, sipping from a fizzing flute of champagne. He has managed to put a slightly less scruffy outfit together and has even ironed the shirt.

Still, he doesn't blend well with the ever-shifting well-to-do crowd clustering around the gallery: collectors and creatives; sparkling ladies, tweedy gents, people with statement hair. Not really Dan's scene.

He watches as Cameron deftly steers Marcus around the party, introducing him to different groups. He eyes the rows of frothing glasses being lined up at the bar. *At least there's free drink.*

Beyond the mingling guests, Dan also catches sight of Reed and Zoya leaning against the wall at the far side of the room. They seem more relaxed with one another tonight, talking and laughing again. He feels hopeful that it might be the end of their bickering and the start of them trying again.

They part as Zoya makes her way to the ladies and Reed heads toward him through the crowd. He makes it through the tangle of art lovers and joins Dan on the bench.

'You two seem to be getting on well?'

'Mmm,' Reed responds noncommittally, but his pursed lips seem to be concealing a smile. 'Where's Marcus?' he asks.

'There he is,' Dan replies, pointing to the centre of the room.

'Ah, the life and soul of the party.'

'It looks that way, doesn't it?' Dan says.

'What are you doing over here?' Reed asks.

'To be honest, I'm feeling a bit out of place.'

'But you've known Marcus for years. You must be used to this sort of schmoozy art-crowd event?'

'He wasn't such a big deal back then.'

They watch Marcus shaking hands confidently with a white-haired man who is wearing a cravat.

'He looks at ease, doesn't he?' Dan says, a playful look on his face.

'Er, yep.'

'He isn't. Hates parties, actually.'

'Then…?' Reed finishes his sentence with a puzzled gesture indicating the party that is bubbling on all around them.

'It's part of his job, I suppose. And, anyway… parties love *him*.'

Reed keeps sight of Marcus. He is now charming a small circle of people who all look delighted to be talking to him.

'Are you sure he hates parties?'

'Positive.' Dan drains his glass. 'He only ever went to parties at uni if *I* said I'd go too.'

'But you didn't *have* to go, either of you?' Reed points out.

Dan has never known someone tread their own path quite as stubbornly as Reed.

'Marcus doesn't like to let anyone down,' Dan explains. 'We've even managed to enjoy a few. Not as much as the part where we went home and listened to records afterwards, but… yeah, good times.'

'Well,' – Reed observes Marcus greeting some man with an enthusiastic hug – 'I think he might be over his shyness now. Or he's putting a very convincing act on.'

'It isn't an act. Comes naturally to him. He's interested in everyone, wants them to have a good time, asks questions–'

'You both do that.'

Dan tips his head in acknowledgement but continues his list. '… Listens to the answers, doesn't talk about himself–'

'And yet he's publishing an autobiography,' Reed says wryly.

'No, I'm serious,' Dan says. 'Just watch. There. It's funny because now he's a big-shot artist, they all want a piece of him, but he doesn't really talk about himself, just gets *them* to do all the talking…'

Reed looks from the group to Dan whose eyes are shining with the reflection of spotlights.

'Most people love talking about themselves,' Dan observes wisely. 'And the thing is, they'll go away telling people how fascinating *he* is, when he barely told them a thing.'

At this moment, Cameron walks away from the group and Marcus begins casting about anxiously for a safety net. Reed notices it too. Marcus manages to spot Dan sitting at the edge of the room, smiles and beckons him over. The beckoning becomes more dramatic as Dan gets off the seat and steps toward the throng.

Marcus seems to be saying to the man next to him: 'Here's someone I'd love you to meet.'

Dan pauses.

'You don't mind, do you? Look, Zoya's heading back anyway – and I don't want to play gooseberry!'

'Not at all.'

Dan joins Marcus in the circle and is welcomed with an arm around his shoulders. Reed turns his attention to Zoya, who is making her way across the room, her beautiful smile flashing at him through the weaving crowd. He can't help grinning.

A man in a blue suit steps in front of her, blocking her route and obscuring Reed's view. He stands up. *Fucking* Douglas *again.* Douglas is holding two champagne glasses and hands one to Zoya. She takes the glass.

'Shit!' thinks Reed, inwardly chastising himself. He was meant to be getting them drinks. Y*ou had* one *job…*

He strides over to join them.

'Oh, hello Reed.' Douglas greets him brightly. 'Not really your thing is it?' he continues, subtly looking Reed up and down.

'Not really…'

'Reed loves art,' Zoya says. She seems to be defending him.

'The parties *we* like aren't quite so' – Reed looks Douglas up and down while choosing his words – 'buttoned-up.'

Douglas raises an eyebrow slightly.

Reed recognises someone. 'Duncan-Fox is here.'

Douglas scans the room jerkily. Alasdair and Cameron are near the entrance, taking turns to talk into each other's ears. The party is getting louder.

'So he is,' Douglas says, neatly.

Zoya spies Dan over by the bar. He is alone but picking up two drinks. She wonders where Marcus has got to, then spots him looking subdued in the middle of the room. Then he beams at someone arriving – Catriona. Douglas has noticed her too.

'And here's Mrs Reece. Excuse me, she'll be wanting to talk to me.' Douglas begins to move in her direction but looks crestfallen when she passes him, heading to Marcus.

'Evidently not,' Reed observes.

Douglas gives him a dark look in response and disappears off into the crowd.

'That was a bit harsh,' Zoya says.

'*Was* it? What's the deal with those two, anyway?'

Across the room, Marcus greets his wife with an embrace.

***

Over by the bar, Dan is returning with the glasses of wine. He isn't feeling so out of place anymore, having been brought into Marcus's glowing circle and introduced as his very best friend. He navigates a course through the party, being careful not to spill the drink in either hand.

His smile fades.

He sees that the scene has all changed now. Catriona is suddenly there, by Marcus's side, taking all his attention. He stops walking. He raises one of the glasses to his lips and drinks the whole thing in one long gulp.

Then he downs the other.

CHAPTER 33

Reed unlocks the guest house door with his key as the taxi drives off into the night. He holds it open in a gentleman-ly fashion for Zoya to step inside. Dan follows, trudging along with heavy footsteps that slap against the tiles. Reed locks the door behind them.

They walk up the stairs. Dan goes first, practically stomping, and Zoya hangs back to exchange a worried look with Reed. They follow Dan upstairs without saying any-thing. Reed takes her hand. It feels soft and warm in his.

They follow Dan around the landing toward the parlour and pause when he opens the door. He hasn't said a word since they left the party.

'Dan. Are you okay?' Zoya asks.

He turns around. 'Me? Yeah, I'm just going to… You two get off, don't worry about me.' There's no sarcasm in his voice, he just sounds weary and flat. It isn't reassuring but he definitely doesn't want their company right now.

'Are you sure?' she says.

Dan goes inside. 'Yeah, of course. I'll see you tomorrow.'

He looks directly at them as he closes the door. They watch as his face becomes a sliver then is gone.

With the clear message that Dan wants to be alone and their hands warming each other's, Reed and Zoya gently lead one another up the stairs to the top floor where their rooms mirror one another at the end of the hall.

Their footsteps slow as they reach the end of the corridor, delaying the moment to come. They stand, looking at each other. Zoya slips her hand from Reed's but uses it to reach for the door handle of his room. Slowly, she turns the handle and releases the latch. Then she looks at him.

Reed nudges the door softly, pushing it ajar and stepping backwards through the frame. He watches her, his focus flickering from her left eye to her right, holding out his hand. Gently, she lays her hand in his.

Slowly, he leads her inside. She closes the door behind them.

***

In the parlour, Dan is pouring himself a whisky. Drops spill onto the drinks cabinet and he puts the bottle down with a thud. The stopper rolls around on the tray.

He walks over to the record player and sees all the Grateful Dead albums stacked up beside it, ready for the listening party that wasn't meant to be. He squats and a little of the whisky slops over onto the carpet. He flips through the records to find *American Beauty* again and picks it out of the pile.

***

Zoya stands up, yanks her top from the chair and hastily pulls it over her head. It hasn't been lying there long.

'Protect him from what?' she demands.

Reed sits up on the bed. 'Marcus. I just don't think he's good for him. I don't think we should even be here.'

'Oh, you're bothered about your friend now?' Zoya says, tying back her hair.

Reed lunges toward the foot of the bed, his unbuttoned shirt flapping as he moves. 'Of course I am. How could you say that? And don't feign concern about Dan – when you only want to stay here to pursue your own little scheme.'

'"*Little scheme*"?!'

Reed clambers off the mattress to stand at the side of the bed. 'Sorry, I just think you're wasting your time. I mean, what do you hope to find out about Fintan anyway? He can't tell us anything; he's dead!'

Zoya is pacing. 'The people who knew him might know more than they realise – and he might have told someone anyway.' She looks at him pointedly. 'Just because *you* never would…'

Reed flings his arms in a gesture of appeasement which is undermined by the wildness of the movement. 'You won't find anything. I just think we should leave. What are any of us doing here?'

'Well, *you* can leave, but I'm staying as long as Dan needs me.'

'Needs you?'

'Yes, if you hadn't noticed, he really needs a friend right now – and *you're* not being a very good one.'

Reed resents the angry point of her finger and the accusation. He puts his hands on his hips and shakes his head, looking at the ceiling. 'What do you mean?'

'I mean, keeping yourself to yourself…' she begins.

'Haven't had much choice, have I? Not since you three formed your cosy little gang without me.'

Zoya presses her eyes closed and takes a deep breath, then she sits on the edge of the bed. 'I'm sorry. It wasn't meant to be that way… and what have you got against Marcus, anyway?'

Reed looks at her before responding with slow, measured words. 'I just think he might…'

Zoya interrupts, standing up again. 'Oh. You're investigating something yourself, aren't you? What else have you found? I mean… about the money… Are you sure you saw what you think you saw? What else have you found while noseying about in other people's things? You do actually have to talk to people to get to know them, you know?' She is shifting her weight from side to side, on the balls of her bare feet.

'Hang on, first you criticise me for not getting involved, and now you're having a go at me for checking things out.'

'When did I ever say *that*?'

'I'm just trying to protect Dan.'

'Protect him from what?' Zoya says, 'It's not like you actually *helped* last year, when I was hanging off a windowsill, fearing for my life…'

Reed takes a step back. A cold expression shutters itself onto his face. 'Just get out,' he tells her.

Zoya collects her shoes. 'I'm *getting* out.'

Reed folds his arms, watching her yank the door open and stomp across the hall to her own room.

'Has it occurred to you,' Reed says, standing in the gaping frame of his door, 'that *you* might be in danger too? I'm trying to protect *you* too.'

She pushes her door open and throws her shoes into her room. 'Like I said–'

'Why do you want to find' – Reed lowers his voice – 'another dreamer anyway? The whole world can be ours anytime we fall asleep.' He glances furtively down the empty corridor.

'Why *don't* you want to find others?' she responds. 'I thought that's what you spent your time doing.'

'I used to. I used to look for other dreamers and then I found you and I don't need to search anymore.' He looks deep into her eyes from across the hall. 'Why do you need others?' he continues, speaking gently. 'Aren't I enough for you?'

It seems like a genuine question. Zoya thinks for a minute, not wanting to hurt his feelings with an ill-considered outburst. She flexes her toes on the carpet. 'Because it's the world!' she exclaims. 'Not everything's romance, you know. Why *don't* you want to know if other people can do this? Why should it be that we are just stuck with each other in the whole entire world of sleeping people?'

'Stuck with me?'

Zoya softly plunges a slow-motion fist at the wall. That's not what she meant.

'Not daredevil enough for you, am I?' Reed says, his voice growing louder. 'Might interest you to know that while you've been having fun… *base jumping*… I've been busy trying to find out if Marcus is who Dan thinks he is.'

'Been spying on me too, have you? It's not actually about having fun…'

'Isn't it?'

'No! And you wouldn't understand.' Zoya grabs hold of the door.

'Wouldn't I? Oh, I'm going to bed,' Reed says.

'So am I! And don't you dare come and find me when we're asleep!'

'Don't worry,' Reed spits angrily. 'Goodnight.'

'Goodnight!'

They both slam their doors.

***

Inside his room, Reed flops onto his bed. He buries his face in the pillows and punches the mattress in frustration. Blood is pounding through his veins.

Once the adrenaline subsides, he rolls over onto his back. He makes a rest out of his hands behind his head and contemplates the ceiling. The argument is still replaying in his mind. He starts to think that a good, brisk night walk might be in order, seeing as he's never getting to sleep now. He could take a sleeping pill, but doesn't like to if he can help it.

But what's the alternative? Lying there all night, fuming, sweating up the sheets?

Just then, he hears Zoya's bedroom door being opened. *Is she coming to apologise, after all?*

He sits up in the bed and listens as her footsteps sound softly in the hall. He waits for the knock at his door. It doesn't come. He gets up and puts an ear to the panel. He thinks he can hear her walking away down the corridor. He opens the door a crack – in time to see Zoya disappearing down the stairs.

He takes care to close his door quietly, not wanting her to know that he has watched her walk away.

***

At the door to the parlour, Zoya taps gently before going in. The only light is that from the street outside falling through the tall windows and cutting across the room. Music softly fills the space.

Zoya goes to the sideboard and switches the lamp on.

'Oh, you're in here,' she says as the soft light illuminates Dan, sitting in the chair by the record player.

He must have been sitting in the dark.

'Are you okay?' she asks.

Dan gives a small nod.

'Just listening to records?' she continues.

Dan resumes his looking out onto the street.

'Mind if I join you?'

Zoya walks across to the sofa and sits down on the seat closest to Dan's chair. She tucks her legs underneath her. Dan doesn't say anything.

'We had an argument,' Zoya says.

Dan turns to look at her.

'We said some things.'

'Not *some things*,' Dan replies. His voice is croaky, but she still picks up on his joke.

'Yeah, 'fraid so.'

'Would it help if I point out that you're just being you – and Reed's just being Reed? At least you both say what you think.'

Zoya's mouth purses at one side. 'It's hard, being with a man.'

'Is it?'

'Yep. For a woman, it is,' she tells him.

Dan shifts in his chair to face her. 'Men are from Mars…?'

'No' – she wrinkles her nose and shakes her head – 'not *that*. Not that *at all*. No, I don't mean that kind of bollocks.'

'Pun intended?'

Zoya laughs and Dan brings his glass of whisky to his lips. The record ends and the needle clicks and clicks and clicks as the turntable keeps spinning. Zoya gets up and switches it off, removing the record and placing it back in its sleeve. She picks up the remote control.

'Shall we see if there are any good films on?' she asks before settling back into her seat.

***

A good while later, Dan is sitting in his place on the sofa, cosy underneath half of the blanket. Zoya comes into the room carrying a tray with coffee and glasses of water.

'Sobering me up, are you?' Dan says.

'Just thought it would help us stay awake. I mean, you *are* waiting up for him, aren't you?'

'Am I?'

Zoya conveys her 'yes' with a simple smile. 'And I'm keeping you company while you do.'

'*Are* you now?' Dan's reply might seem cutting if his expression were different.

'I am.' She places the tray on the coffee table and sits down beside him, wriggling back under the blanket. 'He might not come home again,' she says, using a different tone of voice.

'I know,' Dan says, reaching for one of the coffees. 'So,' – he blows a cooling breath across the surface – 'why aren't you two together?'

Zoya sighs and moves her head. 'I sometimes think it's actually better to just be friends.'

Dan is still looking at her.

'With friends,' she continues, 'you can just enjoy each other and care about each other and nobody's getting upset because their expectations aren't met... so...' She flexes her eyebrows, like a shrug.

'Oh yes,' Dan says, with a mixture of irony and earnestness, 'men are bastards.'

The tone of his voice is comedic but there's no hint of sarcasm and the way he says it makes Zoya laugh. They allow the flickers of light and sounds coming from the small television to drift over them for a few minutes.

'You know what really gets to me?' Zoya says, a new thought bubbling up in her mind.

'What?'

'And I know I'm really lucky in life generally and in not being born in a different society where women are *really*...'

Dan lowers his mug.

'It's just that, no matter how well he knows you or how close you feel to a man, they just can't seem to shake this idea that you aren't actually a person, in your own right; that you're just some... being... put there to supply him with things he wants. You know, they don't even *try* not to wake you if they get up in the night for a pee!'

'*Selfish* bastards, eh?' Dan says, elaborating on his former summary. 'It has been noted before...'

'And there's also this... this... *gulf* of understanding... between you. Like, no matter how like-minded you are, or how close you get, one of you will know what it's like to be a woman in a world that hates women, and one of you will be completely oblivious, because he's a man. I mean, how "connected" can two people be – with all that between them? One of you can't escape it and the other one doesn't even know it exists.'

'And there I was, thinking the "gulf of understanding" was an area of the moon,' Dan jokes, but she can tell from his expression that he isn't mocking what she said.

'Yeah, next to the sea of inequality,' she quips back.

'Maybe the selfish, oblivious bastards can learn, then?' Dan suggests gently.

Zoya cocks her head. 'Well... So, these are my options:' She starts counting them off on her fingers. 'A relationship that's shitty for me on a daily basis; staying single and lonely forever; or delivering an endless lesson about feminism to someone...' She illustrates this last option with a roll of her eyes: not an enticing prospect. 'Or, well, being friends.' She pats the sofa cushion to emphasise that this is the best option and looks to Dan for his response.

'Well, when you put it like that...'

'Yeah. Friends *seems* like the clear winner. But it's not great.' She jerks a thumb to point at herself. 'What, so *I* can't have the support and intimacy that a love relationship brings – just because I'm a woman, and straight?'

Dan lays a comforting palm on her calf. 'Maybe you are just one of life's singletons, like me.'

She squeezes his hand, shaking her head slightly. 'You seem like you could do with some cheering up yourself,' she says.

'Do I?' He sounds sad.

'Wild guess. Sitting in the dark, drinking whisky, waiting for a certain person to come home...'

'I know. Pathetic, aren't I?'

'But you love him.'

Dan breathes deeply. 'Yes… I do… Always have.'

He manages a small, quick smile before darting his gaze away to the far corner of the room. Zoya lays an arm on his shoulder. 'But you've made the friends thing work. How did you manage it? *I'd* like that.'

'You wouldn't.'

'But you've got each other in your lives, you spend time together, enjoy each other's company… it's *better* than a romantic relationship, isn't it? Nothing can take that sort of love away. How *do* you make it work?'

'Well, that's the thing…' Dan rests his head against the back of the sofa. '…I'm not sure it's working so well for me anymore.'

I wake up in my room alone. My head feels groggy from the tablet but at least I got off to sleep.

The bed feels expansive and empty and the patterned duvet that reminded me of a childhood bed I once knew is annoying me with its repetitive, pulsing splodges. It feels heavy. I throw it off me onto the floor.

I half tumble out of the bed and shuffle over to the door. When I open it, there is *her* door, closed. I don't hear anything.

I don't feel like seeing her anyway. Besides, I heard her get up and creep downstairs, so she probably isn't asleep yet. I tell myself not to think about her.

I walk away.

I rub my hands over my head. It feels soothing. I forgot that the dreaming feels fuzzy when I've had to take a sleeping tablet to get me off. My thoughts feel, not sluggish, but like they are falling into a deep, cold well.

I pad along the quiet corridor. It would be exactly this quiet if I were in the waking world.

I curse my clumsiness for banging into the same picture frame as before. I have nudged it out of place. I leave it crooked and continue along, past the 'haunted' bedroom and the bathroom and past Karen's bedroom door. So many of the people who live here aren't here anymore. And here *we* are: three randoms, rattling around the place like squatters. What if nobody ever came back?

I pause and retrace my steps to Karen's door. Where had she said she was off to, that last day in the guest lounge? That's not what her plane ticket to Dublin said. I go in and root about in the pile of things on top of her drawers. I don't find any plane tickets – because, of course, she has used them to fly back to Ireland without telling anyone. Why the secrecy, though?

I open the top drawer and rummage through more papers. My fingers freeze. I do find something familiar here.

Here's another of those weird business cards – like the one Marcus had, with just a phone number and nothing else. Unless, perhaps, it is the same one. Whatever is going on, are they in it together? This time, I pocket the card.

I close the drawer and leave the room. What does it mean? We need to call the number – back when I'm awake.

My head feels woozy. I don't think I'll be taking those pills again. They are making everything feel too dark and too cold – not my body, but inside my head.

Back in the corridor, I continue on toward the back stairs. I could do with another kitchen conference with Dan and Zoya – but this time with evidence to present. We could call the number together. I'd like to know what they think. I place the strange card in the centre of the table, ready.

Beside the kitchen at the top of the back stairs I look at the other door. I haven't really noticed it before. I turn the wooden knob and it falls open, creaking on the hinge.

Ducking my head to get through the stumpy doorway, I find a set of moonlit stairs. They go up.

At the top, I find another small wooden door and open it. It leads inevitably onto the roof. I never knew this was here. Nobody seems to use it. I must bring Zoya up here.

The night throws cool air toward my nostrils, filling them with city smells. I walk out and discover the sharp crunch of small, stray stones dragging under my soles.

Looking around, I see neighbouring buildings casting their window glow down to the streets. The rooftops remain dark, negative blanks. I imagine that in the waking world they are thick with the shadowy shuffling of birds.

I do see some city rooftops – there is an okay view – and the stars are there above me, but the moonlight is hurting the back of my eyes. I lean against the edging wall, the cool ledge sucking heat from my fingertips, and see the terrace way below me. My vision seems to be tunnelling into it.

I stand up again and massage my face, rubbing the heels of my hands over my eyes. This is all wrong. Being alone here. I should be wherever Dan and Zoya are. We should be talking everything through.

I contemplate throwing my dream-self off the roof in order to wake up. Zoya would, but I can't bring myself to do that, so I don't.

I turn on my heel and my foot slips, sliding across the floor. I'm falling, again, in slow motion. I see the hard corner of the wall coming up to meet my eye.

***

Reed is awake again – back in the real world. The sheets are sweaty. He sits up and shakes his head. The muffled headache is still there. In fact, it only feels worse.

He can still see the wall on the rooftop, tilting toward his head, and the sloshing, falling sensation is still churning in his ears. He sits quietly, waiting for it to stop.

He remembers his urge to see Dan and Zoya, gets up and slips on a jumper. He leaves the fusty, lonely room and sets out to be with his friends. Perhaps they are still up.

He dashes along the corridor but has to steady himself against the walls. He takes it slower, carefully walking down the staircase and taking a few breaths before opening the parlour door. He can hear the television quietly bleating away.

There they are together, entwined under a blanket on the sofa. *How did they get so close, so soon?*

They can only be friends, he knows that, but he doesn't like it, seeing them fast asleep and cuddled up together. Reed stands alone in the darkness, sweaty and cold. He forgets what he felt was so urgent anyway and isn't going to wake them up and pry them apart. He closes the door again and carries on, rushing down the stairs that lead to the city outside.

Dan wakes with a jolt and raises his head from the sofa. The fabric's weave has pressed a pattern on his cheek and his neck feels stiff. He tries to open his eyes. The pillow is lying uselessly on the floor and there is a sound he would love to snuff out.

His eyes focus and the room solidifies in front of him. A too-bright morning is forcing its way through the windowpanes and the curtains seem citrus in the light.

He locates the source of the noise – not an alarm, but the telephone. It stands shining in a patch of sunlight, and rings and rings and rings. The fancy gilding reflects rays of sunshine at his retinas. He squints. His eyes water but his mouth stays dry.

The telephone keeps ringing.

Dan's arm feels dead, squashed beneath the bony jut of Zoya's shoulder. He can feel her begin to move. His leg is caught in dishevelled blankets, and he can smell his own sweat.

He gently props Zoya up; long enough for him to extricate his arm from their sleepy pile, kicks his leg free and manages to stand up.

The telephone rings on; annoyingly.

Zoya leans on her elbow, pulls a face and rubs her eyes. Dan strides over to the telephone, desperate to stop its harsh noise.

'Hello?'

His voice is croaky.

'Marcus!'

He opens his eyes.

'Hi! Is everything… The hospital? What happened? Is she alright?'

Zoya sits up, searching for clues about the unfolding conversation on Dan's concerned face.

'Thank God it's nothing more serious…'

Zoya watches as Dan opens his mouth to speak and then waggles the receiver gesturally by his ear. Marcus has evidently rung off. He looks at Zoya with a grave expression on his face.

'That was Marcus. He took a taxi back to South Queensferry with Trinny last night,' – Zoya sees a flicker of emotion cross Dan's tired and puffy face – 'and someone attacked them, getting out of the cab, near her flat–'

'Oh my God! Are they alright? You did say the hospital?'

'They're fine. Except… Trinny came out of it with a broken leg.' Dan returns to the sofa and sits down, heavily.

'Who was it? Do they know what happened?'

Dan spreads his hands and weaves his head from side to side. 'He didn't say much – but it sounds like an attempted mugging, I think.'

'Fuck,' Zoya says. 'So, are they coming back?'

Dan looks blank. 'I'm not sure.'

***

After drinking some water and some coffee and splashing *more* water on their faces, Dan and Zoya are standing in the hallway outside Reed's room. They have taken to leaving their doors unlocked, as they are the only ones here, but they knock.

'Reed?' Dan calls, again, pounding hard on the door.

They look at one another. Zoya puts her fingers on the handle, having a flash memory of the night before. She looks at Dan again. They are both worried that Reed hasn't risen yet.

Dan nods toward the door and Zoya opens it. There is no Reed to be seen.

'Well, he's not dead,' Dan observes.

'Must have gone out first thing.'

'We got that phone call first thing.'

'Well, sometime last night, then,' Zoya surmises.

They look at the rumpled bed.

'Where do you think he's gone?' Dan asks.

Zoya widens her eyes and shrugs. She thinks back on their argument. It wasn't *that* bad...

Dan seems to have an idea. 'He hasn't...?'

'What?' Zoya replies. '*Gone*-gone? I, sort of, did suggest that he should...'

Dan pulls a disgruntled face, half smile, half grimace. 'Doesn't really do what people tell him, though...' he says, stroking his stubbly chin.

Together, they open the wardrobe.

'Well, it's almost hard to tell – because he hardly has any stuff, anyway,' Dan begins, 'but I'm going to say he *hasn't* checked out, so to speak. He's just not here.'

Zoya prods a couple of coat hangers so that the shirts swing in the underused space.

'Shall we go and check his van in the garages?' she suggests.

'Maybe… I just… If Marcus comes back–'

'You want to be here. I know.'

***

In the living room, once more, Dan is standing sentinel by the window.

'You know,' he says, 'considering we're in such a beautiful city, we seem to be spending *a lot* of time in this one room.'

Zoya snorts. 'I know. Rubbish, isn't it?'

Then they hear the front door and go quiet. They listen as muffled footsteps ascend the stairs.

'Is this him?' Dan whispers.

'Reed?'

'*Or* Marcus.'

They look toward the door and watch the handle turn.

Marcus walks into the room. He looks like he has been through some personality-changing ordeal. It can't have been that bad, Zoya thinks. *Just a broken leg? Which isn't good, but…*

Dan launches into a string of concerned questions. 'How is she? What happened?'

Zoya joins in. 'Is there anything we can do?'

Marcus's face looks ashen. He drifts toward a chair and sinks into the seat.

'Well, her leg's broken. I feel awful.'

'*You* didn't attack her,' Dan says, gently.

'Did they arrest whoever it was?'

'No, they got away.'

'So,' Zoya sits forward in her seat, 'what happened, exactly?'

'We got out of the taxi at the flat and someone ran out of the darkness at us. Tried to take her bag, I think, and Tri decided to run after him.' Marcus looks up, revealing his sad eyes to Dan. 'I just stood there, like an idiot, while my wife went after some…' His voice descends into a register of self-pitying moroseness, then fades away.

Dan walks over and puts a hand on his friend's sagging shoulder. 'It probably happened too fast.'

'Yeah… *and* I'm a fucking coward.'

'So, did she catch him?' Zoya asks. 'What happened to her leg?'

'There are some steps and railings near the flat and she ended up falling down the edge of that, somehow.'

Zoya raises her eyebrows. 'I saw the heels she was wearing – I'm not surprised.'

'So… how is she?' Dan asks.

'Well…' Marcus stands up. 'I'm only here to pack a bag – going to stay with her at the flat for a while, to look after her.'

'Why don't you both just come home?' Zoya says.

Marcus swats the idea away with a brusque flick of his hand. 'She'd never manage all the stairs here.'

He walks across the parlour toward the bedroom. Dan paces after him tentatively. 'So, should we…? I suppose we're in the way now. We'll get going. Leave you in peace.'

'No. No, you stay. Doesn't matter.'

'And will we…?' Dan draws an imaginary line from himself to Marcus and back again.

'Look. I don't know. I'll see you soon.'

They watch as Marcus heads to the bedroom to pack. When he has left the room, Zoya turns to Dan to mouth an observation. 'He looks terrified. It's just a broken leg…'

'These things are a shock,' Dan whispers back. 'One minute you're just going about, living your life, thinking about what to have for dinner–'

'Well, *you* are.' She grins.

'And the next, something happens that changes everything. Out of the blue.'

Marcus returns with a leather holdall. 'Okay then. You know where to find me.'

'Sure,' Dan replies.

'Actually, I don't think we have the number,' Zoya says.

Marcus walks across the room without responding. He looks deep in thought.

'So… you'll call us?' Dan ventures.

Marcus turns around at the door. 'I've got to get back to Trinny.'

He leaves. They listen to him plodding down the stairs and wait for the sound of the front door closing before moving to the window to watch the Porsche being driven to the main road.

Zoya looks up at Dan, standing beside her. 'She *is* there, isn't she?' she says.

'What do you mean?'

'Oh. Nothing. Just wondering…' Dan pulls a face.

'You're getting as paranoid as Reed.'

'Oh, paranoid, am I?' Reed says.

'Speak of the devil,' Dan says.

He must have come in the door when Marcus left, Zoya thinks.

'Well,' continues Dan, 'if you've taken to listening at doors, probably, yes.' Dan's face relaxes into a relieved smile, glad to see him back.

'Been visiting your van?' Zoya asks.

Reed smiles coyly. 'I might have been. What's been going on?'

'Sounds like attempted robbery at Trinny's flat last night.'

'Well, on the street,' Zoya elaborates, 'as they got out of the cab.'

'Ended up with Trinny getting a broken leg. Going to stay there for a bit – on account of there not being as many stairs.'

Reed looks from Dan to Zoya a few times. 'So, are we leaving now?'

Dan twists his mouth. 'I don't know if I can…'

Zoya sits and Reed takes the seat opposite her.

'We *are* the only ones living here now,' she says.

'Mmm.' Dan thinks. 'Feels weird, doesn't it – being in someone else's house when they aren't around.' He looks out of the window at the greying skies above, not noticing Reed's eyes drilling holes into Zoya's.

'Yes, feels weird,' Reed says.

After a couple of beats, the three of them start talking at the same time.

'So,' Zoya begins, addressing Reed, 'what was it you found that makes you think there's…'

Dan is saying: 'You know, I'm beginning to wonder if you're right that there's…'

Reed is also speaking. 'So that's two attacks on Catriona. I told you there's…'

They all finish their sentences with the same three words: '…something going on'.

They laugh, releasing all the pent-up tension.

'So, we all agree, then,' Dan states, 'that something's going on?'

'Actually,' Reed says, 'I was coming to tell you last night that I found something.'

'What?' Dan asks, waiting for the next piece of information.

'Why *didn't* you?' Zoya asks.

'I, er… I was going to. I came in' – Reed points toward the parlour door – 'but you were all cuddled up asleep.'

'Reed,' Dan says, addressing him firmly, 'I'm *gay*.'

'I know,' – Reed gestures lightly – 'I just… didn't want to disturb you.'

Instead of protesting that she's free to cuddle up with whoever she likes, as Reed expects she might, Zoya only gives the tiniest sigh.

'So…' she prompts, 'what was it?'

'I found a strange card.'

'Where?' Dan asks.

Reed thinks for a minute then has an idea. 'Up on the roof.'

'The roof?' Dan and Zoya repeat, in unison.

'Yes, you get up there through the little wooden door at the top of the stairs.'

'Let's go up!' Zoya says, jumping to her feet.

'You're alright,' Dan says, shaking his head to decline. 'What's strange about this card?'

'I'll just get it.'

***

Reed comes back in, retakes his seat and leans forward to place the card on the coffee table in front of his friends.

'Here – no words on it at all. And the number seems to be hand-printed.'

He sits back and they lean in to peer at it. Dan then picks it up.

'Hand-*printed*, but not hand*written*,' Reed specifies. 'Printed individually, one number at a time.'

Dan turns the card over in his fingertips. 'I'll give it a call.'

They watch him walk to the telephone table and carefully dial the number. Dan looks serious, holding the receiver to his ear. They try to discern some clue from his expression.

He places the receiver back in its cradle and looks at them.

'*The number has been disconnected*,' he quotes. 'No longer exists.'

Zoya flips her curls away from her face. 'Why keep a phone number that doesn't work?' she wonders.

'And why keep it on a weird card instead of writing it in your address book, anyway?' Reed adds.

Dan comes to a standstill and looks at Reed. He wets his lips. 'I saw something too.'

Reed raises a questioning eyebrow.

'A black sports bag. In Marcus's studio. Could have been full of money. He was being secretive about it.'

Reed glares at him. Then why was he so unwilling to believe what Reed told him about that same money being deposited and collected from Mitchison Square?

'Oh, that reminds me! Be back in a sec.' Once more, Reed unfurls from the armchair and dashes out of the room. He returns, catching his breath and clutching an envelope. He waves the letter at them. 'Look what just came through the door. I picked it up from the hall.'

Dan takes the envelope and surprises them by tearing it open.

'The history report, right?' Reed asks, as Dan reads the contents.

'Yep.'

'A load of ghost stuff, yes?'

'Yep.' Dan quickly skims the report, flipping it over to read the other side. 'Pretty much.'

'What's *that* all about?' Zoya asks.

Reed sucks his teeth, thinking. 'Don't know. Someone wants them to think the guest house is haunted.'

'For *some* reason,' Dan adds.

'And what else has been going on?' Zoya asks.

Reed leans forward, rests his forearms on his knees and clasps his hands. 'The watches. Remember?'

Zoya narrows her eyes. 'I forgot about that.'

'Well,' Reed says, 'both those watches were stopped; the hands pointing to a particular number. The first one was '3', then the second one was '2'...'

'Like some sort of countdown?' Dan suggests.

'To what?' Zoya asks.

'And don't you think that getting Dan up here in the first place was... weird?' Reed says.

Zoya nods, rocking in her seat. 'Seeing as they don't really believe in ghosts?'

Dan looks concerned, furrowing his brow. 'And there's something else too.'

'*Make it look like an accident*?' Reed quotes.

'Yes! How did you know…?'

'I read it in your experiment book.'

Dan sits on the rug and crosses his legs. 'I just overheard it with my bionic ear when I was about to record some audio – in the Strathkeel room – before either of you came. I don't know where it was coming from…'

'So, do you think it might have meant the "robbery" last night?' Zoya asks, looking from one to the other.

'Or the car accident?' Reed adds.

Dan rests an elbow on his leg and plunges his forehead onto his hand. 'Sorry, I've been quite preoccupied recently, I suppose.' Dan swivels his eyes upwards to meet his friend's. 'Reed, I'm sorry I didn't want to listen to what you were telling me.'

'Well,' – Reed shakes his head slightly, dismissing the sentiment – 'we're talking about it *now*. Zoya, have *you* seen anything weird or unusual here?'

'I don't think so. Apart from…'

'Yes?' the men ask.

She wrinkles her brow. 'When I was out with Douglas… I could have sworn someone called him by a different name.'

Reed looks at her, remembering the letter he read in Alasdair's flat. 'Begins with a C, right?'

'Er, yes, "Callum", I think it was. No, it definitely was.'

'How are you *doing* this?' Dan demands, looking at Reed like he's a particularly puzzling stage magician.

Reed and Zoya laugh at the comic outburst.

'Doesn't matter,' Dan continues. 'We should try to find out what's going on here.'

'We should,' Reed and Zoya agree.

They stand up decisively, and Dan follows by scrambling to his feet too. He watches as they begin opening drawers and cupboards and rummaging around.

'Guys, guys…' Dan says, authoritatively, waving his hands at them to stop.

Reed and Zoya freeze.

'What are you *doing*?'

Across the parlour, Reed and Zoya find one another's eyes. Slowly they straighten up and abandon their frenzied searching, remembering that this is real, waking life. They look desperately at one another for a moment. They can't explain.

'You're right,' Reed says, closing the drawer he had been looking through. 'I think we probably need a break from this place.'

'*Anything* to finally leave this room!' Zoya says.

Reed fixes Dan with a knowing look. 'About time we took that magnetometer back, don't you think?'

CHAPTER 36

Inside the SHERPA headquarters, Reed carefully places the boxed magnetometer on the table.

'As promised,' he says.

'Alright, Reed,' Keith says, greeting him in a friendly manner as he comes in from the adjoining room.

'Keith,' Reed acknowledges. 'Ready to sign it back in. All present and correct.'

'Thanks for looking after it,' Keith says.

Dan's eyebrows are set at an angle. He has been looking from Reed to Keith and back again, trying to fathom their new-found cordiality. 'You two friends or something?'

Gregor hurries over with the ledgers, undecided which to have them fill out first.

'Hey, nice T-shirt!' Zoya says. She is tiptoeing along the wooden partition, treating it like a gymnastics bar. He looks up at her with a gaping mouth. She smiles the most radiant smile he has ever seen.

'Hey, what's that?'

Gregor watches as she spies the 1930s infrared camera on the shelving and goes to have a closer look. Gregor wanders over behind her, vaguely pointing a pen in an unspoken attempt to get her to sign in.

'This is our friend, Zoya. Zoya, this is Gregor and Keith,' Reed says, introducing everyone.

Zoya hands the old camera to Gregor and moves along to look inside another vintage box, picking out a succession of brushes and a tub of grey powder. He sets the camera back in its place and hurries after her.

'Careful, don't spill the graphite.'

She looks at him.

'That's an old fingerprinting kit.'

She seems impressed and puts it back on the shelf. Gregor rearranges the brushes in the proper order and then notices that she has opened up a banker's box and is peering inside. She has discovered a couple of wigs wrapped in tissue paper, which she touches gently and folds back into place.

'Spirit Photography Fraud,' Gregor explains obtusely while she tries on a pair of Edwardian spectacles, laughing.

'Pleased to meet you,' she says, in character, extending her handshake to Keith. He doesn't look happy but allows her to shake his hand.

'They're the Society for Historical and Empirical Research into Paranormal Anomalies – Edinburgh and Lothians Chapter,' Reed says, getting the name spot on.

'Paranormal Anomalies? That sounds exciting,' she replies earnestly. 'This is really cool,' she says, looking around the room.

'Thanks...' Gregor replies, accepting the delicate spectacles from Zoya.

Reed sets about filling out the registers correctly while Keith checks the magnetometer. Jim appears from the other room and saunters over, carrying his habitual cup of tea.

'Hi, Dan,' he says.

'Hi, Jim. How was the camping trip?'

'Very nice, thanks. Sally loved Fingal's Cave especially. So, how's things? This your team?'

'Pretty much. Jim, this is Reed and Zoya.'

Smiles and nods are exchanged.

'Hi,' Zoya says.

Reed and Jim look like they might have met before. Keith tidies the magnetometer away in its box, satisfied that everything is in order.

'So,' Reed says, resting his hands on the table, 'any comparable cases?'

'What's this?' Dan asks, joining them by the table.

Gregor is showing Zoya a Victorian Ouija board and pencil planchette.

Reed looks at Dan. 'I hope you don't mind, but–'

'What have you done?' Dan asks, adopting the tone of a disappointed parent. He glances at Keith. 'Not been round with any crackpot theories, has he?'

'Dan, Dan, Dan… you should know they would never entertain such a thing as a crackpot theory,' Reed says.

'So… what is it?'

'Just briefed us about your findings,' Keith explains.

Dan's eyes widen.

'You know, the iron bedframe…'

'Just thought they might be able to look up some similar cases for you,' Reed explains, 'for your report.'

'And we did. Gregor – did you dig out the case notes?'

'Oh. Thanks,' Dan says, accepting the stack of papers.

Dan and Reed look at one another. Dan is wearing an expression of pleasant surprise.

'You *don't* mind, do you?' Reed checks. He also looks a little bit pleased with himself.

Gregor lays another folder on the table. 'Here you go. Really interesting data in this one.' He seems quite taken with it.

Dan opens the folder and begins to read. He blinks a couple of times. He feels the strange mix of warm companionship for these unexpected helpers, yet is put out that Reed has gone behind his back.

'Thanks,' Dan says, folding the cover flap back into place. 'This is... great. Really helpful.'

He still doesn't know why they are being nice to him all of a sudden. He looks around the room. Zoya and Gregor are engrossed in an animated conversation by the window.

Meanwhile, Jim summons Reed to the other side of the room to look at something.

'Well, we are all on the same side here,' Keith replies. 'We are all SHERPAS aren't we? No reason local chapters can't work together.' He smiles.

Zoya is placing some sort of hat she has found on Gregor's head.

Jim seems to be slipping Reed a small, folded note, but Dan is too distracted by what Keith is telling him to pay much attention.

'So, I've been reviewing the literature and, if you are amenable, I've a few ideas about how we can make the article more impactful.'

'Thanks.' Dan turns to his friend. 'Er, Reed…'

'Come on, Dan, you don't have time to do the report by yourself anyway.'

'Don't I?'

'What with the biography and everything.'

'Okay,' Dan says to Keith, 'I'll be in touch.'

He looks at Reed and Zoya. 'Shall we go?'

Dan, Reed and Zoya are squashed into the small office under the stairs. Dan is rifling through documents in the filing cabinet.

'Well,' Dan says, 'there's nothing weird here. How about yours?'

Dan puts a ledger back where he found it and straightens up, ducking his head to avoid colliding with the pendant light that dangles from the low ceiling.

'Hmmm,' mumbles Reed, looking through a box file at the desk.

The lamp casts looming shadows at the wall like folklore figures. It's difficult for them to move without blocking their own light and getting in each other's way.

'Just put it back,' Dan tells him. 'We shouldn't be doing this. We don't even know what we're looking for.'

'You're right,' Zoya agrees, closing a drawer and shuffling around the small table that fills much of the room. She stands, leaning against the wall, but is still close enough to see up Dan's nostrils.

'Let's think through what might be happening here,' she suggests.

Reed spins round in the desk chair and winces as he bangs his knee, *again*.

'Good idea,' Dan replies resting his fists on the table. He ducks his head around the lampshade in order to maintain eye contact with Reed. 'I'll start. I'm sure I heard they were having some money problems – and Marcus told me his career hasn't been going so well… so…'

'So, there's some kind of insurance scam?' Zoya says.

Reed stands up to relieve himself from his twisted position and from the crick in his neck.

'Life assurance, you think?' he says.

The three of them look at one another.

'Or what about the haunted house stuff?' Zoya says, squinting. 'How would that affect things?'

She is standing between the tall men at the side of the table, short enough not to be troubled by the lampshade but too close to avoid being blinded by the bulb.

Reed reaches to the wall switch and turns off the light for her. They are left with the low glow of the desk lamp. The change in lighting prompts them to lower their voices.

'I don't think there's such a thing as *ghost* insurance,' Dan quips cynically.

'No,' she replies, 'but would it put people off staying here? Affect the value of the business?'

'From what I've seen,' Reed says, tilting his head to see Zoya around the lampshade, 'the tourists love a generous helping of "ghost" with their Edinburgh…'

'Well, make the business take off then?' Zoya says.

'Maybe, but they're only empty *now* because everyone's on holiday,' Dan points out.

'And because Catriona can't come back, now she has a broken leg,' Zoya says.

'So, how can they be having money problems?' Reed wonders. 'Or, what if those fake history documents are about something else entirely – about who *really* owns the house?'

'Marcus told me he gave some money to Fintan before he… died.'

'Yes, Dublin…' Reed says, shifting his position to perch on the desk.

They look at him.

'You know how Karen said she was going to France?'

'Yes?' they reply together.

'She wasn't.'

They watch him, waiting for further information.

'I saw her plane tickets – she was going back to Dublin.'

'And we still don't know what *really* happened there…' Zoya points out.

Dan pulls a face and shakes his head.

'I'm sorry but… I don't think it's about the money,' Reed says. 'I think it might be a lot worse than that.'

Zoya's eyes widen.

'*Make it look like an accident?*' Reed quotes, in a whisper, looking from one to the other.

Dan and Zoya exchange glances too.

'And what about Catriona?' Zoya continues. 'I mean… is she really even… *there* – at the flat? Where does she keep disappearing to *really*?'

'Why wasn't she at Fintan's funeral?' Dan wonders, whispering too.

'Is Catriona really still… *alive*?' Reed adds. He shivers.

'Don't,' Dan says, his face stern. 'I think you've gone too far with this.'

'And does she really have a broken leg?' Zoya says. 'Maybe she could manage these stairs, no problem.'

'Like an alibi for something – that hasn't happened yet?' Dan suggests, catching her train of thought.

Reed looks from one to the other. 'Could be her – up to something – could be him.'

Dan looks conflicted and resumes shaking his head. He shifts his weight in the confined space; the largest person trapped at the smallest end of the room.

'No, Dan, I know you don't want to hear it, but,' – Reed leans across the table to touch Dan's arm emphatically, making sure he's paying attention – 'what if he's got more to do with Fintan's death than you think?'

This makes Dan angry. He grabs Reed's shirt in his fist.

'No, hear him out,' Zoya interjects. 'We're just coming up with ideas here.'

'I'm not saying it to upset you, it's just that… What if you're…'

'… Next?' Dan says incredulously, finishing the sentence and dropping his grip on Reed's shirt.

Then Dan furrows his brow. He remembers Marcus telling people in the Claddagh that he hadn't seen Fintan for years and then telling *him* he'd met up with him and fallen out about the money he'd lent. What if Marcus wasn't as honest as he believed?

'But what if you *are*?' Reed continues. 'Makes some sort of sense. First Fintan, then Marcus…'

'If the car accident and the attack were aimed at *him*?' Zoya says, thinking out loud.

Reed nods. 'Then *you*?' Reed looks Dan deep in the eye.

'No,' Dan says quietly, 'you're being ridiculous now.'

'But he has some sort of point,' Zoya says. 'I mean, I was too focused on the lovely, free holiday and the amazing Edinburgh and everything but, now I think about it, doesn't it seem like you are being kept here for some reason?'

'I'm writing the biography, remember?'

'And it's real?' she replies.

'Well, my bank seems to think the advance was real, so…'

'But she has a point,' Reed says. 'What brought you here? Some bullshit job about a haunted bed?'

'It's not bullshit – it's what I do. It's my work.'

'Yes, I know, but did anyone really care about that ghost stuff? I mean, that's the way to snare you, isn't it? That's your thing – work.'

Zoya looks up at Dan. 'Does seem *quite* like an excuse to me…' she says gently.

Dan folds his arms. 'Well, actually, I was commissioned to do that by Trinny – she told me. So, whatever you think is going on, it's *her*, not *him*.'

'Well, she doesn't seem to like you that much… Considering you are old friends…' Reed observes.

'There might be a reason for that,' Zoya says, meaningfully, but Dan ignores the comment.

He turns his head fully from Zoya to Reed and back again a couple of times. 'Ever had that feeling your friends are ganging up on you? Listen. Let's not get carried away with all this. There's no reason to be scared.'

'Then why are we whispering in a tiny broom cupboard?' Zoya asks.

They suddenly feel ridiculous – squashed in around the furniture and underneath the sloping ceiling – and all begin to laugh.

Then they hear the noise. They stop laughing, hardly daring to breathe.

It's the sound of the front door closing. Dan puts a finger to his lips.

The muffled thud of footsteps passes overhead on the stairs. They listen with wide eyes and tense stomachs in the semi-darkness. The noise doesn't identify itself, doesn't seem regular somehow. It could be someone with a broken leg in a cast, could be someone dragging something heavy, could be more than one person.

Zoya leans in to speak and the men to listen. Her voice barely makes a sound. None of them want to reveal their presence, shut away in the small, dim office under the stairs.

'Who is it, do you think?'

'Probably just Marcus coming home,' Dan whispers, but still seems tense.

'But wasn't he going to stay at the flat?' Reed mouths.

'Could be Catriona?' Zoya breathes.

'Or the demon watch collector?' Reed jokes.

Their mouths twitch but nobody dares laugh. The foot-steps seem to have abated.

'Where did they go?' Zoya whispers.

Dan shakes his head. He can't tell.

Reed leans even closer. 'Come on, let's make a dash for my van and get out of here.'

'No,' Dan replies, his voice raspy. 'We'll just come out of the cupboard and go and say hello. Like normal people.' Dan squeezes past them to the door. He grasps the handle and they look at one another.

Dan turns the handle silently and opens the door. Reed positions himself to go next. He turns back to whisper: 'Zoya, you stay here.'

'Fuck off,' she whispers, meaning 'no'. 'I'm coming too.'

The three of them slowly creep out of the office into the shadowy lounge. It is apparently empty.

They follow one another past the reception desk, sticking close to the wall. Moonlight glints from the brass sign like the wink of an eye.

The patter of their feet over the hall tiles sounds too loud in the empty darkness and seems strangely out of sync with their feet. Yet, nobody is following them.

They pause before the steep staircase. It seems to twist above them; angular and dark. They look at one another with wide eyes before continuing up the stairs.

They walk up, treading together, taking the steps one by one. Their slow-moving, fearful huddle feels ridiculous, but no one wants to break away.

'At what point,' Reed whispers in Dan's ear, 'were you going to say hello?'

At the top of the flight, three faces peer around the wall. They see nobody along the landing that stretches to the right, nobody to the left. They advance, just as hesitantly, around the corner toward the parlour door.

It is standing open. Is that the way they left it?

Dan goes first. The tall windows remain uncovered. Shards of moonlight fall across the room. The hard shadows of night-time collect in the corners, concealing what or who, they cannot see.

A noise sounds from the far side of the room. Movement.

The light clicks on and they see it together – a figure.

'Aaaaargh!'

There is a pause.

Reality seeps over them, revealing a strange little tableau. Panting, their eyes adjust to the bright light and everyone starts to make sense of the scene.

Zoya has taken up a karate pose, Reed has ducked and covered, and Dan is holding an improvised weapon aloft, like an iron bar.

Someone has taken shelter behind the sofa and is gradually revealing themselves.

'What. The fuck. Are yous doing. Shuffling around in the dark?'

Karen's face peeks over the back of the sofa and then she slowly stands up. Everyone is getting their breath back. Reed uncoils from his cowering position, styling it out as best he can. Zoya drops her arms and shifts her feet, relaxing from the imminent danger. They are both trying not to look embarrassed.

The four of them look from one to another, processing what just happened.

'You nearly gave us an actual heart attack!' Karen says.

'Sorry,' Dan says, lowering his arm.

Karen and Dan step into a tight hug. They both seem equally relieved.

'Good to have you back,' Dan says.

'Thanks, but you can keep the welcome committee next time,' she replies. 'Jesus.'

Meanwhile, Reed has folded his arms. 'And what were *you* doing, creeping around in the dark?' he asks, narrowing his eyes.

She looks at him. '*I* wasn't.'

He remains suspicious.

'I've just taken my suitcase up' – she points to the door that leads to the back stairs – 'and now I thought I'd watch a bit of TV.'

Reed is still scowling.

'I think you'll find,' Karen tells him, 'that it was *me* turning the lights *on*. Are you alright, Zoya? Where is everyone, anyway?'

She looks at the object in Dan's hand. 'You can stop brandishing the Toblerone now, Dan.'

For the first time, he notices the giant chocolate bar in his grasp. Karen takes it out of his hand.

He clears his throat.

'You mean Marcus and Trinny? She got a broken leg last night – chasing a handbag thief – so they're staying at the flat because of… all the stairs.'

As he hears it coming out of his own mouth, Dan is wondering if any of this even sounds plausible anymore.

Karen moves to the sofa, puts the Toblerone down and sinks back into the seat. She rests one leg, then the other, on the coffee table.

'Chasing a handbag thief?' She raises an eyebrow. 'I'm impressed. Didn't know she had it in her. How did she get her leg broken?'

'Allegedly, she fell down some steps and landed badly,' Reed answers, wrapping his arms around his torso.

Zoya sits down. 'I don't think she was wearing the shoes for it,' she adds.

Karen waggles one of her Doc Martens across the table, drawing Zoya's attention to the sturdy boot. 'Note to self, eh?'

Zoya nods. Karen looks around the room.

'What's all this "allegedly"? Are you taking a criminal law course? Just sit down, all of you. You're making us feel… interrogated.'

Dan sits on the end seat. 'You're back early, aren't you?' he asks.

'Did you have a nice time in France?' Reed asks, cutting in.

Karen smiles and nods. 'Yes thanks,' she says, beginning to unwrap the Toblerone.

Reed, Dan and Zoya all register her lie but do their best not to look each other in the eye.

CHAPTER 38

'So, what do you think she's up to?' Reed says, looking at Dan. '*You* know her.'

It is the next day and the three of them are standing on the roof, arms leaning on the wall, eyes scanning the skyline ahead.

A pale grey sky hovers above the city. Architectural silhouettes jumble before them, massing on the horizon: rows of sloping roofs, slabs of beige stone, endless smokeless chimneys. A siren wails faintly somewhere.

'I don't know,' Dan replies. 'Why is she lying about where she's been?'

'Maybe she just likes her privacy?' Zoya suggests.

'But, Dublin though… again,' Reed says pensively.

Dan sighs. 'Look. Back then, I would have trusted Karen with anything… but it's been years and… well, she *has* been acting weird.'

Reed nods gently. 'Kind of… snappy with people? Doesn't seem like the way you should be in front of hotel guests.'

'Maybe she's just not the obsequious wallflower you think she should be?' Zoya says. She leans her forearms on the ledge and studies the green mosses at her fingertips. Tiny tendrils flutter delicately in the air.

'No, but… I think there's something going on with her. She's… different somehow.' Dan is struggling to find the right words.

The tickling breeze dances across the rooftop while, colossally high above them, weather fronts jostle like gods.

'What was her relationship with Fintan?' Reed asks.

'They were a couple – briefly.'

'What happened?' Zoya asks, raising her head.

'Um… He lied about who he was, and she was… pretty hurt.' Dan checks their reactions.

'Do you think she's maybe been… harbouring something?' Reed asks. 'And what about her relationship with Marcus? Didn't they go out too?'

'Also, a long time ago.'

'But she isn't with anyone now, is she? Or is she?' Reed continues.

Dan's eyebrows shoot up. 'A secret relationship, you mean?'

'Maybe she's got some agenda?' Reed says.

'Maybe she just knows something she'd rather not,' Dan counters.

'Maybe she's just being protective,' Zoya says.

'Maybe she's wondering why people are whispering about her private life on the roof?' Karen says.

They all jump. She is standing behind them.

They turn around to face her. Her expression is a mixture of bemusement and an angry scowl. Her hands are on her hips.

Dan is the first to move, stepping toward her with a placatory gesture. Reed ruffles his hair, interested to see how *this* conversation will unfold.

'Karen – sorry, we–' Dan begins.

'Have you lost your minds?' she cuts in. 'Jesus fucking Christ!' She wheels around and storms across the rooftop, yanking the door open and disappearing down the stairs. They look at one another; Dan looks worried, Reed un-apologetic. Zoya chastises them with narrowed eyes.

They rush back inside and try to catch up with Karen. She is charging down the back stairs angrily. They scurry behind.

In the parlour, Karen sinks onto the sofa. She sits glowering at them, arms folded, one foot tapping the floor.

They sit down, watching her warily, and devising what to say.

'Why don't I just *tell* you what's going on with me?' Karen says, her voice exploding the awkward silence. She looks disdainfully from Reed to Dan. 'So you don't all have to *guess*.'

Zoya notices the men looking sheepish under Karen's gaze.

'You don't have to explain anything,' Zoya says. 'But is everything okay?'

'No. Everything's *not* okay. My very good, old friend just fell off a very tall building and got squashed into a pavement. If you ask me, I'm the only one acting *normal* around here. What's normal is to feel shit about it, you know, and not be able to stop thinking about him, and to miss him, and yes, to be angry and drink a bit and to maybe, just maybe, be a bit of a dick to people around you every now and again. What's *not* normal is to carry on like everything's okay – like the rest of them.'

Dan looks at her. Reed's gaze falls to the floor.

'She's right. Why *is* everyone taking it so calmly?' Zoya asks.

'And just because,' Karen continues, spitting out the words through a clenched jaw, 'I'm a single woman – *happily* single in every way – you don't get to accuse me of fuck knows what. Like I'm some kind of aberration. I'm not any harbouring any *anything* from twenty years ago, thank you very much.'

Zoya leans toward her. 'They didn't mean–'

'Yes, they did.' Karen glares at her, and then at Dan and Reed. She puts an elbow on the arm of the sofa and rests her head in the triangle of her hand. 'I get this all the fucking time.' Her eyes flick up to meet Zoya's. 'And so will you. Though, actually,' – she glares again at the men – 'people don't usually go about suspecting me of murder. Just, you know, of being out to steal their man, or of being mentally ill or lonely or desperate or unhinged in some other way, you know… Like I'm constantly on the edge of going mad and stealing someone's baby! It's the fucking nineties! You would think that sort of thinking had died a death by now!'

Dan swallows and wets his lips. 'I'm sorry. We just got carried away.'

Karen holds her forehead, shielding her eyes.

Dan picks up a framed photograph from the end table beside him. It is the *Wizard of Oz* party photo that has now been put on display. He looks at Fintan's young, happy face.

'Can I ask – where did you get this photo?'

'What photo?' she asks.

'*This* photo… of me and Marcus and Trinny and Fintan.'

Karen removes her hand from her brow and looks at him seriously. 'And me,' she says flatly.

'But you're not…'

'Yes I am. *Right there.*' She stretches her arm to point at part of the picture, then looks at Zoya across the room.

'Fucking hell – if you're not a man or a spouse of a man then you don't exist.' She looks at Dan again. 'There! I'm right there. I've been there all along.'

He moves next to her on the sofa, bringing the frame with him and taking a closer look. He looks at it quietly for a while. 'Sorry – I didn't spot you because you weren't in costume.'

There, in the background of the photograph but very much in the frame, is a younger Karen clad in a simple black sweater, dancing and happy, throwing her head back with laughter. She looks confident and carefree.

Dan doesn't know what to say.

'Don't you like *The Wizard of Oz*?' Zoya asks.

Karen shrugs. 'I've just never been into fancy dress and going to a big effort pretending to be something else.'

Dan looks again at the photograph. The young Karen is wearing her everyday clothes and her loose hair is a bit of a mess. 'No,' he says, 'I remember now…'

Karen plucks the frame out of his hands, looks at the picture, then shoots a sharp look at Reed.

'And no,' she says, as if pre-empting something he might say, 'I wasn't dressed as the wicked witch.' She looks again at the print. 'I love this photo.'

'Me too,' Dan says, putting an arm around her shoulder.

They sit there, looking at it quietly together.

'Nuala copied it for us all to have.'

Reed has a question to ask but tries to moderate his tone. 'But you weren't in France, were you?'

Karen swivels her eyes toward him. 'Wasn't I?'

He watches her.

'You're right,' she says sarcastically. 'I've been hiding up on the roof all this time, plotting my crazed spinster plots. I don't have to tell *you* anything.'

Everyone stays quiet then Zoya shuffles forward in her seat. 'Ignore him. How are you? Are you managing to sleep better at night?'

Karen presses her eyes closed. Then she glances sideways at Dan and her attitude seems to thaw. 'Actually. I was in Dublin,' she says quietly.

'With Nuala?' Dan asks.

Karen nods.

'Have they found anything out?'

'Yes, but it won't help *you* sleep better at night…'

Dan is looking at her. He wants to know.

'Somehow,' she continues, 'and they don't know how, but somehow it's got something to do with organised crime.'

'Gangsters?' Dan asks.

'Yeah. They've traced a vehicle and have some suspects… but they don't know what the connection is – or what it could possibly *be*. Nuala has been having a really hard time of it. I went over to help her out with things and… be somewhere where it's perfectly normal to grieve.'

'So,' Dan says, after a moment's reflection, 'he was *killed,* then…'

They take in the harsh reality of the fact. Reed concentrates on pushing a certain image out of his mind.

Dan looks at Karen. 'I'm sorry we… I never really doubted you.'

'It was Reed with his weird ideas…' Zoya says, making some attempt to lighten the mood ever so slightly.

'Can't help it,' he says, fishing something out of his jeans pocket. 'I've seen a lot of weird things around here.' He holds the strange business card up and looks at it with a frown. 'Like this card. We found it.' He looks at Karen. 'Do you know what it is?'

She looks serious and thoughtful. 'Where was that?'

'But you've seen it before?' Reed asks.

She thinks for a moment. 'I have. But I don't know what it's for either. I called the number a few times when I first found it.' She looks around at their expectant faces and shrugs. 'Never found out. The first couple of times it rang out and wasn't answered. Then, the last time, it was like the number was disconnected or something.'

'And where did you find it?' Reed asks.

Karen looks out of the window. Her face is rumpled, like she is weighing an uncomfortable dilemma. She looks back at Reed. 'Does it matter?'

'It might do,' Dan says.

She holds Dan's gaze, considering her response.

Reed speaks again, attracting her attention. 'Was it in Marcus's study, by any chance?'

Karen turns back to face Dan, her focus darting from eye to eye. Then, reluctantly, she nods.

CHAPTER 39

Dan and Reed are sitting at the table in the small family kitchen, their faces pink with the fiery light of the crimson sun; the death-throes of a bright day plunging toward night.

Footsteps are ascending the back stairs.

'Sounds like they forgot something,' Dan comments. 'Maybe they want us to join them on their night out, after all.'

Reed looks dubious and shifts in his chair. 'I'm not sure I'm Karen's favourite person. Or Zoya's, come to think of it.'

They listen as the footsteps approach.

'It's not *them*,' Dan says, shaking his head.

They look at one another. Dan decides to find out.

'Marcus?' he calls. 'Is that you?'

There is no answer, but the quiet footsteps continue slowly. Dan pushes the chair back with a creak, and goes into the hall.

Marcus is standing by the small wooden door at the top of the stairs.

'Can't we talk on the roof?' he says, inviting Dan to follow him.

Marcus turns and disappears through the small door.

'Everything okay?' Dan asks, behind him.

Marcus is already climbing the stairs, out of sight.

Dan follows. At the top, the door is ajar. He steps out onto the open space of the rooftop and unfolds his spine.

Outside, he finds Marcus. He is standing, watching the sunset, his face upturned to the gorgeous, gloriously painted sky. The blazing, spectacular colours seem to mute the roar of the city.

He walks a couple of uncertain steps toward Marcus and sees the open bottle of whisky hanging from his fingers.

'Everything okay?' Dan asks.

Marcus notices him with a glance, saying softly over his shoulder: 'I'm glad you're here.'

'Is something the matter?'

Dan gets closer.

Fuel-sharp fumes escape from the mouth of the bottle. A trickle runs down the neck.

Marcus begins a slow spin, looking to the heavens and across the cityscape and back at Dan. 'Not a thing.'

Day turns to evening above them: a rainbow palette dashed violently across the sky, falling in billowing swathes of colour and catching on silvery strands of cirrus clouds.

'Listen...' Dan shuffles forward. 'What's been going on?'

'Shhh... Just enjoy it.' Marcus is gazing in the direction of the setting sun.

As Dan draws level, Marcus turns his face to him. 'Enjoy it with me, please. Just this once.'

***

Downstairs in the kitchen, Reed has assumed that, yes, the footsteps belonged to Marcus. He is happy to give them some space to talk. Maybe Dan can finally find out what has been going on.

He stands up and digs out a slip of paper from his pocket – the folded note that Jim gave him yesterday. It's handy that he works for the DVLA.

Reed is glad of the opportunity to leave without anyone asking him any questions. He slips quietly away down the stairs.

***

They are standing together by the roof's edge, taking in the majesty of the sky. Dan hears the contents of the whisky bottle sloshing when Marcus brings it to his lips. When Marcus hands it to him, he sets it down by the wall. Marcus doesn't seem to notice, so taken is he with the sunset. It always was his favourite thing in the world.

There are still a few fuzzy, pink-edged clouds visible against the peaches, scarlets and blues. Marcus points at one.

'That one looks like…'

The surreal jokey description never comes.

'That one's… the two of us…'

The moment drifts along, like the clouds.

'Dan, I've… got something to show you.'

'What is it?'

'Close your eyes.'

Dan dutifully obliges, pressing his eyes closed and trusting Marcus to his reveal. 'Surprise me.'

He waits, wondering, then feels Marcus's lips softly touching his.

Their lips press together and their mouths gently part. He is sinking in the swell of a surprising yet unsurprising kiss; a kiss he has ached for; ever-present, and long-missed.

The sunset swirls around them, centring the cosmos on their embrace. Years of love flow between them, shown and felt in the deep well of a kiss.

Lost in the sweetness, Dan remembers.

He remembers the first kiss and the first rooftop and they could be there again. He feels like a floating cloud, travelling on a string of sunsets back to that intoxicating night in Palermo all those years ago – their night together, under the stars.

He knew that it had happened and clung to it all this time, never letting the memory surface, not even into words. He had pressed it down into the depths of memory; containing it, never letting it see the light of day.

They hold one another firmly, tenderly, and their lips linger on; an out-of-body experience, spinning across the universe just for this moment and for all time.

Slowly, ever so slowly, Marcus's lips leave his. He feels Marcus's hands around his face and his breath upon his skin. Finally, he finds the bravery to open his eyes. The world is still there.

He sees Marcus's eyes twinkling in front of him, deep pools of emotion, dark and fathomless like the open sea on a black night. He sees the passion etched on his endlessly familiar face. Is Marcus crying?

'I thought you had forgotten...' Dan whispers against his cheek.

Marcus backs away and Dan sees his face anew. It is beyond description now; just the face of the man he loves. But there is wildness in his eyes. It feels frightening. How can it be – at the moment of complete togetherness, when they have felt most at one – that Dan can't tell if Marcus is passionately happy or despairingly sad.

Marcus removes himself from Dan's embrace – not regretful, but something else; something unsettling, something strangely resolute. He seems to be trembling. 'You have to go now,' he tells him.

Dan is dumbstruck all over again. He wants to respond, to comfort, to challenge, to ask the millions of questions that he's been hiding for so long. He doesn't say anything.

'Please. For me. Just this once,' Marcus is saying.

Marcus keeps backing away and Dan feels compelled by the imploring look in his eyes. He feels like he is drifting away from Marcus on a dangerous tide.

'But...'

'Just go, Dan,' Marcus beseeches him. This isn't regret but something else. 'Promise. You need to leave me alone.'

Marcus tears his eyes from Dan, spinning away from the deadlock of their gaze.

Dan reaches the stairs but doesn't go. Unseen by Marcus, who is standing, facing the dying light, Dan takes up a hiding place around the corner, behind the wall of the stairs.

The sun has set, and the sky is washed with cooler hues. The eerie glow of the streetlamps grows as the sky dims.

Dan waits and watches from his hiding place – and will wait for as long as it takes.

CHAPTER 40

Reed has found the address – a small house in a suburb toward the bypass. It seemed dark and empty until he crept around to the back garden. Here, he sees a room with the light on, through the slit of curtains not quite closed. He crouches on the patio and crawls toward it, intent upon catching a glimpse of the shadowy figure moving inside. He almost holds his breath.

He inches closer to the window, clinging to the shadows. The dark crawl of night is sweeping from the east. He positions an eye to look through the gap.

There is someone; a man wearing dark clothes. Reed feels certain that this is no more the man's house than the pink Renault is his car. Yes, he could be a father or a boyfriend or a brother or a friend – but the circumstances and his instincts make Reed think not.

The figure passing makes Reed flinch. He jerks into the shadows. The garden behind him is a mystery of bobbing leaves, prickling bushes and loamy darkness. Reed maintains his ankle-straining crouch. The mossy paving slab presses hard into his knee, staining his jeans.

The light from the room steadies and Reed steels himself for another look. It appears that the man inside is methodically clearing up after himself, removing every trace. A hardly-filled bin bag is sitting on the table next to a small case. Reed ducks into the darkness again. The hands he saw were wearing black leather gloves.

The light goes out and Reed feels more exposed. He rolls under the bushes and lies there, frightened, eyes growing wide in the dark. He forces his breath to remain shallow and wills his heart to slow down. He inches further beneath the foliage, the soil cool against his back.

He listens hard.

The side door is opened, quietly. He strains his ears. Someone is leaving the house. The man steps down to the path that runs from front to back.

Reed listens to the footsteps. *Not this way. Please.*

***

Dan waits and watches. The air feels sharper now, spiced with the cool green perfume of garden flowers closing for the night.

Marcus is pacing at the darkest corner of the roof. Dan doesn't know what to do – except he does; he will wait there forever to make sure that Marcus is okay.

The wall by his cheek is disappearing into the darkness. He can hear the scrape of tiny pebbles under his boot as he shifts his weight. He tries to stay silent and still.

When the moment is right, when Marcus has calmed down, he will reveal himself and take him in his arms and see that he sleeps through the night. Tomorrow, he will make him see that everything is alright – *more* than alright.

He watches Marcus drink from the bottle then pour much of the whisky over the wall. He takes something shiny out of his pocket and holds it in his trembling palm. It's just a watch. *Is he waiting for someone?*

Dan can still feel the press of Marcus's lips. His mind races back and forth between that night and this. The day had been spent on the rooftop, listening to music, while Marcus painted his portrait. After hours of sunshine and talking and wine, they came together as lovers; surprising yet inevitable, the most natural thing in the world.

All night, they had stayed on the roof together, caressing each other's skin, tracing the shapes of each other's faces with their fingertips and sleeping under the stars.

By dawn they woke and wordlessly packed up their things. Descending the tiled stairs into the rented apartment, the mood shifted subtly, from love and sensuality to wondering and concern. The apartment was empty and shouldn't have been. *Why hadn't Fintan come home?*

They had washed and changed and busied themselves in the kitchen, and were cooking breakfast by the time Fintan sloped back in. Dan can still see those eggs in the pan. And then it was all about Fintan. He was wearing fisherman pants, carrying a wedge of rumpled dinar and had been out all night. Except none of them mentioned any of it. At all. If Fintan was waiting for a prompt to tell his stories, all he got was a quiet, nonchalant breakfast, exactly like the one the morning before.

And they never mentioned Fintan's untold adventure and they never said a word about theirs. The seismic shift in Dan and Marcus's relationship turned once more; their secret sinking beneath the waves of silence that coloured the morning. It was never mentioned again.

Now, on the cool Edinburgh rooftop, Dan forces himself to stay still. They could be talking about it right now and sketching out a lifetime of love yet to come – but something else is engulfing Marcus and he doesn't want Dan around.

Dan waits and watches. It has been a really long time.

***

Underneath the bushes, Reed's adrenaline has subsided enough that he is beginning to feel cold. He is lying beneath the branches, and the stones in the soil are pressing harder into his back.

He has been lying there long enough that the evening has darkened further. He hears nothing but the deceptive lull of sparse traffic prowling along the suburban estate. Someone drags a rubbish bin along a distant path.

The footsteps hadn't reached the back garden. He heard the man walking down the path and away. He must be long gone by now.

Reed wriggles out of the foliage and stands, stretching his spine. He still feels too wary of making noise to slap the dirt from his clothes. He creeps toward the corner of the house to peer along the path. With the way clear, he walks as casually yet covertly as he can to the safety of the street.

This is the only house where the bin hasn't been wheeled to the pavement edge; nothing suspicious about that if the real resident is away.

He remembers seeing the refuse sack and then the small case lying open beside it. He remembers what he saw inside the case – watches, a jumble of wrist watches, a mysterious collection, simultaneously mundane and strange.

His thoughts turn to Dan. Reed sets off running toward the side street where he left his van. He shouldn't have stayed so long.

****

Dan waits and watches. The night has grown cold. Marcus is hanging about at the darker side of the roof, but he is still there. Dan's leg prickles with pins and needles and his crouching knee is beginning to hurt. He could go and talk to Marcus or he could go inside.

Having watched Marcus for some time now, Dan doesn't feel like he is a danger to himself, just deathly calm and sad. Dan wonders. *Does he know I'm here?*

Then Marcus falls.

Not to the ground below, but to the floor; a sudden, soundless crumpling and a drop. He doesn't cry out. Dan jumps to his feet and his own leg nearly buckles. He races into the darkness where Marcus dropped like a stone.

He grapples in the shadows, aiming to help Marcus up.

Before he knows what has happened, Dan's arm is twisted painfully behind his back, forcing him onto his knees and his face to the ground. And then his arm breaks.

The adrenaline surge kills it for a moment but then: the pain, the pain, the pain.

Dan can hardly see through watering eyes.

The pain.

He hears scrabbling footsteps – not Marcus, but Reed. Reed's feet skid to a stop where Dan is lying. Reed helps him sit up and sees Dan cradling his limp limb.

Reed stands up and looks around. He imagines a shadowy figure slipping over the wall and disappearing across the rooftops into the night. He rushes to the edge of the roof, trying to catch sight of the assailant, then stumbles into Marcus on the floor.

Dan begins to moan.

Reed crouches and takes Marcus by the lapels, shaking him.

'Whatever this is, it's *your* doing!'

Marcus barely stirs.

Dan and Reed are sitting in a waiting area at the hospital. They are waiting for Dan's broken ulna to be set.

Lights shine relentlessly on rows of hard plastic chairs and the mottled lino covering the floor. Health professionals in colour-coded uniforms walk through the corridor between curtained bays and through heavy, fire-resistant doors. The clean surfaces and medical functionality contrast starkly with Reed's grubby clothes.

'Does it hurt?'

'Of course it fucking hurts.' Dan glowers at Reed. 'You didn't need to have come, you know.'

'I didn't want you to be alone.' Reed lowers his voice. 'What did you say happened?'

Dan glances around. A few other patients are waiting on the spread of chairs. A police officer is standing with some paramedics near the entrance. He hears the rubbery tread of another officer's boots as he shuffles by the nurses' station, talking to the staff. Their presence seems to be routine.

Dan gently shakes his head.

'He broke your arm!' Reed hisses, under his breath.

Dan looks at him. The police move, setting off the automatic door. One of them begins to communicate on his radio.

'I just want to speak to Marcus first, okay?' Dan whispers.

A worried-looking relative edges past the seats.

'What happened before I got there?' Reed asks, as soon as the woman has passed.

Dan looks toward the police outside.

'Come on, I saw everything else.'

Reed's green eyes look dark under the sharp lighting. He waits for an answer.

Dan tries to adjust his position but winces with pain. 'I think you should have stayed with Marcus. Are you sure he's okay?'

'Yes. Look, I made him stay in the shower until he seemed alert again. Got him to drink a ton of water. I even dried him off, got him in clean pyjamas and put him to bed.'

Dan purses his mouth. Reed expects him to make some joke about his parenting skills, but Dan doesn't speak. Reed looks all around the waiting area. It's not a busy night, but people are constantly moving about. A swishing curtain sounds from one of the bays.

'How could you let him get so drunk?' he asks quietly.

Dan doesn't say anything. His memory floods with the image of Marcus falling like a dead weight to the floor.

'You're going to have to tell them, Dan. There's a… hitman… on the loose.' Reed says the word 'hitman' even more quietly than the rest. It sounds ridiculous spoken out loud. Another time, Dan might have rolled his eyes, but he doesn't react. He just blinks, looking at the floor.

'If you really thought that, then you wouldn't have left Marcus, would you?'

'Marcus is sleeping like a baby in a locked house. *You're* the one who was attacked.'

The police officers come back inside to meet up with a security guard who has appeared. They all seem to know each other. Dan and Reed look at the floor.

'Well, weren't you?' Reed resumes, in a low, controlled voice. 'So... what happened?'

Dan sighs. It sounds more like a groan. 'I don't know. I want to talk to Marcus... What do *you* think is going on?'

'There was someone else there on the roof – I saw him getting away.'

Dan looks at Reed and arches an eyebrow. Reed leans forward, talking with the corner of his mouth.

'Well. Here's what we know: A big bag of money; watches – stopped at three, two...' He substitutes a wide-eyed nod for the number 'one'. 'A telephone number...' He adopts a meaningful expression. 'And, under what circumstances in the last, say, eight months, have you heard of someone dropping like a stone, falling into a deep sleep?'

Reeds eyes bore into Dan's.

'When I go back up there,' Reed whispers, 'I bet I find a dart...'

They become aware of a policeman standing nearby, at the vending machine, waiting for coffee to fill a disposable cup.

Reed stops talking. He's not sure how to describe the man he saw or anything he witnessed that make him sure that he's right. He shouldn't have kept that address to himself in the first place, could have done something sooner. Always too late to save the day.

The policeman's coffee is spurting pathetically into the polystyrene. When it stops, he takes it from the machine and then waits for a second coffee to pour. Reed begins to feel awkward, as if it is obvious that the reason they aren't talking is because of the policeman in earshot. He wonders how to break the silence.

After a few minutes, Dan is the one to speak. 'I think you should get back and look after Marcus.'

Reed tries to signal with his eyes that he has more to discuss but Dan directs a dismissive scowl at him. He doesn't want to hear it, whatever it is.

'And what about Karen and Zoya?' Dan says.

Reed's brow furrows and his mouth squashes into a line. 'Go on, you get off back to the guest house. It's pointless you waiting here. I'll call when they've patched me up,' Dan says. 'Pick me up in the morning.'

The policeman walks past, a coffee in each hand.

Reed looks at Dan, his face rumpled with concern. 'But, don't you think…' he begins, 'it was meant to be *you*?'

Dan remembers Marcus's face coming into focus as the endless kiss fell away. He remembers the tears in his eyes and the awful insistence that Dan leave. *Was he trying to protect him from something?* Could *someone else have been there?*

Dan's jaw tightens. Couldn't he, just for once, keep hold of the moment? Now, that wonderful, tumultuous, beautiful moment beneath the sunset has been snatched away by smothering questions – and the evening twisted into something else. He can believe that the accident was a drunken tussle, but everything lurches away from him at the suggestion that there was another dark figure cracking his bones.

He feels angry with Reed and fights to contain the emotion, frustrated by the impossibility of talking frankly, irritated by the fathom-deep pain in his arm.

His head begins to hurt too.

Mentally, he tries to shake off the impression that it had all been some kind of tragic goodbye kiss. He feels a rage welling up, deep inside him. He struggles to hold on to the memory of that moment; of the love flowing between them and the years of repression falling away.

Reed is still there, looking at him. He is about to say something else. 'I don't mind waiting with you.'

'Well, *I* do,' Dan says.

Reed stands up and leaves.

CHAPTER 42

By morning, Dan is sitting, waiting, near a different entrance in the hospital, beneath a sign pointing to 'Critical Care'. The exit is quiet and leads to a small pick-up bay. Distant ranks of cars recede to greyness in the car park beyond.

Dan looks at the day with bleary eyes. The skylights reveal a blank strip of clouds and there is the trace of dull thudding in the back of his head. The drag of the cast-heavy sling catches at hairs on the back of his neck.

He sits watching for the arrival of his lift. He feels empty and hungry and doesn't care.

He watches and waits.

A man on crutches walks past, accompanied by a woman. The automatic doors at the end of the foyer swish open as they pass outside, bringing a sigh of fresh air.

The woman talks to a waiting taxi driver and then helps to get the man and crutches into the back seat.

Dan is beyond thinking. His eyes follow the Volvo as it drives away. His gaze drifts down toward the floor tiles. He stares at the pattern for a while.

He rubs his eyes with his good hand and sits up straighter in the plastic seat. He cranes to see the traffic making its way along the approach road, eventually spotting what looks like Reed's camper van in the distance. He seems to be going the wrong way.

Dan leans his head back against the wall and closes his eyes, resolved to wait where he is.

The doors swish open and he hears the pad of rushing feet. He opens his eyes to discover Marcus standing before him and feels a sudden, sharp pang at seeing the man he loves.

Marcus is panting slightly, his face a mixture of elation and nervous excitement, his steps faltering as he pulls up from his dash.

'Marcus!'

'I've come to pick you up,' Marcus announces, his voice wavering slightly.

Dan swallows and looks beyond Marcus to the traffic outside. He spots the Porsche 911 pulled haphazardly into the kerb.

'Actually… Reed's out there – somewhere in the car park with his van…'

'I've brought the Carrera.' Marcus smiles uncertainly. 'Take you for another spin…?'

His sentence trails away. Marcus stands where he stopped speaking, just inside the foyer.

'Are you okay to drive?' Dan asks, 'I mean, last night you were…'

'I'm fine. Reed looked after me.'

Marcus nods but Dan just looks at him.

'Yeah, he made me drink water, stuck me in the shower and put me to bed. Wouldn't leave until I could answer his questions properly.'

'What questions?'

Marcus laughs. 'Art movements of the twentieth century.'

Dan raises an eyebrow. 'Is that the way the police test for drunk drivers now too?' he jokes. 'General knowledge quizzes? I'm going to have to swot up…'

Marcus smiles, then takes a couple of steps toward the seats. His face falls into sadness when he looks at Dan's plastered arm. He walks a couple more steps toward him and sits down in the next chair.

'No, I'm fine. I wasn't that drunk, I was just… upset.'

Dan considers the soft thud Marcus's body made on the rooftop last night when his body dropped to the floor. A sudden rush of cold sweat prickles his skin as he thinks about what happened after he fell.

'Marcus,' he begins, gently, 'what happened last night?'

They look at each other. The minutes seem to tick away. Marcus bites his lip then makes a shape with his mouth as if wrangling words that won't come out.

Dan cannot read his expression.

Does it mean that Marcus knows but won't tell him? Or that he can't figure out what's going on? It feels odd not being able to read him, the telepathy they share all gone. Dan feels an expansive distance growing between them, their closeness cooling on the air.

'You can tell me,' Dan says, unsure how best to respond.

Marcus's eyes seem to be brimming. 'I can't,' he says, softly.

They sit quietly together.

'Your arm!' Marcus says, loudly, remembering the injury. 'How did it happen? Shit. That's your writing arm too, isn't it?' His concern pours out in overflowing questions.

Dan watches Marcus closely as he talks. It looks like the broken arm has surprised and shaken him. *Does he not remember doing it? Wasn't it him? Doesn't he remember at all?*

Dan decides to trot out the same explanation he has grown accustomed to giving during his night in the hospital – but this time, he doesn't even try to make it sound convincing. 'I fell down the stairs.'

The words tumble flatly from Dan's mouth. He keeps watching Marcus for a response.

'Come on,' Marcus says, 'I'll take you home, or… we could go to the beach again, or somewhere else. We could take a trip…?'

Dan watches Marcus babbling, unsure what to think.

'There's something I want to ask you,' Marcus says.

Dan watches as Marcus looks up through the window to the shifting sky, his face lightened by a pulse from the weak sun. The foyer brightens momentarily. Dan subtly sweeps his head from side to side in gentle dissent.

'Ask me now.'

Marcus turns his gaze on him, looking like his mind has strayed far from thoughts of a day trip, his face now wild and serious at the same time.

'We always…' He tries again. 'Why can't…?' The sentence halts and his lips quiver.

Dan's throat feels dry.

What is Marcus asking him – this friend, this lover, with his sad, elated smile? Does he want a life with him, or a friend to prop him up or a distracting escape? Has Marcus forgotten the kiss all over again?

Dan notices Marcus's lips parted in almost breathless anticipation. It would be the easiest thing in the world to lean in and kiss him – soft and firm and forever – but he doesn't. It would also be too hard.

The unasked question floats between them still.

He doesn't know what Marcus means or what question to answer or how, even, to begin. Is Marcus asking for a future together or lamenting that it could never be?

As much as Dan is filled with impossible longing, swept away with the promise that Marcus's fluttering '*always*' might bring, there is also the sharp echo of his '*can't*', puncturing Dan's hopes.

The two men look at one another, frozen between an explanation and a kiss.

Marcus watches and waits. The faintest shadow of a soft cloud, drifting above, falls over his face. The echoes of that slight, suggested future fall away, sinking under that same old, familiar discomfort of unspoken love, like a ravenous hunger forever endured.

Of course, Marcus can't be thinking of a life of love and passion together, Dan realises. *Why would anyone want that with him?*

'It's been a really nice visit…' Dan says.

The polite, mundane sentence tails off. He sees the spark of something fading in Marcus's dark eyes; a trail growing cold. Then his friend's focus flickers away from his and the long, hopeful gaze is gone forever.

The foyer doors swish open and someone pauses in the doorway. Dan follows Marcus's gaze to see Reed standing there hesitantly, having spotted the two of them. He seems to think that Marcus might be sharing his secrets and doesn't want to interrupt, but it is too late for him to retreat.

The doors begin to close but Reed is standing in the way. They slide open again, then repeat the abortive closing, stuck in a strange rhythm, like a heartbeat running slow.

Dan and Marcus have both stood up. Reed tries to assess the situation. He sees the Porsche parked outside and looks from it to Marcus and Dan.

'Are you going with Marcus?' he says, eventually, when nobody speaks.

Dan shakes his head. 'No. We're not...' He doesn't finish the sentence.

'Thanks for putting me to bed last night, Reed,' Marcus says, walking toward the doors, 'I'm actually... I'm going somewhere else...'

Dan feels he is moving away too fast and trails after him. 'When will I see you?' he asks, hoping to anchor Marcus with some kind of plan.

Reed notes the desperate edge to Dan's voice.

'Tomorrow,' Marcus says, now hurrying out of the door.

Reed turns around to see Marcus opening his car door and Dan striding out of the exit.

'We could…' Dan calls after him.

Marcus looks back and flashes a weak smile.

They watch him disappear into the Porsche and drive off too fast.

Reed wonders if Marcus is drunk again but Dan only wonders where he is going. They stand there, long after the car has disappeared from view.

Reed looks at Dan, waiting to hear what he has learnt.

'Didn't you two talk?'

The next morning, Reed clambers out of bed and goes to the window. He grasps the limp fabric and gently tugs the curtains open, allowing the daylight to fall across his eyelids before taking in the new day.

Squinting, he wipes a crumbly speck of sleep from the corner of an eye and feels waves of tingling as the follicles of his legs bristle in the cold of the new day. The thin curtain crinkles in his clutch.

It is still early. The light of morning shows up tiny scratches in the glass. The soft sheets of his comfy bed are calling him back to nap in its cottony embrace, but he stands there, waking up.

He sees the dew-laden grasses shimmering in the daylight, as the shadow of the roofline slowly draws across the ground. Things come into focus. His gaze sweeps across the plain of tufty grass alighting on a shape nestled at the foot of the small slope – not far from the place where he lay looking with lonely longing at the stars.

He remembers Zoya and Glenda and their dawn therapy session, but this looks more like something blown off a roof. One of the terrace tables has been smashed to the paving and a couple of the chairs thrown out of place.

Reed rubs his eyes. From his vantage point, he sees the bulky figure of Dan darting outside. Dan runs across the terrace and dashes down the slope to the dark, still shape. He falls to the floor and thrusts his arms underneath it.

Only when Reed sees Dan cradling it, does the awful reality snap into place. Only when Dan holds it in this uniquely human way, does he see it for what it is – an unresponsive body. And he instantly knows *who* it is.

Without stopping for clothes or shoes, Reed tears himself away from the window and begins to run through the house. He shoots along the hallway and down the long set of stairs, skipping steps and leaping to the landings as he goes.

He bursts through the terrace door into the cold morning and the deathly stillness outside. Dan is now kneeling by the body, having let it fall back into the long grass. Reed stumbles down the slope toward him, wary of getting too close.

It can only be death, the way Dan is motionless, looking; the way he isn't shouting for an ambulance or trying to wake him up. Reed watches as Dan leans closer to Marcus's body and softly kisses him, for a few long seconds, on the cheek. Then Dan draws back to look.

Reed has never seen the expression on Dan's face before, but he understands what it is. It's the face of a person who knows that they are looking at someone they love for the very last time.

Then Dan tears himself away, pushes off up the slope to the terrace, past Reed, and into the house. And somehow, Reed knows, just knows, that Dan is out of there – into the city and away.

Reed takes a couple of steps toward the body, planting his bare feet carefully between the uneven tufts. Marcus looks like he is merely sleeping in the soft embrace of the grass. Reed steps closer. Now he can see the other side of Marcus's face, the side of his head, broken and bloody. Reed winces and averts his gaze before finding the ounce of bravery he needs to look back.

Marcus's eyes are closed – perhaps Dan closed them, putting his friend to bed in the grass.

Up close, there is a twist to his body that belies any sleep pose. Everything looks wrong. He doesn't look like Marcus anymore; all traces of life are gone. It isn't like the monuments and archives that endure after the fact. It's the gut-wrenching abjection of Marcus being not-Marcus, lying like an object on the ground.

This is the third dead person that Reed has seen – and two of them seemed to fall from the sky. He looks up to the roof slowly. A horrible question is dragging at the back of his mind: *Did he slip or was he pushed?*

It must be down to Reed to call the authorities, but he finds himself frozen, his feet growing icy in the grass.

CHAPTER 44

Reed closes the front door and flicks his storm-blown hair from his eyes. His feet feel leaden as he climbs the staircase. He approaches the parlour and wonders if there's been any news.

The door opens with a slight creak. Inside, the room is steeped in a smoky gloom and he sees that almost every seat has been taken. None of the people are Dan.

He answers those who look at him for a report, with a small shake of the head. Others stare at the floor, at their hands, or at nothing in particular. He can hear the wind whistling savagely outside.

Cameron sits hunched in one armchair, running his cravat through his fist over and over again. His hair has unslicked itself and hangs over his furrowed brow. Douglas and Alasdair Duncan-Fox sit next to each other on the sofa, exchanging occasional glances. Douglas has kicked off his shoes. Karen is sitting in the other armchair, still wearing her pyjamas. She is crying into her palm. Zoya perches on the arm of the chair, her hand laid comfortingly on Karen's back. Nobody is sitting in Catriona's elegant chair by the telephone table.

As Reed moves further into the room, Zoya is still watching him, concern dragging at her pallid face. She has tied her curls back and Reed notices that her eyes look puffy. He wants to take her in his arms.

'Do you know you are all sitting in the dark?' Reed says.

His query is mostly met with stifled sniffs and wet blinks but Zoya turns the standard lamp on. The orange glow illuminates the scene but fails to change the mood. On the coffee table, clenched tissues unfurl like blossoms.

'You didn't find him?' Zoya asks.

Karen looks up too.

'No,' Reed answers simply. He scans the group. 'Any news?' he ventures, quietly.

When nobody answers, Alasdair Duncan-Fox sits forward. 'No. There's no news,' he says. 'Catriona's still with the police and, well, there was an empty bottle of whisky on the roof...'

Douglas puts his head in his hands. It sounds like he is mumbling something about Catriona, but Reed can't be sure.

'I was here when they found that,' Reed says.

He had searched the roof terrace himself the morning before – after getting Dan home from the hospital – but didn't find any kind of tranquiliser dart. Even the whisky bottle that Dan had mentioned seeing had gone. The police found a different one today.

Alasdair unclasps his hands and forms them into a questioning gesture. 'No luck finding your friend, then?'

'No,' Reed confirms.

He has been driving around all day, searching. He massages his neck and Zoya catches his glance.

'He'll come home,' she says softly.

They look at one another, nodding.

Reed watches Alasdair tugging at his collar and loosening his bow tie. He wonders what the curator is doing here. Alasdair catches his glance.

'I was with… Douglas here… when we heard the news,' he explains, without being asked.

Reed almost asks what they were doing together but finds that he really doesn't care.

'Callum,' Douglas says, quietly but definitively, the word dropping softly into his lap.

They look at him.

'Callum,' he repeats, sitting up.

'Just call me Callum, Uncle Alasdair. After all, it is my real name.'

Douglas – or Callum – rubs his head vigorously as the information permeates everyone's grief. His rubbing leaves his hair sticking up wildly and he seems to sigh with relief.

'I… er…' Alasdair falters, his eyes looking warily at the young man, now revealed as his nephew.

'I thought I heard him call you by that name,' Zoya exclaims, 'that friend in the fancy dress place.'

'It's true,' Callum says. 'My real name's Callum Duncan-Fox.'

'Then why go by "Douglas Anderson"?' Karen asks, wiping her nose with a tissue.

'My ma's an Anderson,' he says.

'But why the false identity?' Reed asks.

'The crooked lawyer,' Cameron says, hoarsely, balling his silk cravat into his fist.

'It's not the boy's fault,' begins Alasdair, laying a hand on Callum's arm. 'My brother might be a lying–'

'… selfish,' Callum interjects.

'– criminal, but the lad shouldn't have to suffer because of his name.'

'Quite right,' Cameron responds, looking at Callum. 'I don't blame you in the slightest. Choose your own name, make your own way in the world.' He lets the crumpled cravat fall in front of him to the carpet where it lands without a sound.

Everyone seems to be reacting sympathetically. Even Karen is looking at Callum differently, and not just because of her swollen, reddened eyes.

Reed folds his arms, shifting his weight from foot to foot. 'And it's nothing to do with the history scam you two are pulling?'

Zoya looks at him with alarm.

'I'm sure I don't know what you mean,' Alasdair replies.

'I do,' Callum says, interrupting his uncle's lie. 'Just something for the business. A ghost story for the tourists, that's all. I thought Catriona might appreciate it.'

Alasdair looks to the floor, embarrassed, but Callum remains serene. He is looking at Catriona's empty chair.

'And it's my fault she had that car accident. Because I didn't take the Astra in for its MOT. Somebody should be with her.'

It's obvious that Callum thinks that that someone should be *him*.

The group fall quiet for a long time, considering what Catriona is going through, processing the information that Douglas is really Callum, shocked that Marcus is gone.

Reed remembers the last time he saw the artist; wild-eyed at the hospital. He remembers the last time he touched him; putting him to bed. Dan is the only other person who was there, and he doesn't seem to know or believe half of it – and Dan, also, isn't here.

Reed sits cross-legged on the floor instead of taking Catriona's seat – even though she is not the one who has died. He feels a warm hand on his shoulder and sees Zoya sitting down next to him on the floor. She rests her head against him, and he takes her hand.

'It's *my* fault,' Cameron says. They hear the sob catching on his breath. He composes himself effortfully. 'I see him all the time. I should have known he was... I didn't think he was *that* worried about... the work... I should have... We're friends.'

'No,' Karen says sternly. 'Our friend Fintan just died like that – and he *didn't* jump, he was *pushed.*'

Her eyes are wet and flashing. She rushes from the room, holding out a palm instructing Zoya not to follow.

Cameron is shaking his head. 'No, there was nobody else up on that roof.'

Reed stares at a tuft in the rug pile, remembering what he saw in the suburbs and what he thought he saw on the roof. But the man had been packing up and leaving, hadn't he?

The telephone rings but nobody dares pick it up. Zoya looks around the room and stands up but it stops before she can get to it. She perches on the empty chair.

'What if that was Dan?' she says.

Reed shakes his head. He doesn't feel like it was.

'Why weren't they together?' Cameron asks.

Only Reed looks at him with shock. 'Dan... and...?'

'Marcus, yes,' Cameron responds.

'You think they should have been a couple?' Reed says, confusion rumpling his long, pale face.

'Darling, they were in love with each other,' Cameron says. 'As plain as the nose on my old, queer face.' Cameron's voice sinks back into despondency. 'Too late now.'

Dan is standing by the window in his room. He is facing the cityscape and the sunny street outside, but his eyes aren't focussing on the view.

The stone setts gleam brightly outside. A passing car reflects a glancing beam of sunshine at the window. Dan doesn't even blink. His eyes stay dull and dry. The light flickers around the walls of the room and sparkles in the crystal glass of whisky in Reed's hand.

Reed is standing in the doorway, not knowing what to do or say. Zoya brushes past him into the room.

'Okay, I've got the scissors – if you want to get the shirt on over your cast?'

Dan doesn't respond to her question, doesn't move, doesn't speak.

He is wearing the same faded, grey Grateful Dead T-shirt. A smart shirt and jacket have been laid out on the bed, but not by Dan. The sling weighs heavy with his broken arm.

Zoya is still waiting for him to speak. Gradually, she looks around at Reed. He leans against the door frame.

'I don't think he wants to wear the shirt,' Reed says quietly.

She picks it up and thinks for a minute. 'No, I don't think he does, either.'

She lets it drop to the bed and puts the scissors down on the bedside table. Dan stares out of the window.

'Right,' Reed says, pushing himself off the doorframe with his hip, 'I'll go and fetch the van around.'

Zoya nods. Reed raises his voice to reach Dan's ears.

'Is there anything you want before we go? Dan?'

Dan doesn't answer.

'There's a drink here for you…' Reed holds out the small whisky he had poured to fortify his friend. 'I'll just leave it here for you.' He places the glass on the chest of drawers.

'I'll see you at the front door in a bit,' Reed continues, talking to Zoya, who nods.

As Reed walks out of the room, Zoya picks up the suit jacket from the bed. 'I'll help you get the jacket on,' she says.

She considers the logistics for a while. Dan doesn't even turn his head.

Zoya takes hold of Dan's left hand. It hangs like an inanimate object between her slim fingers. She lifts his heavy arm and begins to feed it through the sleeve of the jacket, standing on tiptoes on account of Dan's height. He doesn't even seem to notice.

Once she has the jacket on his left shoulder, she takes the other lapel and drapes it over his right, curving her arm around his back like an embrace. She lets her hand linger gently on his back.

***

Later, they are sitting on a park bench, Dan and Zoya, side by side. Reed is finding somewhere to leave the van. There are rustling trees dappling the sunlight and, beyond the gate, a view of the church across the road. Zoya can see a string of mourners going in.

She looks at Dan, still staring into a veiled future. He doesn't seem to notice the leaves and flowers or the pond, thick with reeds and teeming with life. Rushes pierce the water's edge.

'We don't have to wait for Reed, you know,' she says. 'He'll come into the church when he gets back.'

Dan doesn't respond. She takes this as his answer. He wants to sit there a while longer.

Beneath the sporadic rumble of vehicles on the road, she hears the chatter of wrens. She catches sight of one – a tiny brown speck flitting through the low bushes.

'Well,' she looks back toward the church, 'we've got lots of time yet.'

A pigeon walks around the bench.

'And… it's okay if you don't want to go,' she adds.

She looks again at Dan's face. His gaze is slowly drifting skywards. He is watching a small cloud floating across the blue, spring sky. There's still no real expression on his face. She observes him long enough to notice the momentary shadow cast over him as the cloud passes in front of the sun. His eyes are dry.

Zoya takes some very deep breaths. She is thinking how best to say something. It's important but might not come out right.

'I want to tell you something…' She studies the profile of his face. The gentlest breeze tugs at his hair. 'It's going to sound fucking trite, to be honest, and thousands wouldn't say it… or wouldn't say it to you right *now*…' She swallows. 'But it's important… and I don't know when I'll get another chance.'

She collects herself and her words and takes a couple more deep breaths. She spots a pair of ducks nestled in the reeds.

'The thing is… when my mum died… Dad told me something it took me years and years to understand.' She brushes a wriggling strand of hair from her face and tucks it behind an ear. 'I don't think I *could* understand it when he told me – because I was young and… because it just takes time.'

She watches the leaves of a bush rippling in the sunlight.

'But he meant it… and felt it – feels it *still*.' She turns to look at Dan who continues to stare blankly ahead. She rolls her eyes to the sky again. 'Fuck. This is going to sound like the worst platitude in the world.'

She takes another deep breath.

'Look it's not earth-shattering – just that Tennyson thing about love and loss – only that's not how my dad put it. *He* said that we don't only have to grieve for losing someone, but we can also be happy for having had them in our lives at all. And I get it now. I honestly do. And it doesn't matter about the words. People come and go from our lives – for all sorts of reasons, not just,' – she sighs – 'death.'

She looks at the shiny surface of the pond.

'And I *had* to say this to you now because the thing about love and loss is true. *I* feel it now. I really do.'

When she raises her head and turns to him again, she sees that Dan is looking at her now. Her babbled words, or their sentiment, have brought him back to the present moment. She scans his expression, looking from eye to eye.

'But you *were* together,' she says, interpreting his unspoken thoughts.

Dan is looking intently at her, but he doesn't say a word.

'You talked, you laughed, you shared everything about yourselves, you ate and drank and sang and danced together. You lived under the same roof. You got into and out of trouble together. You went places and made memories together...' Her words build momentum. She waves her hands around and looks to the sky. 'You had hours and days and *years* of knowing one another... You understood each other... You had affection... You had love!'

Her arms drop softly to the bench. She spots a distant cloud of her own.

Then she feels Dan's hand on hers. He squeezes and it feels warm.

Dan thinks of the kiss goodbye and that one summery, sensual night in Sicily when he and Marcus had made love.

*****

After the service, they follow the coffin to the grave. Dan has made it known that he didn't want Zoya and Reed babysitting him by evading their concern and striding off.

Everyone is there: Karen, Cameron, Rab, Muriel, Callum, Alasdair and, of course, Catriona. She is managing to look elegant in dark glasses, coat and dress, despite the fractured fibula and the crutch and the life-shattering shock of her husband's death.

There are many other mourners clustering by the graveside, many of them Dan has never met. He faintly registers their low conversation and the soft scrape of shined boots on dry cobbles as they approach the cut of deep, dark earth.

Glenda has arrived from Ireland and Zoya and Reed walk beside her. She smiles to see them holding hands.

Dan is squinting. The sun is shining, and nothing feels right.

The brightness hurts his tired eyes that have no more tears to give. He stops walking. With his working arm he reaches into a jacket pocket to retrieve his sunglasses but has difficulty opening them with one hand.

Then Catriona is by his side. She takes the sunglasses, folds out the arms and helps Dan to put them on. They acknowledge one another with a calm, wordless gaze. The plaster cast on her leg seems so cumbersome on her small frame. Dan sees that the crutch she has propped up is about to slip down the stone wall. He manages to catch it before it falls to the ground.

As he hands it back to her with his good arm, she instead slips her arm through the crook of his. Together they make their way toward the long, dark hole in the ground.

CHAPTER 46

Reed and Zoya step from the bright glare of the daytime into the sombre shadows of the hall. Dan is with them, his footsteps following quietly across the tiles.

Walking into the guest lounge, they see bunches of black-clad mourners standing around with glasses and plates. Dan doesn't seem to notice anyone. He makes for the armchair by the window, sits down and stares ahead.

Reed and Zoya exchange a look. They don't know what to do.

Glenda joins them.

'I'm so sorry,' Zoya says.

Glenda gives her a heartfelt hug. Then she moves to Reed, pulling his awkward frame into another. He locks wide eyes with Zoya over Glenda's head.

Glenda draws back. 'Thank you. How are you two holding up?'

Zoya attempts to form words. Glenda regards her with soft, bright eyes, giving her space to think.

'It's such a horrible accident,' Zoya says. 'Do you think he was up there thinking about Fintan?'

'Had you known him a long time?' Reed asks.

'Fintan? Goodness, all his life. I was his godmother. Marcus – since they were at university together.'

She glances to the corner. 'And Dan there.'

He is staring out of the tall window.

Mourners glide glacially around him, a kaleidoscope of shadows with respectfully hushed, velvet voices.

'He isn't talking,' Zoya says.

Glenda considers him. 'He doesn't have to,' she says gently.

'Were you his therapist?' Reed asks.

Zoya looks at him strangely.

'Dan?'

'No, Marcus,' he answers.

'Actually, I was.'

Zoya is surprised. 'Are you meant to be telling us this?'

Glenda shakes her head, causing her hair to sway. 'I don't care, so I don't. I have some letters Marcus wrote – as part of his therapy – so *everyone* will know then.'

'You're going to give them out?' Reed asks, frowning.

Glenda looks from Reed to Zoya and back again. 'Marcus was intending to deliver them,' she says, simply, 'but now he'll never get the chance.'

'Is it ethical?' Zoya asks.

Glenda lays a hand on Zoya's shoulder. Her touch is feather-light. 'Some things are too important to remain se-cret. Besides, it *is* what he wanted – he was just working up the courage to see it through.'

They think about what she is saying without responding.

'Will you excuse me?' Glenda continues. 'I want to talk to Karen.' She smiles and crosses the room.

'Like the Lion,' Reed says.

'I'm sorry?' Zoya queries, confused.

'The Cowardly Lion. Like the photograph. It was the Cowardly Lion that wanted courage.'

Zoya tilts her head up at him. 'I never had you down as a *Wizard of Oz* fan.'

'But… you know I like old films.'

'Yeah, the black-and-white ones…'

A smile plays at the corners of his eyes. 'I have my technicolour moments…'

Zoya thinks for a minute, picturing the photograph and remembering which character Dan had been.

'So, what was it that the Tin Man wanted?' she asks.

Reed's expression falls as he takes in his friend by the window – a lonely void at the edge of the gathering. He looks back to Zoya, meeting her questioning gaze.

'A heart.'

***

Later, half the mourners have gone, and wet rings pattern the furniture. Dan remains sitting in his chair.

Reed finds himself in a circle that includes Glenda, Cameron, Alasdair and others. Cameron is getting something off his chest. His face looks pink and sweaty.

'All I'm saying is, dear man, it's the opposite – Marcus was making his best art when he was *happy* and, when he *wasn't* in such a good place, well, he found creating tough…'

Alasdair decides to pipe up. 'So, what was the root cause of his malaise, then? If not the soul of the tortured artist? Was he' – Alasdair's gaze sweeps around the circle – 'living a double life?'

'Here we go,' barks Cameron, waving his glass in gesture.

Alasdair plays with his tie. 'But for a fellow to drunkenly stumble off a rooftop... Something must have been gnawing away at him.'

Reed's eyes flicker straight back to Cameron.

'But not necessarily his sexuality,' Cameron says, curtly.

'No, it wasn't that at all,' Glenda asserts. 'Marcus never had a problem with who he was in that respect, and neither did anyone around him.'

Alasdair looks mildly surprised.

'You might be getting it confused with the movies, dear,' Cameron says, loosely, but with a pointed stare. 'Where the homo has to die in the end.'

Alasdair has the sense to look at his feet. Cameron walks away.

Reed sees Zoya returning with plates of food from the buffet. She sets one down on the small table besides Dan's chair. He doesn't acknowledge her. The drink they placed there earlier remains untouched.

Reed meets her in the middle of the room and takes a vol-au-vent, thanking her with a quick smile. Karen appears besides them but shakes her head at the offer of food.

'How are you?' Zoya asks.

Karen's eyes widen with the darkest of darkly comedic stares. 'Just don't let Dan go on any rooftops anytime soon, or that will be the set!'

Her words come out like a crass joke, but they know she means it.

Zoya picks a tiny piece of quiche from the plate she is sharing with Reed. 'Any news from Dublin?' she asks, before taking a bite.

'Yes. They got them,' Karen answers, spitting out the words. 'The bastards.'

Zoya swallows. 'Well, that's' – she searches for the right word but there isn't one – 'good.'

'Do they know how it… came about?' Reed asks.

'Not really.' Karen shakes her head.

'The perpetrators thought Fintan was someone else.'

'But how…?' Zoya begins.

Karen pulls a wide-eyed expression. 'Maybe we'll never know.'

Karen looks around the room. Reed slips his arm around Zoya's shoulder. Then they follow Karen's gaze. She has spotted someone coming down the stairs.

'Hey Douglas!' she calls. 'Er… *Callum*!'

She indicates that he join them with a jerk of her head. He walks over.

'What *do* we call you now?' Karen asks.

'Callum's fine,' he says.

'Why are you skulking in the hallway? Come talk to us for a while.'

He flexes on the balls of his feet and glances back to the darkness of the stairs. 'Catriona's in her bedroom,' he explains. 'Wants to be alone for a while – but I'm… well, I'm here if she needs anything.'

They imagine what she must be going through.

***

Later still, the guest house is quieter. Most of the visitors have gone, leaving only a select group. Glenda is standing in the middle of the lounge, having gathered Karen, Cameron, Rab and Muriel on the chairs. Reed and Zoya are there too, perching on a small bench at the back of the room. Dan forms part of the circle only by default, having never moved from his chair. An empty seat has been left for Catriona, but she hasn't left the bedroom.

Glenda is holding several letters, clutched preciously to her chest. She watches expectantly as Callum enters from the hall. In answer to her unspoken question, he simply shakes his head.

'Right,' Glenda says. 'So.'

Everyone looks at her.

'A part of my therapeutic process is to get clients to the stage of writing really honest letters to the people in their life.'

They eye the envelopes in her clutch. Some seem thicker than others. Glenda's gaze sweeps the group. The usual glint sparkles in her eye though today it could be the beginnings of a tear.

'Some of you may be thinking that I shouldn't be giving these letters to you – because Marcus isn't here, himself, to tell us it is what he wanted.'

Cameron raises his arms to support the back of his head on interlaced fingers. He is trying to contain a conflicting mixture of emotions, his expression stuck somewhere between concerned and sad.

'But, you know, I *am* going to deliver them for him,' Glenda says, 'because I *know* he was resolved to do it.'

Karen looks sceptical. Muriel sniffles and Rab strokes her arm. Glenda's slight frame swells with a large intake of breath.

'And, you know, it's my *gift* to Marcus to be his final piece of courage and make something he wanted to happen come into being.' She inhales again. 'Okay. Douglas – Callum, I should say – this one is for Trinny.'

She picks out the thickest envelope and holds it out. Callum walks forward to collect it.

'And this one is for you,' she tells him, handing over a second letter.

He takes both letters and walks slowly out of the room. He has a weighty delivery to make.

'Here's yours… and yours… and yours…' she says handing letters to Rab and Muriel, then Cameron, then Karen.

Rab and Muriel take their letter respectfully and hold one another, looking at it. Cameron stands up and immediately begins ripping open his envelope and pacing the room. Karen sits there, clutching her envelope tightly, almost crumpling it with her hands.

Glenda takes a deep breath. 'And this last letter is for me,' she says, holding it in both hands, studying Marcus's distinctive handwriting apprehensively.

Reed and Zoya stop watching everyone so intently, wondering if they should really make themselves scarce.

Then Dan slowly stands up. They haven't seen him move all afternoon. He walks past them out of the lounge, through the breakfast room and toward the back stairs.

They look at one another, then rise and follow him, leaving the others to their letters.

As they reach the top floor, they find Dan already halfway through the passage that leads to the roof. Turning to close the door behind him, Dan sees them; worried and hesitant to follow. He looks each of them in the eye and then slowly and intentionally closes the door. They can tell from his expression that he is sending them a message – *don't follow me* – and he means it.

He slots the creaking door into its frame.

Zoya turns her face to Reed's. 'Do you think he'll be okay up there?'

They stare hard at one another, searching for the answer to their worries deep in one another's eyes.

'I think he just wants to be alone,' Reed says finally.

They stand on the landing, feeling uncertain, holding hands and looking at the door.

'Do you think it's because he didn't get a letter?' Zoya asks.

Reed taps a squeeze on her hand with his fingers. 'Come on, I've just remembered something.' He leads her down the stairs again and takes her into Marcus's study.

Reed pulls on one of the desk drawers, but it remains stuck. 'It was in here.'

He holds it firmly and yanks the drawer again, this time breaking the lock. Zoya knows he'll have his reasons but is hoping, wide-eyed, that they are good.

Karen comes into the study. She had taken her letter to the parlour to read. 'Are yous two breaking things in here?'

Zoya notices that Karen has put her letter from Marcus in the top pocket of her black jacket, perhaps unopened still.

Reed is rifling through the opened drawer. He retrieves a battered envelope. 'You might want to read this one too…' he says.

'How did you…?'

Zoya, meanwhile, has taken the wrinkled envelope from Reed's hand and is examining it. The envelope remains intact. 'It's from Dublin,' she says.

She holds it out for Karen, who accepts it with a shaking hand. 'Oh, my God! I remember this!' she says. 'I was here when it arrived. Right after we got back from the funeral – it was waiting for us. For Marcus. But…' Karen goes quiet.

'He couldn't face reading it?' Zoya suggests.

'No, not then.'

Reed looks from one to the other. 'And he *can't* now.'

Zoya knows this is Reed's way of urging Karen to open it, even though it wasn't addressed to her. He leans back against the wall of the study to watch. Karen contemplates the envelope some more.

'You should read it,' Zoya says.

'*Someone* should…' adds Reed.

Karen looks at them, pausing to think, and then decides that, yes, she will. She slips her finger under the flap and rips it open with a jagged tear.

***

Soon, they are sitting at the table in the family kitchen upstairs; Karen, Zoya and Reed. The letter from Dublin lies spread out on the table. They are staring at it, although they are already familiar with what it says.

They sit, digesting the contents.

'So, that's it,' Reed says, the tone of his voice settling somewhere between incredulous and underwhelmed.

Zoya feels the need to summarise what they have learnt – one more time. 'He just answered a note meant for someone else and then a few days later he was dead.'

Karen shivers slightly.

'And he used to do that sort of thing?' Zoya questions. 'Why?'

Karen shakes her head and shrugs. 'I don't know. I've never understood it. Because he was a canny fella as he was.'

'Well,' Reed begins, 'there was all that stuff about how he thought there might be some money in it.' He points to a section of the letter. 'He was promising to pay Marcus back.'

'If only he hadn't met them,' Zoya says sadly.

'If only Fintan had had some fucking sense,' Karen replies. She calms down again. 'I don't know how to feel about this.' She looks from Zoya to Reed for a clue. 'It's like he's still here, for a moment. I can hear his voice coming off the page.'

Zoya puts a hand on Karen's arm. 'Are you alright?'

'I don't know about that.'

Karen pushes the chair back and stands up. She crosses to the doorway. 'I'm just going to my room for a while.' She pats the jacket pocket with the envelope. It looks like she's placing her hand on her heart. 'I've got another letter to read.'

She disappears down the landing to her bedroom and they hear the sound of her door closing.

Zoya and Reed are left alone in the kitchen. Their eyes meet again. They hold hands across the table.

'At least they've got *some* closure now,' Zoya says. 'About what happened to Fintan, at least.'

'Do you think it's better for people to know things like that?'

'Than to wonder forever? Yes, I do.'

Reed looks pensive, almost pained. 'But what if–'

He sees Zoya place a finger to her lips. He follows her gaze to the landing, seeing Catriona through the doorway, climbing the stairs. She is holding a parcel wrapped in brown paper and her letter from Marcus, the pages bunched in her grip. She sees them in the kitchen and approaches – close enough for them to hear her parched, feeble voice but remaining in the shadow of the landing. She looks as drained and frail as they'd imagined she would.

'Where's Dan?' she asks.

Zoya swallows, ready to reply. 'He's…' She gestures upwards, slowly, with a pointing finger. She couldn't bring herself to say the word 'roof' to Marcus's widow out loud.

Catriona closes her eyes and nods once to show she understands. Nevertheless, she retains her composure and places the package on the narrow table that stands by the small wooden door.

'He wanted Dan to have this,' she says.

She turns and walks back down the stairs.

Reed and Zoya wait for the shadow of her presence to fade before talking but, as they relax, they hear the wooden handle turn and the hinges creak.

They move into the hall.

Dan is standing, staring at the parcel. The sight of something the size and shape of a painting is clearly having an emotional effect. The object seems to hold power over him.

Reed clears his throat. 'That's something that Marcus wanted you to have. Catriona left it there for you.'

'I think it was mentioned in her letter, maybe…' Zoya adds softly.

Dan stands looking at it and not speaking. He doesn't notice Zoya lean into Reed's shoulder, turning her face away and burying her brimming tears in his shirt. Reed curls an arm around her. Seeing Dan like this *is* hard to take.

Dan edges away, leaving the parcel untouched where it is. He walks slowly down the stairs.

'I can't stand it,' Zoya says, when Dan has gone, lifting her face to Reed's.

They squeeze one another, smothering the pain of it all, emerging from the embrace in an emotional kiss.

***

At the foot of the staircase, a wedge of light illuminates Dan's face in the shadows. He sees that Catriona is holding the bedroom door ajar; her face, at first a sliver, slowly revealed as she opens the door. They look at one another with sad eyes.

***

Upstairs at the far end of the landing, Reed and Zoya slip quietly into his room. The door closes gently behind them as they disappear inside.

***

At the door to Marcus and Catriona's room, she steps slowly backwards, and Dan, wordlessly, follows her in.

<h1 style="text-align:center">CHAPTER 47</h1>

The morning comes and Reed wakes up in a soft, warm bed. The cotton cools at the outer reaches of his searching fingertips. He rolls across the wrinkled sheets toward Zoya, but she is not there. On the pillow, there is only a crumpled empty space that smells of her hair – and a note.

A thin crack of morning light shines between the curtains, pointing to the note. He reaches for it.

'*Dear Reed,*' it begins.

He squeezes his eyes closed. The formality is not a good sign. He opens one eye and then the other. Zoya's handwriting swims into place.

*Thank you for yesterday and for yester*night *– but, as you will have realised, I had to go. I can't help thinking about what you told me last night. I don't know, either, whether it is worse for Catriona to think that Marcus died in a stupid and horrible accident or whether it is worse for her to think he killed himself. But I can't stay around to be part of a lie. I won't be able to look her in the eye in the morning, so I had to leave tonight.*

And if I stay now, and learn to rely on you, then I might never be able to leave.

Don't wait for me. I have to stretch my wings for a while.

Please look after Dan.

I love you, Zoya.

Reed lays the paper down and contemplates the rays of light falling through the drapes. This isn't the tender, loving morning he had anticipated, but Zoya's leaving somehow doesn't shock him. He can understand it.

They had loved and comforted one another, and found a connection stronger than before. They had whispered across the pillows, their secret, fragile thoughts. She thought Reed's version of events was far-fetched, but she had listened all the same. If Marcus had paid someone to kill him, was it right for Catriona not to know? But, if he couldn't prove anything, and Marcus died a different death a different day, was it wrong to put the idea in her head?

He had eventually seen the woman who really lives in that house: the rightful resident, leaving home and getting into her pink car; safe and sound and oblivious. And, having seen her alive and well, he could now sleep easier in his bed.

Reed throws off the covers and his bare feet find the carpet. Zoya told him she loves him, at least.

He reaches up to open the curtains, letting the soft glow of the still morning warm his body. Beyond the slide of the curtain rail, there is not a sound.

Only today does he notice that, far beyond the city, he can see the distant hills.

He pulls on underwear, reaches for a pair of jeans and finds a clean T-shirt in the drawer. Then, slowly, he makes the bed, smoothing out the sheets and taking up Zoya's note again.

On the landing, he sees her room unlocked and gently pushes the door. It is no surprise that all her things are gone. The guest room is a mirror-twin of Reed's, except it has been vacated. The wardrobe door hangs open, showing its empty rail. He makes out the shallow trail of a suitcase dragged across the carpet. It disappears by his feet.

He tears off the bottom strip of her letter – the part that says *'I love you'* – and puts it in his wallet. Then, he screws up the rest of the note into a tight, tiny ball. He will dispose of it sometime and someplace else – when it is safe from prying eyes and wounded hearts.

He thinks it is a noble secret to keep.

He ambles along the corridor, finding the house filled with a serene lull. In comparison to the wake yesterday, the place feels empty, but he knows that it is not. The others must all be fast asleep. It should do everyone good.

This morning, his shoulder manages to avoid the print on the wall, the one he left pushed out of place. He stops to look at it, noticing for the first time that it is a photograph of a ballerina. He takes hold of the frame and straightens it against the wall. The dancer is Catriona and she looks happy and strong.

He pauses at the family kitchen. Nobody is about. He continues, past the table with its mystery package, past the small wooden door to the roof, and walks, step by step, down the back stairs to the floor below.

Of course he will look after Dan.

Walking soundlessly through the household, Reed feels like a friendly ghost.

In the dreaming, it often feels like *he* is the one haunted by the traces and intrusions of another dimension but, on this soft, golden morning, he feels like a phantom become flesh, finding his place in the waking world.

At the bottom of the small staircase he notices that Catriona's door is ajar. He sees dark shapes on the bed beyond and shuffles to the gap for a closer look.

Catriona is sleeping on the bed, her fair hair splayed out on the pillow, and the person she is cuddling is his curly-haired, broken-armed friend.

Dan is tucked up with Catriona beneath a tangled sheet. His cast remains in its sling and he is wearing the Grateful Dead shirt. From the look of Catriona's shoulder, she looks to be wearing her funeral dress. They must have fallen asleep like this – in the place where they talked and cried and found a friend.

Reed looks at the peaceful scene, understanding how much Catriona must be in need of that sleep.

He considers her face, half buried in the pillow, relaxed and open and young.

He sees Dan's blue eyes regarding him. His friend is awake.

Slowly and gently, Dan untangles himself, sliding his leg, then body, out of the bed. Once he has freed his good arm, he puts a finger to his lips and then points upstairs. Reed nods and creeps away.

He climbs the stairs again and then settles in the small kitchen on a chair, waiting for Dan.

Dan appears upstairs a few minutes later. He looks rested and pink. Although Dan hasn't said a word yet, the ashen silence he had been carrying with him for so many days seems to have vanished overnight.

Dan pauses at the landing table and reaches toward the package. He almost cannot touch it. Then, he carefully picks it up. He walks into the kitchen, looking at it with a furrowed brow. Reed watches as he places it on the table uncertainly. After a few minutes, Dan stops looking at the brown paper and pulls a chair out for himself.

Reed decides to try a question. 'What's that?' he asks, meaning the parcel.

Dan doesn't answer but looks out of the tall, bright window, blinking a couple of times.

'Want some breakfast?' Reed asks, leaping into action and finding a frying pan.

Dan's expression seems to say 'yes'.

Reed busies himself cooking them a breakfast of bacon sandwiches and coffee. He looks down to the smooth sea of grass in the garden, innocent again today.

He finds some plates and begins buttering the bread as the meat sizzles. Although they don't converse, the mood feels comfortable and calm. He boils the kettle for their coffee as Dan sits, happy enough to be looked after.

They sit elbow to elbow at the table corner, eating the butties and raising mugs of steaming coffee to their mouths. Reed is pleased to see Dan eating with gusto, despite the broken arm, hungrily biting into the sauce-oozing sandwich and getting grease on his chin.

Dan pushes his empty plate away with a grateful smile. Reed picks up the dirty crockery and begins to run water into the sink, squeezing washing-up liquid into it. A couple of tiny bubbles fly up into the air.

'Zoya's gone, hasn't she?' Dan says.

Reed turns back to face him and nods. 'I think she had to,' he replies, and smiles. 'Told me to look after you – so I am.'

'You don't seem so glum about her leaving this time,' Dan says.

Reed shuts off the tap and turns around fully, leaning against the unit. 'You know what she once told me? "Don't let the past define the future." I didn't get it then, but now I do.'

Dan raises an eyebrow, signalling that he is impressed. 'She knows some things, that one,' he says.

They contemplate the statement. Then Reed notices that Dan's eyes have strayed to the packaged painting at the end of the table. Reed folds his arms across his chest – hugging himself in proxy of the embrace he wants to give Dan.

'He knew you loved him,' Reed says.

He watches Dan's head begin to bob in a small nod, which grows and grows. His eyes stay on the parcel and his nodding swells.

Reed turns back to the sink and sets the tap running again. He drops their greasy, sauce-smeared plates into the warm bubbles and locates the sponge.

'We can take our time,' Reed says, brightly, 'you know, driving home. It takes – what? – six weeks for a broken bone to heal? We can… see where the fancy takes us. Stop off at a few places. Even go to Stonehenge?'

When Reed turns around to check Dan's reaction, he sees his friend smiling a warm smile.

'Well, I've had the spin but not the road trip. Are you sure there'll be enough room for both of us?'

'It is possible to share a bed with a friend, you know,' Reed says, quoting Dan.

Dan looks again at the parcel and lays a hand on the paper wrapping. Reed continues to wash the pots in the sink, dunking the mugs into the water with a plop.

'Trinny said this had been under their bed all along, apparently. For years and years. She's never seen it unwrapped.'

Reed's movements slow as he listens, and Dan's voice continues behind his back.

'It was *Trinny* who invited me here,' Dan is saying. 'She said…' His words catch and the voice runs out of strength. 'She said,' – he resumes the thread, slowly piecing his sentence together – 'she thought… that if Marcus and I could… get together… then he might finally be…'

'Happy' is the only word that could have finished Dan's sentence, Reed thinks. But the darkness running through Marcus must have been deeper than love. If only he could have talked about it.

He abandons the washing up and wheels around to give Dan his full attention. He sees Dan's eyes, watery now. If only Dan could have felt worthy of all that love.

Dan clears his throat. 'Listen, man… Do you mind if…?'

Reed quickly dries his hands on the tea towel and tosses it onto the side. 'Of course, man.'

He doesn't need further instruction and makes his way to the kitchen door. 'I'm here if…'

Reed doesn't need to finish his sentence either. He knows that Dan understands. Reed sees Dan's head nodding again and leaves him alone with the package.

When Reed's footsteps have retreated out of earshot, Dan readies himself with a deep breath. He places his good hand on the edge of the package, feeling the framed canvas beneath.

He breathes again and pulls the painting toward him, staring at the blank wrapping for a long time. In a quick movement, he tears into the folds of the paper. His heart beats fast.

What he couldn't put into words, if someone asked him, is just how much seeing Marcus's work is like seeing the man himself. Dan doesn't know if he can take it, but is curious – no, *compelled*.

He couldn't have looked at it, last night. No way in the world. But today, something is different. Now or never. And because it is Marcus – 'never' would *never* do.

Dan peels off the remaining wrapping and holds the painting, its backing toward him. He summons the final

drops of bravery to look at it and turns the canvas over –
but, at the last minute, can't help closing his eyes. He takes
another deep breath, eyelids still squeezed shut. *Surprise
me.*

There it is, as he knew it would be – the portrait Marcus
painted of *him*, that glorious day on the Palermo roof.

He rests it on the table.

There he stands, a younger man. He remembers that
wide-lapelled shirt.

After briefly studying his own image, Dan's focus
dives into the paintwork: the brushstrokes, the movement,
the finger-smudges of Marcus's physical touch.

He follows the swirls and dashes and caresses of colour
that Marcus used to form the image of him – the solidity of
his shoulder, twists of his hair, the tanning flush on his skin.
Gently, he touches the daubs of paint, unable any longer to
touch *him*. He traces the detailed brushwork in the shadow
of the sitter's neck, *his* neck, and it all mingles in memory
with the touch of the real man on his actual skin.

Pulling back before emotion overwhelms him, Dan
considers the depicted image again. He looks at the figure
conjured before him; his younger self, transported through
time. He sees how he had looked that day, *to Marcus*, as
they spent the day together on that roof under the exotic,
summery sun.

This is who he was to Marcus: reluctant to be looked
at, but also happy and comfortable being with the man he
loves. The picture is so simple, so obvious, so him – and
so *them*.

He notices the reflection in portrait-Dan's mirrored sunglasses. He leans closer to examine it, holding his breath.

The image of the artist reflected in the sunglasses has been rendered through clever perspective play. It's not easy for Dan to look at it now, yet he can't tear his gaze away.

There Marcus is, his tan skin glowing. He is flourishing a paintbrush and looking at his subject with an artist's intense gaze, yet he is evidently also happily listening to Dan talk. Dan recognises that grin and hopes to see it in his dreams forever; Marcus looking happy.

He peers even closer and sees yet another painted reflection captured by Marcus's gold aviators. And again; an infinite regression of reflections suggested by finer and finer touches of paint.

Dan falls into the painting. It becomes impossible to separate the layers of reflected reflections, fused as they become in a blob of colour; a vanishing point – not to the horizon, but into oneness; merging that moment in time with this.

The painting becomes a time portal between the world of Dan's memory and the monumental presence of the artefact in his hand; a magical conduit between the life they shared and the ongoing feelings that Dan will forever carry alone; the infinite regression and progression of love.

CHAPTER 48

Outside the guest house, Dan looks up to the window and smiles. Catriona is there, a still figure in the parlour watching him in the street below. Dan winks and she reveals a small smile.

Birds are returning from Africa and filling sunny gardens with song. Purple blossoms embellish a wisteria down the road and Dan realises that the calendar has flipped forward into May. A May that's cool with North Sea breezes, but he can sense the swell of summer all the same.

Reed and Karen each place luggage on the stone flags. She fixes Dan with her gaze.

'So, you're off then?' Dan asks her.

'Yep,' Karen replies. 'First my holiday' – she turns to Reed – 'I'm actually going to France this time. And then detective school. Turns out they actually *want* more women to join up. WPC for a couple of years, then…' She raises her eyebrows, connoting a sense of 'we'll see'.

'I hope–' Dan begins, about to wish her well.

'What's *your* dream, Dan?' she asks, cutting him off.

He opens his mouth slightly.

'You should really go for it,' she says, '*when* you know what it is.'

They look at one another, readying themselves for a hug. She flings herself toward him but manages to be careful of his broken arm. Dan scoops her up. When he sets her back down on the pavement, there is some moist-eyed blinking on both sides.

'Take care,' Dan says eventually. The words seem more meaningful, in the circumstances. 'It's been…' he continues – but the sentence never ends.

'Hasn't it?' Karen replies, nodding and shifting her feet on the pavement.

'At least I got to hang out with you again,' Dan says, 'despite… everything.'

Karen turns toward Reed. 'You *will* look after him, won't you?'

Reed smiles and picks up one of Dan's bags. 'We've got everything we need,' he replies, jerking his head demonstrably toward his van.

There, by the kerb, is the Neptune Blue camper van, already packed with most of Dan's luggage. Reed always travels light.

He is excited to be reunited with his van again but thinks he is keeping it under wraps. Reed carries Dan's bag to the vehicle and stows it inside.

'So, you're finally taking a holiday?' Karen asks.

'Well, maybe a few detours on the way home. Not so much the A to B.'

Reed re-joins them and picks up the final piece of luggage – Dan's case of paranormal investigator kit. 'Dan's got some recuperating to do,' he says.

The ever-threatening ghost of a sad mood flickers over them for a second as they think about their departed friends.

'Right,' Karen says, breaking the moment, 'I'm going to get moving.'

She picks up her own bag and slings it on the passenger seat of her heavily laden Polo. As she walks out into the cobbled road to open the car door, she looks up and sees Catriona waving her off, wearing a sad smile. Reed and Dan see her too.

Callum walks into the frame, handing Trinny a coffee in a gilt-edged cup. He raises a hand to wave them off and wish them all well. He and Trinny seem so comfortable together, side by side at the window, holding their matching cups.

Once more, Dan and Trinny's eyes lock. Their mirrored expressions seem to say so much.

He drags himself away and makes for the van. Karen is turning her car around and beeping her horn goodbye. He waves until her Polo disappears around the corner at the end of the road.

A dark-blue Espace turns in. The small people carrier pulls up opposite the guest house and a few familiar faces pile out. First is Gregor, sporting a pink seahorse sweater, then Keith, wearing a warm smile. Next comes Jim, strolling toward the van. He is holding not the usual mug of tea, but the hand of Sally – a beautiful woman with jaunty blue pigtails decorated with tiny black bats.

Dan walks across to see them. They meet in the middle of the street.

'Come to see me off?'

Keith laughs warmly. 'Just making sure you leave town.'

Dan eyes his cheeky expression and the two men share a laugh.

'No, the opposite really,' Gregor says in his literal way. He looks healthier out of doors. 'We wanted to catch you,' he explains, 'before you left.'

Jim nods. 'We've got a job for you. Oh, you remember Sally?' he says.

'Hi, Sally.'

She raises her hand in a little wave. 'Hi, Dan. I'm so sorry for your loss.'

Dan nods, acknowledging the sentiment. 'So, what is it?' he asks Jim.

'Yeah, we're planning an investigation up in... oh, *I'm* chapter co-ordinator now,' Jim says.

'The boss?' Dan asks.

'Yep,' Keith says. 'Time for some changes.' He seems happy about it, like perhaps it was even his idea.

'So,' Gregor says, wanting to get back to business and spit the proposal out. 'It's your basic new-house effect haunting up by Kirkaldy, except it's...' His description trails off as he hears Dan decline.

'No, thanks. Anyway, you realise I'm kind of out of action?' Dan strokes his plastered arm in the sling.

'No need to write,' Keith says. 'We just respect your experiment design and data-collection expertise. Might be a good article in it?' He raises an eyebrow, temptingly.

'Listen. Thanks – I really appreciate it. Maybe we can work together some other time, but Reed and I have got plans – or actually – *no* plans.' He says it emphatically enough that they understand what he means.

Reed is standing, arms casually folded, leaning against the van. 'We're going to follow our noses, do some sight-seeing,' he calls.

'Not like you, Dan?' Jim observes matter-of-factly but with a friendly frown.

'Well,' – Dan shrugs slightly with his good shoulder – 'it *might* be.'

'Okay, well,' Keith says brightly, reaching out to shake Dan's hand. He swaps his right for his left palm on account of Dan's broken arm.

Dan shakes it and then shakes the hands of everyone else. 'Thanks. Well. We've got to get going.'

'There's no rush, Dan,' Reed says, but Dan is already heading back toward the van.

Reed opens the passenger door for him in readiness. The paranormal investigators stand by Jim's Espace, waiting to see them off.

'I thought we might be able to make a stop somewhere before it gets dark.' He thinks of Mr and Mrs Jenkins on their whirlwind anniversary trip. After all, Arthur was right: life is short.

He turns to wave again at Keith, Gregor, Sally and Jim. 'See you at VIGIL, if not before!'

They wave back.

Reed and Dan get into their seats and pull the doors shut. Reed helps Dan with his seatbelt then adjusts the mirror and inserts the keys.

'So, they *can* survive outdoors,' Reed jokes, but not meanly. 'Nice of your fan club to come and say goodbye.'

'Well, I *am* very loveable. That reminds me,' Dan says, 'I meant to tell you…'

Reed looks at him.

'Remember the night of the experiment?'

'When we got drunk and abandoned the scientific method?' Then Reed's expression changes, inviting Dan to go on.

'Yes, well, the magnetometer picked up some very strange readings – late in the night…'

'I know,' Reed says, 'the experience-inducing frequencies – from the bedframe.'

'Yes, but as well as that, a different pattern of frequencies – after we passed out…'

Reed masks his reaction by turning away again, ostensibly to wave at the SHERPAS. *Just what had it been picking up?*

Then, remembering, he reaches behind the seat, retrieving a big, black hat.

'You kept the hat!'

It is Dan's old, wide-brimmed fedora, the one he had gifted to Reed last year in Shilly-on-Sea.

Reed's eyes crinkle and he wriggles his shoulders as if to say 'of course'. He places the hat on Dan's head. 'There. Now you are your old self again.'

Dan looks up at the guest house. Tiers of glinting windows fill with bright reflections of blue sky. 'No... I'm not.'

Then Reed releases the handbrake and drives to the junction. 'Left or right?' Reed says, asking for inspiration rather than directions.

'Surprise me,' Dan says.

Reed makes a turn and the van rumbles into the road. He switches on the radio and starts tapping his fingers on the steering wheel. Dan sees the city passing by, no idea where they are headed.

Then he remembers a thought; the opening gambit of a conversation he had pegged for later. He leans toward his friend.

'So, Reed... You never told me about *your* dream...'

THE END

If you enjoyed this book, please leave a review.
You will help other readers to find books they love and
make the author very happy.

Follow Jenny Cutts on
Goodreads, Bookbub and Patreon.
www.jennycutts.com

Titles in this series
The Invisible Body
The Long Lost Sunset
The Never Ending Fall

Read on for an excerpt from *The Never Ending Fall*…

THE NEVER ENDING FALL
CHAPTER 1

Blood seeps slowly from the skull, darkening hair and pooling on stone. The black, rushing river splashes the rocks; a tearing torrent dashing by deaf, dead ears. Night shadows wash the blue dress grey.

The body sprawls in its resting place, limbs limp, deformed by boulder-snapped bones. Icy fingers trail in the tugging water, yet unpierced by the bite of perch.

A break in the clouds reveals a pattern of printed white daisies. The blossoms crystallise like stars pricking a pitch sky.

The eyes are open, shining with moonlight, bright against the muddied, bloodied face.

CHAPTER 2

Zoya is watching the window. On the other side of the glass, the sparrow seems to hover, an impossible suspension, before its wings flutter and it swoops dramatically out of sight.

'So,' continues the interviewer.

Zoya's attention snaps back to the thin, grey woman and the frowning man sitting across the table, their notes neatly positioned before them in two parallel piles.

'… aside from your administrative experience,' the woman continues, 'what makes you a good fit for Charlotte Carre?'

'Well…'

Zoya's eyes flit from one serious face to the other.

'I love dance. I mean, I love to dance myself – as an amateur. I've taken a lot of dance classes, particularly over the last year, and been to see a lot of shows – er, performances.'

She looks up to the vacant patch of sky.

'I love it. It's like… the world just melts away and time itself stops… just hangs there floating…'

Zoya realises that this isn't much of a job interview answer and brings her focus back to the room – the neat furniture, pale walls and neutral expressions of the man and woman waiting for her to say something that will score some points.

'So, I just really feel that… I just think that by contributing to a – *this* – dance company, by bringing my administrative skills to the company… it would help me to feel' – she searches for the word – 'fulfilled.'

Zoya clasps her hands together neatly on her lap, straightens her spine slightly and smiles a close-lipped smile.

***

Reed's mouth hangs open, a spot of saliva pooling at the corner. As he wakes, he instinctively wipes it away with the back of his hand and then wriggles free of the tangled covers. Sitting up in bed, he reaches for the retro patterned curtain and pulls it aside to check out the morning. Sycamore trees fill the camper van window with green shadow, the leaves hanging still as a photograph. He runs his fingers through his hair. It slowly flops back into place.

Beyond the leaves lies the wide, grey suburban street and another flat August day. Nobody seems to be about. Eventually, he spies a faraway walker, circled by the curious snuffling of his dog.

Once dressed, Reed opens the cabin door, the sound soon dissipating in the quiet street. He hops onto the pavement and pulls the door shut. A car drives past the distant junction and a blackbird begins to sing somewhere, out of sight.

Reed stretches his spine, his long arms reaching toward the treetops in a wide span. He sets off on the short walk toward Dan's house, thinking about breakfast.

***

'Thank you, Miss Carmichael. That concludes the interview.'

The thin, grey woman, whose name Zoya can't remember, replaces the cap on her pen with a click.

'As mentioned,' the grumpy man adds, 'we expect to make our decision by the end of the day. Thanks for coming in.'

Zoya follows their lead in standing up, extending her arm for handshakes and exchanging polite thanks.

A loud bang at the windowpane startles her. She sees the stunned sparrow plummet to the ground, like a stone.

***

The thud of the car door sounds too loud in the quiet, still street. Dan stands on his doorstep watching Robin drive away. In the open doorway, Dan's skin prickles as cool morning air seeps into the house.

He watches as the blue Ford Fiesta quietly trundles down the street and rounds the usual corner – and he watches long after it has gone. Dan's thick, dark brows sink slowly over his stare and his pursed mouth settles in a small, pained frown.

***

In the corridor, Zoya manoeuvres herself out of the way. The thin, grey woman is calling for the next interviewee. A thin, blond woman – almost a mirror image – rises from the waiting area. Zoya notices that they embrace.

'Hi, darling – we said you'd be back!'

Zoya struggles to stash her resume in her bag and her cheeks feel hot. She stuffs the papers in and hurries down the stairs.

Hitting the open air, she turns a corner to find the back of the building and leans against the wall. She looks up through the muggy, greying skies to the windows rising above her, imagining the affectionate greetings continuing in the interview room above. She already knows that she won't be getting this job. She steps out of her uncomfortable interview shoes and flexes her feet on the grass.

***

Reed's Converse make a slight slapping sound on the drive as he ambles up to Dan's front door. The familiar suburban semi seems quiet today, no signs of life or Dan. He remembers that Sarah and Matty don't live there anymore, Dan's sister and nephew having moved in with her new boyfriend, Nathan.

He reaches for the doorbell and presses. As he waits, not hearing anything, he glances up and down the road. Someone along the street is hanging washing out to dry.

He hears faint footsteps inside the hall. Dan opens the door. He has a preoccupied look on his face.

'Reed!' Dan says, mustering an enthusiastic greeting that doesn't land quite right.

'Had you forgotten?' Reed answers, following him inside. 'We were going to go through the vanishing necklace case today...'

'No, no,' Dan says. 'You're just a bit earlier than... I suppose I lost track of time.'

They head down the hallway and into the kitchen.

'Oh, have you got company?' Reed asks. 'Is Robin still here?'

'No.'

Reed waits for the explanation, wondering what caused Dan to lose track of time. Dan intuits the unspoken question.

'I was just… thinking,' he answers.

They sit at the table.

'Right,' Dan says, planting his hands on the tabletop, 'here's what we know.'

***

Zoya leans against the wall, feeling directionless in life. As her pulse slumps back to normal, she becomes irritated by the stifling stillness of the London morning and the stiff, heavy cling of her stupid interview suit.

Not far from her feet, she sees the body of the fallen sparrow, motionless on the grass. She looks at it glumly for a few minutes, wondering what to do with the rest of her day.

Then there is a flutter. The stunned bird rights itself, takes a few faltering hops and then flies away.

***

Sharon perches at the edge of the storeroom above the nightclub, tolerating the smell of tobacco, beer and disinfectant that has sunk deep into the walls. The room is crammed with shadowy, decrepit equipment, thick with dust and sweated grime. The music rises in muffled beats and the wasp-swarm hum echoes in the biting buzz of loose screws. One foot rests on a heavy wheel of cable, the other on the grubby floor.

The door to the office is speckled with peeling varnish and stays shut. She can't hear the men talking inside.

She peers at the paper form she is working through, resting it on the edge of an old mixing desk. She fills in the boxes of the application form in chunky capitals, glancing furtively to the corridor and the door. All she can hear is the thud of the music being played downstairs.

She works her biro carefully, filling in the bursary section, just finishing before a sixth sense tells her to check back with the office door. Her fingers scrabble to fold away the application and hurriedly stuff it out of sight in her bag. She sees the handle turn and the latch release before he emerges slowly, shoulder and hip first, still talking to the men inside.

She adjusts her position, zipping up her bag and smoothing her hair. Alex is half out of the room, still wrapping up his conversation. She sees that he is holding a bag now, one that falls with weight toward the floor. His arm looks muscular holding it. She always liked the way he stands like that; slim hips, poised for action, carrying his weight on one leg.

She tries not to wonder about the bag too much, but the thought keeps pricking her: *maybe he is finally going to pay her back*. All that money, all those years: it wasn't his, it was *hers*.

The music comes to a stop.

Alex steps fully into the corridor and looks around. Sharon stands up, making herself available.

'Sorry, babe,' he says. 'Bit of business. We're leaving now.'

Alex scoops an arm around her and nudges her forward with a hand at the small of her back. She walks ahead of him down the dark, sticky stairs.

As they move through the club below, Alex nods to all the staff. John is darting around collecting plastic glasses from the floor and Garry pauses with his broom to let them pass. They walk through the cavernous, sweat-sheened room and say goodnight to the bouncers who are crowd-managing clubbers away from the cloakroom and into the nipping, northern night. Alex and Sharon exit through the fire door.

Soon they are outside by his car, a 1977 orange Ford Capri. She watches as Alex puts the bag on the back seat.

'Babe. Hurry the fuck up,' he barks.

She opens the passenger door and glances back to the club. 'I thought we were giving Darren a lift home?'

Alex shrugs. 'Fuck him,' he says nonchalantly.

Then he leans toward her with a stern look on his face. She becomes aware that his lips are moving, that he is muttering something at her through gritted teeth. The words become clearer as his voice grows in volume and anger.

'… five, six, seven, eight…'

She cuts off his counting by quickly getting into the car.

***

My feet shuffle to the edge of the concrete. I can see the River Thames carving its wide passage through the city. I see Somerset House all lit up on the far bank and all the low, wide bridges crouching above the chill water. You cannot imagine how eerie London feels when you're the only person here.

I look at the illuminated towers in the distance and wonder what it would be like to take off from there. But this is enough.

I look to the toes of my trainers touching the void beyond the theatre roof. It's enough to get my heart pumping, faster and harder, but I'm not doing it for the adrenaline rush.

I look around at the gust-riven, empty city. I have seen it all before.

There's still a sick, cloying feeling collecting in the pit of my stomach, the sediment of a day that didn't go exactly as I'd hoped.

I think of the interview. I was clearly not their cup of tea.

I ready myself to step off now. Nothing fancy, just a step. It still shocks me; that first instant when there's no ground beneath me – just me and the fall.

I step, leaning my weight forward and soon I'm drifting head-first into the night. The air cools my face and I feel the churn of time slow around me as I fall and fall and fall…

The Invisible Body

A strange ability. A discovered corpse. But will his supernatural sleuthing skills lead him into a killer's trap?

England, 1990. Reed has travelled his whole life in search of someone who understands him. So he's thrilled when his journey brings him to free-spirited Zoya, who shares his rare ability to dream-walk. But after his gift leads him to a hidden corpse, he becomes the prime suspect in the murder.

Despite the setback, Reed resolves to use his power to help crack the case.

When the real perpetrator delivers a violent threat, he's tempted to give up, slip into his camper van and hit the road again. After all, who would miss him?

Will Reed flee the tiny seaside town and abandon his new friends – or will he risk everything to expose the murderer?

The Never Ending Fall

A risky habit. A dangerous drop. But will a murderer make her watch her step?

England, 1992. Zoya is a free spirit with a risky habit trying to find her place in the world. When she lands a place at an isolated dance school, it seems like the perfect fit. But, following a mysterious death, the countryside doesn't seem so idyllic anymore.

When the police aren't making progress, she starts asking questions of her own. By refusing to accept it was an accident, she finds herself walking a lonely, dangerous path.

Can Zoya bring the murderer to justice or should she tread more carefully?

www.ingramcontent.com/pod-product-compliance
Lightning Source LLC
Chambersburg PA
CBHW030948190726
48285CB00004BB/1278